Penguin Books

JAKE'S THING

Kingsley Amis, who was born in Clapham, England, in 1922, was educated at the City of London School and St John's College, Oxford. At the age of eleven he embarked on a blank-verse miniature epic at the instigation of a preparatory school master, and he has been writing verse ever since. Until the age of twenty-four, however, he remarks: 'I was in all departments of writing *abnormally unpromising*.' With James Michie he edited *Oxford Poetry 1949*. Until 1963 he was a university teacher of English; he is a keen science-fiction addict, an admirer of 'white jazz' of the thirties, and the author of frequent articles and reviews. His novels include *Lucky Jim* (1954), *That Uncertain Feeling* (1955), *I Like It Here* (1958), *Take a Girl Like You* (1960), *One Fat Englishman* (1963), *The Anti-Death League* (1966), and *I Want It Now* (1968). Of his other fiction, *My Enemy's Enemy* (1962) was a book of short stories; he wrote *The Egyptologists* (1965) with Robert Conquest; *Colonel Sun* (1968) was published under a pseudonym. *A Frame of Mind* (1953), *A Case of Samples* (1956), and *A Look Around the Estate* (1967) are the titles of his books of poetry, and he is also the author of *New Maps of Hell* (1960), a survey of science fiction, and *The James Bond Dossier* (1965), which he terms 'belles lettres'. His more recent publications are *The Green Man* (1969), *Girl, 20* (1971), *On Drink* (1972), *The Riverside Villas Murder* (1973), *Ending Up* (1974), *Rudyard Kipling and His World* (1975), *The Alteration* (1976), winner of the John W. Campbell Memorial Award, and *The New Oxford Book of Light Verse* (edited, 1978). Kingsley Amis has two sons and a daughter.

Kingsley Amis

Jake's Thing

Penguin Books

Penguin Books Ltd, Harmondsworth,
Middlesex, England
Penguin Books, 625 Madison Avenue,
New York, New York 10022, U.S.A.
Penguin Books Australia Ltd, Ringwood,
Victoria, Australia
Penguin Books Canada Limited, 2801 John Street,
Markham, Ontario, Canada L3R 1B4
Penguin Books (N.Z.) Ltd, 182–190 Wairau Road,
Auckland 10, New Zealand

First published in Great Britain by
Hutchinson & Co. (Publishers) Ltd 1978
First published in the United States of America by
The Viking Press 1979
Published in Penguin Books in Great Britain 1979
Published in Penguin Books in the United States of America 1980

LIBRARY OF CONGRESS CATALOGING IN PUBLICATION DATA
Amis, Kingsley.
   Jake's thing.
   I. Title.
[PZ4.A517Jak   1980]   [PR6001.M6]   823′.914   80-13178
ISBN 0 14 00.5096 5

Printed in the United States of America by
George Banta Co., Inc., Harrisonburg, Virginia
Set in Times Roman

To Pat Kavanagh

Contents

'When did you first notice something was wrong?'

'Well, notice, it must be five or six weeks, I could give you the date if I had to. But then as soon as I did notice I realized something had been wrong much further back than that.'

'How much further back?'

'Oh . . . A year? Year and a half?'

'About the time your other trouble started to become acute, in fact.'

'Yes. There must be a link.'

By way of answer the doctor gave a quiet sigh. His patient, a round-faced bespectacled man called Jake Richardson, was left to wonder whether this meant that the link was all too grimly real, that only a fool would suppose one existed or that the task of explanation seemed altogether daunting. Jake didn't wonder for long. To have gone on doing so would have been to concede the doctor (Curnow by name) too much importance. When asked why he persistently went to a man he had so little time for, Jake would say that disliking your GP was a good insurance against getting dependent on him.

Now Dr Curnow shook his head a few times and swallowed. In the end he said, 'There's nothing I can do for you.'

'Oh, but surely you must have a –'

'No. The only way is for me to send you to someone.'

'That was rather what I –'

'Excuse me a second, would you please?'

Funny how it's got ruder to say please than not, Jake thought to himself as the doctor began to turn slowly through a small leather-bound book on his desk. He seemed to find its contents of unusual interest, even novelty. One page in particular absorbed his attention for longer than would have been necessary if he had been doing no more than reading the whole of it with care. After this interval he lifted his head abruptly and looked Jake straight in the eye for a quarter of a minute or so. Then he returned his gaze to the book before him, keeping it fixed there while he reached for his telephone. It had buttons instead of a dial.

'Dr Rosenberg? Dr Curnow here.' This information was enough to provoke a considerable speech from the other end, though Jake couldn't make out anything of what was said. 'I have a patient you might be able to do something for,' said Curnow at last. 'I have him here in the room with me. Name of Richardson, J. C. Richardson . . . Well, you'll remember the Mr Pickering I sent to you last autumn . . . Oh did he, I'm sorry to hear that . . . Yes, I'm afraid so . . .' What Curnow heard next made him stare at Jake again but more consider-ingly, look him over rather than look at him. 'Certainly not. No question of anything like that . . .' Curnow's face changed, except for the direction and quality of his stare, and he started nodding emphatically. 'Oh *yes*, very much so . . . Yes, the perfect description . . . Oh really? You will? . . . I'll ask him.' Curnow arranged an appointment for the following week, listened with a grave, responsible expression to a final passage of words from far (from not all that far, actually, just a couple of hundred yards up Harley Street) and rang off.

'A very able man, Dr Rosenberg. Very able.'

'Good,' said Jake. 'Rosenberg. Presumably he's some sort of –'

'Would you excuse me a second, please?' Curnow lifted a switch on what he no doubt called his intercom, which had started to hum hoarsely. 'Yes, what is it?'

'Sheikh Qarmat bin Ezzat el Sha'ket is here,' said a version of a girl's voice.

'Bring him in in thirty seconds precisely and cash as he leaves of course,' said Curnow, getting up. 'Well, Mr

Richardson, you'll be letting me know how things go. Insides behaving themselves?'

'Oh, mustn't complain.'

'That's right. No pain in the abdomen?'

'Just a twinge or so, nothing out of the way.'

'Urine satisfactorily pale?'

'Yes thank you.'

'Faeces satisfactorily dark?'

'Yes.'

'What about the haemorrhoids?'

'You mean piles. I haven't got piles,' said Jake truthfully. 'I don't have them.'

The doctor chuckled and shrugged his shoulders, tolerant of his patient's nervous or whimsical avoidance of the topic. 'Getting plenty of exercise?'

'I thought I was supposed to take it easy.'

'Mild exercise. Walking. Gardening. Didn't you say you gardened?'

'Yes I did. I do.'

'Keep on with it. It can't fail to do you good. Whatever's wrong with you.'

'Thank you, Dr Curnow.'

In the hall the man of the East, clad quite as if he had just arrived from there, without even time to freshen up after the journey, was approaching across a carpet that looked as if it had once taken a similar course: no doubt the gift of some greatful emir or caliph. The receptionist, a girl of twenty or twenty-five, was in attendance. Jake noticed that her breasts were either remarkably large or got up to seem so by a professional. He tried to reckon the chances of Curnow's knowing which and felt downcast for a moment, because any chance at all was too much. But almost at once he cheered up again: between the front door and that of the waiting-room there moved a fellow-patient he had seen at least once before under this roof, moved with new and extreme labour, one leg straight and stiff, the other bent and stiff. Teach him, thought Jake. Not me yet, he also thought.

As one who did what doctors said while still rather looking

down on them, he decided to walk to Warren Street and catch a 127 bus instead of taking a taxi. That in any case wouldn't have been as easy as winking in this area. No sooner had one black, brown or yellow person, or group of such, been set down on the pavement than Americans, Germans, Spaniards were taken up and vice versa. It was just after four o'clock on a fine afternoon early in April. Jake lengthened his stride and crossed the road in front of a double-parked car, large, black and with CD plates. An unmistakable witch-doctor, in equally manifest need of outside help, was doing his best to alight from it. Portland Place turned out to be easily as full of north-bound vehicles, most of them cars, as might have been expected at this hour on Wednesday in Holy Week, no less so than it would doubtless turn out to be on 23rd December or, this year, more likely 22nd. Despite their intermittent and slow progress, Jake waited for the lights to change before he left the kerb. He had made this a rule ever since a momentously near miss by a motor-bike the previous year. The traffic going the other way was much lighter but no faster, thanks to some extensive road-works with nobody working on them.

By contrast, though not altogether by contrast, Euston Road resembled a motor-racing track, or a network of such. Jake felt some relief at reaching the northern side undamaged. He waved and smiled cheerily at an old friend he couldn't have named for the moment and the old friend, who had just come out of Thames Television House, waved and smiled cheerily back a couple of seconds before Jake realized he wasn't an old friend but the chap who played the super-intendent in that police series. Oh Christ, thought Jake; still, the bugger must get a lot of that.

Half an hour later, having been carried up through Camden Town, Chalk Farm and Hampstead, Jake got off the 127 at the stop outside the Orris Park National Westminster Bank. He was about to start the five-minute walk to his house when his eye fell on the window of Winesteals Ltd and an ill-written notice that nevertheless clearly proclaimed Crazy Cuts: 10p in the £ off everything this week only. He hesitated only a moment. He had brought himself to go and see his doctor, he had responsibly taken a bit of exercise, he had saved something like £1·20 by not taking a taxi home, and he was fed up with Tunisian Full-Bodied Red Table Wine (Dry) every night of his life. Into the shop he darted and over to the French corner. Côtes de Nuits Villages 1971 at £2·05 less presumably 20½p? Beaune Clos de la Mousse 1972 at . . . To hell with it: Château Talbot at £4·09 less whatever the fuck. On his way to what people probably meant by the check-out he noticed a pile of boxes of liqueur chocolates and hesitated again, longer this time. £2·17, but that wasn't what was at stake. In the end he took a box.

Ahead of him at the till stood a customer in very dirty whitish overalls smoking a cigar and chatting to the senior of the two shopmen present while the junior cast up what he was buying.

'Is it worth it?' he asked a couple of times. 'This is it. If it isn't, I don't want to know. If it isn't, I'm not interested. If it is, then this is it. I mean, this is it. Right?'

'Right.'

'And it is. It bloody is. Like everything else.' As he talked the overalled man took a roll of £20 notes from his side pocket and counted some out; Jake thought five but wasn't sure. 'It bloody is. Twelve-year-old's better than eight-year-old and '61's going to be better than '62. I mean, you know, this is it. Ever tried Jack Daniel's Green Label?'

'No.'

'Worth trying.' Change was handed over, not much. 'Ta. Yeah, worth trying. Shows you the Black's worth it. Green's good, though. Well, cheers.'

'Cheers.'

Jake moved along, put his two items down on the stub of counter and set himself to see which buttons on his machine the junior shopman would prod. 3, then one he missed, so he gave up and waited for the receipt slip to be torn off and wordlessly handed to him. He screwed up his eyes. 003·69, 002·17, 006·86. He went on looking while the senior shopman drew in air through his nose.

'Er, the . . . You've charged the full price for the chocolates.'

'Right.'

'But your notice says 10p in the pound off everything.'

'Everything bar chocolates and smokes.'

'But it says everything.'

'It means everything bar chocolates and smokes.'

'But . . .'

'You want them, do you, squire?'

'. . . Yes.'

'Right.'

After a short pause, during which he took a blow on the kneecap from the corner of a wire basket in the hand of a man in a blue boiler-suit, Jake paid, picked up his goods and left, remembering he should have said Cheers just as the exit door swung shut after him. Out in the street he noticed that away from the sunlight the air was chilly: the spring had begun late and wet. There were still a few dead leaves half beaten into the triangular patch of bare earth bounded by concrete, probably due to become a communal flower-bed any day, at the corner of the High Street and Burgess Avenue. The near end of the latter consisted of two longish brick terraces put up a hundred years before to house the workers at some vanished local industry and these days much in demand among recently married couples, pairs of homosexuals and older persons whose children had left or never existed. Jake had bought no. 47 in 1969; he couldn't have afforded to now.

2   The Farting Ploughboy

The house stood out among its neighbours by not having had anything done to its outside: no stucco, no curious chimneys, no colourful shutters, no trailing ferns in wire baskets, front door and window-frames and drain-pipes not painted cinnabar or orpiment or minium or light mushroom, and garden neither turned into a tiny thicket nor altogether removed to accommodate a car. Having no car had made it comparatively easy for Jake to prevent that last option but some of the others had taken toll of his powers of resistance. He opened and then shut the gate, which was not of wrought iron or imitation bronze, walked up the eight yards of gravel path and let himself in.

A great deal had managed to get itself done to the inside of no. 47 because so much of it was in items small in themselves and capable of being introduced a bit at a time. He was also at the mercy of the view that whatever rights a man might have over the exterior of his dwelling lapse by definition once its threshold is crossed. The place was full of things. It had to be admitted that some of these weren't as small as all that, like the heavy-duty cheval-glass near the front door and the giant's-coffin-sized Dutch (or some such) clock in the alcove by the sitting-room fireplace, but a lot were. No flat surface except the ceiling and parts of the floor was free of ashtrays bearing quotations from poem and song, serious souvenir mugs and antique paperweights, and screens supplemented the walls for the hanging of small pictures enclosed in large mounts and photographs of dead strangers. It was hard to find a square foot that hadn't been made nice.

The person who had brought all this about was Jake's fat

wife Brenda, who stood up, brushing cake-crumbs off her knee-length fisherman's-knit cardigan, to be kissed on the cheek by him. He went over and greeted similarly her old friend Alcestis Mabbott, who was fat too, not as fat as Brenda but short with it. And then Alcestis's hair stood away from her head in a stiff dun froth while Brenda's, though no more vivid, was smooth and abundant, so that almost anybody would have decided that Brenda had the better of things between the two of them.

'Hallo, Allie dear,' said Jake. 'What a nice surprise.'

'I told you she was coming,' said Brenda.

'Did you, darling? I must have forgotten.'

One way or the other the presence of Alcestis was certainly a surprise to Jake. If it hadn't been he wouldn't have come carting his recent purchases into the sitting-room like a boy back from the fair. It was on them, as he could have predicted without the least trouble, that Alcestis's round-eyed gaze instantly fell.

'Been shopping, have we?' she asked gruffly. It wasn't a tone or vocal quality adopted for the occasion. On their first meeting, round about ten years earlier at a dinner-party in some cultural crapper south of the river, Jake had come really close to congratulating her on a marvellous imitation, unasked-for though it was, of the way retired colonels were supposed to talk. All that had deterred him was puzzlement about why she thought it went well with the detailed account she was giving him of how she had made the unpleasant dress she had on. Then, soon after she had switched the focus of attention to the new wallpaper she was going to have in her dining-room and kept her voice the same, he had got it. Whenever he considered he had done something particularly foolish, which wasn't often, he would cheer himself up by remembering that at least he'd never made a pass at Alcestis ('Smudger' to him in his thoughts).

He answered her questions, or anyhow spoke while looking at her. 'Just one or two odd things.'

'One of them looks to me like a very odd thing indeed.' She meant the bottle which, though wrapped in brown paper, was obviously either a bottle or an object shaped just like a bottle.

Forewarned of he knew not quite what, Jake put it down on a tiled coffee-table slightly to his rear and said to his wife, 'Got you a little something.'

'Ooh . . .' Brenda moved her spectacles from the top of her head to the region of her nose and uncovered the liqueur chocolates. 'Oh, darling, you really shouldn't.'

'Nonsense, everybody deserves a bit of a –'

'I mean you *shouldn't*, darling,' said Brenda. Her eyes, unlike her friend's, were long from corner to corner and also bright, both in the intensity of their greenish colour and in the shining of their surfaces even through glass. Jake had never forgotten the first time they had been turned full on him: not where or when, just how they had looked. 'You know, this is exactly what I'm not supposed to have because they're sugar and booze and I can't resist them. It's very sweet of you but honestly.'

'You haven't got to dispose of the whole –'

'I'm sure good old Jake'll give you a hand if you're well and truly stuck. Always ready to help out, our Jake, eh, what?' Alcestis didn't actually utter the last two words but they were there in the way she rocked her long head to and fro and pushed her lips up afterwards.

'I should jolly well hope so, I can tell you,' said Jake, and saw Brenda give him a sharp glance over the top of her glasses. He added hastily, 'I mean that's right, I can always –'

'What absolutely fills me with the most burning curiosity is the question of what's inside the other parcel, the chappie over there.'

'Well, it's a . . . a *bottle* actually of all things, Allie. With drink corked up inside it.'

'Absolutely agog.'

The two women waited. Jake reached out and snatched up the bottle and tore the paper off it as fast as he could. In wine-waiter style he displayed the label to Alcestis, who nodded several times and gave a grunt or so of approval. There was another pause.

'I wonder . . .' said Alcestis. 'Of course it is a bit on the early side.'

'Would you like a glass?' asked Brenda.

'Well, I must say, I don't normally, I –'

'Come on, do you good, why not, fill your boots, great stuff, that's the spirit.' It wasn't (Jake saw) that Alcestis had guessed he had been going to give himself a treat which she had maliciously decided to impair, nor that she had simply fancied a glass of wine: she had sensed, without realizing that she had sensed, that he hoped she wouldn't ask him for one and so naturally had asked him for one, or better still had got herself asked to have one. 'Shan't be a jiffy.'

Along in the kitchen he got going fast. Off with the vile plastic foil they put round the necks of bottles these days and out with the cork; same treatment for a bottle of Tunisian Full-Bodied Red Table Wine (Dry). Now a jug, or rather pair of jugs.

'I remember as if it were yesterday,' he said as he worked. 'Jerry had given our lads a fearful pasting round St Quentin and Compiègne and most of us thought that when the big push came in the spring we'd be done for. Not a word of a lie. Literally. I said done for and I meant done for.' He raised his voice. 'Where's the bloody corkscrew? Oh, here it is – all right – got it.'

By this time he had the two wines in jugs of their own and was pouring the Château Talbot into the Tunisian bottle. A jet aircraft came into earshot.

'There were men in my battalion who'd gawn six months without sleep and the average life of a subaltern in the front line was thirty seconds. Absolute gospel. Literally. Then one day in the shithouse at Division I ran into old Bugger Cockface who I'd known at Eton and Sandhurst and in the Crimea and at Spion Kop.' The jet was almost overhead. 'And I said to him, I said, "Are we done for, Bugger?" and he said, "By George not yet, Smudger," and I thought, damn fine soldier, damn fine Englishman, damn fine feller, what? What? *What?*'

'I said what on earth are you doing? You've been simply ages.'

Brenda had spoken. Alcestis was at her side. The two must have stolen up on him under the noise of the aircraft, which had begun to recede. Jake hoped he hadn't turned round too abruptly. There stood near him the two bottles each filled with what had been in the other and the jugs not noticeable. He said,

'Just . . . It took me a while to find the –'

'Two bottles,' said Alcestis. 'I say, are we having a piss-up?'

'That one's for dinner-time. These cheap plonks, if you take the cork out a couple of hours before you –'

'Tunisian Full-Bodied . . . This is good enough for me.'

'No really, it won't have –'

'Suit me down to the ground. I'm not a connoisseur chappie like you.'

'No, the other one's much –'

'No, you have that with your dinner. Able to appreciate it, mm?'

'I'd far rather –'

It was no good: she had noticed, again unconsciously, that he now wanted her to have what a minute earlier he hadn't wanted her to have, and maintained the appropriate reaction. (She must have grasped too that something was going on in the kitchen because he hadn't been out there that long.) Back in the sitting-room she took a sip and raised her unabundant eyebrows.

'I think this is awfully good, Jake. What did you pay for it if you don't mind my asking?'

He took a gulp. Although he much preferred drink with food he was fucked if he was going to, etc. 'I don't know,' he said a little wildly. 'One twenty-five . . . ten . . .'

'Where? No don't tell me, no point, memory like a sieve. Of course, I suppose with your experience and your palate, easy. Brenda love, aren't you drinking?'

'No, I'm cutting down,' said Brenda. She went to the

tea-tray, poured herself a cup and added milk and three lumps of sugar.

'But you're . . .' said Jake and stopped.

'I'm what?'

'You're . . . entitled to break the rules once in a way.' He was acting on the principle that every drop of claret outside Alcestis was a drop saved. 'Let me get you a glass.'

'No thank you.' She spoke sharply.

'What have you been up to today, Jake?'

Distracted by Brenda's tone, which had led him to start reviewing his words and actions in the short time since he'd entered the house, he answered Alcestis without thinking. 'Seeing the doctor.'

'Oh.' She drew him down to sit beside her on the padded bamboo settee. 'Anything . . . troublesome?'

'Not really,' said Jake, who had recovered his wits enough to try to spread a little embarrassment. 'What you might call a man's thing.'

'I see.'

'I don't expect to die of it exactly.'

'Good,' she said, laying her hand on his shoulder for a moment. 'Do you care for Curnow terribly?'

'No, but I trust his judgement.'

'Neither do I, but Geoffrey swears by him.' She referred to her husband. 'He's Cornish, Curnow, you know. Like Michael Foot.'

'Is he?'

'Oh *yes* my dear, in fact his name's Cornish for Cornish. Worse than the Welsh. Oh yes.'

'Ah.'

'Can I finish my story now, Brenda love?'

'Oh yes Allie, do.' This time Brenda's tone was warm but the warmth was firmly vectored on her friend.

'I was just getting into it when you turned up, Jake.'

'Sorry.'

'Well, just to put you in the picture very briefly, Brenda's probably told you about the trouble we had with our drains last year. Well, the plumber was simply charming. Young fellow, very good-looking, extremely intelligent, all that. Now I can't quite explain it, but he rather fell for old Geoffrey and me. Nothing was too much trouble any hour of the day or night, brought us some little cake affairs his wife had made – cookies, brought *her* along one evening, said she'd been making his life a misery, always on at him to take her to see the people he'd told her so much about. Anyway, some time in the summer he said he'd had enough, of this country that is: no freedom, take all your money off you, won't let you work harder and better yourself. If you want to put it crudely, he felt his initiative was being strangled. Well, to cut a long story short he got a job in Nigeria and went off there with wife and two young kids for good. Emigrated. Out. Gone. Bang. This was last October, that's nearly . . . six months . . . ago.'

Alcestis paused, put the palms of her hands together and rested her chin on her thumbs. Jake asked himself which way it was going to go: Minister of Plumbing, uranium strike, massive diamond find, fleet of Cadillacs, gold bed? Surely not, and preferably not too in the case of a moron and pervert on the present scale: wild-life reserve trip, safari camp, freedom fighters, tribal ritual, cut off his, forced to eat . . .

'And then, just last week, we had some news. A letter. I knew straight away who it was from by the stamp. I mean we don't know anyone else out there. I just opened it without thinking, as one would. No idea what was in it. Geoffrey was with me. And what it said, quite simply and straightforwardly, was this. Everything had gone fine, they have a lovely house, got on splendidly with all the people there, job's evidently exactly what he wanted, the whole thing. Now don't you think that's marvellous?'

'*Oh* how exciting,' said Brenda.

Jake was close to tears. In that moment he saw the world in its true light, as a place where nothing had ever been any good and nothing of significance done: no art worth a second look, no philosophy of the slightest appositeness, no law but served the state, no history that gave an inkling of how it had been and what had happened. And no love, only egotism, infatuation and lust. He was glad when, two or twenty-two minutes later, Geoffrey Mabbott turned up, and not just because the fellow's purpose was to take Alcestis away; he was actually glad to see Geoffrey himself, even offered him wine. By now this seemed almost natural, unimportant: Jake's feelings of self-identification with Graham Greene's whisky priest, who sat helplessly by while greedy berks drank the wine he had meant to use at a communion, had reached their peak when old Smudger, what there was of her eyebrows again raised, silently held out her glass for a second dose after bringing her plumber story to its climax.

Rotten bastards might have said that Geoffrey was Alcestis's third husband just as Brenda was Jake's third wife, but they would have been getting the just-as part all wrong. Just as was just as it wasn't. Jake had had two unsatisfactory former wives, or so he would have put it; Alcestis had exercised a mysterious attraction and then an unmysterious repulsion on two former husbands, the second of whom had had to resort to fatal coronary disease to get away from her. It was to be presumed that Geoffrey was in some uncertain intermediate state. That would at any rate be typical: he was in uncertain states of one sort or another far more than not. One of his specialities was the inverted pyramid of piss, a great parcel of attitudes, rules and catch-words resting on one tiny (if you looked long and hard enough) point. Thus it was established beyond any real doubt that his settled antipathy to all things Indian, from books and films about the Raj to Mrs Gandhi, whom by a presumably related crotchet he took to be a daughter-in-law of the Mahatma, was rooted in Alcestis's second husband's mild fondness for curries. His preference for Holland's gin over the London and Plymouth varieties, often-mentioned partiality for cream cakes and habit of flying by K L M had been less certainly connected with his possession of a sketch by Van Dyck, whom on a good day he might very well have supposed to have been a Dutchman. How he managed to be a buyer for a firm of chutney-manufacturers, or indeed be paid for doing anything, was an enigma, a riddle. His taste in clothes was odd too.

He frowned, as he so often did, when he looked at the wine bottle, and said nothing at first. Jake waited expectantly, running his eye over Geoffrey's conventional dark-grey suit, self-striped orange shirt, pink bow-tie and thick-heeled white shoes: what far-distant event, rumour or surmise was plodding on its way to decide the issue for him?

'It's frightfully good, darling,' said his wife.

'Mm.' Then all at once his brow cleared and he spoke with his usual liveliness. 'First-rate notion. Thanks, I'd love some. You know, these Middle East wines are about the best value there is these days. Algerian, of course. And some very, very decent Moroccan red I had the other day.' (He must have remembered being annoyed by a Jew, or meeting or seeing one, thought Jake as he handed him his glass.) 'Oh, thanks most awfully. Mm. Well, it's no vintage claret, but it's a good honest drink. Better than tequila, anyway.'

'It's certainly that,' said Jake. 'But aren't they rather different types of drink?'

'Aren't which?'

'Wine and tequila.'

'Well of course they are, that's what I'm saying. Wine comes from grapes and tequila comes from cactuses.'

'Well actually it's a –'

'Vile stuff. Make it in the Argentine, don't they?'

'Mexico, I think.'

'Really? Ever been there?'

'No, never,' said Jake lightly, and added even more lightly, 'You, er . . . you been there, Geoffrey?'

'Me? But . . . Why should I have been there?' Geoffrey's frown was turning his forehead white in patches. 'I've never even been to the States, let alone South America.'

'Actually Mexico's in –'

It must have been that Alcestis felt she had done enough in the way of holding her mouth open in a smile and blinking her eyes quickly to show how bowled over she still was by her husband even after all these (five? seven?) years.

Certainly she changed her expression to one of a kind of urgency and said, 'Some of this modern architecture they've got in Mexico City, finest in the world you know, especially the museums and the university. *And* some of the blocks of flats and offices. Something to do with the use of materials. Just nothing like it anywhere.'

She ended up looking at Jake, so he said, 'How did you, er . . . ?'

'Common knowledge.'

'Oh I see.'

'How are you, Brenda dear?' Geoffrey spoke as if in greeting, but the two had exchanged warm hugs and several words on his arrival; it was just that he hadn't noticed her since then.

'Fat,' said Brenda, and everyone laughed; Jake saw that Alcestis put her head back further than usual, to show that she knew what had been said was a *joke*. Brenda went on to ask Geoffrey how he was.

'About the same, thanks. Yes, very much the same. Well, no, actually, not really. All right if I have a slice of this? One of my weaknesses, this sort of stuff.'

On Brenda's nod he picked up a large slice of cream cake and ate it carefully, his eyes fixed straight ahead of him. He was concentrating either on what to say next or on the cake, a small problem cleared up when he swallowed finally, said 'Quite delicious' and emptied his glass.

'In what way aren't you the same?' asked Brenda.

'Not what?'

'You said you weren't –'

'Oh, that's right. Well, that's a jolly good instance. Physically no problem, just getting older as who isn't. It's concentration. You know the sort of thing I mean – you go up to your bedroom to get a clean handkerchief and when you get there you've forgotten why you've come and have to go back downstairs to where you started. Quite normal up to a point. But with me, I've got to the stage where I take a cup over to the stove to pour some tea into it and find there's one there already, from . . . half a minute before. And then I have

24

to taste it to see if I've put sugar in. Now that's still just annoying. As I say, it just adds on a few seconds to some of the things I do. But . . . er . . . the . . . silliest part is what I'm thinking about instead of what I'm doing. It's me I'm thinking about, and that's not a very interesting subject. I mean, if a chap's thinking about his, er, his mathematics instead of his teacup, or his . . . symphony, then that's all right, that's reasonable. It's in proportion. But me – I ask you!'

Geoffrey had not departed from his cheerful tone. The two women laughed affectionately. Jake held up the wine bottle, which still held about a glassful, but Geoffrey smiled and shook his head and went on as before.

'And the stupidest thing of the lot is, I don't think poor old me, or poor old me in the financial sense, though I jolly well could like everybody else these days, and certainly not *brilliant* old me. Just, just me. It's not enough, you know.'

'It certainly is not by a long chalk,' said Alcestis, going up to her husband and putting her arm through his. 'I only married you because you were the most boring chap I knew so nobody but me could stand you. Now I'm going to take you home, or rather you're going to take me home and we'll leave these good people in peace.'

'Why don't you stay to supper?' asked Brenda. 'There's nothing very much but I'm sure you and I could knock something up. Allie.'

' . . . Yes, do,' said Jake.

'No, sweet of you, but we've tried your patience long enough already.' Alcestis embraced Jake briefly. 'Come along Mabbott, let's hit the trail.'

By custom Brenda saw the visitors out while Jake stayed behind in the sitting-room. Normally at such a time he could count on a good five minutes to himself, but today it was only a few seconds before he heard the front door slam and his wife approach along the passage.

'When the bishop farted we were amused to hear about it,' said Jake. 'Should the ploughboy find treasure we must be told. But when the ploughboy farts ... er ... keep it to yourself.'

Brenda had started putting the tea things together, not very loudly. With her back turned she said in her clear soprano, 'Did you make that up?'

'Free translation of one of Martial's epigrams.'

'Quite good, I suppose.'

'It enshrines a principle poor old Allie would do well to –'

A saucer whizzed into the empty fireplace and broke. 'You leave Allie alone! You did quite enough when she was here!'

'What? I didn't do anything at all.'

'Much! I know you can't be expected to like my friends, that isn't reasonable, why should you, we can't all be the same, I don't necessarily like your friends.' Brenda was talking very fast, though not for the moment quite at the pitch to be expected from someone who had reached the crockery-throwing stage. Now she paused and bit her lower lip and gave a shaky sigh. 'But I don't see why you feel you have to make your low opinion of my friends so devastatingly crystal-clear!'

Jake heard the last part with annoyance and some self-reproof. He had thought his behaviour to the Mabbotts a show-piece of hypocritical cordiality. And now he came to think of it, hadn't Brenda said something of this sort the last time they had seen Alcestis, or the time before? 'I haven't got a low opinion of Allie,' he said with an air of slight surprise, 'I just find her a bit of a –'

'She knows exactly what you find her, she's not a fool

whatever you may think, though even a fool could tell. The way you imitate her and take the mickey out of her and the way your face goes when she tells a story and the way you *sit*, I didn't think it was a very terrific story either but she wouldn't have told it if you hadn't shut her up and absolutely sat on her about the doctor and brought the whole conversation to an absolute full stop. You used to quite like her, I can't understand it.'

'I didn't want to discuss the doctor with her, obviously.' Jake poured out the last of the wine. He longed for a smoke but had given it up four years previously and was determined to stick to that. There were no cigarettes in the house anyway.

'You still had no need to sit on her and be crushing,' said Brenda in about the same tone as before. Although she was standing above him she talked with her chin raised, a mannerism that had stood her in good stead since she began to put on weight. 'And I don't know what she thought when she finished her story and you just *sat* there as if you hadn't heard a word, or rather I *do*.'

'I didn't realize it was over at first. I honestly thought that couldn't be the end. And what do you mean she wouldn't have told it if I hadn't shut her up about the doctor? She'd already started to tell it to you before I got back, that was quite clear.'

'I meant she wouldn't have gone on with it. She'd been telling it to me because it was a tiny little thing in her life that she thought might interest me for about five seconds. That's what old friends do when there's just the two of them together, or didn't you know that? I tell her the same sort of thing all the time. We don't go on swapping translations of epigrams by Martial hour after hour.'

'No of course you don't, I quite see,' said Jake mildly, as opposed to saying harshly that that would be all right if the story didn't take fifty times as long as it was supposed to be interesting for.

Brenda's expression softened in response but a moment later it had hardened again. 'And the way you treat poor old Geoffrey, as if he's off his head or something.'

'I think he is a bit off his head, always has been as long as I've known him. Look at those bloody silly clothes he –'

'That's no excuse for treating him like that. You should have seen the way you were looking at him.'

'When?'

'*When?* Whenever he said anything or was getting ready to say anything, when he said he'd like some wine . . . And what was all that about the wine in the kitchen? What were you up to?'

'Nothing, just opening it. The other bottle was . . .'

'No, you were up to something but I know it's no use going on about it. When he said something about Mexico and when he said he was absent-minded, Allie saw the way you were looking at him, and then when I asked them to stay and after about five minutes you said what a good idea as if it was your own funeral. You should have heard yourself.'

She paused. Jake looked up at his wife. Her breasts were about as large as Curnow's receptionist's but her hips were large too. And, partly concealed by the loose-fitting cardigan, one of her favourite forms of dress over the last couple of years, her waist, her thighs and her upper arms were also large and her paunch was fairly large. But her face, as he had recently noticed from a photograph, had hardly changed in ten years: it was still the face of a woman anxious not to miss anything good or happy that might come her way in the future. That anxiety in it had been the second thing he had observed about her, after her eyes. She turned their glance on him now. He reached out his hand and she took it; he considered getting up and putting his arms round her but somehow decided not to. Without hostility she soon withdrew her hand.

'I'm sorry,' he said. 'I'll try to do better next time.' Of course he meant do and nothing more: how could anyone change his attitude to a pair like the Mabbotts? But next time was going to have to include next time they came up in conversation as well as in person, and that meant fewer of those jocular little sallies about them which had so often cheered up his half of the breakfast or lunch table. A few moments earlier he had thought of telling Brenda that in fact the idea of those two having noticed anything in the least objectionable was a load of rubbish and that she was cross with him for what she knew he felt about them, not for how he had behaved to them, but that too he decided against.

She had moved to the fireplace, he now saw, and was carefully picking up the pieces of china. 'How did it go with the doctor, darling? I should have asked you before.'

'That's all right. Oh, he . . . asked me the sort of questions one might have expected and said *he* couldn't do anything and fixed up an appointment for me with some fellow who might be able to do something.'

'When? I mean when's the appointment?'

'Tuesday. Right after Easter.'

'Good,' said Brenda, going back to the tea-tray. 'Anybody interesting at the club?'

The club was a long way from St James's in more than the geographical sense and existed for the benefit of unprosperous middle-aged and elderly men of professional standing. In order to survive it had recently had to sell half of itself, of its premises that is, to a man who had constructed a massage parlour there. 'Just the usual crowd,' said Jake, accurately enough.

'I see. Ooh, the Thomsons have asked us round for drinks one evening next week,' she said, mentioning one of the comparatively few couples in Orris Park who didn't go on about their cars or their children the whole time. 'I've put it in the diary.'

'Well done.'

'You know, we ought to give a party some time. We can't go on just taking other people's hospitality.'

'I quite agree, but it's so bloody expensive. Everybody drinks Scotch or vodka these days.'

'They can't do much about it if you just offer them wine.'

'I suppose not.'

'I was thinking.' Brenda stood with the tray held in front of her stomach. 'I thought we might give that new Greek place a try.'

'Tonight?'

'I just thought . . .'

'I don't really like Greek food. I always think Greek food is bad Turkish food and Turkish food isn't up to much.'

'What about Sandro's? We haven't been there for ages.'

'They charge the earth and they never seem to change their menu. Isn't there anything in the house?'

'Only the rest of that chicken.'

'Sounds fine. You could fix up a salad, couldn't you?'

'I suppose so . . . Then we could go to a film.'

'There's nothing very marvellous on, I looked at the *Standard* yesterday. Oh, apart from that thing about Moloch turning up in the crypt of a San Francisco church and having children fed to him alive, *The Immolation*, that's it, I wouldn't mind seeing that.'

'Well I would.'

'You are funny, I keep telling you it's all pretend. Look love, I vote we pull up the drawbridge tonight. I know it's selfish of me but I don't honestly feel quite up to stirring out and that probably means I shouldn't, don't you think? Let's be absolute devils and have the heating on and huddle round the telly.'

So when the time came, Brenda went and sliced the chicken and made a salad and a dressing and got out the rather swarthy Brie that needed eating up and put it all on trays and brought them into the sitting-room. The TV was a colour set, small but all right for two. On it she and Jake watched episode 4 of *Henry Esmond*, the News, including film of a minor air disaster in which a good half of those involved hadn't even been hurt, International Snooker, with a commentary that laid great stress on the desire of each player to score more points than the other and so win the match, World Outlook, which consisted largely of an interviewer in a spotted bow tie being very rude to a politician about some aspect of nuclear energy and the politician not giving a shit,

and Rendezvous with Terror: *The Brass Golem.* Or rather
Jake watched that far; Brenda gave up at the first soccer
result and opened her Simon Raven paperback. At the start
of the col-legno violin passage advertising the approach of
the rendezvous just alluded to, she got up from the sofa
which she had herself covered with crimson velvet.

'You off, darling?' asked Jake. 'These things are always
innocuous ballocks, you know. About as frightening as
Donald Duck.'

'No, I'll be off anyway. Still the spare room?'

'I think while we're still sleeping badly.'

'Mm. Ooh, I'm sorry I didn't thank you properly for the
chocolates.'

'The . . . Oh yes. Oh, I thought you did.'

'If the scales aren't too bad in the morning I might treat
myself to one tomorrow night. Well . . .'

'Good night, love.'

She bent and kissed him on the cheek and was gone. Jake
washed down his Mogadon with some of his second glass
of what was supposed to be claret. He was sorry now that he
hadn't done what impulse and habit had suggested and told
Brenda about the abortive wine-switch. Done properly the
tale would have amused her, its confessional aspect given her
pleasure, the row over the Mabbotts been prevented or
disposed of, not merely broken off. But to have done it
properly would have meant taking trouble, not much, true,
but more than he had on the whole felt like taking at the time.
Well there it is, he thought.

Despite everything the background bass clarinet could do,
and it did indeed get a lot done in quantity, terror as expected
failed altogether to turn up at the prearranged spot. Sum-
moned by an ancient curse but otherwise unaccounted for,
the metalloid protagonist ran his course in twenty minutes
less commercials. His most mysterious endowment was the
least remarked: that of always coming upon his quarry alone,
out of sight and hearing of everyone else, in a blind alley, in a
virtually endless tunnel, in a room with only one door and
no usable window, etc. He ground to a halt finally through

gross overheating of the lubricants in the Turkish bath where Providence, in the form of total chance, had led his last intended victim to take refuge. Very neat.

As he went round the room turning everything off, Jake reconstructed the brief script conference at which the creative producer had outlined the story to his colleagues. 'Right,' he snarled, stabbing at the air with an invisible cigar to point the turns in his argument, 'got this guy made of like brass, see, buried somewheres for a coon's age, okay, comes like an earthquake or explosion or whatever, right, anyways he done get gotten dug up, see, this old like parchment says any motherfucker digs me up gets to done get gotten fucked up good, okay, he fucks up three-four guys around, right, chases the last guy into somewhere fucking hot, see, now the brass guy done gotten oil like instead of blood, okay, so *he* gets to done get gotten fucked up, right, Zeke and Zack get on it right away, see, they don't get to done get gotten done it by tomorrow, they lose their asses, okay, and any number of cunts all over the world who know a bloody sight better will watch the bloody thing. Right.'

Upstairs, Jake unhurriedly cleaned his teeth and peed, feeling a comfortable drowsiness at the edge of his mind. Light showed under Brenda's door: she liked to read for a time before settling off, which he didn't. He went into the spare room and undressed. There were pictures in here no less than everywhere else, most of them non-modern black-and-white unoriginals; in almost every case he could have said whether or not a given one belonged to the house but he would never have missed any of them. He put on his pyjamas, turned off the light and was about to get into bed, then changed his mind and went to the window.

Looking out, he remembered with no great vividness doing the same thing one night some shortish time after Brenda and he had come to live here. Then as now there had been plenty to see, mainly by the street-lamp that stood no more than twenty yards off: houses, trees, bushes, parked cars, the bird-table in the garden diagonally opposite. Then, too, some of the windows must have been illuminated and it was quite possible that, as now, the only sounds had been faint voices and distant footsteps. After some effort he remembered further his feelings of curiosity, almost of expectation, as if he might find himself seeing a link between that moment and things that had happened earlier in his life. He remembered, or thought he did; there was no question of his re-experiencing those feelings, nor of his wishing he could. What was before him left him cold, and he didn't mind.

The next Tuesday morning when Jake set off down Burgess Avenue it was raining, but not very hard. Even if it had been very hard he would have more or less had to set off just the same. Four or five years ago there had been a taxi-rank at the end of the High Street by St Winifred's Hospital and a telephone-call fetched one to the front door within a few minutes in any weather. The sign and the shelter were still there but they served only to trap the occasional stranger into a fruitless wait. Minicabs either didn't come or had drivers you had to pilot street by street to places like Piccadilly Circus. And there was the expense. And the Underground was only worth while for long journeys, over the river or out to Chelsea: Jake had established that 47 Burgess Avenue NW16 was about as equidistant as anywhere could be from the stations at Golders Green, East Finchley, Highgate and Hampstead. He had several times read, though not recently, of plans to extend one or other branch of the Northern Line to a contemplated Kenwood Station in the 1980s.

Every 6–7 mins was how often 127s were supposed to turn up at the stop by the Orris Park Woolworths, so to be given the choice of two after only 10–11 was rather grand and certainly welcome in the increasing rain and squirts of cold wind. Jake got on to the second bus, one of the newish sort distinguished by a separate entrance and exit. The doors closed after him with a swish of compressed air that resembled to what was almost a worrying degree the sound of the off-licence bugger and his overalled customer saying Cheers to each other. The conductor too was one of the newish sort, which in this case meant that he chucked you off if you hadn't got the exact money. But Jake made a great point of not being caught out by things like that.

Whenever he could he liked to sit at the back on the offside, where there was a niche just wide enough for an umbrella between the emergency door and the arm of the seat, but someone from Asia was there that morning so he took the corresponding position upstairs. Among the people he had a good or fair view of, there was none he remembered having seen before. They were divided, as well they might have been, into those older than him, round about his age and younger than him. In different ways all three groups got him down a bit. Only one child seemed to be about the place but it was making a lot of noise, talking whenever it felt like it and at any volume it fancied. Far from admonishing or stifling it, its mother joined in, talked back to it. Like a fool he had forgotten to bring anything to read.

Although there was no shortage of his fellow human beings on the pavements and in and out of shops, other places and spaces were altogether free of them, so recurrently that his mind was crossed by thoughts of a selective public holiday or lightning semi-general strike. A railway bridge revealed two or three acres of empty tracks and sidings; large pieces of machinery and piles of bricks stood unattended on a rather smaller stretch of mud; no one was in sight among the strange apparatuses in what might have been a playground for young Martians; a house that had stayed half-demolished since about 1970 overlooked a straightforward bomb-site of World War II; nearer the centre, the stone face of a university building was spattered with rust-stains from scaffolding on which Jake had never seen anybody at work. Even Gr nville Co rt, Collin woo C urt and the others, angular but lofty structures of turd-coloured brick resting on squat stilts, seemed to be deserted. Even or especially.

Warren Street was at hand; he climbed warily down the stairs, holding on with all his strength when a deeper cavity than usual in the road-surface lifted him heel and toe into the air. He got off by Kevin's Kebab, crossed over and fought his way westward against a soaking wind that blew now with fatuous indignation. 878 Harley Street. Proinsias

Rosenberg MD, MA (Dip. Psych). The door opened in his face and an Englishman came out and stepped past him and was away. A small woman in a white housecoat showed Jake into a room where folk from many lands and of nearly as many creeds sat in chintz-covered armchairs reading *Punch* and *Private Eye*. But it was no more than ten minutes before she came back, took him along a corridor to another room and shut him in.

Jake found himself closeted with a person he took to be a boy of about seventeen, most likely a servant of some kind, in a stooped position doing something to an electric fire. 'I'm looking for Dr Rosenberg,' he said.

It was never to cut the least ice with him that the other did not in fact reply, 'Ah now me tharlun man, de thop a de mornun thoo yiz' – he might fully as well have done by the effect. ('Good morning' was what he did say.)

'Dr Rosenberg?' said Jake again, a little flustered. He saw now that the youth was a couple of years older than he had supposed at first, short-haired and clean-shaven, wearing a sort of dark tunic-suit with a high collar that gave something between a military and a clerical air.

'Rosenberg it is. How do you do, Dr Richardson.' Jake got a hearty handshake and a brown-eyed gaze of what looked like keen personal admiration but in the circumstances could hardly have been the genuine article. 'Do come and sit down. I hope this room'll be warm enough – such a wretchedly cold spring we've been having so far, isn't it?'

When he failed to add what Jake was in a way expecting and would certainly have accepted, that his master or father if not grandfather would be down in a minute, things eased quite quickly. 'I'm sorry, I'm afraid I . . .'

'You're not the first by a very long chalk indeed, Dr Richardson, I can assure you of that.' He who must after all be conceded to be Dr Rosenberg didn't really talk like an O'Casey peasant, his articulation was too precise for that, but he did talk like a real Irishman with a largely unreconstructed accent, even at this stage seemed no more than twenty-one or -two and had shown himself, between finishing with the fire and sitting down behind his desk, to be about two foot high. He said in an oddly flat tone, 'I understand very well how strange it must be to hear my style of talk coming out of a man with a name straight from Germany.'

'Or Austria.' Which would be rather more to the point, thought Jake, and thought too that he had conveyed that meaning in his inflection.

'Or Austria.' The doctor spoke as one allowing a genuine if rather unimmediate alternative.

Jake went back to being flustered. No sooner had he managed to bring himself to have this tiny Emerald Isler palmed off on him instead of the bottled-at-the-place-of-origin Freudian anybody just hearing the name would have expected than he was being asked to believe in a student of the mind who didn't know where Freud had come from. He said quickly, 'Dublin man, are you?'

'Correct, Dr Richardson,' said Dr Rosenberg, in *his* inflection awarding his new patient a mark or two for knowing that many Irishmen were Dubliners and virtually all Dubliners Irishmen. 'Perhaps it might be of interest,' he went on, though not as if he had any very high hopes of this, 'if I were to explain that an ancestor of mine was a German consular official who liked the look of the old place, married a local girl, and no doubt you'll be able to fill in the rest of the story for yourself. I charge seventeen pounds fifty a session – is that acceptable?'

'Yes,' said Jake. Christ, he thought.

'Good. Now Dr Curnow has sent me a report on you.' The psychologist's manner had changed and he opened a file with an alacrity that would have been quite uncharacteristic of his colleague. 'There's just one point I'd like to have clearly understood before we get down to business. You do realize that in our work together I shall be asking you a number of questions.'

'Yes.'

'And you have no objection.'

'No,' said Jake, suppressing a different and longer answer.

'Good. First question then. What is your full name?'

'Jaques [Jakes] Cecil Richardson.' Jake spelt out the Jaques. And I reckon I got seventy-five per cent on that, he thought, in mind of a comic monologue a decade or two old.

'Jaques. Now that's an uncommon name for an Englishman.'

'Yes. *My* ancestor came over from Paris in 1848.'

'1848! You must have made a close study of your family history.'

'Oh, I wouldn't say that. After all, 1848 was 1848.'

'Just so, but the date would seem to have lodged in your memory.'

'Well, they did have a spot of bother there in that year, if you –'

'Ah, when did they not the horrible men? Do you know, Dr Richardson, I think those French fellows must have caused *nearly* as much trouble in the world as we Irish?' Rosenberg gave a deep-toned laugh, showing numerous very small white teeth. 'Oh dear. Your age.'

'Fifty-nine.'

'Sixty,' said Rosenberg as he wrote.

'Well, it is actually fifty-nine, not that there's a lot of difference, I agree.'

'We always enter the age next birthday. We find it makes for simplicity.'

'Oh I see.'

'Your profession.'

'I teach at a university.'

'Any particular one?'

'Yes. Oxford. I'm Reader in Early Mediterranean History there and a Fellow of Comyns College. And by the way I have got a doctorate but I don't normally use the title.'

'So it's *Mr* Richardson. Now your trouble is that your libido [lib-eedo] has declined.'

'My what?' asked Jake, though he had understood all right.

'Your libido, your sexual drive.'

'I'm sorry, I'd be inclined to pronounce it lib-ighdo, on the basis that we're talking English, not Italian or Spanish, but I suppose it'll make for simplicity if I go along with you. So yes, my lib-eedo has declined.'

'Are you married?'

'Yes.'

'How much does your wife weigh?'

'*What?* No I beg your pardon, I heard what you said. How much . . . I don't know. But you're right. I mean she weighs a lot. She's quite tall but she weighs a lot. Fourteen stone? I don't know. How did you know?'

'Oh, it's just one of the most statistically common reasons why men lose sexual interest in their wives. I couldn't say I knew.'

'All right. I mean I see. But it isn't that, or rather it may well be that too, or *there* may well be that too but it's general, I simply don't –'

'Your wife's age?'

'Forty-seven.'

'Does she know you've come to see me today?'

Good God yes, of course. We're still, well, on close terms.'

'It's important she starts losing weight as fast as it's safe to do so. May I telephone her?'

'No, don't do that. Write her a letter, but leave it a couple of days. Not that I can see it having much effect.'

'Ah, one never knows, one can but try.' The doctor hurried on; the conversation about weight, however necessary, had been an obvious check to his interest. 'You were saying you'd suffered a general loss of drive.'

'That's right. I don't fancy anyone, not even girls I can see are very attractive. And it wasn't always like that, I promise you.'

'I think Mr Richardson, before we go any further you might tell me when you first –'

'Let's see, I first noticed something was wrong,' began Jake, and went on to talk about the year or more he had spent in continual, at times severe gastric pain being treated by Curnow for an ulcer, drinking almost nothing, watching his diet, taking the antacid mixture prescribed him and telling himself that pain, discomfort, general below-parness had temporarily reduced his desires to some unestablished low level. In the end he had developed jaundice, had had diagnosed a stone in the common duct (that into which the canals from the liver and the gall-bladder unite) and had had this removed by surgery, another set of experiences decidedly not associated with satyriasis. Out of hospital his recovery had been steady but slow, marked by periods of fatigue and weakness, a third period in which it seemed to him natural to postpone sexual dealings with his wife, let alone going in pursuit of other ladies. He had still somehow not got round to either branch of activity, though admittedly beginning to feel rested and fit, when there came that fatal Saturday in late February – the night of *Thunderball*.

There was no point in telling Rosenberg the full story, but Jake remembered it with great vividness. Brenda had gone to stay with her grand cousins in Northumberland, one of the places where by tradition he didn't go with her. She had left on the Thursday; she was due back on the Monday evening; she had actually telephoned that lunchtime to ask him to find and read over to her a recipe for quenelles she had meant to take with her. Given ten years of his precept and example in the matter of each being kept informed of where the other was at all times, her dislike of changes of plan, the non-existence of anything likely to bring her back prematurely which he wasn't bound to hear of first, she couldn't have been away in a more armour-plated, hull-down, missile-intercepting fashion. Arriving back from Oxford on the Thursday night he had found her already well gone, had spent most of Friday self-indulgently and yet dutifully writing to some of the old friends and ex-pupils who had fled from the England of the 1970s and had made Saturday a remorseless build-up to the time at which, an avocado pear with prawns, a trout with almonds supported by Brussels sprouts and chestnuts and a bottle of his beloved Pouilly Fumé (£1·99 while stocks last) before him, he would settle down to watch the film of *Thunderball* on television.

When, twenty minutes before the off, the telephone brought him hurrying from the bog he had felt no pre-monitory stirrings: Brenda most likely, checking that it was indeed six pinches of powdered baboon's balls in the sauce, and if not, even Alcestis could hardly talk him out in Brenda's de luxe absence. A female voice he at once recognized but couldn't at once name had asked him if he was there.

'Speaking.'

'Jake! You stinker. This is good old Marge. Remember me?'

Christ yes, as what seven years earlier had been a bosomy thirty-five-year-old from Baltimore, the source of a strenuous and reprehensible couple of months before some now-forgotten necessity had plucked her away across the ocean. He had gone on to say enough to show he did remember her.

'You sound as if you're alone.'

'I am.'

'Completely?'

'Yes.'

'Oh, that being so, why don't I just grab a cab and come toddling up to your place and we could get along with kind of renewing our acquaintance if you've nothing better to do?'

'Fuck me wept!' he had cried, regressing to an oath of his Army days: he had clapped his hand over the mouthpiece in the nick of time. 'Shit!' he had added. And then he had been filled with alarm and horror.

'You're telling me it was a failure, is that right?' asked Dr Rosenberg.

'Not in the sense you probably mean, no. I . . . performed. Not with any distinction, but adequately. No worse than many a time in the past. No, the striking thing was after-wards, immediately afterwards. I kept thinking about the trout and whether we could –'

'Hunger is a normal reaction on completion of sexual intercourse.'

'I'm not talking about hunger, I was thinking about miss-ing my dinner or it being spoilt or there not being enough for the two of us, no, it was more there being enough for me if she had some too and what else could she have. In fact the evening as I'd planned it for myself, very much included what was left of *Thunderball*. I reckoned that if –'

'I wonder if you'd kindly explain about this thunderball thing you've been constantly referring to. I don't believe I –'

'Well, you know, *Thunderball*. Film, didn't I say? Sean Connery. James Bond. Ian Fleming. Barbara something, was it?'

'Ah to be sure, James Bond,' said Dr Rosenberg without producing much conviction in Jake. 'Do you want to tell me what happened later?'

'I will. We lay around for a bit, not very long, and then she said brightly she was hungry and what about dinner, and I said we could eat at home, and she said if I didn't mind what she felt like was a long lazy rather greedy evening somewhere with a lot of pasta and a lot of vino, and so that's what we did, and it was quite good fun really, and we said good night in the restaurant. She was marvellous, she did it very well. The only thing she couldn't do was make me think she didn't know. Of course she couldn't. They always know things like that, not that much acumen was called for in this case. Yes. She knew I knew she knew I knew she knew.'

Rosenberg seemed to think this last part was important; at any rate he went in for a good deal of writing while Jake's memory fastened against his will on the hours he had lain awake that night and on how he had spent most of the next day: unable to read, unable to attend to radio or television, eating almost nothing, staring into space, hardly thinking, trying not so much to accept what had happened to him as just to take it in. To distract his mind from this he glanced round the small and by now slightly overheated room with artificial interest. He saw a couch of a height inconvenient for anyone much under eight foot (to use it himself the doctor would pretty well need a rope ladder), a green filing-cabinet, no books beyond diaries and directories and, on a fluted wooden pedestal, a life-sized human head in some shiny yellowish material with the surface of the skull divided into numbered sections. That distracted his mind like mad.

'Right,' said Rosenberg at last, 'I think I have that clear. And you've had no intercourse at all since then. Have you masturbated?'

It took Jake a little while to get the final participle because the Irishman had stressed it on its third syllable, but he did get it. 'Er . . . yes. Well, a couple of times.'

'Do you have early-morning erections?'

This time Jake responded at once, with a desire to tell the bugger to mind his own business. Then he saw that that sort of wouldn't do and said, 'Yes. Usually anyway.'

'Do you have fantasies?'

'Sexual fantasies. A bit. Not much.'

'Have you over these last weeks used written or pictorial pornography or visited a sex movie?'

'No to the lot. I haven't read any pornography for years and I've never been to a, a sex movie.'

'I see. Going back now to before your illness, how was your libido in those days?'

'Well, not what it was when I was a youngster, obviously, but my wife and I were having a – performing sexual inter-course at least once a week and more at special times like holidays, and I worked out that in '74 I had two affairs, one of them only a couple of, er, occasions but the other lasting several months on and off.'

'And longer ago, how active were you sexually in your forties and thirties?'

'Just put it this way, in my time I've been to bed with well over a hundred women.'

Rosenberg had made some notes of the answers to all his questions until this last one, at which to Jake's distinct annoyance he merely nodded. More questions followed and more notes were taken. Parents, characters of, probable sex-life of, attitude to; knowledge of sex, how acquired; masturbation, frequency of (high); homosexual activities (none); first sexual experience, to what degree a success (bloody marvellous, thanks very much); then, at a less leisurely pace, subsequent sexual experience, marriages, divorces, causes of, present wife, relationship with, sexual and non-sexual. As far as he knew Jake kept nothing back here, but he had the feeling that a series of negatives was all that was established; still, necessary work, no doubt. At last the scientist of mental phenomena looked at his watch and said,

'Ah now, just one or two final points. What is your height, Mr Richardson?'

'Five foot eleven.'

'And your weight?'

'Twelve stone six' – noted by Jake only the previous week to be exactly right for his height and age, according to whatever chart it had been.

Rosenberg gave a small frown. 'Is that all?'

'Yes, that's all.'

'Mm. Well I think all the same you'd do well to lose a few pounds. Try to get down to twelve stone. Cut down on starchy foods and take more exercise. And of course, how much do you drink?'

'Sometimes a glass of beer with lunch, sometimes a glass of sherry before dinner, three or four glasses of wine with dinner rising to a whole bottle on special occasions, say once every three or four weeks.' This was the exact truth.

Rosenberg frowned more deeply. 'No more than that? No spirits?'

'I haven't drunk any spirits for over thirty years. I found they didn't agree with me.'

'Try not to go beyond three glasses of wine in future.'

'All right.'

'Would you care to make a note of those points? There'll be more to come.'

'Okay.' Jake scribbled on the back of his cheque-book in his shameful handwriting. 'Starch. Exercise. Wine.'

'Good. Now Mr Richardson, there is a certain programme of tasks that you have to work through with me. We call it inceptive regrouping. Is this time next week convenient? Very well. Between now and then I want you to do the following. Buy some pictorial pornographic material and study it on at least three occasions for a minimum of fifteen minutes at a time. See that this leads to masturbation at least once, preferably twice. Write out a sexual fantasy in not less than six hundred and not more than a thousand words. Oh, and fill this in – there we are – making sure you give only one answer to each question. I'm not going too fast for you, I hope? Good. I also want you to have a non-genital sensate focusing session with your wife. You understand what I mean by non-genital?'

'Yes, I understand that.'

'In a non-genital sensate focusing session the couple lie down together in the nude and touch and stroke and massage the non-genital areas of each other's bodies in turns of two or three minutes at a time for a period of up to half an hour. They don't perform sexual intercourse. That's exceedingly important: sexual intercourse is strictly forbidden at this stage. You'll find it all set out here.' He handed over a second sheet of sleek paper. 'Now we come to the use of the nocturnal mensurator. If you'd just step over here, Mr Richardson.'

Dr Rosenberg turned and took from a narrow table behind him an object Jake had not noticed before, a heavy wooden box outwardly of much the sort women keep sewing or embroidery in. When the lid was raised it could be seen that a black composition panel covered most of the inside. On the panel were a brass turntable with a short thick spindle, an arm on the gramophone principle with a stub of pencil in place of the needle, a two-point socket, two electric switches and two lengths of double flex with various attachments at each end.

'If you'll pay attention,' said the doctor, 'you'll find this is quite straightforward. Mains here.' He put the plug at one end of the fatter length of flex into a socket in the side of the box and the plug at the other end into a socket in the wall behind him. 'Mains on.' He snapped one of the switches. 'This in here.' He put the much smaller plug at one end of the thinner length of flex into the socket on the panel and showed that attached to the other end was a broken hoop of light plastic an inch and a half or so across and apparently stiffened with wire. Then, neatly enough but with rather more force than might have been expected, he tore off a corner of paper, pushed a ballpoint pen through it and fastened it by way of the hole just made to the spindle. 'You'll be wanting to run up nice neat little discs like gramophone records for your own use but this'll show the general idea. Now we lower the pencil on to the paper so, press the other switch so, and the turntable is now revolving, too slowly for you to see, but you can take it from me it is. Now: this fellow here' – he held up the plastic loop – 'is what they call a circuit-breaker. At the moment the wires in it are touching and so the circuit is closed. Now watch the pencil when I pull the wires apart and break the circuit.' The pencil together with its arm moved an undramatic but definite tenth of an inch inwards, towards the centre of rotation. 'Close.' The pencil moved back. 'Break. Close. And so on. So: when you go to bed you fasten the ring round the root of your penis, you go to sleep, the turntable revolves maybe half an inch, you get an erection, which pushes the wires apart and breaks the circuit and bingo! the pencil moves and stays in the same position until the erection passes. And so on. And in the morning, there we have a complete record of your nocturnal erections. Ingenious, don't you think?'

'Very. What use is it?'

'It's of use, or I wouldn't be asking you to go through all this riddle-me-ree, now would I? Every night, please, until further notice. Bring the discs with you when you come next week. Oh, and be sure to keep a note of the times you go to bed and wake up. Erections when you're awake don't count. And don't forget to turn off *both* switches when you get out of bed.'

While he talked the doctor had been swiftly dismantling the nocturnal mensurator. He shut the lid and put the box into a Harrod's plastic carrier, explaining with a smile that Jake wouldn't be wanting to have people in the Tube or wherever ask to see his tape recorder. On request, Jake supplied his address and telephone number, taking a visiting-card in exchange.

'Proinsias. Is that a German name?'

'Irish. It's pronounced Francis. The correct Gaelic spelling. I take it you've no objection to exposing your genitals in public?'

'I hadn't really –'

'It's only semi-public. All qualified personnel. We have a first-rate sex laboratory at the McDougall Hospital in Colliers Wood. I venture to say it's the finest in the world at this time. Professor Trefusis runs a splendid team. We'll be running the rule over you.'

'Will you?'

'I will, I'll be there too. It'll take a few days to fix it up – I'll let you know. And I'll write to your wife.'

'Just one question, doctor, if I may. Can I take it that there is a connection between my illness, convalescence and so on and my loss of, er, lib-eedo?'

'We don't generally find it helpful to talk in those terms.'

'Perhaps you'd talk in them this once just to please me. Connection?'

'Physical pain and fatigue do not in general inhibit libido.'

'Thank you.'

It was almost with eagerness that Jake embarked on his programme of inceptive regrouping. A kind of savour attached to the official, by-order-in-council doing of things often thought inappropriate, even unseemly, in those past their first youth. To the idea of doing them, at least. But first there was the Brenda side of the question to be settled. How much, if anything, was she to be told of the bits that didn't directly involve her? With the nocturnal mensurator his mind was made up for him by the impossibility of concealing it about his person on arrival back home, nor could he think of a plausible false description of it. And what after all did it matter? No accountability could be apportioned anywhere for how his tool behaved, or failed to behave, while he slept.

Its conduct in waking hours was a horse of another colour. Any woman, even the most severely rational in intention, a category that excluded Brenda, must feel slighted to some degree when the one she regarded as her own property was turned to a different sexual use, not by any means least in cases where her successful rival existed only on paper, so to speak, or in the mind. And he felt sure that all the talk he could devise about the entire point of it being the restoration of their sex-life, however well argued, however carefully listened to, would only end up with her asking him to promise to try not to enjoy it. Besides, sneaking off on the quiet with some pictorial pornographic material would be like old times.

The next morning looked like giving him as good a chance as he was likely to get: Brenda had gone off early with Alcestis to probe a new kickshaw-mart in New King's Road, an operation any male could have polished off in three hours at the most, bus there and back, but was going to last those two, travelling in the Mabbotts' Peugeot though they were, most of the day with lunch thrown in, no doubt at one of those places where they really worked on you to get you to have a glass of wine with your food. (Alcestis: he had whimpered and gone all shaky for a while at the thought – unentertained the previous day – of what would have happened without fail if she'd been at no. 47 when he got back from Rosenberg: him – Jake – flat on his back on the bamboo settee ballock-naked with the plastic whatsit round his john thomas and the other end of the flex plugged into the plugged-in nocturnal bloody mensurator in one minute flat.)

Once a keen buyer of tit-magazines, he realized as he left the house that he hadn't even glanced at one for what felt like about three years but was probably a bit more. He did know, though, that the old order, of Venus Films Ltd and Visart Dept 100, of *Kamera*, *Pagan*, *Zoom*, *QT* and *Solo* no. 3 (featuring Rosa Domaille) sold alongside science fiction in the little shop in Newport Court, had yielded place to the open and widespread sale of large glossy journals that went further and also elsewhere, in the sense that they included supposedly serious or at least non-ruttish short stories and articles on probably cars and clothes. However widespread, their sale could hardly be universal; better make for the Blake Street end of Orris Park, by tradition the cheaper and nastier end. At first glance this wasn't apparent: the buildings were no grimier, the proportion of derelict shops with corrugated iron in the window-frames no higher, the amount and variety of litter underfoot no greater. Then he saw the hand-done poster on the door of the Duke of Marlborough – Pub Live Family Entertainment with Bridie on drums, The Cowboy Himself, Mick on Duovox – and reflected that not all distinctions had been effaced.

The shop was on a corner next to a place with a lot of corroded refrigerators and rusty gas and electric cookers on the pavement outside it. Jake pretended to peer at one of these while he spied out the land. Confectionery counter –

kids' toys and things – greeting-card stand – the stuff. In he went and started trying not to read what it said on the cards and looking the stuff over. Not easy: it was arranged in an overlapping row so that only the one at the end was fully visible. In Newport Court, under the headmistressy yet motherly eye of the white-coated lady in charge, limited browsing had been the rule, half-a-crown's worth of purchase per five or six minutes. Here there were no other customers to give guidance, though some was provided by the look of the bloke behind the confectionery, just the kind of squat bald forty-year-old to jump at the chance of asking Jake menacingly if he could help him. So one fell swoop would have to do it. *Mezzanine* – hadn't they seized a couple of issues of that in Australia recently? The rest of the lettering wasn't encouraging: The Gay Lib Game, Through the Insurance Maze, Exclusive – Britain's Secret Police Network. The picture was different. It showed a girl with the kind of angular good looks that suggested a sound business head and the kind of clothes, though in some disarray, that real girls wore. In one hand she held a tipped cigarette, but what counted for much more, especially on a cover, was where the other wasn't quite. One, thought Jake. Further along he caught sight of the fragment *sington* and took it to be part of *Kensington*, the name of a periodical recently described by its proprietor (in what connection Jake had forgotten) as entirely educational in character. Two. Directly to the side he caught a glimpse of half an outsize bare breast and decided that had better be three and the lot before the bald bugger asked him if he wasn't tiring his eyes with all that reading.

As it turned out he had been hard on this man, who politely didn't smile or leer when he saw Jake's selection, named a cash sum once and said Cheers five times, the first time when he noticed the approach of his customer, again when handed the magazines, again when he took money, again when he gave change and the last time when bidden good-bye. Better than arseholes to you, thought Jake.

He set off home with quite a spring in his step. Dirty girls approached and passed him, overtook him, moved across his front. When he observed this it occured to him to take stock of them and so lend some background and depth to the study he would shortly be making of the relevant portions of *Mezzanine*, *Kensington* and whatever the other one was called – he hadn't liked to look and was carrying the things rolled up and back outwards. So, as the creatures cruised about him on the split and loosened paving-stones, advanced and receded between skips full of rubble at the kerb and fat black plastic bags full of rubbish against or near the shop-fronts, he took a bit of stock of them.

They differed from the ones he had used to know within quite a wide range and yet unmistakably, as a random bunch of passers-by in Prague would have differed from the Brussels equivalent. Apart from their dirtiness, which was often no more extreme than a look of entire neglect as in a hermit or castaway, they tended to have in common smallness of frame that wasn't quite slimness, smallness of feature that went with roundness of head, dark-blonde colouring and nothing to shout about in the way of tits, so much not so that the odd one here and there was probably a boy: anyhow, there were enough such to point to a large secret migration from (as it might have been) Schleswig-Holstein. The favoured attire suggested a lightning raid on the dressing-up chest or actual deprivation of clothing as normally thought of. They were wearing curtains, bedspreads, blankets, table-cloths, loose covers off armchairs and sofas. A sideboard-runner hung round one neck in the manner of a stole, a doubled-over loop of carpet round another in that of an academic hood. And somebody's fucking them, thought Jake.

The pageant continued unabated throughout the walk back to Burgess Avenue, so there had been no malign Blake Street influence at work. Perhaps there was one which embraced Orris Park in general and even, it could be, surrounding territories too; he must keep his eyes open on his travels and compare. Turning in at his gate he realized there was one thing shared by the whole crowd, the larger as well as the smaller, the ones in clothes no less than the ones in household textiles, the black and the white and the khaki: they had all not looked at him.

Jake wielded his latchkey and opened the front door slowly, cautiously. As soon as he had created an aperture wide enough for it to do so, a human head came into view at about the level of his knee and no more than a few inches from it. The eyes caught his and showed astonishment. He wanted to kick the head, which ascended and receded as part of a move from a crouching to a standing posture. It belonged to Mrs Sharp, the woman who came in three mornings a week to clean the house. He had told her about three-quarters of an hour earlier that he was going out for about three-quarters of an hour, so it was no more than natural that after about forty minutes she should have settled down (as he now saw) to polish the brass frame round the mat immediately inside the front door, nor that astonishment should have visited her to find him of all people entering the house at such a time and by such a route. It was sensing enough of this that must have led him to open the door in the way he had.

He had had plenty of practice at that kind of thing in the four years Mrs Sharp had been working here. Obviously she had been recommended by Alcestis and might even have worked for her at some stage. He was unsure about this and likely to remain so, since he had asked Brenda and forgotten the answer too many times. What he was sure of was that she (Mrs Sharp) bore marks of being Alcestis-trained or alternatively was Alcestis continued by other means. A round-shouldered woman of about forty with prominent but otherwise rather good teeth and a trick of murmuring indistinguishably in tones of self-reproach or mild alarm, Mrs Sharp was always in the way, his way at least. On the stairs, on the thresholds of rooms, in the narrow bit of passage from between the foot of the stairs and the dining-room door to the kitchen door (especially there), dead in front of whichever part of whichever shelf held the book he wanted – always, always. She monitored his shits, managing to be on reconnaissance patrol past the lavatory door or standing patrol in sight of it whenever he went in and out; he couldn't have said why he minded this as he did. Keeping at him in this way meant so much to her that she took 10p an hour less than the going rate and so, in these thin times, rendered herself virtually unsackable.

Today offered her special opportunities. The first of course concerned the nocturnal mensurator. Debarred from what would have been old Smudger's approach – direct questioning for as long as necessary – Mrs Sharp would if she could have led with something like 'I'm afraid I may have broken your record player or whatever it is, Mr Richardson, look. Would you see if it's still working, then I can get it repaired if it isn't.' At the moment the apparatus was in Jake's study, which he was able to keep locked on the vague grounds that it contained some rare books and without this precaution, supposedly, the milkman would rush up and pinch them. (In fact the rarest book there was a copy of his own early work on the first Greek settlements in Asia Minor: most of the small only edition had been pulped in the post-war paper shortage.) A locked door wasn't anything like a hundred-per-cent protection against Mrs Sharp – he wouldn't have been much more astonished than she just now if he had found her on the roof setting fire to petrol-soaked rags and dropping them down the study chimney – but it was a hell of a sight better than nothing.

On his entry she had flattened herself against the wall to allow him, and any twenty-stone friends he might have brought with him, to pass. He got out of range of her, so that if she fell over at this point she wouldn't be able to knock the magazines out of his hand in the process, and said weightily,

'I'm going up to my study now, Mrs Sharp.'

'Yes, Mr Richardson.' (Already a most unusual exchange: it was her habit never to speak except while she was being spoken to.)

'I've got some very important work to do.'

'Yes, Mr Richardson.'

'I don't want to be disturbed for the next hour.'

'No, Mr Richardson.'

Somebody who knew her less well than he did might have thought that this would put ideas into her head. Perhaps, but they would have come of their own accord, born of that mysterious power, shared with Alcestis, of *unconsciously* sensing how and when and where to be obstructive and acting on it. He had said what he had said merely to forearm himself against whatever way she might rise to her second special opportunity of the day, for rise to it she would: the readiness was all. The same somebody as before might have deferred matters till the afternoon or next day: no good: she would have stayed on to make up for hours not worked last week, come tomorrow so as not to have to come on Friday when her daughter, etc. *And* he was fucked if he was going to, etc. He knew the Alcestis-Mrs Sharp gang counted a lot on that reaction but sod it.

As he went upstairs he sang under his breath a ditty learned in those Army days of his:

> Get older this ...
> Get older that ...
> When there isn't a girl about
> Yer feel so lonely,
> When there isn't a girl about
> Yer on yer only ...
> Get older this (bash! bash!)
> Get older that (boom! boom!) ...

It certainly didn't take him back. Locking himself in with a load of new-bought wankery, on the other hand, did, as predicted, but the distance was far smaller in the second case. He settled down comfortably in his handsome brass-studded red-leather armchair, a present from Brenda on his fiftieth birthday, and opened *Kensington*.

After looking through it at colour-supplement speed he put it aside. It was full of chaps and parts of chaps, or rather of course it was full of girls but with chaps very much in the picture. *Zoom* and its contemporaries had occasionally included the odd chap dressed as a policeman or rustic, only he had been dressed, and the point of him had been the mistaken though innocuous one of something like comic relief, and you could usually get rid of him or most of him by folding the page. No amount of ingenuity of that order would have got rid of the chaps here.

The journal he had picked up in the shop almost at random turned out to be called *Agora*, and the breast he had spied on its cover turned out to be part of a drawing, more precisely part of a drawing-within-a-drawing that a chap in the outer drawing was drawing. He was the only visible chap throughout *Agora*, but there were dozens of his sex in the letterpress of which, apart from small or smallish advertisements and some more non-erotic drawings, it entirely consisted. The range was from she ran her dainty fingers up and down my, by way of the other night my girl-friend took hold of my, to can anything be done to straighten out my. Some of it wasn't supposed to be true and some of it was.

Lastly and with renewed expectation he came to *Mezzanine*. It was about the size of the Liverpool telephone directory but was printed on much nicer paper. As part of the fun-delaying ritual that was itself part of the fun, he began at the beginning. Car. Cigarette. Soft drink. Hard drink. Mezzanine Platform – this was some more on the lines of said she'd never seen anything like my. Cigarette. Car. Article on speedboats. Article on Loire wines. He was over halfway through this, finding it sound enough if rather jocosely written, when he so to speak remembered where he was. Guiltily he flipped over the page and came upon a small photograph and a large photograph, both a bit misty on purpose, of a very pretty girl who at the same time looked like President Carter, in the sense that her face looked like his face, and who had almost no clothes on without giving much away. Over the next page, three more photographs, arty angles, unlikely poses. Over the *next* page, well this is it folks. Wham. And (there being two such) bam. And thank you most awfully mam.

Jake stared, though without amazement. Tit- was not what this magazine was. In one sense he was on very familiar territory, even if the familiarity was slightly dated; in another he'd never been here before. His mind searched slowly. It was all a matter of how you looked at it, in two senses again if not more. In itself it was a bit . . . And for some reason you found you had to consider it in itself, even though most of the rest of her was there, including her face. In itself it had an exotic appearance, like the inside of a giraffe's ear or a tropical fruit not much prized even by the locals. He turned on and found more of the same, on again and found more art, again and came to an article on hair-pieces. Men's. To put on their heads.

In the days of *Zoom* – when, that is, *Zoom*-style had been as far as you could easily, safely and not expensively go – he had believed that to come across, by some stupendous accident, one of his favourite *Zoom* girls, Anne Austin, June Palmer or Rosa herself, in a pose such as he had just seen would have constituted the summit of human (or at least male) felicity. Well, *then* no doubt it would have done. That had been *then*.

He turned on yet again through various commemorations of the unfree good things in life until he came to the expected series of photographs with the girl on the cover as model. There was quite a lot of stuff alongside about her personal habits, including a clear statement in large letters and between quotation marks of what she regarded as the best thing in *her* life. Jake found this slightly offensive; her holding such a view was at least unobjectionable but he would have preferred to reach that conclusion about her under his own steam. In some of the accompanying pictorial pornographic material her hand was quite where it hadn't been quite on its cover and her mouth was open and her eyes shut. Right. Now that should have been just what the doctor ordered. Why wasn't it? What made it, to a very small degree but unmistakably, off-putting? Before he could get his censor out of bed the thought popped up in his mind that she was no lady. By Gad sir, he said to himself, country's going to the dogs, time and place for everything, but without squashing that thought, which even attained the clarification that while what this girl was up to or at any rate was trying to be mistaken for being up to lay well within the scope of a lady, being so photographed didn't. But, he reminded himself, the girls he imagined to himself got up to things that were much more, more – come on, out with it: more degrading than this. Yes, but that was him. And those girls did what they did because, however perversely, they enjoyed it, not because they were getting paid. He had imagined better than he knew when he credited this one with a sound business head. All rationalization and self-deception, he said to himself; you wouldn't have thought of any of that *then*. Ah, but supposing it had been *then* that you . . .

Jake did a mental about-turn. He had decided that the only picture of business-head that he really liked was one of her shopping (fully clothed) in a vegetable-market and was about to junk the whole project when he remembered with a start what the flesh-and-blood doctor had ordered. Fifteen minutes had he said? Oh Christ. Well, knock off five for time already put in. He set himself to pore grimly over business-head and Carter-face in alternate bouts of two minutes each, fighting off as best he could the distractions of the possibly-Roman ring worn by the one, the pleasantness of the rural scene in which the other wallowed, the uncertainly identifiable ornament or utensil in the shadows behind the one, and so forth. After a while, this way or that he was getting interested. Then the dead silence was broken by a tremendous rattling of the lock on the door.

That fairly hurtled him back not far off fifty years. He went into a kind of throe and made wild self-defensive motions. 'What is it?' he asked. He had to ask most of it twice or more.

No answer, further rattling, but the door itself did seem to be holding for the moment.

'What do you want? Mrs Sharp?' This was louder and steadier. 'I told you I didn't want to be –'

'– thought your knob looked as if it could do with a polish.' No no, *of course* she didn't say that, couldn't have done; she must have been talking about th' door-knob or y' door-knob, but it had sort of come through to him different.

'Oh I see. I mean it probably does, still surely there's no need for you to start on it –'

'– come back and finish it later if I'm disturbing you.'

'Yes do. No don't.' It would be anything from two to a hundred and two minutes later. 'No, finish it now you've –'

'– easily come back after I've –'

'No. No. Finish it *now*, Mrs Sharp.'

'Well . . . if that's what you really want, Mr Richardson.'

The buffeting resumed and went on for a minute or so, then stopped. Moving only his eyes, and them not much, Jake sat and waited for another half-minute. At the end of that time he executed a playful lunge, a feint. Instantly the buffeting re-resumed. He rocked triumphantly in his chair. 'Gotcha!' he hissed. 'Now try and tell me it's all imagination.'

But the funny part came when the polishing was well and truly over and he could go on where he had left off, or rather more or less where he had begun. As if acting on orders committed to memory and carried out many times in rehearsal he went to the top drawer of his desk, took out an unused long envelope, turned to the picture of Carter-face that he liked most of best, put the envelope so that it covered the less endearing part of her and went on from there.

Later he said out loud, 'And that's only the beginning. No. It's a start.'

'What does it mean?' asked Brenda.

'Well, sensate ought to mean endowed with sense or senses, as dentate if it occurs must mean endowed with teeth, but I don't see how any sort of focusing can be endowed with any sort of sense. I think they wanted an adjective from sense and noticed or someone told them sensuous and sensual were used up and they noticed or someone told them a lot of words ended in -ate. Makes it sound scientific too. Like nitrate. And focusing, well. Homing in on? No? Concentrating? Something like that.'

'I see. But what does it mean?'

'Christ, love, I don't know. Getting you, getting one interested in the other person physically, something like that I should think. Anyway, we know what we're supposed to do.'

'Yes. Darling, you're not to be cross but I must ring Elspeth before we start. She said she'd ring me today or tomorrow and I *know* it'll be while we're doing our focusing if I don't get in first. You know.'

'Check.' As just disclosed, Elspeth was of the Alcestis-Mrs Sharp sorority though, living as she did on the far side of London at Roehampton, less to be feared. 'You take as long as you have to. I'll be in the study.'

Jake finished putting the lunch plates in the rack on the metal draining-board and went where he had said. The study had been made out of what had been not much more than a spacious box-room and the kneehole desk, the celebrated red-leather armchair and a pair of Queen Anne bookcases left little space for anything else, but even he could see that the turquoise carpet was a pretty shade and went well with the wallpaper and Madras cotton curtains.

With the intention not so much of getting in the mood as of keeping up the good work he glanced at a couple of papers that lay on the desk, had been lying there in perfect security since the previous Thursday, even though it was now Monday and Mrs Sharp had by standing arrangement attended the house on the Friday and that very morning. For both times Brenda had been at home and, as in many a (or many another) case of hypernormal powers, Mrs Sharp's were severely curtailed or even curbed altogether by the presence of a third party. Jake picked up one of the papers.

M27 (he read) I find the thought of sexual intercourse with a willing female somewhat under the age of consent, say 14–15 yrs

    1 very pleasant
    2 fairly pleasant
    3 a little pleasant
    4 very unpleasant

In so far as he could make himself address his mind to the problem, he found he thought all four. The age thing didn't come into it: the attractiveness of any willing female past puberty depended for him on her attractiveness, though as far as he knew he had in practice confined himself to those of 16 yrs and over. What counted was the immediacy or lack of it. Some time or other in Hawaii or somewhere, very pleasant; on his next trip to Italy, fairly pleasant; by the end of next month in Orris Park, a little unpleasant; here and now, very unpleasant. Even that wasn't quite right because of the difference between the thought of sexual intercourse and the thought of the thought of it. If he could snap his fingers and boof, there he was in mid-job, very pleasant; if she were really actually in fact standing a yard away on the precise point of starting to show how willing she was, very unpleasant. Not unpleasant, either, just as much as his old man needed to set it trying to haul itself up into his abdomen. But he couldn't write all this down, especially since the question was obviously nothing to do with any of it. Like the good examinee he had always been (best classical scholarship of his year at Charterhouse, First in Mods, best First of his year in Greats) he asked himself what was expected here, what was being looked for. A means of sorting out the child-molesters from the gerontophiles, why yes, and no doubt of making the finer distinction between the inhibited who welcomed any accepted restriction and the robust sturdy husky hardy hearty etc. He ticked 2 and picked up the other paper.

A fantastically beautiful girl with an unbelievable figure wearing a skin-tight dress cut as low as it possibly could be is looking at me with eyes blazing with uncontrollable passion (he read). With lazy languorous movements she peels off the dress and reveals herself as completely stark naked and utterly nude. Her breasts are so enormous that there is hardly room for them on her thorax. They are rising and falling with irresistible desire as with her shapely hips swaying lazily she glides over and stands insolently before me with her hands on her curving hips and her colossal breasts jutting 100 words out at me. I tear off all my clothes and she gives a tremendous gasp of astonishment and admiration and awe. She lies down on a bed which is there.

There was more, but he was still 73 words short of the 600 minimum set by Rosenberg and had already been compelled to introduce two additional girls, the first with immense breasts, the second with gigantic ones, for the sake of variety. He felt that this must violate some important canon of the genre but could find no other alternative to direct repetition. It was not that he had been idle; this was the fourth draft. The first, which had said all he really wanted to say on the matter, had consisted only of nouns, verbs, prepositions, pronouns and articles and been 113 words long; gamma minus at best. Well, he had to find those 73 somewhere before setting off for Harley Street the next morning. What about a black girl? With Brobdingnagian breasts? No no, with gleaming ebony skin. Mm ... The trouble was that being white himself he tended to think about white girls when he thought about girls at all.

Brenda tapped softly at the open door. 'All right?'

'Right.'

He followed her across the small landing, where a Bengal rug lay, and into their bedroom. Here, in a drill they had been through many times together, they lifted off, folded and laid down on an ottoman the patchwork quilt she had expertly made. Again by tradition, lapsed in this case, she slipped off to the bathroom and he quickly undressed and got into bed. He felt calm and yet uneasy, quite resolved to carry out orders but unable not to wish that something harmless in itself would prevent what was in prospect. After a minute he turned over so that he would have his back to Brenda when she reappeared. She had treated with exemplary seriousness Rosenberg's letter about her need to lose weight, had joined the local group of Guzzlers Anonymous at the first opportunity and had already taken off six ounces, but that wasn't going to be enough to make her feel all right about being seen naked, which she had avoided for the past year or more, he supposed.

There was a patter of arrival behind him (she moved lightly for so large a woman) and she got in and snuggled up to him with wincing and puffing noises.

'Ooh! It's freezing. It's supposed to be the middle of April and it's like January.'

'Would you like to turn the other way?'

'No, this is fine for me. Had you heard of comfort eating before?'

'What?'

'Comfort eating. What Dr Thing said I'd been going in for because of feeling sexually inadequate. Had you heard of it?'

'I think so, anyway it's clear enough what it's supposed to mean, which is all balls. If there's anybody who feels sexually inadequate it's me and I haven't started eating my head off. Just another example of thinking that if you name something you've explained it. Like . . . like permissive society.'

'I don't think you're always meant to go in for comfort eating when you feel sexually inadequate. And in any case what makes you think you're the one who feels it so terrifically you leave everybody else standing, how adequate do you think *I* feel when I think about things and look back, that's what I'd like to . . .'

Brenda, who had started talking at some speed, stopped altogether because a jet was passing and even at this range she would have to shout rather and she was bad at shouting. A part of the window-frame buzzed for a short time as it always did on these occasions. Eventually Jake said,

'My fault. I just got fed up and guilty and ashamed. Of course you must feel inadequate if we have to use the word, but I can tell you there's no need for you to, it's all me, we went into that.'

'I know we went into it, but we decided it must be me as well as you.'

'You may have thought so, but it wasn't what we decided.'

'Well *I* think it was. And of course it is, it's obvious. Anyway I'm warm enough now. Hadn't we better get on with it?'

'All right.' Grunting, Jake turned over so as to face his wife. They intertwined their legs in a friendly way.

'Tell me again what we're meant to do.'

'We take it in turns to stroke and massage each other anywhere but what you used to call down below.'

'Did I? Anyway I bags you start.'

'Okay. Lift up . . . Put your arm . . . That's right.'

He started stroking the back of her neck and her left shoulder and upper arm. She sighed and settled herself more comfortably, moving her head about on the pillow. A minute or so went by.

'Is that nice?' he asked.

'Yes. Are we meant to talk?'

'He didn't say we weren't to, the doctor, so I suppose it's all right.'

'Good.'

But neither did any more talking for the moment. With his glasses off, Brenda's face was a bit of a blur to Jake but he could see her eyes were shut. By his reckoning, the second minute was just about up when she said,

'Did the doctor say we weren't to have a kiss?'

'No.'

'Let's have one then.'

He couldn't have said how long it had been since they had kissed each other on the mouth, probably less than twenty-four hours, but it was longer since he had noticed them doing that. Their mouths stayed together for a time, again showing friendliness, this time roughly of the sort that, on his side, he would have shown an amiable acquaintance in public at a New Year's party. He thought Brenda was putting about the same into it. The kiss ended by common agreement.

'Well, that was all right . . .' he said.

'. . . as far as it went. We'll get better, darling. Lots of ground to be made up.'

'Yes – your turn now.'

'To what?'

'Stroke me the way I was stroking you.'

'Oh yes. Will the same sort of place suit you? Round here?'

'Fine.'

'I'm sorry I'm so fat,' said Brenda after a moment.

'That's all right, I mean you couldn't help it and you've started doing something about it.'

'Yes. Do you think I ought to do something about my hair?'

'What's the matter with it?'

'Matter with it? It's all grey, or hadn't you noticed?'

'Of course I'd noticed. It's a very nice grey. A, an interesting sort of grey.'

'Wow, you make it sound terrific. I could have it dyed back to something like what it used to be. They do jolly good dyes these days.'

'Oh but you can always tell.'

'Not if it's done properly. And supposing you can tell, what about it, what's wrong with that?'

'Well, it looks a bit . . .'

'A bit what? A bit off? A bit bad taste? A bit not quite the thing? A bit mutton dressed up as lamb?'

'Of course not. Well yes, a bit, but that's not really what I . . . I just think it looks ugly. Because it's unnatural.'

'So's make-up unnatural. So's shaving armpits. So's you shaving.'

'All right, just ugly then.'

'I wasn't going to have it bright red or bright yellow or bright purple, just something like what it used to be like, which was brownish mouse if you remember. No I think you think it's sort of out of place.'

'I doubt if we're supposed to talk as much as this.'

'Not that you care.'

Jake looked mildly startled. 'What do you mean?'

'You're not enjoying this are you, me stroking you? Your face went all resigned when I started. Are you?'

'I'm not disenjoying it.'

'Thanks a *lot*,' said Brenda, stopping stroking.

'No don't. What else could I have said? You knew anyway. And it isn't you. With this it really isn't you. You said we'd got a lot of ground to make up. We've only just started.'

'All right, but I reckon it's your turn again now.'

'Fair enough.'

'Did the doctor say you weren't to stroke my tits?'

'No.'

'Well, you can stroke them then, can't you?'

'I suppose so.'

'Only suppose so? They aren't down below are they?'

'No, but they're sort of on the way there. Put it like this, if down below's red and your arm's green, that makes your tits amber.'

'Yes, I see. Perhaps we'd better be on the safe side and not.'

'On the other hand of course, it'd be a natural mistake to make, so if it is, if it would be a mistake you'd think he'd have made sure of saying so, you know, oh and by the way non-genital includes tits, excludes them rather, I should say breasts. No, mammary areas.'

'You mean we can?'

'I don't see what harm it could do, do you?'

'Fire away.'

He fired away for a full two minutes. She stayed quite passive, eyes shut, breathing slowly and steadily, giving an occasional contented groan. No doubt what he was doing, or how he was doing it, bore a close resemblance to its counterpart of a couple of years before, but there was no means of comparison because he had felt so different then, in particular felt more. What he felt now was an increasing but still never more than mild desire to stop doing what he was doing. In itself each motion he made was unequivocally if only by a little on the pleasant side of the pleasant/unpleasant borderline; the snag was there were so many of them. Patting a favourite child on the head or indeed stroking a beloved animal (to single out two activities he had never felt much drawn to) became unnatural if continued beyond a certain short time, however willing child or animal might be to let things go on. My God, another twenty-five minutes of this? – it was a good job he was such a faithful doer of what doctors told him to do. Hadn't Rosenberg told him to carry on with this bleeding sensate-focusing carry-on for *up to* half an hour? Twenty minutes was that, wasn't it? So was ten. And five. But to argue so was to use advertiser's mathematics. Amazing reductions at Poofter's, up to twenty per cent on all furnishings. Daily brushing with Bullshitter's fleweridated toothpaste reduces cavities by up to thirty per cent, in the case you happen to be looking at by only point-nought-one of one per cent but what of it, and also of course helps fight (not helps *to* fight) tooth decay, alongside drinking things and not eating toffee all day long. Daily brushing with candlewax or boot-polish would also reduce cavities by up to something or other and help fight tooth decay. There were enough laws already but surely there ought to be one about up to, restricting it to, oh, between the figure given and half of it. Helping fight things would be rather more of a –

'Isn't it about time for my turn?' asked Brenda.

'Oh, er ... yes I suppose it is. I sort of lost count of time.'

'Carried away. No I don't mean that darling, forget I said it, I was just being frightfully silly. Now on this round I think we might ...'

'Hey!'

'What's the matter?'

'Supposed to be non-genital.'

'That's non isn't it, there?'

'Well yes, but only –'

'Genital's genital and non's non.'

'But the spirit of the –'

'Sod the spirit. And even the spirit doesn't say you're not supposed to enjoy it.'

'I don't think we ought to –'

'Shut up.'

After a little while, Jake began to breathe more deeply, then to flex and unflex his muscles. Forgotten feelings, located in some mysterious region that seemed neither body nor mind, likewise began to possess him. Brenda sighed shakily. He pressed himself against her and at once, try as he would, the more irresistibly for his trying, which was like the efforts of a man with no arms to pick up a pound note off the pavement, the flow reversed itself. In a few more seconds he relaxed.

'Oh well, that's that,' he said.

'No it isn't. Only for now. It shows there's something. What do you expect at this stage?'

'What I expect at *this* stage, and what I shall no doubt get, is about twenty more minutes of an experience I wasn't looking forward to and which has turned out to justify such ... mild forebodings. It isn't you, it's me.'

'Don't think you're the only one, mate. It isn't you, it's me cuts both ways, you know. You're not blaming me, that's how you mean it, but you're not taking me into consideration either. What about that?'

'Yes. Yes, you're right.'

'If you had – been considering me, you might have wondered what I was doing telephoning Elspeth when all I needed to do to make sure we weren't interrupted was take the receiver off. That's right. Putting off the evil hour. Giving way to mild whatnames. It wasn't you, it was me. Now you'd better start stroking again, uncongenial as it may be. The doctor said you were to.'

'It's not un*congenial*, it's just –'

'No, not there. Do my back.'

He started doing her back. 'You said it was nice before, when I was on your shoulder and arm. Was it? Is this?'

'Oh yes. Not tremendous, but nice.'

'Sexy?'

'No,' she said as if he had asked her whether she had said yes or no. 'Nice all the same. I like all that sort of thing, massages and sauna baths and whatnot. You don't, do you?'

'Never been able to see the point of it.'

'I suppose it's just how you're made. I suggest what we do now is go on for however long it is and not mind too much how we get there, talk or recite or sing as long as we put in the time.'

'Yes. The idea must be to get used to touching each other again.'

'Start to get us used.'

That was on the Monday. On the Tuesday Jake went down
to see Rosenberg again, taking his homework with him: the
completed questionnaire, the sixth and final draft of his
fantasy and the paper discs that recorded the doings of the
nocturnal mensurator. These troubled him slightly. Each
disc bore a faintly pencilled arc with, at intervals, a thicker
line or perhaps a pair of contiguous ordinary lines in a radial
position. They were no more than a millimetre or two long
and must represent movements of the metal arm on the
breaking and making of the electrical circuit. But by this time
Jake had forgotten which way the thing was supposed to go
when, so he didn't know whether he had had a series of
virtually continuous erections, broken only by breathing-
spaces in a continuous-performance dreamland orgy, or half
a dozen flickers of mild interest per night.

Though he inspected the discs thoroughly, Rosenberg
made no comment on this or any other point about them
and Jake didn't care to ask him. He took even longer over
the questionnaire, nodding as he looked through it with a
slow regularity Jake began to find offensive: was he (Jake)
such a predictable mess? He had only just begun to find this
when the doctor suddenly raised his head and, Curnow-like,
stared hard at him for God knew how long. Could this be a
reaction to the breach of discipline in his answer to $M41$ I
think children should receive sex education 1 as soon as they
can understand 2 before puberty 3 at puberty – *never* scrawled
at the bottom? More likely it was his regarding ($M49$) the
thought of being watched while engaged in sexual intercourse as not very pleasant nor fairly pleasant nor even a
little unpleasant but very unpleasant that had produced the

stare, on this view a signal much less of hostility or alarm than of wonder, of a desire to fix in the mind something to tell one's grandchildren.

It was soon clear that the fantasy was altogether on the wrong lines. Rosenberg's chubby little features filled with deep disappointment. Once or twice he screwed up his eyes and frowned as if in actual pain, whether bodily or mental. But in the end he laid aside the neatly typed sheets with a muttered promise to take a more careful look later and asked Jake a lot of questions about his childhood and adolescence, some on new topics like any dreams, wet and non-wet, he remembered from that period and how he had felt about the physical changes he had experienced then, others over already-traversed ground, his parents' relationship and such-like, in the evident but vain hope of eliciting significant con-tradiction of previous responses. Together with his detailed account of the non-genital sensate focusing session, inter-spersed with further questions from Rosenberg which con-tinuing to listen in silence would in most cases have rendered needless, these activities filled up the hour. Or very nearly: there was time at the end for three momentous directives. One – Jake and Brenda were to go on to practise genital sensate focusing, a term which Rosenberg explained with a wealth of well-known words derived from the classical tongues. Two – Brenda was to accompany Jake on his next visit to the consulting-room. And three – before that could come to pass, the following Thursday afternoon in fact, Jake was to visit the sex laboratory at the McDougall Hospital. By way of reassurance Rosenberg again asked him to say, virtually with his hand on the book, whether he had any objection to exposing his genitals in public and was given the answer no.

The nearer it got to Thursday afternoon the less that answer squared with the truth. In the past he had been very willing indeed to carry out such exposure to selected indi-vidual females in private, though not of course just like that, but in the Army, in sports changing-rooms and so on he had been one of the majority who preferred where possible to keep themselves to themselves. At the time he had followed that policy without thinking of it as a policy or as anything at all, but now it looked as if he had better start thinking of it as something. This change of approach was just part of the steady progress towards more sophisticated awareness which had come to fuck up (so it seemed to him) most kinds of human behaviour in the last however many years it was. Preferring to keep himself to himself must be allied to the quirk whereby he regarded the thought of being watched while engaged in sexual intercourse as very unpleasant. And that was going to have to do for the minute.

His bus map told him that having taken the 127 to Gower Street he could change there to a 163 and, via Chelsea, Putney Bridge and Southfields, be transported to Colliers Wood. That was what he did. On this journey he had remembered to bring the *Times* crossword puzzle but the lurching and plunging of the vehicle at the various irregularities of the highway, together with the difficulty of the clues, led him to stop it soon. He was also distracted by the very loud unsteady wailing noise to be heard whenever the driver used his brakes. The view out of the windows south of the river, after the 163 had passed under a couple of dozen railway bridges in a mile or so, was definitely less attractive than what was to be seen from the 127. Here were derelict churches covered with grime, yards of hoardings with no posters on them, dining-rooms and small draper's shops such as he hadn't seen since the '30s, waste lots big enough to accommodate a shopping complex barely to be dreamed of and, beyond them, hulking greyish towers of offices or dwellings that loomed in the smoky distance. He supposed that people who lived here might well vote for or against somebody at an election, neither of which he had bothered to do since 1945 (Liberal). The ones he saw had an archaic look too, dumpy, dark-clothed, wearing hats: the infiltrators from Schleswig-Holstein had not reached here yet.

Sitting near the front of the bus on the upper deck he became aware by degrees that a sort of altercation was going on behind him, the sort, as it soon proved, in which only one voice was to be heard, a woman's, deep and powerful, projected with that pressure of the diaphragm used by actors.

'It isn't right, is it? I mean do you think it's right? After all these years and all I been through? I said I've had enough, I done everything you told me and I've had enough, I said. I told him straight. What's in it for me, I said, yeah, what's in it for me? I've had e-bloody-nough. Now that's my rights, isn't it? I reckon that's my rights, don't you? I said don't you?'

He looked over his shoulder to see what kind of unfortunate was having to put up with this, and found that nobody and everybody was, staring hard out of the window or at a newspaper or into space. The speaker wore a dark-brown coat flecked with green and a very pale lilac-coloured silk scarf round the neck. That neck looked too slender for the job of connecting the broad-shouldered trunk to the large round head. The woman's complexion was dull, her chin pointed, her nose thin, her hair straight and dry, standing out and up from her scalp. While she continued to talk she seemed never to look directly at anyone, always between people.

'I'm not going to stay there,' she repeated several times in the same tone as before, accusing rather than angry. 'I told him so. I said, I don't mind coming along, well I do, but I will. I don't mind coming along but I'm not going to stay. I've had enough of that. Where's it got me, that's what I'd like to know. It's not fair, it's taking advantage, that's what it is. He's got me where he wants me and there's nothing I can do about it. I been given a raw deal, haven't I, a raw bloody deal. Don't anybody think I've been given a raw deal?'

Jake had turned back to face his front after one good look. The sound-quality of the last couple of dozen words told him that the woman had got up and was moving towards the top of the stairs, presumably on the way to getting off the bus. On an impulse he didn't at once understand he shifted round in his seat and said, 'Yes, I do.'

Now she did look straight at someone and he saw with

unusual clarity that everything about her face was wrong. The tip of her nose was a narrow white peak above a pair of ill-matched nostrils partly outlined in red; her eyes didn't so much protrude or glare as have no discernible sockets to lie in; her eyebrows were irregular streaks of bristle; her ears were set a little too far back on her skull; the borders of her lips were well marked at one corner and blurred at the other; the state of her skin showed him for the first time what it really meant to say that someone was pale and drawn. That's right, he thought to himself: they're not just mad inside their heads, they're mad to their fingertips, to the ends of their hair. And he had spoken to her to make her give him the straight look he had needed in order to see that in her.

What might have been the beginnings of a smile showed on the woman's face in the second before she stepped clumsily to one side and passed out of view down the stairs. Soon afterwards the bus stopped and from his position above the pavement he saw her walk away, swinging her arms a lot. Some distance ahead lay a small piece of park or public garden, a grassy triangle where, with a show of energy unexpected in these latitudes, a group of men in helmets and jerkins were attacking some trees. Products of their labours were strewn about them in the shape of much sound timber and vigorous foliage. The peevish wavering groan of their saws could be clearly heard through the noise of the traffic. At first idly, then with concern, Jake took in a rusty street-sign that said Trafalgar Place. Distracted by the incident of the madwoman, he was about to overshoot the stopping-point he had picked out on his de luxe *A to Z*. He toiled his way downstairs at his best speed but no kind of speed shown by him would have affected the progress of the bus, which finally dropped him a couple of hundred yards beyond the turning he wanted.

It was raining slowly but, with his umbrella and navy-blue light mackintosh, he found this no great infliction and set off with a brisk stride, a touch elated at having successfully brought off what was for him an out-of-the-way journey. There were six minutes to go before his appointment, which should be enough if the hospital was reasonably close to the main road. He had nearly reached the corner when he saw something he did find a great infliction, a figure he recognized standing on the opposite pavement and looking at him. Of course the McDougall was a psychiatric as well as a psychological joint; of course those who attended it regularly knew the nearest bus-stop to it; of course chaps who were fool enough to speak to people like that deserved all they got. And of course his first thought was of flight, but he loathed being late for anything. If he had known the district even slightly he might have risked a detour but again he didn't. So he turned the corner and quickened up to light-infantry speed.

'Excuse me!'

It was harsh and hostile and he ignored it.

'Excuse me.'

This time he thought he detected a note of appeal and found himself half-turning and slowing down so that the woman could catch him up. 'Yes?'

'I seen you on the bus, didn't I?'

'I believe so, yes.'

'You said you thought I been given a raw deal.'

'Yes, I . . .'

'Why d'you say that?' she asked merely as if she wanted to know.

'Well, I thought you seemed a bit upset and I wondered if I could cheer you up, that's all.'

'You're the first one as said I been given a raw deal for I don't know how long. They all say I get the best attention and all they want to do is take care of me but they got a funny way of showing it is what I say. I was in the hospital for five months and all they done was boss me around. The doctor just give his orders and never took a blind bit of notice of how I felt or what I thought. It's not fair, it's taking advantage.'

All this had been said in a tone that showed a sense of injury but none of the bitterness noticeable on the bus. Poor devil, thought Jake, a complete stranger throws her a kind

74

word and she calms down immediately – these bloody doctors are all the same. Not that he had stopped looking for the hospital, of which at the moment there was no sign.

'Are you disturbed?' went on the lunatic.

He grasped at once that to her there could be no other reason for coming this way than her own. 'No, just, er, tension.'

'I been disturbed for . . . a long time. Ever since my mum died but they say it's nothing to do with that. Do you think it's to do with that?'

'I don't know. It must have something to do with it, I'd have thought.'

'You're the first one as ever said I been given a raw deal.' She turned her head towards him and smiled, showing a wide variety of teeth. 'That was real nice, that was. Real nice.'

'Oh I think most other people would have done the same,' he said, trying not to gabble it, to stay calm, to work out what to do if she pounced on him.

'I get very lonely. I'd like someone to come and see me. After I've had my tea, that's when I wouldn't mind someone, that sort of time. They don't, though, not them, no fear, they got better things to do, the lot of them. Dead selfish, the lot of them. Six weeks it's been since Harry come, and as for that June . . .'

Just then there was a sign of the hospital in the form of a hospital sign, and the monologue on selfishness kept up satisfactorily while the two approached Reception – All Patients, stopping only at the swing doors. Inside, Jake's companion, swinging her arms in her awful way, went straight on without a word or a look while he made for the desk. A girl in a grey uniform standing behind it called over his shoulder,

'Excuse me dear, are you sure you know where to go?'

The words were delivered with unimpeachable gentleness but it was as if – no, to hell with as if: the madwoman had heard something different. She stopped dead and sent towards the desk a look of great fear and hatred. In that moment Jake recognized that, with the sole exception of the three words he had spoken on the bus, she had heard nothing of what he had said to her; he also withdrew what he had been thinking a couple of minutes earlier about bloody doctors.

'Who are you going to see, dear?'

'Holmes. Dr Holmes.'

'Good, he'll be waiting for you.' The girl blew out her cheeks as she turned to Jake. 'I'm new – they told me everyone was supposed to report here. Sorry – can I help you?'

'I was told to ask for Professor Trefusis.' He squared his jaw, took darting glances round the hall and tapped his rolled newspaper against the palm of his hand, trying to look like the vital, dynamic, thrusting head of a giant transcontinental sex consortium. 'I'm Dr Richardson.'

'Oh yes, doctor, room 35, third floor.'

In the lift, he asked himself what the hell he was doing there. Then he realized he hadn't noticed anything at all about what the girl at the desk had looked like except for her grey uniform, and told himself what.

'Mr Richardson? Do come in. I'm Professor Trefusis.'

After the Rosenberg business no mere Yap Islander or Kalahari Bushman going under that name would have disconcerted Jake in the least, but a woman did rather, especially one that even he in his reduced state could see was very attractive, in her middle thirties probably, with thick blonde hair parted at the side, blue eyes and a figure that would not have thrown *Zoom* into abject disgrace. Her manner was quiet and friendly. In succession she introduced him to Dr Thatch, a boyish-looking boy with mnemonically helpful abundant long hair, Dr something he missed, another boy but still distinguishable from his colleague by being nearly bald, Miss Newman, a lumpish, gloomy girl of about twenty(?), and Mr something he couldn't believe was a name, which didn't matter much because the man it referred to, tall and of dignified bearing, stood out at once from everyone else in the room by being black; he was said to be a citizen of Ghana and present only as an observer. Oh, so everyone else was going to twiddle with him, hey?

'And Dr Rosenberg of course you know.'

Seen by Jake for the first time in the company of others, the Irishman looked unexpectedly less small than on his own; he could have been as much as five foot, even perhaps an inch or two more. He shook hands and gave a cheerful smile.

'The purpose of this preliminary encounter,' said Professor Trefusis in the tones of a lecturer, but of an outstandingly good lecturer, one interested in the subject, 'is to establish amicable relations on an informal basis. We find the quickest way of doing this is for me to quote a few personal details relating to each member of the team. Now we know about you, Mr Richardson, that your first name is Jaques or Jake, that you're sixty years old, you're married, you're employed at Oxford University and you have a house in Orris Park. My first name is Rowena, I'm thirty-six years old, married to a photographer, we have two children in their teens and we live just up the road from here in Tooting. Dr Thatch is called Bill . . .'

Jake stopped listening then. He meant to switch on again to hear the bald doctor's name but forgot to. This part was easy enough; what was to come? What *sort* of thing? Before he could ask, Rowena Trefusis (Daphne du Maurier? No, more like Barbara Cartland) got there on her own.

'. . . people you're going to work with in a relaxed atmosphere. The work itself is quite straightforward. We hook you into an electric circuit – the current passed is minute, so even if everything went wrong at once you'd be in no danger even of discomfort – and then we present you with a series of sexual stimuli and measure your responses to them. It's an essentially simple process and the procedure is totally informal.'

'That's good,' said Jake, thinking it was something to be spared a totally formal procedure of measuring his responses.

'We try to use dress as a way of promoting informality. No white coats here, you'll have noticed.'

He just about had; now that he looked further he saw that the boys were wearing zipped-up jackets of imitation leather and trousers of some stuff like oakum or jute, Miss Newman the same sort of trousers and a light pullover with a Union Jack on it and the head of the team a smartly cut suit in what might have been highbrow mackintosh material. The African of course was turned out like a Japanese businessman. Jake made some approving noises.

'Well, I think we might as well –'

'Just one moment if I may, Professor Trefusis.' Rosenberg's manner had turned grave. 'You're sure, Mr Richardson, you've no objection to exposing your genitals in public?'

If you ask me that again, my little man, Jake thought to

himself, I'll expose yours right here and now and your weeny bum for good measure. He said, 'Quite sure.'

'Very well, so let's be getting along to the theatre.'

'The what?' Images of operating tables and surgical masks rose in Jake's mind. 'Isn't that going to be rather . . .'

All of them except Miss Newman laughed. Professor Trefusis stopped almost at once and looked self-reproachful.

'I'm sorry, Mr Richardson, we've made that mistake before. Have no fear – you won't have to face any spotlights or rolls of drums. Dr Rosenberg meant the lecture theatre.'

'The *what*? Look, if you think I'm going to . . . expose my genitals to a whole crowd of God knows –'

'There'll be no crowd, I promise you. The number is eight, and one of those is doubtful.'

'All medical students,' said Thatch. 'Think of them as doctors, like us.'

'They won't get in anybody's way,' said Rosenberg. 'They've been carefully briefed on being as unobtrusive as possible and things are so arranged that you'll hardly know they're there.'

Jake reflected: there were six of them here; another seven or eight wouldn't make much odds, true, but it was a bit thick to be treated as mid-Victorian for not favouring a come-one-come-all admissions policy at the impending show. When he signified that on consideration this could go ahead they switched to treating him like a child just bravely out of its mopes or dumps. So, as the party trooped along a corridor that had the look of being identical to several hundred others in the place, he was not best pleased when Rosenberg moved him a little apart from the others and said,

'I found your attitude just now quite interesting.'

'Oh you did, did you?'

'You reacted somewhat violently to the notion of a large number of persons witnessing our investigations.'

'Mm.'

'Why?'

'Well, to start with, it's not inconceivable I might be recognized.'

'Would that be so disastrous?'

'Most things people object to aren't so disastrous or even disastrous, doctor. I object to somebody who knows me seeing me having this done, whatever it may be.'

'You mean the exposure itself?'

'Well – needing treatment for sexual . . . inadequacy.'

'Really now? You wouldn't object to being known to need treatment for, er, diabetes, which arises from insulin inadequacy?'

'Of course not. That's different.'

'Would you call that a mature attitude?'

'Perhaps I wouldn't and then again perhaps I would, and either way it's my attitude. Like my genitals.'

'We'll discuss this again, Mr Richardson,' said Rosenberg as they approached an unluxurious lift in which the others already stood.

The lecture theatre was of a type familiar to Jake chiefly from American films: semi-circular tiers of seats rising up from a level space on the other side of which were blackboards and a projection-screen attached to the wall. Near the middle of the space there stood a metal framework mounted on struts and castors and with electric cables attached to several of its components; Jake assumed that what he saw was the back of the apparatus, which as he soon gathered bore dials or other measuring devices on its front. He found himself sitting on an ugly and expensive-looking straight-backed chair without his trousers and underpants. Otherwise he was neatly, almost formally dressed on the clean-linen-for-the-scaffold principle: dark-grey suit jacket, cream shirt, well-knotted regimental tie, grey socks and much-polished black shoes. The promise of immunity from spotlights given him a little earlier had been kept in the letter but not so much in the spirit: though there were several sources of light, all of them overhead or somewhere near it, their illumination was concentrated on him and the couple of dozen square yards round him; the one exception shone on the faces of Thatch and his bald colleague as they peered at their machine and clicked a switch here and there. Professor Trefusis stood near Jake at a metal table taking folders, typewritten sheets and a hardbacked file-cover of some kind out of a briefcase and arranging them on the table. Her expression was serious almost to the point of grimness, like that of an official about to announce a threat to the security of the kingdom. What was her husband like? What did he photograph? Did she do this instead of sex or was she so barmy about it that she had to spend her whole working day on this sort of substitute or semblance, keeping herself quiet, so to speak, until she could scuttle off for several uninterrupted hours of the real thing? Could anyone really tell? What about the visitor from Ghana, the only other person in plain sight? Which raised a question.

'Are your students here, Professor Trefusis?'

'Yes, all eight of them.'

'So the doubtful one made it after all; I'm so glad. Tell me, how can they see to take notes?'

'They don't have to. All the technical information and a full account of the procedure have been circulated to them already. From their point of view, this session provides an opportunity to watch the work actually being carried out under field conditions.'

'Oh I see.'

'I think we're about ready. Miss Newman?'

Miss Newman came into the light carrying a length of flex that ended in what looked to Jake like a classier version of the plastic hoop on the old nocturnal mensurator. Without looking him in the eye she hung it on him and withdrew. Was that all she did?

'Bill?'

'Okay.'

'Now Mr Richardson, I want you to try and concentrate entirely on me, on what I tell you and what I show you. Forget about everybody else. If there's anything you don't like for any reason you're to say so immediately, and you can stop the whole session at any time simply by saying Stop. Right? Now. Shut your eyes. Have a sexual fantasy. Think of something that really turns you on.'

What Jake wanted to say immediately was that nothing really did that and if anything within reason really did then he wouldn't be there and hadn't Rosenberg told her so, but he followed doctor's orders and thought away like mad. Or tried to. Girl. Beautiful girl. Fantastically beautiful girl with an unbelievable ... No. *Girl*. Girl with slinky dress which she slowly draws up over her head. Underclothes and stockings. No, tights these days. Bugger these days. She slowly takes off one stocking. But he'd never been one for that kind of thing: off with the lot in short order had been his way. Off with the lot, then. Kiss. And so forth. He was well, or as well as he could manage, into the so forth when Professor Trefusis said,

'All right, Mr Richardson, hold it and relax for a moment. Bill?'

'Point-nine and thirty-three point-nine.'

Perhaps these figures displeased or disquieted the boss; anyway, she went over and joined the two at the apparatus, behind whom Jake could now make out two or three or more dim shapes. He could tell there was at least one other person to his left rear but didn't look round. Only the Ghanaian observer was now in full view; he had got in a lot of observing when Miss Newman did her bit and even now was still at it on and off. Jake wanted to tell him to pull up a prayer-mat or whatever he fancied and be his guest. He yawned and stretched. It could hardly be that he had broken the machine by overloading it – no no, here came Professor Trefusis with a satisfied expression.

'Sorry about that.' She picked up the file he had noticed and passed it to him. 'Would you read aloud what it says on the first page? I should explain that the object is to make sure you're turned off after each stimulus.'

'Ah.' He found that the thing was actually a loose-leaf book containing sheets of typescript. Clear enough. He read aloud,

'Apart from the peculiar tenets of individual thinkers, there is also in the world at large an increasing inclination to stretch unduly the powers of society over the individual, both by the force of opinion and even by that of legislation; and as the tendency of all the changes taking place in the world is to strengthen society and diminish the power of the individual, this encroachment is not one of the evils which tend spontaneously to disappear, but, on the contrary, to grow more and more formidable. The disposition of mankind, whether as rulers or as fellow-citizens, to impose their own opinions and inclinations as a rule of conduct on others, is so energetically supported by some of the best and by some of the worst feelings incident to human nature that it is hardly ever kept under restraint by anything but want of power; and as the power is not declining, but growing, unless a strong barrier of moral conviction can be raised against the mischief, we must expect, in the present circumstances of the world, to see it increase.'

He shut the book and handed it back, aware as he did so that no more observing was going on in his immediate neighbourhood. Whatever was next came out of one of the folders and was held up so that the group near the machine could see it. A moment later the professor was showing him a magazine photograph of one of the business-head-Carter-face sisterhood displaying her giraffe's ear.

'I don't like that,' he said.

It was out of sight in an instant. 'What don't you like about it?'

'It's ugly.'

'You find the model ugly?'

'No, not at all. I mean her . . . parts.'

'They repel you?'

'Yes. What I see there repels me.'

She hesitated and glanced momentarily to his left. That must be Rosenberg standing there, perhaps among others, and were those questions his, put on his behalf instead of directly out of what, etiquette? Never mind: with no more said the second exhibit was exhibited after the same fashion as the first. It was much more up Jake's street, a nice-looking girl who also looked nice, possible too in the sense that you met girls like her, and arranged or shown in what might be called neo-*Zoom* style – advantage taken of some of the freedoms of the last few years without the surrender of decency.

'Better?'

'Fine.'

'Concentrate on it.' Trefusis leaned towards him, lowered her voice and said kindly, 'And remember this: by now nobody's thinking of you as an individual or a person. You're just an object.'

'Thank you.'

He concentrated and quite soon it started being rather a success, nothing to cause any wild surmising at the instrument panel, but still. This part went on for some minutes. Then he was told to forget about that and given the book open at a different page. He read aloud,

'If all mankind minus one were of one opinion, and only one person were of the contrary opinion, mankind would be no more justified in silencing that one person than he, if he had the power, would be justified in silencing mankind. Were an opinion a personal possession of no value except to the owner; if to be obstructed in the enjoyment of it were simply a private injury, it would make some difference whether the injury was inflicted only on a few persons or on many. But the peculiar evil of silencing the expression of an opinion is that it is robbing the human race; posterity as well as the existing generation; those who dissent from the opinion, still more than those who hold it. If the opinion is right, they are deprived of the opportunity of exchanging error for truth; if wrong, they lose, what is almost as great a benefit, the clearer perception and livelier impression of truth, produced by its collision with error.'

The third offering showed two girls being familiar with each other, no more than that, on a piece of very clean and neat garden furniture. That went down reasonably well too. Before his third bout of reading Jake said,

'May I ask a question?'

'Certainly.'

'I'd just like to make it clear' – he resisted the temptation to look over his shoulder – 'that what, well, appealed to me there wasn't what they were getting up to really, it was just the fair one, the look of her face and her breasts.'

'I'm sorry, what's your question?'

'Oh. Oh well I haven't really got one, I just wanted to say that.'

There was no reply apart from an undecided nod of the head, which he felt was quite as much as his non-question had deserved. Why had he bothered? Perhaps the same problem was exercising others: he heard whispers from the far side of the apparatus and a murmur behind him. But in a short time he was reading aloud,

'We take care that, when there is a change, it shall be for change's sake, and not from any idea of beauty or convenience; for the same idea of beauty or convenience would not strike all the world at the same moment, and be simultaneously thrown aside by all at another moment. But we are progressive as well as changeable: we continually make new inventions in mechanical things, and keep them until they are again superseded by better; we are eager for improvement in politics, in education, even in morals, though in this last our idea of improvement chiefly consists in persuading or forcing other people to be as good as ourselves. It is not progress that we object to; on the contrary, we flatter ourselves that we are the most progressive people who ever lived. It is individuality that we war against: we should think we had done wonders if we had made ourselves all alike; forgetting that the unlikeness of one person to another is generally the first thing which draws the attention of either to the imperfection of his own type, and the superiority of another, or the possibility, by combining the advantages of both, of producing something better than either. We have a warning example in China.'

The next thing was that the lovely Rowena was showing him a photograph of a girl doing what he didn't want to see any girl doing ever except to him – school of *Kensington*, in fact.

'I don't like that,' he said. 'And what I don't like about it isn't the activity itself, far from it, but being shown it going on between other people. It's not that I disapprove. Well yes actually come to think of it I do disapprove rather. Of that photograph being published I mean.'

'Fair enough,' she said, but spent the next minute or so looking through her folders, presumably in search of material that wouldn't offend his susceptibilities. At last she handed him a sheaf of seven or eight pictures and asked him to pick the two he liked best. That was easy: he chose one girl who, by the look of her, could have had no idea in the world why those men had asked her to lean against a tree wearing just a straw hat, and one with a faintly intellectual expression who reminded him of a *Zoom* favourite of his. The procedure had an end-of-session feel to it and some nuance of the professorial manner, he thought, suggested the same thing. So he was surprised and a little fed up to be told, after both girls had been disposed of, that he could take a short rest.

He put on a smile. 'Before what?'

'Before the second part of the programme. Do smoke if you want to, Mr Richardson.'

'No thanks, I've given it up.' The same thing only live? 'What happens in the second part?'

'We stimulate you artificially.'

'As opposed to –'

'With an artificial stimulator,' explained the professor.

'Oh I see.'

She went across and seemed to confer with the group by the machine. Although they were so near he couldn't hear a word of what they were saying. Rosenberg came strolling out of the shadows, followed by the Ghanaian.

'Well now, and how's it going?'

'I thought you were supposed to tell me that.'

'I meant your personal reaction in mental and emotional terms.'

'How I feel, you mean. Well, I suppose one can get used to anything. Look here, what's this stimulator?'

'Ah, there's a cunning little gadget if you like.'

'No doubt, but what is it?'

'Let's see, it's metal, and it's powered by electricity, and it . . . revolves rapidly.'

'You brave man,' interposed the observer.

Jake gave up Rosenberg and nodded appreciatively, hoping to be told what for this fellow said him brave man.

'Your ego has been subjected to a massive onslaught. Of the events in detail inducing you to set your foot on the path that has brought you here this afternoon, I know nothing; but of this I am quite sure, that they were of a sort to injure your pride most severely. So it must have gone with all the intervening events. Today, given among other factors your age and class, was the supreme test. I confess to having done a little to aggravate it; I apologize, and can plead only the excuse of scientific curiosity. I salute you, sir, and would ask you to do me the honour of allowing me to shake your hand.'

They shook; Jake had been about to get up from his chair to do so but remembered the state of his clothing, which indeed had seldom been far from his thoughts over the past half-hour and which now, for some reason, decided him against getting up. He was still most interested in the question of the artificial stimulator and was satisfied soon enough. Professor Trefusis, with Miss Newman at her side, again stood before him. She was holding up an object of yellowish metal about the size of a pepper-pot with a small protuberance at the top.

'This,' she said, 'is the artificial stimulator.'

With a neat movement she tripped a switch on the device and a thin high-pitched whine started up. To Jake it sounded like a dentist's high-speed drill and some of his reaction to the thought must have shown in his face, because Trefusis smiled and spoke reassuringly, took his hand and laid the metal protuberance, which he now saw was spinning rapidly, against it. He felt an agreeable stroking sensation, not intense, as if something between a finger-tip and a feather were being applied with superhuman regularity. He nodded appreciatively again.

Part II now went ahead with businesslike dispatch. Artificial stimulator in hand, Miss Newman knelt before him. Professor Trefusis looked quickly through the contents of one of her folders and said,

'You'll now be subjected to the same stimuli as before while also being stimulated genitally. No doubt you'll appreciate that should your response come to climax the programme would have to be discontinued.'

'Yes,' said Jake, thinking this was a bit mealy-mouthed of her in the circumstances.

'So if you raise your hand the genital stimulation will cease at once.'

'Fine.'

What followed was physical pleasure in its purest form, unaccompanied, in other words, by any of the range of feelings from tenderness to triumph normally embodied with it. Even the desire for its continuance was missing, so that every minute, every dozen seconds he had to strive not to send the damned contraption flying and run for the door, no trousers or no no trousers. How can she do it? he kept asking himself, not rhetorically: what sort of woman does it take to measure what happens to chaps' willies for a living? What does your mummy do? And how can her husband cope? The she he meant was entirely the fair professor; Miss Newman never entered his thoughts. It was that, he saw afterwards, that made the whole shooting-match bearable: by luck or amazing judgement they had passed over for the artificial-stimulator-wielding spot all the impossible kinds of person, to wit males, attractive females and unattractive females, and come up with somebody as near nobody as anybody could be, somebody totally unmemorable, somebody who did nothing at all except as ordered. Or perhaps her behaviour, or absence of behaviour, was the result of her having been carefully briefed in the interests of relaxation of atmosphere and total informality.

The girl in the straw hat went back into the folder and the whine of the cunning little gadget sank in pitch and disappeared. Jake sighed and swallowed. His eyelids felt heavy; in fact so did most of the rest of him. Professor Trefusis came and muttered into his ear,

'Would you like a climax? We can give you one, not out here of course, or we can arrange for you to give yourself one in private.'

'I don't think I will, thanks very much all the same.'

When they parted a few minutes later she said to him, 'I hope to see you again soon.'

'Again? Soon?'

'After the successful completion of Dr Rosenberg's treatment.'

Jake and Rosenberg went together across the hospital hall, which had a fight going on in it near one of the side walls. Two medium-sized men in white suits were struggling to hold a largish man in a fawn raincoat who seemed to be doing nothing more than trying to free himself from them. Not many of the people standing about or passing through bothered to watch.

'If it's been like that all the way here,' said Jake, 'those two are earning their money.'

Rosenberg smiled leniently. 'They're ward staff. The poor fellow's objection must be to being made to leave. There, you see?'

The man in the raincoat, at liberty for a moment, ran back towards the lifts where the two nurses caught him again. Jake had a glimpse of the captive's forefinger straining to reach, and being held back from reaching, the call-button with great intensity, as if this were no call-button but, TV-style, the means of activating a bank alarm or nuclear missile. Outside it wasn't quite raining but was damp and chilly. Rosenberg looked to and fro a couple of times in a furtive sort of way, swinging his unnaturally large black briefcase about, then he said,

'How were you intending to make the return journey, Mr Richardson?'

'Bus.'

'Ah, it's not the weather for that. I have my car here, I'd be happy to give you a ride.'

'That's very kind of you.'

But the other stayed where he was a space longer, looking down at his disproportionately small feet. There was that in his manner which meant that it came as no complete surprise when he flung back his head and produced one of those stares he and Curnow went in for, had perhaps developed together as part of some research project. Jake met this one and waited. When Rosenberg spoke it was in a strained, almost querulous tone, as if he was at great moral cost dragging out a deeply overlaid memory.

'Am I quite mistaken or did you tell me you were sometimes known to take a glass of sherry before dinner?'

'I must have. It's true anyway.'

'I thought so. I thought so. And it's before dinner now. Some time before, I grant you, but before. You see I find a small amount of alcohol at this time of day distinctly beneficial. Tell me, have you any objection to drinking in a public house?'

In its tone and much of its phraseology the last part of that so closely resembled the bugger's favourite question that Jake started to want to hit him, but he soon stopped and said, 'Not in principle.' He could have added that in practice he found the activity distasteful, especially of late; it was also true that nothing would have kept him from seeing the little psychologist in the proposed new setting.

With a peremptory sideways movement of his head Rosenberg led off ⸱t a smart pace. A minute's walk up towards the main road brought them to a pub called the Lord Nelson which Jake, occupied with his madwoman, hadn't noticed on the way down. The exterior, royal blue picked out in yellow, was promising, and the interior had no more than half a dozen youngsters in it, wearing their offensive perpetual-holiday clothes, true, but not laughing and talking above a mild shout. The noise from the fruit-machine was that of an intermittent and fairly distant automatic rifle, and even the juke-box thumped and cried away well below the threshold of pain; all in all a real find. Of course it was early yet.

Rosenberg had said they might as well look in here, but any pretence of unfamiliarity was at once undone by the whiskered and tee-shirted fellow behind the bar, who greeted him as doctor and without inquiry picked up a half-pint glass tankard and began to fill it with beer. When this was done he looked at Jake with a slight frown and narrowing of the eyes, as if less interested in what he might want to drink than in what form of lunacy possessed him.

'And you'll have a sherry, will you not?' asked Rosenberg.

'Thank you, medium dry.'

'Is sherry still the great Oxford drink or is that all folk-lore?'

Jake made some idle answer. At the mention of Oxford any hint of misgiving or antagonism left the barman's manner; he was evidently satisfied that his customers were not doctor and patient but doctor and colleague. His underlying assumption that having to do with Oxford somehow vouched for sanity might itself be said to imply derangement, but it would be more interesting to consider what had made Rosenberg a habitué of this place. One's first assumption, that being Irish he would naturally be rushing round the corner all the time to get a lot of strong drink inside him, wasn't borne out by that modest half of bitter. Could there be a convivial side to him? It seemed unlikely, though Jake couldn't have told why.

Again taking the lead, Rosenberg moved decisively across the room and sat down with his back to the wall on a padded bench enveloped in black artificial something. Jake, always in favour of getting a good view of anybody he might be talking to, looked round for a chair, but there was none to be seen, only long- and short-legged stools. He fetched a short-legged one, finding that its top was covered with the same stuff as the bench. Apart from being so covered it was too convex to suit a normal bum like his, pleasing as that convexity might well have been to the trend-blurred eye of whatever youthful fart had designed it. He sat regardless and faced Rosenberg across a circular table made of semi-transparent amber-coloured substance. Huge photographs of Wild West people and scenes covered the walls.

'I had lunch recently with a friend of mine,' announced Rosenberg.

'Oh yes?' said Jake encouragingly, but not just encouragingly in case what he had heard had been deemed worthy of remark in itself, which he thought was possible.

'Have you ever come across a magazine called *Mezzanine*?'

'Yes, in fact –'

'This friend of mine is the editor. He's been in the job for about four years would be my guess. That's a long time in that sort of journalism, he says. The pace, you know. I doubt if he'll stick it much longer. I'll be sorry when he goes, because he and I have been fortunate enough to build up an excellent working relationship. In practice it benefits me distinctly more than him.' The doctor gave his deep laugh; the present rendering gave an effect of reluctant self-congratulation. 'Oh dear. Of course he has a very acute social conscience, which makes him anxious not to publish any material that might in any way be harmful.'

'What sort of material would that be?'

'Encouragement of anti-social fantasies involving violence chiefly but also such matters as simulated hanging which can be dangerous.'

'You mean physically dangerous.'

'I do. Death from that cause is not uncommon.'

'Mm. So what people see and read in that way does affect their actions.'

Rosenberg put down his glass, which was still nearly full. He laughed again slightly. 'Why my dear sir, of course it does. If it didn't, my work would have to take a very different form. You must realize that, even from the little we've done together.'

'I suppose I do. But going back – can't your editor pal spot what to steer clear of for himself? I mean for instance I can tell straight away that a chap whipping a girl involves violence.'

'It's not always as simple as that,' said the doctor rather peevishly, then went on in the sunniest of spirits, 'Where *I* score is having access to the unpublished *Mezzanine* correspondence, which is most valuable. They write things they'd never dare say to fellows like me.'

'For fear of bursting out laughing in your face.'

'Ah not at all, not at all. You can always spot the ones who're trying to take you for a ride.'

'Always? How?'

'Let me put it to you the way my friend put it to me. If you say when you write, if you call something warm, or soft, or firm, or moist, or hard, or anything like that then you're not serious. You don't use adjectives when you're serious. Which brings us by a long way round to the fantasy you wrote for me, Mr Richardson. But first let me get you another drink.'

'My turn. Same again?'

'No thank you, I'll just nurse this.'

Jake would have cancelled his own drink at that but he wanted a couple of minutes to reflect. Standing at the counter he decided it was dull of Rosenberg to have moved with such speed and determination from what had sounded like the start of a nice credulity-stretching story or two about *Mezzanine* to that bloody fantasy. And there had been something dull too, dull in a different sense, about the tone of voice in which he had mentioned the editor and the four years in the job and the pace and the working relationship. More than dull. In the act of ordering his sherry Jake became conscious that he had heard that very tone elsewhere in the last couple of weeks, and at the same time that Rosenberg reminded him of someone. He went on trying to think where and who until he got back to the table and saw that the typewritten pages of his fantasy were spread out on it.

'Uncontrollable passion. Irresistible desire.' Rosenberg sipped slowly at his beer. 'Colossal breasts. Quivering thighs. Delirious response. Do you know if I hadn't heard different from you I think I'd be wondering whether you'd ever performed sexual intercourse?'

At the first phrase Jake had looked hurriedly about. No one was in earshot, not yet, although the bar now held twice as many youngsters as before and an additional two, moustached and flat-chested respectively, were entering at that moment. He sat down, spreading his arms slightly to try to screen off Rosenberg and his reading-matter. 'Would you?' he said.

'I think I would. As the friend I was mentioning to you would put it, you're not serious.'

'Good God, do you imagine I'd have come to you in the first place and gone through all that ... rigmarole this afternoon if I weren't serious?'

'Why did you come to me in the first place?'

Jake started to speak and then found he had to consider. 'I realized something that used to be a big part of my life wasn't there any more.'

'And you miss it.'

'Of course I miss it,' said Jake, instantly seeing that the next question ought to have to do with how he could be held to miss what he no longer wanted; you don't miss a friend you'd be slightly sorry to run into, do you? Can you miss wanting something?

Perhaps Rosenberg already knew the answers. 'Any other reasons?' was what he asked.

'Well, there's my wife to consider. Obviously.'

'There is, obviously. Very well. I didn't mean you weren't serious in your overall approach to your condition, I meant you weren't serious when you wrote this. You weren't in a state of sexual excitement.'

'These days I very rarely am. That was in another sense why I came to see you in the first place.'

'No doubt it was, but the state under discussion can be achieved with the aid of pictorial pornographic material, manual manipulation and so forth. You clearly omitted to use such aids. It's my view that consciously or unconsciously you avoided doing so. Because you sensed that if you did use them you'd almost certainly write something you'd have been embarrassed to let me see. You'd have used different words – none of your quivering thighs and delirious response. I'm sure you know the kind of words I mean.'

For all the Irishman's ridiculous accent, his articulation was as distinct as ever and he had not lowered his ordinary conversational volume. Another glance over his shoulder showed Jake that the moustached shag and the flat-chested bint, whose skull as he now saw was about the size of a large grapefruit, had moved away from the bar with their drinks and were now standing just near enough, given goodish hearing and less than full absorption in each other, to catch some of whatever Rosenberg might say next. 'I'm sure I do too,' mouthed Jake faintly, rolling his eyes and raising and lowering his eyebrows and pointing through himself at the couple.

For the moment it was hard to tell whether the doctor had heeded or even read these signals. 'We often find it best to avoid them in a consultation context for socio-psychological reasons,' he said at his previous pitch, 'especially in the earlier stages of therapy. But they tend to be useful in the kind of work you were doing here. I suppose I might have . . .' He dismissed without apparent trouble the thought of whatever it was he might have done and continued, 'I strongly recommend you to use such words when you try again, which I want you to do between now and next Tuesday. They may help you to resolve your main difficulty. You see –'

With the effect of a great door bursting open the noise of the juke-box increased perhaps fourfold in mid-beat. Rosenberg's voice mounted above a swell of half-human howling and mechanical chirruping and rumbling. 'As well as what you wrote, your attitude before our investigations this afternoon commenced, you remember, and your response to some of the stimuli during them – it all suggests to me that our society's repressive attitude towards sex has engendered an unrelaxed attitude in you. You've been conditioned into acceptance of a number of rigid taboos.' Perhaps now he did notice Jake's expression, which had turned to one of impatience or weariness, because he went on to bawl, 'You're suffering from guilt and shame.'

'*What?*'

'I said you're –'

'I heard you. Look, can't we discuss this somewhere else?'

'Please let's finish. I know this is uncomfortable for you but that's why I brought you here. Certain states of feeling can be brought to the surface more efficaciously in this type of environment than in a consultation situation. Now just one moment if I may.'

The clamour changed somehow, perhaps became more measured or emphatic. Rosenberg opened his briefcase and fingered through its contents, taking his time in a way that once more recalled Curnow. He was getting ready, Jake knew, to say or rather shout something unsayable at the instant when the noise ceased, which it must be on the point of doing. The instant came; Rosenberg was silent, but he had taken from his case and tossed down on the table between them a coloured magazine cutting pasted on to thin cardboard. The object landed with a soft click which seemed amplified in the first moment of silence. Jake saw that it was the photograph of the girl wearing just a straw hat, apart from which and in a way partly because of which she was without doubt completely stark naked and utterly nude. Her breasts were not in any true sense gigantic but they were large enough, and the rest of her made appropriate all manner of unserious adjectives. Everything about her for some reason struck him more forcibly here in the Lord Nelson than it had in the lecture-theatre.

'That's the one you liked best,' said Rosenberg with un-improvable clarity. 'According to that clever little machine back there.'

Jake sensed there were a number of people close behind him; he heard a movement, a grunt, a giggle, a whisper without knowing whether they referred to him or the picture or something quite different and naturally without turning to see. The temperature of the skin on the back of his neck changed, though he couldn't have said in which direction. He still had his *Times* with him. In a manoeuvre that sent his sherry-glass rocking he shoved the newspaper over and round the picture and scooped it up and laid the package thus made on the floor. Then he gave a deep sigh.

'Guilt and shame.' Rosenberg's voice was so low that it could have been audible only to Jake, who acknowledged in time that the little bugger could be effective whatever you might think of the effect. But for now all he said was,

'No. There are some things that are too ... No, you're wrong. You've got it all wrong.'

That Saturday was the first day of the Oxford summer term Jake had to go up there to supervise a collection, no charitable enterprise, this, but an examination set and marked by himself and intended to assess the extent to which his pupils had done the reading set them for the vacation just ended, or more practically to deter them a little by its prospect from spending every day of that period working in a supermarket and every night fornicating and smoking pot or whatever they did now. A drag, yes; all the same, satisfyingly more of a drag for them than for him and over just in time for him to be back at Burgess Avenue for Saturday Night at the Movies, of course not actually *at* the movies but in front of the television set.

The following Tuesday Jake went back to Oxford after he and Brenda had kept their appointment with Rosenberg in Harley Street and eaten something, in her case very little and in his not much more, at a place called Mother Courage's off the Marylebone Road. The food wasn't much good and they were rather nasty to you, but then it cost quite a lot. After walking part of the way in the interests of health, Jake got to Paddington a good twenty minutes before the departure of the 3.5, a train otherwise known to more than a few as the Flying Dodger for being the latest one even the most brazen and determined evader of his responsibilities would dare to catch at the 'start' of the 'working' week at the university, or 'university', and in consequence much esteemed among senior members of that institution. It was sometimes not easy to get a seat for the neglectful philologists, remiss biochemists and other lettered column-dodgers who swarmed aboard it; hence part of the reason for Jake's early arrival. He stood in a queue that by its diversity would have served quite well as model for a Family of Man photograph, laid out his fifty quid or whatever it was for a second-class ticket and went along to the book-stall. Here he searched carefully among the paperbacks and in the end came up with something called *The Hippogriff Attaché-Case* by an author unknown to him. He couldn't understand the jacket-design, which consisted chiefly of illuminated numbers and different-coloured little light-bulbs as well as a quantity of wasted space, and turned to the matter on the back of the cover.

To the heart of a vast computer complex buried miles deep in the earth's crust beneath America's Rocky Mountains come a brilliant cybernetics engineer, an international thief whose specialty is by-passing sophisticated alarm systems, a disillusioned CIA hit-man and the beautiful but enigmatic daughter of a US general who has disappeared in mysterious circumstances (he read). Their mission? To extract from the computer's banks the identities of American society's most dangerous enemies with the aim of unofficially executing them. Only trouble is ... *one* of the team of four is a psychopathic killer ...

Just the job, thought Jake as he handed over his few more quid: right up the street of a past-it ancient historian about to be on his way by unsophisticated train to one of England's premier seats of learning. Roll on wrist-watch television.

Time to get aboard the train; it was already filling up, with younger persons for the most part, undergraduates, junior dons, petty criminals. Jake found a lucky corner seat in one of the dozen identical uncompartmented carriages of the type he had by now almost grown used to after years of vaguely imagining it had to be a stopgap measure adopted while something less desolate was under construction. He wondered, not for the first time, about the irremovable tables between each pair of seats: what unbriefed designer, Finnish or Paraguayan, had visualized English railway travellers beguiling their journey with portable games of skill or chance, academic study, even food and drink? Well, he would beguile the first part of this one with reading, or letting his eyes run over, a *Times* article on the Soviet armed threat to Western Europe. He kept at it until the train had slid out of the station and begun to pass the rows of dreadful houses that backed on to the line and all his fellow-passengers had settled down. The chances were quite high that this particular mobile other-ranks' bun-shop held two or three people he knew well enough to talk to, and as high or higher that the moment he saw who they were he wouldn't want that. When he lowered the paper he found he was safe enough with a young couple opposite in a loose half-embrace, eyes bent on vacancy, mouths and jaws slack to a degree that suggested heavy sedation, and next to him an old bitch with a profile like a chicken's who obviously hadn't talked to anyone for years.

He opened *The Hippogriff Attaché-Case* but several things made concentration difficult: the small print, the sudden directionless lurches of the train, although it wasn't yet going very fast, and thoughts of the session with Rosenberg and the lunch that had followed. To get away from the last lot he started on thoughts of his job and his work, topics he seldom investigated consciously. The job side of his life presented no difficulties, called merely for constant vigilance; it was perhaps the one such side he could afford to feel a tingle of complacency about. After years of effort and much nerve and resource he had got the job sewn up almost to the point of not being underpaid; one more work-shedding coup, to be mounted at an early opportunity, and for the next academic year at least he would be able to consider himself well remunerated for his efforts – not counting inflation of course.

The work, in the sense of his subject and his attitude and contributions to it, gave less grounds for satisfaction. If challenged he would have said that he tried fairly hard and with fair success to keep up with developments in his chosen sphere, Greek colonization from the first Olympiad to the fall of Athens, and did a sporadic something about the, to him, increasingly dull mass of the rest; but he hadn't revised his lectures and his seminar material except in detail, and not much of that, for how long? – well, he was going to say five years and stick to it. Learned articles? He must get that bit of nonsense about Syracuse off the ground again before too long. Stuff in the field? According to a Sunday newspaper, the kind of source he sneezed at less and less as time went by, two Dutchmen had found a pot or so near Catania and he was going to have a look in September, but since he knew there couldn't be much more to find round there and he wasn't an archaeologist anyway, the look would be brief, its object far less the acquisition of knowledge than to get off tax his travelling expenses for a fortnight's holiday with Brenda. Books? Don't make him laugh: apart from the juvenile one about the sods in Asia Minor there had been three others, all solidly 'researched', all well received in the places that received them, all quite likely to be on the shelves of the sort of library concerned, all combined still bringing in enough cash to keep him in bus fares. Three or, in the eye of charity, four books were probably enough to justify Dr Jaques ('Jake') Richardson's life. They were bloody well going to have to.

That life was unlikely to run much beyond the end of the present century. Never mind. Jake's religious history was simple and compact. His parents had been Anglicans and right up to the present day the church he didn't go to had remained Anglican. As far as he could remember he had never had any belief, as opposed to inert acquiescence, in the notion of immortality, and the whole game of soldiers had been settled for him forty-five years previously, when he had come across and instantly and fully taken in the Socratic pronouncement that if death was unconsciousness it was not to be feared. Next question. It, the next question, did bother him: how to see to it that the period between now and then should be as comfortable and enjoyable as could realistically be expected. The one purpose raised the problem of retirement, the other of sex. Oh bugger and bugger. Talking of sex, the girl across the table, moving as if buried in mud, had shifted round in her seat, put her arms across the young man and given him a prolonged kiss on the side of the neck. A perceptible lifting of the eyelids on his part was evidence that he had noticed this. Jake produced a very slight gentle smile, which just went to show what a decent chap he was, not turning nasty like some oldsters when they saw youngsters who were presumably having it off, on the contrary feeling a serene, wry, amused, faintly sad benevolence. Like shit – all it just went to show was how far past caring he'd got. Nought out of ten for lack of envy in colour-blind shag's feelings about other shag's collection of Renoirs.

These and related topics, together with another uninformative glance at *The Hippogriff Attaché-Case* and a short involuntary nap, filled most of the journey. After the houses and the factories and the clumps of presumably electrical stuff standing in the open it was sometimes worth glancing out of the window. Much of what should have been green was still brown after the drought of '76, but past Reading it turned pretty decent, with the Thames running beside the track and once, for some seconds, a swan in full sight; bloody good luck to you, chum, thought Jake. Eventually the train stopped as usual outside Oxford station by the cemetery. This sight, although quite familiar enough, reminded him of his bus journey to Colliers Wood, or of that later part of it before the advent of the madwoman. He had been carried past mile after mile, probably getting on for two anyway, of ground given over to the accommodation of the departed, stretching away for hundreds of yards on one side of the road or the other, sometimes on both at once, interrupted by a horticultural place or one that sold caravans only to resume, covered with close-order ranks and files of memorial stone arranged with a regularity that yet never repeated itself, so extensive and so crowded that being dead seemed something the locals were noted for, like the inhabitants of Troy or Ur. The thought of shortly arriving in some such place himself and staying there meant little to Jake, as noted, but this afternoon there was that in what he saw which dispirited him. In the circumstances he was quite grateful for the yards of rusty galvanized iron fences, piles of rubble and of wrecked cars and, further off, square modern buildings which helped to take his mind off such matters.

The train pulled up at the platform at 4.29 on the dot, which was jolly good considering it often didn't do that till 4.39 or 49 and wasn't even supposed to before 4.17. Jake descended into the pedestrian tunnel that ran under the line to the front of the station; once, there had been an exit on this side too, but it had been discovered years ago, not long after he got his Readership, that the only people who benefited from this arrangement were passengers. An amplified voice blared something at him as he made the transit. He saw nobody he recognized in the taxi queue, not that he looked about for such. When his turn came he found himself sharing with a fat old man who said he wanted to go to Worcester College and a girl of undergraduate age who evidently made her needs known without recourse to speech. She had the other type of young female physique, the one being that of the bullet-headed shrimps he had identified on his visit to Blake Street: this genus was strongly built with long straight fair hair which, an invariable attribute, had been recently washed and, seen from the rear, hung down over not an outer garment but a sort of collarless shirt with thin vertical blue-and-white stripes. The old man shook slightly from distinction or drink or both. The driver put him down some yards short of the gate of Worcester, not, or not only, to disoblige but to avoid being inexorably committed by the city's one-way system to driving the two or three miles to Wolvercote before being permitted to turn right.

They were soon entering the north end of Turl Street and joining a line of traffic that moved forward a few seconds at a time. There were still forty or fifty yards between it and Jake's destination, the front gate of Comyns College, when the driver stuck his head out of his window and peered forward.

'Trouble there,' he said.

'What is it?' asked Jake.

'Picket or demo or whatever you like to call it.'

'Outside Comyns?'

'Right. Better if I drop you here.'

'What's going on?'

'Some crowd.' The driver pulled up. 'Better if I drop you here. Forty.'

Puzzled and annoyed, wishing he knew how to insist, Jake paid and got out. He approached cautiously, able to make out nothing at first for vehicles and passers-by and the slight curvature of the street, then caught glimpses of dull blue and straw colour and black and white. Peering through his bi-focals from a few paces nearer he made out the blue and straw colour as belonging respectively to the clothes and hair of girls resembling the one in the taxi, who as he was soon to see might indeed have doubled back after being dropped round the corner. The black and white belonged to placards, one of which was turned in his direction for a second: it said Piss Off Comyns Pigs.

Jake knew where he was at once without liking it there. Before he could think further there was rapid movement ahead of him, a scuffle as somebody tried to enter or leave. At a brisk pace but without hurry, Jake crossed the momentarily clear road with the intention of recrossing it when opposite the gate, thus striking from an unexpected angle while attention was still diverted. This turned out to be a bad idea. With the sound and a touch of the speed of a smallish aeroplane, a motor-cycle, headlight glaring, rider got up like a riot policeman, seemed to be coming straight at him down the street, illegally too he fancied. As he hesitated the girls round the gate, their erstwhile victim dispatched or escaped, all turned and saw him, seventeen or eighteen of them, blonde and wearing blue. Shouts arose.

'Admit women as undergraduates!'

'End medieval discrimination!'

'Down with élitist chauvinism!'

'I know that bugger!'

'Fall into line with other colleges!'

'Richardson! Bloody Richardson!'

'Wanker!'

'Wanker Richardson!'

Jake lost his head, though short of running away at once and creeping back after nightfall there wasn't a lot he could have done. With his suitcase held up in front of him he charged, to be easily halted by three or four muscular female arms. The uproar continued but in a changed form, that of cries of simulated passion or ecstasy, some involving low terms. Instead of the blows he had foreseen, kisses descended, breasts were rubbed against him and his crotch was grabbed at. There was a great deal of warmth and flesh and deep breathing and some of the time he could see no more than an inch or two: My Body Is Mine But I Share, he read at close quarters, holding his glasses on with his left hand and his case with his right. He felt frightened, not of any physical harm or even of graver embarrassment, but of losing control in some unimagined way. There seemed no reason why this jollification should ever stop, but after what felt like an agreed period, probably no more than fifteen or twenty seconds, he found himself released, stumbling over the wicket in some distress of mind but no worse off physically than for a couple of smart tweaks of the hampton.

The head porter Ernie, as fat and yet as pale as ever, stood in his habitual place at the entrance of his lodge. He gave Jake a savage wink that involved the whole of one side of his face and everything but the eye itself on the other.

'Nice little lot of young gentlewomen come up to our university these days, eh sir?'

'Wonderful.' Jake put down his suitcase and straightened his tie and smoothed his hair.

'No problem to you though, I'll be baned.' Bound was what most men would have said but this one came from Oxfordshire or somewhere.

'I don't quite see why you . . .' Oh Christ, he had forgotten again.

The porter chuckled threateningly and wagged a forefinger. 'Nay nay, Mr Richardson, you know what I'm talking abate. Plenty of people remember the way you used to weigh the girls, I can tell you. A ruddy uncraned king you were.

You fancied something – pay! you got it. And I bet you still know how to mark 'em dahn.'

The lodge entrance was only wide enough for one person, which was why it was Ernie's habitual place. He would vacate it at once on the approach of the Master, the Dean, some senior Fellows and luminaries like the Regius Professor of Latin, who happened to be a Comyns don, but almost anyone else could safely count on a minute or two of enforced conversation. Jake said rather slackly,

'We're all of us getting on, Ernie, you know.'

'*Aitch!* Don't remind me sir – we are indeed. And hay!'

Ernie still showed no sign of moving yet but just then the buzzer on the telephone switchboard sounded and with a grunt of something close to apology he turned on his axis, which showed a marked declination, like the Earth's, and creaked off towards the inner lodge. From behind the glass partition of this he was soon to be heard confidently declaring that someone was not in college, nor likely to be for an immeasurable time. All porters are the same porter, thought Jake as often before. By now he was at his pigeon-hole in quest of mail, driven chiefly by habit, not expecting that much or any would have arrived since his fair-sized pick-up on Saturday. But some had: the Historical Society's programme for the term, a publisher's catalogue and an oddly shaped package addressed in large light-green characters. The first two he threw away on the spot, the package he shoved unopened into his mackintosh pocket, for Ernie could bar his exit in a few strident strides. He picked up his case.

It was a hopelessly established tradition that Ernie should be licensed to chaff him about his amatory career, and in some senses a justified one. They were the same age; they had been acquainted for over forty years, since Jake's arrival at Comyns as an undergraduate to find Ernie already employed as a servant in Hall and on staircases; elevation to junior porter had come just when Jake, first marriage about to collapse, was starting out on his most ambitious round of sexual activity since youth, using his college rooms to pursue parts of it too, discreetly enough to escape notice in every

quarter that mattered but of course not in the lodge, by a
larger tradition the clearing-house of all internal gossip.
Another bond between the two men was the similarity of
their careers in the war, Jake rising in a rifle regiment to
command one of its companies in France and Germany in
1944–5, Ernie becoming a warrant-officer of light infantry
and picking up a decoration after Anzio. At his times of
gloom, which were frequent, the ex-sergeant-major would
use barrack-room catch-phrases to describe his wonder at
what the world was coming to. Jake, who was feeling a bit
cross, united these two themes now in a mumbled monologue as he set off across the front quad.

'Assit, lad, give her the old one-two. Take your bloody
finger eight and get stuck in. Lovely bit of crackling. Shit-
hot slice of kifer. Go on Joe, your mother won't know, are
you a man or a mace? There you are old boy, take a good
look around, and if you find anything you fancy I'll buy it
for you. You've seen the mighty piston-strokes of the giants
of the CPR, with the driving force of a thousand horse so
you know what pistons are, or you think you do. Better
than pork. I *am* the vicar. With his bloody great kidney-
wiper and balls the size of three, and half a yard of . . .'

At this stage Jake was moving towards the arch communicating with the further quad where his rooms were and
was passing the gift shop in the cloisters by the chapel. This
popular source of revenue offered for sale all manner of
authentic stuff, tea-sets with the Comyns coat of arms on
them just like the Master drank his own tea out of, Comyns
beer-tankards made from genuine English pewter, Comyns
paperweights, Comyns corkscrew-cum-bottle-openers, not
Comyns neckties on account of some stuffed shirt had put a
no on that one but Comyns head-scarves and Comyns hand-
kerchiefs and all kinds of Comyns postal cards showing the
insides of some of the buildings, including the chapel, and
different parts of the campus, and then there was this
extremely interesting historical one of some document in
old-fashioned writing supposed to be written by was it

Edward II? A number of tourists were clustered round the doorway of the shop. As Jake drew level they all looked at him, very much as the girls outside the gate had done. This time there was a short pause before the shouting started, but it started.

'Da geht ja einer!'
'En v'là un!'
'Ach, man, daar gaan een!'
'Och där har vi en!'
'Hey, there's one of them!'
'Ha, asoko nimo iruyo!'

They began to move towards him in twos and threes, slowly at first, the men unslinging their cameras with grim professionalism, the women pleased, all agog. Jake quickened up, got to the arch, in fact more of a short tunnel under the first floor of the library, and ran like hell through it and at an angle across the lawn of the quad beyond. Behind him he heard a babel of voices, more literally such than most and gaining added force from the echo-chamber properties of the tunnel. By the time he reached the shelter of his staircase the leaders were almost upon him, but before they could actually bring him down he was safe behind his oak, that outer door with no outer handle. The windows of his sitting-room looked directly on to the quad. Through them he could see his pursuers walking or standing disconsolately about, shrugging their shoulders and shaking their heads, reslinging their cameras. All right, he thought.

He switched on his standard-lamp and moved it and a padded chair as far forward as he could, took a bottle out of the cupboard and poured a glass of what was semi-sweet sherry, not port – all one to them though. His academic cap lay where he had put it after Saturday's collection; in an instant he was wearing it, sitting in the chair, holding the glass up to the light. A muffled cheer sounded from outside and the cameras clicked and fizzed once and again, one lot, then another. He gave them a simulated in-the-act-of-drinking pose, a here's-to-you pose and a glass-out-of-sight pose for the religiously scrupulous. Then he switched off the light to signal the end of the show and acknowledged the grateful smiles, waves and thumbs-up.

'No, not at all, fuck *you*,' he said. 'Fuck you very much, ladies and gents, fucks a million. And a fisherman's fart to all at home.'

He had poured the untasted sherry back into the bottle, which was only there for visitors, and was going to hang up his raincoat when he noticed a bulge in the pocket – the thing he had collected at the lodge. He felt interest, curiosity, a nice change for one given to knowing all too well and at first sight whatever the post might have brought him. The outer cover, reinforced with sticky tape, was resistant. When at last he got it off he had come to a roughly cylindrical object wrapped in many thicknesses of purple lavatory-paper. After unwinding these he found himself holding an imitation phallus made out of some plastic material or other with the words Try This One, Wanker! written on it in the same large green letters as the outside. Moving faster than he had done for some years Jake locked the object up in his desk, then looked briefly and without result at the wrapper, went not at all fast to his armchair by the empty fireplace, sat down and put his hand across his mouth and sighed. All he needed now was a visit from the madwoman, dropping in on her way to catch Harry or June as they came off shift at British Leyland, or more likely find them on strike.

Jake didn't know how long he sat on in the armchair. He roused himself at the sound of a light step on the stone flags of the corridor outside. Anyone coming to visit him would clear off without further ado at the sight of the shut outer door, a convention that had stood him in unimprovable stead in the days Ernie had referred to but not wanted at the moment. He hurried to open that door, looked out and saw the figure of a girl retreating.

'Miss Calvert?'

She turned back. 'I'm sorry, I thought . . .'

'No, my fault. The door must have . . .' He found he had started to suggest that half a hundredweight of forest giant had swung through something like a hundred and fifty degrees at a puff of wind, and changed tack. 'I had to shut it to keep some tourists out.'

'Tourists? Out?'

'Yes, they chased me from the gift shop. They wanted to photograph me. I mean not me in particular, just a don. Any don. An Oxford don. So I put my square on and let them. Photograph me, I mean. Might as well. Do sit down, Miss Calvert. Now I'll just find your essay – your collection paper.'

They had moved into the sitting-room, where his suitcase, containing Miss Calvert's collection paper and everybody else's collection paper and much else besides, stood on the otherwise empty dining-table. He went over and put his hands on the corners of the case. Should he open it in here or take it through the communicating door into his bedroom and open it in there? The first would be quicker if the scripts were at or near the top, as he was almost certain they were. Or rather the first would be quicker wherever they were, only if they weren't near the top he would have to unpack the lot of his belongings on to the table and then at some stage put them back again before finally unpacking in the bedroom. How certain was he that the scripts were near the top? Had he perhaps put them in first to make sure of not leaving them out? Realizing that he must have been standing there with his back to the girl for close on half a minute, he unclicked the catches of the case and at the same instant became almost certain he had indeed put the scripts in first. Then he had better reclick the catches and do the necessary unpacking in the bedroom after all. But one of the catches, the left-hand one, was hard to fasten securely, always had been. Would the other one stand the strain if he carried the case by its handle in the normal way? – he didn't want his belongings all over the floor. So should he try to carry it held horizontally out in front of him? He could. Then he must. Quick. Now. He wriggled his forearms underneath the bugger and, no doubt looking rather like a man who risks his life to remove a bomb from a place of public resort, took himself and burden off at top speed. Thank Christ the communicating door wasn't latched.

The scripts were on top, as he could have seen earlier with little trouble. Miss Calvert's wasn't among them. Yes it was. There was something worrying about it but he took it straight back into the sitting-room, where Miss Calvert had failed to sit as requested. Although she had been his pupil for two terms he had never properly looked at her before. Now he did. He saw that her eyes were darker than most fair-complexioned girls' and that her jaw was firm, not much more than his original vague impression of generic blue-clad blondeness; he certainly made no progress in estimating whether she could be, should be, surely must be considered attractive or not. This failure wasn't the result of loss of interest, in the way that morbid failure of appetite for food might be expected to impair the palate: he had had no trouble over Professor Trefusis. That was because the comely scientist was in her middle thirties, well above the decisive age-limit.

No, it wasn't an age-limit in the usual sense, because the ones just below it were getting older all the time. The whole thing was a matter of date, of year of birth: 1950 would be about right. So when he was seventy he wouldn't be able to tell whether any female under thirty-seven was attractive or not. A curious world that would be.

Enough. He tried to bring himself round. 'Ah. Of course. Miss Calvert.'

'Yes, Mr Richardson?'

The sound of his name reminded him of the last time he had heard it uttered by a female, not long ago and not far from here. Someone in the picket had known it, had recognized him, and he was an obscure person, never on TV or in the papers, in no sense an Oxford character, more or less of a stranger even to many undergraduates of his own college, one who taught a subject neither soft nor modish nor remunerative. Was it this girl who had identified him? And of course what had bothered him about her script was that it was written in green ink, like the words on the object he had locked up in his desk. He glanced at the script, saw immediately that the respective hands were quite different and even the ink was a bit different, then looked wordlessly at the girl.

'Are you all right?' she said, taking a short pace towards him.

The movement brought to mind what he must have noticed before, how slim she was, her middle hard-looking and yet flexible, more like a thick electric cable than any thin living creature. He had embraced slim girls in his time and could remember consistently finding them more substantial then than the sight of them suggested. Perhaps fellows found the same thing today. 'Oh – yes,' he said. 'Yes, thanks. Do sit down. Been rather a hectic day one way and another. Here we are.'

He pushed the padded chair back to its usual place. It wasn't very comfortable and it certainly looked nasty but it was the second-best in the room to the battered old dining-chair at his desk, its leather scuffed by generations of academic bums. Everything else was wine- or ink-stained, fire- or water-damaged, extruding springs, possessed of legs or arms that fell off all the time, impossible to open, impossible to close and repulsive. For years he had lived here most of the week, most weeks, not only in term-time, and without meeting Brenda's standards the place had been quite decent. Since then, by ruse, hard bargaining and straightforward theft-and-substitution the Domestic Bursar had plundered it into the ground. Well, not easy to complain when you spent no more than a tenth of the year in it.

'I hope you had a pleasant vacation?'

'Yes thank you.'

'Settling down all right this term?'

'Yes.'

'Good.' He picked up a lecture-list. 'Now I presume you went to Sir Clarence Frankis yesterday and will continue to do so.'

'I didn't actually.'

'Why not?'

'Well, there's a lot to do, you know, and a lot to get through, and it isn't in my special subject, Minoan, and you said yourself it would be more detailed than I needed.' For some reason she had a deep voice.

'Yes. I did. But, er ... Minoan ... *civilization* is fairly interesting, and Sir Clarence is probably the most – er, rather good. It's not really a question of need, not totally. You ought to go. Sorry, I mean try to go whenever you can. No difficulty with the others? Right. Now your collection paper, Miss Calvert. I don't quite know what to say to you about it.'

But he quite knew what he wanted to say to her about it and related matters. One, see if you can't work out some way of getting yourself just a bit ashamed and scared of not wanting to know anything about anything or to be any good at anything. Two, if that fails, at least try to spell a bit and write legibly and write a sentence now and then – you can forget, or go on never having heard, about punctuation. Three, when you see a word you recognize in a question like Greek or Tyre or Malta, fight against trying to put down everything remotely connected with it that you may have – oh stuff it.

And four, go away and leave your place at St Hugh's to someone who might conceivably – oh stuff it.

Jake didn't say any of this because he wanted Miss Calvert's benevolent neutrality at least in the coming struggle for power at his Wednesday lectures, where that little bastard from Teddy Hall seemed about to escalate his campaign of harassment into a direct bid to seize the lectern. So he said as gently as he thought he could,

'Your handwriting. You do realize, don't you, that we're allowed to ignore anything we can't read or else have it typed up and make you pay the typist?'

'Why could a typist read it if you couldn't?'

Once, he might have been able to tell if this was defiance or ingenuous inquiry. Now, he couldn't or couldn't be bothered. 'Because the typist would have you there with your script reading out to her what you'd written. With incidentally an examiner looking over your shoulder to see you didn't correct anything or put new bits in.'

'Her? Why not him? Why shouldn't a typist be a man?'

Oh for . . . 'No reason at all. It's just that in fact the typists in this case are as far as I know all women.'

'I didn't know that. And I'm sorry, I didn't understand about the typing.'

'That's all right. You do now. Don't forget either that I know your writing pretty well by this time, but it won't always be me reading it. Now your spelling. I'm quite tolerant about that,' because a policy of being quite intolerant would multiply the failure rate by something like ten, which would never do, 'but the same thing applies. I know some of these names are difficult; even so, I think it might pay you for instance to remember that Mediterranean is spelt with one T and two Rs and not the other way round. Especially,' he went on, striving not to shake from head to foot with rage and contempt as he spoke and summoning to his aid the thought that in the Oxford of the '70s plenty of his colleagues would share Miss Calvert's difficulty, 'since it appears in the actual title of the subject and is very likely to come in the wording of some of the questions – four times on this paper, in fact.' Was she listening? All right, call it the fucking Med! was what he wanted to shout, but forbore. 'I've put a wavy line under some of the other examples.

'In general, you clearly have a concentration problem,' are an idle bitch, 'and I was wondering whether there was anything in your personal life that ... I'm not asking you to tell me about it but you could mention it to your Moral Tutor. Or if you like I could –'

'No it's all right thanks. There isn't anything really. Except the point.'

'What point?'

'The point of going on.'

'With the subject.'

'Well ...'

'With Oxford?'

'All sorts of things really.'

Jake said in his firmest tone, 'I think most people feel like that from time to time. One just has to hang on and have patience and hope it'll put itself right.' He couldn't remember now why he had started to ask her; habit, something to say, show of concern to assuage possibly wounded feelings. Yes, habit, a carry-over from the days when he might have gone on to suggest discussing her problems under more informal conditions. Oh well. 'Now you answered only two questions but I'm going to give you a beta-double-minus all the same,' like a bloody fool. 'You must try for three next time. Now which of the other questions would you have tried if you'd had longer?'

Muttering to herself, Miss Calvert studied the paper for a space. At last she said, 'I think "Culture is the most profitable export." Discuss with reference –'

'Oh yes. Well, suppose you take that as your subject for next week.' This favourite tactic not only gratified his perennial need, strangely exacerbated today, to avoid having to think up essay subjects whenever remotely possible, it also relieved him, having just marked several exam answers on the topic, from the slightest mental exertion about it till next week came, if then. He tried to turn his complacent grin into a smile of friendly dismissal, but before the process was finished felt his face stiffen at the tone of the girl's next remark.

'Mr Richardson ... you know that article of yours in JPCR you asked us to look at? On Ionian trade-routes?'

'Yes?'

'Well, the copy in the Bodleian's all ... well, people have been writing things on it.'

'Writing things? What sort of things?'

'Like graffiti.'

'Really.'

'I sort of thought you ought to know.'

Malice or goodwill? Those two should on the face of it be no trouble to tell apart, but not much thought was necessary to recall that in practice they mixed as readily and in as widely-varying proportions as coffee and milk, no sugar, no third element needed. But then what of it? He would look in at the library on the way to or from his lecture the next morning; for now, he thanked Miss Calvert, gave her her script back and sent her off, noticing at the last moment that she bore a handbag like a miniature pack-saddle, all flaps and buckles. He watched out of the window to see if she tossed the script over her shoulder as she left, but she held on to it at least until after she had vanished into the tunnel. Her walk showed that their interview had entirely left her mind.

Jake stood at the window in thought, though not of any very purposeful description, for a couple of minutes. It took him as long to make quite sure that the locked drawer of his desk was indeed locked, secured, made fast, proof against anything short of another key or a jemmy. Then he collected himself and went into the bedroom to unpack. It was small and dark but dry and not particularly draughty, and had in it the only decent object in the set, the bed that filled about a third of it, his own property from long ago and as such safe from the Domestic Bursar's depradations. By the time he had finished in here and glanced through his notes for the next day, the chapel clock, the nearest among innumerable others, was striking six. He slung his gown over his shoulder and sauntered across the grass, looking about at the buildings, which had once been attributed to Nicholas Hawksmoor; recent research, after the fashion of a lot of recent research, had disproved this without producing any certain re-attribution. Never mind: they were pleasing to the eye for two sufficient reasons – someone had put them up well before 1914, and no one, out of apathy, lack of money, instinctive conservatism or sometimes even perhaps deficiency of bad taste, had laid a hand on their exterior since except to clean them. Until about a quarter of a century back, Jake had had no architectural sense that he knew of but, like every other city-dweller in the land with eyesight good enough to get about unaided, he had acquired one since all right, had one doled out to him willy-bloody-nilly. So it was no great wonder that he halted and looked about all over again before entering the staircase in the far corner.

Here, on the first floor, there lived an English don called

Damon Lancewood, like Ernie in being an almost exact contemporary of Jake's but unlike him in an incalculable number of ways. One of the fewer ways in which he was unlike Jake has already been mentioned: he lived where Jake only popped in and out. Lancewood belonged to the lonely and diminishing few who still treated college as home. It was true that he had a cottage near Dry Sandford and also true, while less well known, that he was joined there most weekends by the owner of a small business in Abingdon, a man of fifty or so to whom he had been attached for the past twenty-two years.

Jake knocked at the door, which had a handsome brass finger-plate and other furniture on it, and obeyed the summons to come in. He saw that Lancewood had somebody with him and spoke up at once.

'I'm sorry Damon, I didn't realize you were –'

'No no no, my dear Jake, I was expecting you. I'd like you to meet a colleague of mine . . .'

Introductions were made. Jake failed to gather or shortly forgot the Christian name and college of the visitor, a tall long-haired sod in his thirties, but caught the surname – Smith. Lancewood, himself tall but with neatly cut white hair and a bearing and manner of dress that suggested a retired general rather than a don, turned his blank-looking gaze on Jake.

'I think you could do with a glass of sherry.'

'I think so too. Thank you.'

Quite possibly it was Jake's sherry: he brought Lancewood a bottle now and then, a much nicer arrangement for everyone than returning hospitality in his own place. It came in a solid bit of glass that went with the way the room was fitted up, which in turn reflected its occupant's military style: nothing overtly martial or imperial but suggestive of bungalow here, club there, mess somewhere else, the many pictures showing horses, dogs, an occasional parrot or monkey, what could have been a troopship, what could have been a cantonment, portraits of dark-skinned persons no one had the authority to say were not sometime servants.

They even included three of four water-colours of aggressively English scenes given that niggling, almost effeminate treatment characteristic of men of action.

'Thank God,' said Jake, sipping. 'I've just been closeted with a female pupil.'

Lancewood cocked his head. 'Was that such an ordeal for you?' This question Ernie would have understood perfectly, though his phrasing of it would have been quite different.

'You don't know her.' Jake was beginning to feel like an inefficient impostor, constantly putting his foot through his cover. 'Attractive enough, I . . .' – no, not suppose – 'grant you, but – well, you know the sort. A kind of celestial indifference to being seen to be, oh, lazy, stupid, ignorant, illiterate, anything you please.'

'Do you find the women worse than the men in that way?' asked Smith in an expressive adenoidal voice.

'I hadn't really thought about it,' said Jake, who if he had been strictly truthful would have gone on to say that now he had had a second and a half to think about it of course he bloody did.

'Well I bloody do,' said Smith. 'As a matter of fact we were on that very point when you turned up. Naturally Damon was taking the opposite view. He seems to have some sort of thing about women.'

'Indeed I have. Which reminds me of one of my favourite ones. How's my darling Brenda?'

'Fighting fit,' said Jake. And hay, he added silently.

'John had a rotten cold with all this vile weather but he's fine again now.'

This was of course the Abingdon chap. 'Good, give him my love,' said Jake, registering the adroit passing of the message that Smith knew about that. He (Jake) surmised that that sort of adroitness came in jolly handy for people like Lancewood, must be well worth the trouble of acquiring.

Lighting a French cigarette, Smith pursued his point. 'I mean, the levels to which they'll sink. And go on sinking because they stay the same and the problem stays the same, which is: a whole literature, six hundred years' worth, and virtually all of it written by male chauvinists. So, Wordsworth was no good because he abandoned Annette Vallon, no good as a poet that is, the Brontës and George Eliot went over to the enemy by adopting male pseudonyms so they were no good, Doll Tearsheet is the heroine of *Henry IV*, Part 2 at least, and of course the real –'

Lancewood gave a guttural sigh. 'Have a heart, she was joking.'

'Not this one,' said Smith firmly. 'The one who told her might have been, but not this one.'

'Well then somebody was or, or might have been. You really do –'

'Damon, it's nothing *in them*, it's forced on them. The men would probably be just as bad if you could find a way of making them think of themselves as men all the time, if such a way were conceivable.' Smith caught sight of Jake. 'I say, this must be rather –'

'Go on, I want to hear.'

'Well – the bright ones can't help seeing that, right, Sappho . . .'

'Who was untypical?' said Lancewood.

'And who's mostly folk-lore anyway. Then you really come to, as far as they're concerned, the Matchless Orinda. Sorry, Katherine Philips, born in the same year as Dryden, died young, not as young as Shelley though, for instance, anyway she's quite good. Of course she is. What would you? Having taken the precaution of not being born with the digits one nine in front of her decade, but that's a . . . Anyway, after her, let's stick to poetry for the moment, you get the Countess of Winchilsea, even more of a household name, and then you sit around for a couple of centuries waiting for Christina Rossetti, who's quite good, and that's that. If no female had ever emerged they'd have been able to put it down to male oppression but Katherine spoiled all that. Back in the middle of the seventeenth century she showed it was *possible*. As I say, it works down from the top, so that the ones who don't know what the seventeenth century was feel it as much as the others, well, insofar as they can, hence collective inferiority feelings, hence collective aggression. Admittedly with the novel it's not quite such a –'

'All this *they* talk.' Lancewood gestured with the decanter at Jake, who was all right as he was, then poured sherry for Smith and himself. 'The ones and the others. From the way you go on, most people would say you were the one with the thing about women.'

'Let's just nail that one right away. My relations with them, with women that is, have been and are normal to an unparalleled, even preternatural degree. Three-point-seven premarital affairs, the precise average, married at twenty-five-point-whatever-it-is, lived happily ever after, or since. Perhaps that's not so normal.'

'It's probably a bit early to tell,' said Jake. 'What does your wife think about poetry?'

'She's a biologist,' said Smith. He seemed puzzled at the question.

'Curious you should mention centuries,' said Lancewood. 'One of *them*, which you must admit sounds like something quite different, brought me a new interpretation of *Hamlet* yesterday. Now this, I want you to understand, is a thoroughly sweet, good-natured, charming little girl, no aggression in the wide world. As to brightness, well you shall hear. Hamlet was a woman.' He gave them both his blank look.

Smith gave a great groan but said nothing.

'Even I know that's not very new,' said Jake. 'Didn't Sarah Bernhardt play him, or her?'

'Indeed she did, and I'd said as much before I realized that of course my little girl would never have heard of her. Quite senseless to expect it. Cruel in a way. Well what could I do, great actress of the nineteenth century, quite natural she should want to play one of the greatest parts, different approach in those days, all that, but I needn't have bothered because I'd lost her, as she would have expressed herself, at the nineteenth century. Now she'd clearly heard of it, she even knew it was something to do with a tract of time but all the same there was more to it than that, just as the Age of

Johnson or the Nineties, say, don't refer merely to a pair of dates. To her it was, the nineteenth century I mean was, not exactly when old people were young because there can be no such period, but awful and squalid and creepy, with all sorts of things going on – she could easily have come across figures like Dracula and Frankenstein and Jack the Ripper and Dr Arnold and realized they were nineteenth century. Well, the look she gave me, you should have seen it.' Lancewood half turned his face away, narrowed his eyes and peered out of their corners. 'Suspicion and morbid curiosity and a hint of distaste.'

'If you're doing it properly it was more like ungovernable lust,' said Smith to Jake's agreement.

'In that case I'm not. She was wondering what I used to get up to with Sarah Bernhardt, whom I must have known at least or why bring her up? Actually quite funny it should have been the great Sarah, in view of her reputed ... I think if one actually challenged my little girl up to the hilt, as it were, she'd say that the years beginning with nineteen were in the nineteenth century up to about 1950, after which it became the twentieth. That would cover the years of birth of even her most senior contemporaries. One understands very well. All these references to people being dragged kicking and screaming into the twentieth century when it's agreed that that's the number of the century we're in, it must be most frightfully confusing. One does sympathize.

'Well. Her ... her *case* was roughly that since Hamlet is far too nice and intelligent to be a man, he must be a woman because there's nothing else for him to be. I was ready to come back smartly with what about the way he treats Ophelia, male chauvinism if there ever was such a thing, but she'd thought of that – that was how all the men went on in those days, still do really, and it would have been suspicious if she, Hamlet, had behaved differently. What about old Hamlet and Gertrude? – you'd have expected them to notice. Old Hamlet had noticed, but he needed an heir, so he got Polonius to rig things, which gave Polonius the leverage he needed to be kept on at court when all he was fit for was talking balls. I liked that, quite as good as any other explanation I've come across if you think that's what he did talk. Gertrude hadn't noticed because women weren't allowed to bring up their own children then, any more than they are now really. I must say I thought that part was a little weak. Horatio guessed, naturally, but he couldn't say anything. And what did I suppose it was that had driven Ophelia mad? Obviously a sexual shock, eh?

'I shouldn't be going on like this because it'll only feed your prejudices, but, well, I said what about the whole of the play, there's nothing in it that suggests that things are any different from what they seem. She didn't know about that, she said; *she thought* Hamlet was a woman.'

'I hope you told her she needed weightier authority than that,' said Smith. 'A Radio 1 disc-jockey thinks Hamlet was a woman. An unemployed school-leaver in Wapping thinks Hamlet was a woman. A psychiatric social worker –'

'That's just sneering, my boy. What she also *thought*, in a different sense, was that Hamlet was a woman in some other . . . realer sphere than the play or Shakespeare's sources or anything that might historically have taken place at Elsinore or any other actual spot. Some third domain beyond fiction and fact. That's the terrifying thing.'

At the end of a short silence Smith said, 'I used to get that from one of my three-point-seven as it might be after films. How did they get on when they started having kids in that place? Did she come back to him in the end? Not might, assuming for fun and for the moment that it's life we're talking about. No – did.'

'Not too dull for you I hope, Jake?'

'It's exactly what they're like. I didn't know anybody else had realized, it's never been said, not in my hearing anyway. Absolutely hit it off to a T. When you get past all the poise and the knowingness and the intimacy there's a tiny alien particle that doesn't understand.' It came to Jake that he had been speaking with some warmth and he altered his tone. 'You'll have to bear with a very ancient historian who spends most of his time coping with drop-outs from Kettering Catering College. Well, what a rarity, listening to two dons discussing their subject,' and so on and so forth.

Not long afterwards Lancewood suggested that they should go over. Smith asked for a quick pee and was shown where. As soon as possible Jake said,

'Damon, what's a wanker?'

Lancewood hunched his shoulders with a jerk, showing that as well as being amused by the question he wasn't totally surprised by it. Again in a way uncharacteristic of dons, or perhaps of the popular idea of them, he spent no time on prolegomena but went straight to what was intended.

'These days a waster, a shirker, someone who's fixed himself a soft job or an exalted position by means of an undeserved reputation on which he now coasts.'

'Oh. Nothing to do with tossing off then?'

'Well, connected with it, yes, but more metaphorical than literal.'

'That's a relief. Up to a point. Well. I got called it today.'

'No really? By that pupil of yours?'

'No, by that picket of women's-lib women at the gate.'

'Oh yes of course. It's quite clever, all that, their campaign to make people feel old and senile and clapped out and impotent – that's where the literal part of wanker comes in.'

'Clever? As a means of persuading us to admit women?'

'Certainly. I can think of several colleagues of our sort of age who'd be troubled and frightened by such treatment and inclined to do what they could to put a stop to it. Can't you?'

'I suppose so.'

'Have you had anything unpleasant through the post? I gather there's been a certain amount of that.'

'Yes, today I was sent a . . .'

Although Jake considered Lancewood one of his closest as well as oldest friends he found himself perfectly unable to tell him what he had been sent that day. Luckily Smith came back just then and the three set off. In the quad a fine drizzle was falling, so fine that it hardly had the weight to fall and wandered almost horizontally. The zenith was a weak grey but the sun showed for a moment or two. Lancewood mentioned that the question had come up of the admission of women to men's colleges.

'Oh yes, you're one of the last-ditch trio here, aren't you?' said Smith. 'Comyns, Merton and Oriel. Rather grand in a way.'

'How long have you been letting them in at your place?' asked Jake.

'Oh, we haven't let them *in*, what do you take us for? At the end of '75 we published a Declaration of Intent that declared our intent to do something or other about it some time, and since then we've been consulting away like mad, pretty well without stopping, the JCR, the porters and the rest of the staff, the other colleges in our awards group, and the women's colleges of course, bloody funny that, and it all seems to have cooled off. We might just ride it out until the next thing turns up, World War III or whatever it might be. I often think my namesake in Rhodesia could have done with a touch of the Oxford spirit.'

'What's bloody funny about the women's colleges?'

'What? Oh, just our Governing Body is about as solidly against the idea as any, nearly all for Victorian anti-feminist reasons in effect, and there they are or were in a secret alliance with the crowd who want to block it for Victorian feminist reasons. Like something out of who, Damon, C. P. Snow?'

'Or Shaw. Jake,' said Lancewood rather patiently, 'letting women into the men's colleges will damage the women's colleges for ten or twenty years, perhaps longer, because they'll only get the men and the women the men's colleges don't want. *Jake*, because no man or woman is going to go to St Anne's when he or she could go to Balliol.'

'I'm sorry, I don't seem to have been keeping up with things.'

'It's tough,' said Smith, evidently alluding to the likely state of the women's colleges, 'but overall the case in favour is unanswerable.'

'I thought you didn't care for women undergraduates, at least in your own subject,' said Jake.

'As they stand I don't.' Smith seemed slightly cross. 'That's the whole point. Living and working among the men is bound to improve them. It's the only way they'll ever forget they're women and start behaving like, I know, not students, but –'

'You make them all sound the same,' said Lancewood, seeming slightly cross himself. 'Anyway, it'll mean the end of this.'

This must have been in the first place the Senior Common Room, where they had just arrived. Considerable parts of the building that embodied it dated from the fifteenth century; the room itself had been radically reconstructed in the 1870s under the influence of a Master of advanced artistic taste, and was well known to those interested in such matters for its carved pillars, multi-coloured floor tiles, authentic Morris wallpaper and pair of stained-glass windows depicting respectively The Progress of Art and The Progress of Science. There were also some paintings from that period, a Burne-Jones, two Poynters, a Calderon, a Simeon Solomon and others and, from an earlier one, a Romney of an otherwise unnoted Fellow of the college; recent research had been at that too, though so far without managing to dislodge the reputed artist. Jake had liked the room and its furniture on sight in 1936, when his tutor had invited him up to dessert, and still did, despite certain changes he could not now have defined.

Its occupants for the moment were rather less to his taste, starting with Roger Dollymore, the Senior Tutor, and an elderly chemist called Wynn-Williams. Jake went over to them not because he much wanted to but to give Smith and Lancewood, whom he hoped to sit with in Hall, a rest from him meanwhile. Little enough was required of him by the other two, who seemed quite happy, or not significantly more unhappy than might have been expected, telling each other about the plays they had seen in London during the vacation. Jake thought briefly how he hated plays, then tried to remember how each of them stood on the women-in-or-out thing. He knew how they ought to stand if they had any sense;

all he could remember about Wynn-Williams's wife was that she was impossible, but he knew Naomi Dollymore fairly well, or had done in the days when there were dinner-parties, and could have gone on for quite a long time without repeating himself about her readiness to share most details of her experience, recent or remote, with whoever she might be talking to, not in Alcestis's pseudo-sequential, fool's-anecdote style but by as free a process of association as you could hope to come across. So both husbands ought to be ready to lay down their lives for the status quo: the feminization of college, once begun, would lead irresistibly to the taking-over of common-room and High-Table life, of college life, by the wives. Just imagine the way . . .

'What?' said Jake. 'I'm sorry?'

'I said,' said Dollymore in his sheep's voice, the only one he had, 'where are you going.'

'What? Well at the moment I . . .'

'Away. Abroad.' Wynn-Williams might have been a Shakespearean king or other hero encouraging his followers into the saddle but of course he wasn't really, he just sounded like an old-style actor. 'We go to Venice at the end of June.'

'Naomi and I have rather fallen out of love with Venice,' said Dollymore. His interest in Jake's holiday plans had perhaps never been deep. 'So commercialized and full of Americans. That is the perennial struggle, to find a place that isn't. Naomi and I have been moving on almost every year for . . . years. We've been driven out of one Greek island after another. It seems Nisiros is still comparatively unspoiled.' After a long pause he went on at a reduced speed, 'Though I'm sure it's very different nowadays from . . . from the time when . . .'

Wynn-Williams came in quite quickly. 'The time when Jake's . . . Jake's . . .'

'Jake's pals from the . . . the . . .'

'From the long-ago were . . .'

'There. Were there.'

'Were there, yes.'

The two laughed in simple pleasure at having jointly

recollected Jake's subject and succeeded in bringing that fact to utterance. He laughed too. It was at any rate nicer over here than it could possibly have been in the larger group by The Progress of Art. They were all young, under about thirty-five anyway: the philosopher who was co-editor of a London weekly paper, the political scientist who ran a current-affairs programme on TV, the historian of drama who put on plays full of naked junior members of the university torturing one another, the writer in residence with his look of eager disdain for his surroundings, somebody's guest with his look of unearned eminence – a wanker of the future, if when the future came it tolerated any judgements of worth.

'Good evening, Master,' said Dollymore, and Wynn-Williams and Jake said something very similar.

They did this because the Master of Comyns, Marion Powle by name, had come up to them. He was fifty-five, a distinguished crystallographer, recent successor to a mad Graecist, serious, well liked even among the arts men: Jake quite liked him. Or didn't mind him. Not really. He opened his mouth with tongue against top teeth and held the pose for a few seconds, an effective way of calling for attention. Then he said,

'I must draw Jake aside briefly. I have to consult him about women.'

The other two responded like two immensely respectful and discreet versions of Ernie, if such a thing could be imagined. Jake wondered how Don Juan would have stood up to this sort of thing. He also wondered whether recent research might not have uncovered a historical prototype of that character and found him to have been a timid, anxious recluse like Isaac Newton, ending up married to his cook.

'And the desirability of admitting them to this college,' added the Master.

This time the two sighed noisily and flapped their hands, and Jake wondered what stopped them from seeing that, for good or ill, this was the most interesting matter ever likely to come their way, short of death.

'As you know, it's on tomorrow's agenda,' said the Master when he and Jake had moved off.

'Yes,' said Jake. Now he did. He had already known, though he had forgotten, that a College Meeting, i.e. of its Fellows, not of teachers and taught alike, was to take place the following afternoon.

'It's a bore, we agree, but we have to settle something before the end of the year. All I propose doing tomorrow is to announce a full discussion in two weeks' time and to nominate two Fellows to summarize the cases for and against just to set the ball rolling. A couple of minutes apiece, no more. I'm going to ask Roger Dollymore to put the anti point of view and I'd like you to put the pro. I thought of you partly because of your long experience and the fact that the small number of your pupils means you're not going to be personally affected either way. You won't have to say anything tomorrow except yes you'll do it, that's if you agree. I didn't want to spring it on you.'

Powle refrained from stating what another part of his grounds for asking Jake to do this job might have been, nor did he imply anything of the kind by his manner, which was entirely free from both jocoseness and it's conscious avoidance. Jake agreed to serve.

'Good lad. Oh, you needn't bother with any fact-grubbing, state of play in other colleges and such. I'll hand that to one of the youngsters. Yes, I think probably Whitehead. He's still a bit pleased with himself over the reception of that paper of his last year. Do him good.'

Soon afterwards the members of the college and their guests went down the worn stone steps into Hall. Jake sat near the middle of the table facing the body of the room with Lancewood and Smith directly and diagonally opposite him and Dollymore beside him. Gossip started on the events leading to the premature retirement of the head of another learned foundation. Lancewood knew more than Dollymore about this and so was able to keep him almost completely quiet. Later, while host and guest conversed together, Dollymore got back by going on about rising prices in a markedly personal style, suggesting either that he was the first to have spotted the phenomenon or that the increases were being levied on him alone. Out of the idlest curiosity Jake began counting those recognizable as females on the benches before and below him, stopping before he reached ten. Bloody nice cheap trouble-free way of victualling your girl-friend between pokes, he thought to himself with tremendously unwilling respect. The food and drink at High Table were excellent as usual. Over the savoury he considered whether or not to go on to dessert back in the SCR. If Lancewood hadn't had a guest there would have been no issue; as things were there was the risk of a further dose of Dollymore and/or, worse, of Wynn-Williams, fifteen minutes of whom might be thought enough to keep any man topped up. The Feisal Room it was, then.

In this chamber, adjacent to the main SCR, the Regius Professor of Latin, the Fellow and Tutor in Oriental Studies and the Principal Demonstrator of Anatomy were watching a colour-television screen on which a man with a woollen sort of mask over most of his face was using a pick-helve studded with nails to hit on the head an older man in a dark-blue uniform, or was at least feigned to be doing so. The Reader in Early Mediterranean History silently joined the audience.

About three hours later the gownsman just referred to descended the same stone steps as before but this time went out into the open. Not so many years ago at this time, the right side of midnight, the place would have been alive with activity, undergraduates fighting, vomiting, illicitly playing pianos or gramophones, setting fire to the JCR, throwing bottles of brown ale at the Dean's window, wrecking the rooms of Jews or pinioning them to the lawns with croquet-hoops. So at least it seemed to Jake. Now all was quiet. What were they doing instead? Fornicating? Taking drugs? Working? Writing poetry? He had no idea and didn't want to know.

An obstruction in his ear, catarrh or wax, clicked in not quite exact time with his footsteps on the stone. It would probably get all right left to itself. He entered his staircase and then his bedroom without having had to turn on any lights on the way, a skill acquired during some barely recalled business of fuel economy or power cut. After taking his Mogadon and putting on his pyjamas he had a thought, decided to forget it and then decided there could be no harm in just making sure. He went into the sitting-room and assured himself that nobody had burst or blown open his desk. Half a minute later he decided there could be no harm in just making sure, returned to the bedroom for his keys and opened the relevant drawer. The plastic phallus lay there snug as a bug in a rug, heart-warmingly undisturbed. Vowing to dispose of it the next day he turned off all the lights and settled down to sleep.

Time went by. Jake tried to remember some of the ladies who had shared this bed with him in the past and was quite successful in two or more cases, except that what he remembered was all a matter of their bracelets and their cigarette-lighters, the way they sneezed or asked for a drink, where they lived and how he used to get there and they here, the time he and one of them bought an evening paper or he and another of them went into Blackwell's bookshop. For a few seconds he had lying beside him some sort of image of that fair-haired South African who had worked in the University Registry, but what there was of it went before he could pretend to himself that he was even touching it. He did no better with just *a* woman or with merely considering in a general way business-head, Carter-face and the *Zoom* stable: his mind kept drifting away to other things. So then there was nothing for it but to give in and have his attention turned to what had been lined up for it ever since it had happened, Brenda's convinced but unexcited statement before Rosenberg and him, somewhat amplified over whatever they (she and he – Jake) had eaten at Mother Courage's, that she had had no pleasure or other benefit out of her marriage for a not very small number of years and only acquiesced in its continuance out of habit, laziness and dislike of upsets and, in particular, that she considered her husband to be at best indifferent to all women except as sexual pabulum. In fact she had put her point more shortly than that, adding that the biggest mistake of her life had been to understand her mother's maxim about men only wanting one thing as applying no further than to transactions with them outside marriage.

In the end he fell asleep, woke up about five and spent a couple of hours going over what Brenda had said and thinking about it, and then again fell asleep and dreamed he had to go on parade but couldn't find his boots, equipment, rifle or cap and didn't know the way to the parade ground.

Not very long afterwards Jake got up and went over to the buttery for breakfast. The cafeteria system here was most efficient and in no time he had settled himself at one of the waxed oak tables with his plastic tray. Nor did it take him long to dispose of the sausages that went to coarse powder in your mouth, electric-toaster toast charred round the edges but still bread in the middle, railway butter and jam, and coffee tasting of dog fur. When he had he went back to his rooms, dictated some letters into a cheap tape-recorder and took the spool over to the College Secretary's office, where someone would eventually type its contents. As often he looked in on the Secretary's secretary, a woman of about Brenda's age called Eve Greenstreet. Years ago she had gone to bed with him for a few weeks, something which a great many members and ex-members of the university could say for themselves. When the time came for him to move over he had felt no resentment, probably wouldn't have even if he hadn't already started on another lady, but had missed and gone on missing what he clearly remembered as her liveliness and quick common sense. Since her marriage some time in the '60s (was it?) she had supposedly turned respectable, not that she had become sedate in her manner or stopped taking care of her slim dark good looks – marvellous teeth and nice way of holding herself too.

She was on the telephone when he put his head round her door but at once she frowned theatrically and beckoned him in. 'Well, whoever seemed to think that seemed to think wrong, I can assure you: the Estates Bursar is the ... Yes, I can – extension 17 ... Not a bit. Good-bye.' After ringing off she looked wonderingly at the telephone and said, 'I told the same bloody fool yesterday.' Then she jumped up and came round her desk and kissed Jake, whom she hadn't seen since before the end of the previous term. He asked after her husband and was told he was fine and she asked after Brenda.

'Fine.'

'Oh? What isn't, then?'

'How do you mean ?'

'Oh, come off it, love. What's she done, flown the coop with somebody?'

'Of course not.'

'There's no of course about it the way you sounded.' Her expression changed. 'You're not ill, are you?'

'No, I'm fine. I mean really fine.'

There was an awkward silence; then Eve said abruptly, 'Sorry, I seem to have got off the mark a bit fast. I just thought you . . .'

He spoke abruptly too, without forethought. 'Actually there is something. Could I talk to you about it?'

'Not now, I presume?'

'Can I take you out to dinner?'

They arranged to meet the following Tuesday at La Sorbonne off the High Street where the old Chinese place used to be. As Jake was going Eve said to him,

'Just one thing, my old Jayqueeze,' and went on without pissily waiting to be asked what it was, 'I'm Mrs Greenstreet now, Mr Greenstreet's wife, if you get what I mean.'

'I do.'

'Because it would be such a shame, and so on.'

He was going to trumpet something about anything like that being off the cards in a big way, but before he could thereby let out to Eve what he wanted to discuss with her a girl knocked and came in with a couple of folders, so he just declared that he thought so too and took himself off. He couldn't have stayed much longer in any case if, in order to heed the state of its copy of his JPCR article as mentioned by Miss Calvert, he was to look in at the Bodley before his lecture. With a pupil coming at twelve, he realized, there would be no time afterwards, and then there was lunch, and ... and anyway he somehow wanted to see what was in store for him as soon as he could. When he did see, he wished he hadn't been so keen. Apart from Wanker! rather tastefully executed in orange and Prussian blue and various more familiar obscenities, there were marginalia of an altogether different order. Copied from Grossman, PAHS, vol. xlvi, p. 44 – when he hadn't even heard of Grossman, let alone read his article. Not possibly before 900, unlikely before 800; see Nardini, MES, vol. xxx, p. 524 – when he knew pretty well the sort of thing Nardini would be saying and had no time for it. Refuted by Silvester, RHSF July 1969 – when nobody could be expected to read everything. After a quick glance, or glare, round he ripped out the offending pages and hastened from the scene.

His lecture, delivered in a windowless room off Parks Road belonging to the Department of Criminological Endocrinology, went down like a bomb: well, he came through it with a whole skin. Even the little bastard from Teddy Hall had no very violent objection to his answer to a question about the Median legal system. When all was over for that week he walked back to Comyns through a shower of rain that stopped abruptly, like a tap being turned off, when he was a dozen yards from his staircase. The expected pupil turned up within half a minute, having followed in his wake from the lecture-room. He was a fat little fellow from Bradford who nevertheless showed both some curiosity about early Mediterranean history and some respect for Jake's standing in that subject, a combination so dazzlingly rare that Jake had come near to looking forward to their tutorials. Today discussion of the collection paper and of a single point from the lecture kept them going till they were interrupted by the chapel clock striking one. Still able to come occasionally that way, Jake thought to himself. He walked over to the SCR and ate some bright yellow soup with globules of oil on the top and a layer of farinaceous material on the bottom, two rectangles of ham of a greyish as well as pink complexion, a rudimentary salad and a segment of wrapped Camembert, and drank a tankard of beer because you couldn't get wine at lunch because that was easier for the staff. From half-way through the soup to the start of the Camembert, Roger Dollymore stood at his right rear and read out to him an article in *The Economist* about the economy. After Jake had drunk his coffee, which tasted of licorice and its own grounds more than dog fur, and glanced through the daily papers it was time to go into the Grade Room for the College Meeting. These conventions, held weekly in term, had once started at five o'clock and ended at a point which enabled the members of the college to stroll into the main SCR and drink a glass of sherry before going down to the best Hall, i.e. dinner, of the week. Now all that was changed and the thing started at two on the dot to let people bugger off as sharp as they could.

That afternoon's portion held nothing that lodged in Jake's mind after it was over except the Master's request, notified the previous evening, that he should briefly put the case for the admission of women into Comyns at the meeting to be held a fortnight on, and his saying he would. In fact the two utterances not only lodged in his mind, they weighed on it too, slightly but to a degree he couldn't put down to anything. It meant extra work, too little though to oppress even him. More likely he was not fancying the prospect of the rallying, chaffing, twitting, bantering smiles, winks, nudges and grimaces to be seen, or fancied to be seen, when he duly spoke for the ladies. There had been a touch of that this time.

He took tea in the SCR and bloody good it was as usual, one of the bits they hadn't got to yet, like the Halls: toasted bun, cucumber sandwiches and Jackson's Earl Grey. At five minutes past five he went over to his rooms, there to conduct his seminar on Lydia – the region of Asia Minor and ancient empire of that name. Doing that put him in just the right frame of mind to receive his guest for the evening at 6.30. This was an ex-pupil, a graduate student from St John's who had been short-listed for an assistant lectureship at the University College of South Wales at Cardiff, largely no doubt on the strength of the laudatory but quite fair reference provided him by Jake. For a reason that will be seen in a moment, he had fought as hard and conscientiously as he could to clobber the chap's chances by praising him with faint damns, but in vain: integrity, curse it, had triumphed as it so often had in the past, long ago condemning him, with some assistance from laziness, to the non-attainment of a professorial chair. But in this case there was still a chance of undoing its ravages. Tonight he would tell his man that while Cardiff was a thoroughly respectable place there might be better things in store for him here in Oxford. If he stayed on and – point coming – ran or helped to run Jake's seminar for a year or so, he would be in a much stronger position to walk into Jake's readership when in due course it fell vacant. Integrity was going to demand that he made it clear to the chap that he would be warmly supported for that post whether he went to Cardiff or not, but he felt he could submit to that demand with a comparatively good grace.

When it came to it the operation was painless, though the young man gave no sign of being drawn towards or away from Cardiff. Jake took him on to dessert and gave him port; to help to seem to be giving rather than plying with he took a small glass himself. Not that plying with of various sorts and intensities wasn't raging about the two of them. Far to seek was the guest invited for his company rather than for some turn he might serve – back a candidate for a college place or a university lectureship, agree to publish a book of dolled-up learned articles, endow something, withhold support from something else – or perhaps had served: Lancewood, who might have provided an exception, hadn't been in Hall. Jake wondered what was being asked of the only woman in the room, distantly known to him as a fellow-historian with interests in medieval Scandinavia. There had been senior women guests at Comyns for years now: all things considered, among them her age and general condition, the present one was most unlikely to hurl herself diagonally across the polished walnut and snatch at his winkle; nevertheless he was put out to see her there, as if she knew something about him that he would have preferred to keep hidden.

The evening ended quite agreeably: guest thanked host and

said he would think things over and let him know. Jake went to bed and, aided it might have been by the port he had drunk, slept much better than the previous night. He was up early, in good time to face a string of tutorials starting at nine, or rather 9.10. During the intervals he wrote a short note to whom it might concern that said here was a copy of the Ionian-trade-routes thing for the recipient's personal use. This, together with an off-print of the article and a slip asking for twenty copies please, he took over to the Secretary's office and handed in at the place where they kept the photostat machine. Miss Calvert would probably talk around among her thick pals and the little bastard from Teddy Hall would probably whip across to the Bodley to go over the ground and hence to deduce further who must have mutilated the relevant number of JPCR and to laugh, if he ever laughed, but what of it?

Jake was between Didcot and Reading in the earliest of the three usual return Flying Dodgers (the choice was less confined than on the outward journey) when it came to him that the plastic phallus was still in his desk drawer. Unless somebody else had already taken it out, of course.

'What exactly is it?' asked Brenda.

'It's like what we did before, only this time it's *genital* sensate focusing, so down below is all right, in fact the whole point so to speak.'

'I see. There is a thing called a feel-up, isn't there? I mean of course there is, but that is an expression, feel-up?'

'It certainly used to be. I expect it still carries on.'

'Okay. Now: how is this genital whatname different from a feel-up?'

'It's a feel-up by numbers,' said Jake in a sneering tone.

'Don't sound like that about it. What's by numbers? No I see, so many minutes each, sort of like a drill.'

'Exactly like a drill. They must think that takes the anxiety out of it, everything being predictable, no decisions to take.'

'That seems quite sensible to me, as far as it goes.'

'I don't know, perhaps it is. Well . . .'

'And we're allowed to have sexual intercourse but not required to.'

'Yes. There goes predictability. I must have muddled it up, that part.'

Jake and Brenda got up from their seats in the sitting-room at Burgess Avenue and clasped hands with an air little different from that of a couple shaking them before going off to face some minor social ordeal like boss to dinner or speech to local society. Upstairs they put the patchwork quilt on one side, she went out to the bathroom and he started undressing. At first he tried not to think of what was in store; then he decided that was silly and thought. Thinking passed quickly and imperceptibly into feeling. What feeling? Reluctance? Yes. Revulsion? No. Fear? No. Embarrassment? No. Boredom? Er, no. Dejection? Yes, but still not the right section of the thesaurus. Disfavour? Yes, but not much further forward. *Dismay* – of a peculiar kind, one not encountered before in any of his admittedly unhabitual attempts to analyse his emotions: it was profound ... and ... unalloyed ... and ... absorbing ... and ... (Christ) ... very very mild, like so much else. Well, what did he know about that?

He finished undressing and got into bed with his back towards the door. Brenda pattered in and joined him.

'Ooh! Let's get warm first, shall we?'

'Sure.'

'I've lost another five ounces. Mostly going without potatoes last night, that must be.'

'Good for you.'

'I am trying, you know.'

'Of course you are. I said good for you.'

'Will you remember the programme all right, do you think?'

'I won't have to, I've got it here.'

'Oh marvellous.' After a silence, Brenda said, 'Well, shall we start?'

'Okay,' said Jake cheerfully. 'Now the first thing is five minutes each of sensate focusing, that's the non-alcoholic sort. Who's going to go first?'

'Me. Remember you're to say if I'm doing it right and what I'm not doing that you'd like me to.'

'Check.'

Brenda did it right rather than wrong and he couldn't think of anything she wasn't doing that he'd have liked her to, except for falling asleep, going to answer the telephone etc. Then he called time and took his turn. He put in a solid, conscientious performance that must have gone down quite well, because she evidently couldn't think of anything he wasn't doing that she'd have liked him to do.

'Right,' he said at last, still cheerfully, reached for the xeroxed sheet on the bedside table and put his glasses on. 'Yes – now you stimulate my nipples and breasts by stroking, tickling or gentle pinching, or the whole breast area may be gently rubbed. Off you go.'

And off she went. After a couple of minutes he said,

'Let's scrub this. It says fifty per cent of males respond sexually to such stimulation. That probably means up to fifty per cent. Anyway, I must be one of the other fifty per cent. Now it's my turn, or your turn. I'd better just . . .' He put his glasses on again. 'Female breast area, here we are. Yes, you're supposed to explain to me just how you like it done.'

This proved to be unnecessary. Brenda plainly liked it done how he was doing it, responded perceptibly more than last time. He was glad about that: he felt pleased, though without feeling pleasure. That was to be expected: if he had been getting pleasure out of what he was at there would be no need for him to be at it, or alternatively he would have been at it anyway without ever having heard of genital sensate focusing or been near bloody Rosenberg. But to have not the slightest expectation of any pleasure whatsoever undoubtedly eased the strain. Grating a carrot or polishing a spoon would be far more tedious if you had to keep on the alert waiting for it to 'turn you on', as he had gathered it was called. Somehow, too, not talking helped. It made the whole business more serious, more like the Army. When he did say something it was out of the book.

'End of Phase I. Now with Phase II either partner can begin, so shall we swap round? It seems more . . .'

'If you like.'

'Okay. That means I sit with my back against the head of the bed with my legs spread out and you sit between them with your back to me. Then I' – glasses – 'I use gentle tickling, stroking or kneading movements in long, even, rhythmic strokes and you, well what it boils down to is you guide me and after a bit I . . . yes, I conduct a gentle but persistent invasion . . . and mustn't be afraid to stop for rests. That sounds pretty straightforward. Shall we go?'

The first part of Phase II was completed according to instructions. At its conclusion the partners changed their positions as follows: the woman sat with her back against the head of the bed with her legs spread out and the man faced her, put his legs on either side of her and lay back with his genital region accessible to her. After a period of stimulation, beginning with gentle tickling, stroking, pinching and scratching, the man showed signs of arousal and excitement. In due course an act of intercourse took place, in the course of which both partners achieved climax and evinced various signs of relaxation in the course of time.

Afterwards the male partner lay on his side in a reposeful posture, his facial area in close proximity to the facial area of the female partner and his right upper limb partially surrounding her trunk. Well, he thought to himself, that (the taking place of the act of intercourse) ought to prove something. The question was what. That he could if he would, at any rate. What more? That there was nothing organically wrong with him. But he already had Dr Curnow's word for that.

As if she sensed that he was in a questioning frame of mind, Brenda kissed him warmly on the cheek. That was nice.

'You see?' she murmured. 'All just worry and tension.'

'Was it all right for you?'

'Yes.' After a pause she added, 'Like old times.'

That was nice too, but the male partner didn't think much of it as a statement of fact, or at least of how he felt, he himself speaking personally as of then and there. What had finished a minute earlier had been pretty much like old times, physically at least and as far as he could remember – the remembering trouble having less to do with the oldness of the times than the inherent difficulty of remembering a lot about any such experiences or series of them; so at least plenty of people would say. But over the last minute, now extending itself to two or three more of the same, he could find in himself rather little, hardly enough to be worth mentioning, of the old-time mixture of peace and animation. That might be round the corner: early days yet, long way to go, walk before we can run, etc.

'Would you like a cup of tea?' he asked.

'Ooh, *yes.*'

'And a slice of toast?'

'Oh *darling*,' she said as if he had added a gold chain or something to his original offer of a diamond necklace, which was agreeably far from taking things for granted but also rather convicted him of having done bugger-all for the preceding decade. Then she added immediately, 'I daren't. Guzzlers Anonymous would kill me.'

'I won't tell them.'

'I know, but still . . .'

He tossed a coin in his mind and said sternly, 'I didn't think, I shouldn't have suggested it. Of course you mustn't have toast.'

'All right.' She put her face under the bedclothes.

The post-coital cup of tea was very much an old-time institution, with assorted origins or purposes. It satisfied Jake's need at this stage to be up and doing instead of going on lying about; its making and fetching gave Brenda the chance for a short nap; it was a small token of his appreciation; drinking it together brought a pleasant cosiness. Or rather all these things had once been the case; at a more primeval period, the interval that ended with the laying down of cups had turned out to be just right for his thoughts to start returning whither they had started turning half an hour before. No surprise was expressed or felt when that didn't happen this afternoon, or more precisely early evening. After the tea was drunk Jake went and had a bath, as usual leaving the water for Brenda so as to save fuel. Then he dressed himself with a certain care in clean pale-pink shirt, mildly vivid tie, the Marks & Spencer suit he betted would fool anyone he had much chance of running into, and the grey suede half-boots that had been all the rage in some relatively recent era like that of Hitler's rise to power. He hadn't a lot of hair left on his head but he tidied what there was with the touch of complacency this exercise always tended to arouse in him: better bald as a badger than train it over from side or back and be afraid to sneeze. That done, he went downstairs and watched Crossroads. Just as it was finishing Brenda came into the room.

'Ready,' she said in exactly the same way, eager and yet nervous, as he remembered from when he had taken her out to dinner in Oxford for the first time after they were married, at the Dollymores' house in St Margaret's Road; she had worn a sort of coppery-coloured dress of some shiny stuff and bright green slippers with gold clasps and pointed toes. Jake felt more than one kind of pang, at how time had gone by, what quantity and in what way, and at how long it had been since anything much about Brenda had struck him. He got up quickly.

'You look beautiful.'

She smiled delightedly and without reserve. 'That's good. You look all right yourself.'

'It's the tie. Brings out the blue in my eyes.'

'Off?'

'Yes.'

They were indeed off that night, not however to anyone's house but to a fairly classy Chinese restaurant called the Bamboo Bothy and situated almost round the corner from them in Vassall Crescent, easy walking distance anyway so no trouble or expense over transport. The idea – in general: the choice of premises had been left entirely open – was Rosenberg's, indeed his instruction. Weekly until further notice, the Richardsons were to engage in interpersonal recreative sociality, in other words to 'go out together'. It had been and would remain Jake's part to initiate the enterprise, though Brenda had an equal voice in determining its nature. Since what he would have liked best, granted he had to leave the house at all, was a straight-there-and-back attendance at the most violent and/or horrific film on show in Greater London while what she would have liked best was drinks at the Ritz followed by dinner at the Connaught, things might seem to have gone her way of the two, if not by much, but he had really scored by vetoing the below-subsistence-level man's, the famine-relief-beneficiary's version of the Connaught that was all they could afford: cooling bad quasi-continental food served tardily and rudely in hot dark noisy smelly dirty crowded surroundings. 'We won't go *there* again,' Brenda would say, but they did in all but name, admittedly less often in the last year or so.

The Bothy was almost empty, to Jake's knowledge its invariable state: turning up at eight or nine o'clock, walking past at eleven showed the same three unpeopled files of immaculate white tablecloths. It must be just the lid of an arsenal for use when. The proprietor's grandson or father greeted them pleasantly and showed them to a booth or berth at one side of the room. The composition covers on the benches or banquettes made your bottom give awful snarling, farting noises as you squirmed it along, forced so to squirm it by the overhang of the lowish table. Would they like a drink? No, they would like to order, though having done so they, in the person of Jake, also ordered a bottle of stuff called Wan Fu which they had tried and liked before. Among the welter of what must be Chinese on the label it said, in English, that this wine was specially selected to accompany Chinese dishes, and added reassuring references in French to negotiants, Bordeaux and cellars. Jake pictured a negotiant, or the appointee of one, walking round a cellar in Bordeaux with his mind bent hard on spare ribs, sweet and sour prawn, fried crispy noodle and chicken with bamboo shoots and every so often suddenly and infallibly selecting. Well worth the mark-up.

'Ooh, I was going to say, the garden's in a bit of a state I thought today,' said Brenda.

'There's always rather a lot to do at the beginning of a term.' It was true that he had a little more to do then than at some other times. 'Anyway I've finished pruning the roses and I'll do the chrysanthemum fertilizer over the week-end. Weather hasn't been very inviting you must admit. Ah, thank you very much, that looks delicious.' As soon as the waiter had gone Jake said, 'Well, darling, we've got something to celebrate.'

'Something, yes.'

'Oh I agree it isn't very much, but . . .'

'No it isn't. Well, it's just something.'

He groaned to himself. 'It's only supposed to be a start.'

'What is? What's *it* exactly?'

'Well, a . . . successful . . . what Rosenberg would call act of intercourse.'

'What's that? What's a successful one of those?'

'Just . . . one where the man gets it up and eventually comes, and the woman comes too.'

'How important is that, the woman coming too?'

'Very important, I mean it wouldn't . . .'

'It wouldn't be Grade A without that, would it? Not strictly kosher. Not quite all present and correct. It might mean you weren't able to hold back for the number of minutes and seconds laid down in Screwing Regulations for Mature Males section fourteen sub-section D.'

'You know it's more than that,' said Jake a little absently. He was going over in his mind what he had said since leaving the house, because it must have been since then.

'Nobody would have known it from the way you asked me just afterwards if it had been all right for me. You should have heard yourself. Talk about any-complaints-carry-on.' Brenda had been looking down at the food through her spectacles, sorting out for herself the less calorie-crammed items; now her eyes met his. She had spoken and continued to speak in the same unheated tone she had used in Rosenberg's consulting-room when making similar points more generally. 'I've taken in quite a lot of that Army stuff of yours. It might have been the best time of your life.'

'If we're going to get on to that level we might as well –'

'That's not on a level, you think about it, not now, and you see if it wasn't. Anyway if it's of any interest, sorry no I know it's of interest, it was all right for me, just, what you might call technically.'

'You said it was like old times.'

'So it was. I meant it.'

Jake's spirits fell sharply. 'Gee thanks,' he said.

'Don't misunderstand me, that's better than nothing, and I wasn't thinking of the real old times, when we started together. They were –'

'But you didn't sound as if you meant it, well, disappointedly then. You sounded friendly and affectionate then.'

'That was then. Even after your any-complaints thing I wanted to make you feel as good as I could . . .'

'Which you're losing no time in duly reversing.'

' . . . *so* that you might start showing a bit of physical affection to me, instead of which you shot out of bed and started getting some tea going.'

'You didn't sound as if you minded the tea idea, quite the contrary, and surely you remember we always used to have tea afterwards, it isn't that long ago good God, and what do you think I'd been doing before but showing you physical affection – putting you in your place socially? I think you might –'

'I was making the best of a not frightfully good job, and I fancied a cup anyway, though a large gin would have been more like it just then quite frankly,' – Brenda was warming to her theme a little now – 'and of course I remember how we used to have tea once, but that was different, and . . . what was the other thing?'

'Er . . .' Jake looked away diagonally across the aisle of the restaurant and saw that the three youngish men he had vaguely noticed a couple of minutes earlier, men whom by their open-necked shirts and pullovers or leather jackets he had vaguely taken for a group of gasmen or dustmen on emergency call, were peering at menus. One of them was in the middle of a tremendous unshielded yawn. *Really*, the way they . . . 'Er . . . Christ . . . physical affection.'

'Oh yes. Well I don't count a poke as physical affection, I'm thinking of before that, the non-genital stimulation or whatever it's called. That's part of what that's meant to be, you realize, it's meant to be partly affectionate, or rather you don't realize, not like grooming a horse or more like pumping up a bicycle-tyre. You were like – I've never heard anybody gritting their teeth so loudly in my life, when you were doing it to me *and* when I was doing it to you. And not saying a bloody word.'

'I thought that would help us concentrate. And you didn't say anything yourself either.'

'I took my time from you to start with and then I just hung on out of curiosity to see how long you were going to keep your mouth shut.'

Jake started to speak with resentment and defiance, then checked himself. 'Now look. I know I've said it before, I'm merely reminding you, this is all me or, all right, mostly me largely me, it starts with me, not you. I'd be the same with anybody.'

'I don't care about anybody. I'm meant to be special as far as you're concerned.'

'You are, and that's bound to make a difference but it's not going to happen all at once, we must accept that. And we have made a start. After all, biologically we've –'

'Screw biologically. We've made one sort of start, but there's another sort we haven't made,' said Brenda with an emphasis he had never heard her use before, or else had forgotten, 'and this really is you. You've got to find out whether you feel any affection for me or whether you're the sort of man who can only feel affection for women he wants to go to bed with or wouldn't mind going to bed with or thinks of in a sort of bed whatname, context. If you're not that sort, if you do feel some affection for me even though you don't want to go to bed with me you'd better start working on it and trying to show it. And remember I can tell.'

'What about your affection for me?' he asked after a silence.

'It's there but it's keeping itself to itself. It tends to watch its step a bit after the knocks it's taken.'

'When did it last take a knock?' This was playing for time while he tried to recover a memory.

'Ooh, about two hours ago, when I kissed you and tried to start talking to you and you came back with any complaints and put your arm round me as if I was an old sow you were having to keep warm till the vet arrived.'

'I didn't mean it like that.'

'I don't say you *meant* it like anything. I just might as well have been an old sow.'

'I suppose you think this is a good time to bring all this up.'

'Yes I do. Check. An excellent time. After you've taken the first step towards getting your, well, your confidence back and before you sell yourself the idea that that's all you have to do. I mean before you absolutely stop wondering what went wrong. Dr Rosenberg seemed to think they go together, you know, screwing and being affectionate, as far as I could make out what he meant, and so do a lot of other people.'

'Yes of course.' Jake had remembered, 'You believed me when I said you looked beautiful in the sitting-room just before we came out.'

'I believed something. Something nice. What made you say it?'

'Just remembering how things used to be, sort of suddenly.'

She dropped her gaze to her plate, which was now quite empty, and pushed her hand out towards him between the dishwarmer and the soy sauce. He took the hand and squeezed it, telling himself it was amazing how after all these years one went on forgetting the old truth that women meant things differently from men. They (women) spoke as they felt, which meant that you (a man) would be devastated for ever if you took them literally. (The compensation, in fact bonus on aggregate, was that they thought you operated in the same way, so that they forgave and forgot the devastating things you said to them. He had once, in the course of one of their rows about her relations, called Brenda an illiterate provincial, which had gone down at least as badly as expected at the time but had never since been thrown in his face, thank God; just think what he would have done about and with an accusation of remotely comparable nearness to the bone. And felt about it too.) So what she had said last Tuesday to Rosenberg and him, what he had lain awake going over in his mind in the medium-sized hours the following day, what had then seemed to him to write or at any rate rough-draft finis to their marriage – all that that had boiled down to was saying in bold sans-serif Great Primer italics that she was seriously fed up with him and he had bloody well better stop feeling sorry for himself and take a bit of notice of her for a change. And she had been and was absolutely right. So there they were.

'I think all this might sort itself out in the end with a bit of luck,' he said.

'So do I, darling.'

'Good ... We must have earned at least a beta-double-plus from Dr Rosenberg for this evening's work.'

'If not beta-alpha query.'

'If he could see us now he'd be nodding his little head in approbation.'

'Rubbing his tiny hands with satisfaction.'

'Showing all his miniature teeth in a benevolent smile.'

'Dancing on the tips of his microscopic toes.'

'Shaking his filter-passing buttocks.'

'I quite like him really.'

Jake lifted the corner of his lip and sighed. 'What's this do he's got lined up for us next week-end?'

'The Workshop?'

'Oh *Christ*, I'd forgotten it was called that, I must have censored it out of my memory.'

'What's wrong with it?'

'*Wrong* with it? If there's one word that sums up every-thing that's gone wrong since the War, it's Workshop. After Youth, that is.'

'Darling, you are a silly old Oxford don, it is only a word.'

'*Only* a word? – sorry. No, this whole thing is all about language.'

'Whole thing? What whole thing?'

'Well, the ... you know, bloody Rosenberg and his jargon, and beyond that, the way nobody can be bothered to ... Anyway, what is this fucking Workshop? I may say that if it's a *fucking* Workshop you can all count me out. I'm buggered if I'm going to start taking part in exhibeeshes in my condition, or even trying to.'

'It's nothing like that, it's a sort of group where everyone has a different sort of problem and says what it is and the others talk back to them. It's meant to help you unburden yourself and gain insight. But Dr Rosenberg explained it to us. Weren't you listening?'

'I suppose unburdening yourself might be a good thing in some cases. No, I was too bored.'

'You must try and make it a success, you know, and take it seriously.'

'I promise you I'll try, but at this distance it does give off a distinct smack of piss.'

The following day week, Saturday, at a quarter to ten of an overcast but so far not actually wet morning, Jake and Brenda made their way on foot to a house in Maclean Terrace some five hundred yards from their own. The events of the intervening eight days may be briefly summarized. There had been two further sessions of genital sensate focusing, the first slightly, the second considerably less successful than the initial one; the consultation with Rosenberg had thrown further light on Jake's sexual behaviour and attitudes but made visible thereby nothing in particular, or so it seemed to the patient; Brenda had told Jake, this time over tandoori chicken and bindhi gosht at the Crown of India in Highgate, that if he wanted to show affection for her he must try harder and then had discussed their holiday plans for September; Eve Greenstreet had cancelled her dinner with Jake because it looked as if her mother had started dying; and Mrs Sharp had tried to break down Jake's study door in order to admit a woodworm authority while he (Jake) was deeply engaged with business-head and Carter-face. Oh, and Brenda had had lunch and been to a film about peasants with Alcestis.

The house that was to house the Workshop was a little older and, to judge by its front, a little larger than the Richardsons'. That front had also had nothing done to it but in a bigger way: parts of the stucco facing had fallen off and there was a quite interesting-looking crack running down from the corner of an upstairs window. The front garden had no flowers or shrubs in it but quite enough in the way of empty beer-tins, fag-packets and cardboard food-containers thrown over the low hedge by tidy-minded passers-by and not removed by the inmates. What were the latter going to be like? Jake, who would have had to confess unwillingly to suffering slight twinges of curiosity and expectation as well as uneasiness at what might be in store for him, felt the uneasiness start to mount and become better defined. He noted successively the broken window-pane mended with a square of linoleum, the lidless dustbin in which a thick slightly shiny off-white vest with shoulder-straps and a bottle that had held Cyprus sherry caught the eye, the bucket half full of what you hoped was just dirty water and the comfortable-looking two-legged armchair in the passage that led to the rear. Agoraphobic stockbrokers, dentists afflicted with castration anxiety, anally-fixated publicity consultants he had been prepared for; mixed-up berks from building sites or off those lorry things that pulped your rubbish were quite a different prospect. Nor was he one whit reassured by the child's bicycle propped against the side of what was doubtless known as the porch.

No knocker or bell-push was to be seen on or near the peeling front door, so Jake pounded on it with the side of his fist. In the interval that followed he and Brenda embraced, briefly and without looking at each other. Then the door opened quite normally to reveal a long-haired middle-aged man holding a glass of what looked like whisky and water which he swirled all the time.

'Yer?'

'We're looking for something called the Workshop,' said Jake.

'Doctor you wanted, was it?'

'Yes. Yes, I suppose so.'

The fellow motioned with his head, his locks flying. He said in a lowered tone, 'Second on the left down there,' stood aside and carefully shut the door behind the Richardsons. Apart from what might perhaps have been a bead curtain the interior was featureless, also rather dark; there was a faint sweetish smell, not unpleasant; in the distance an organ, probably but not certainly through one or another means of reproduction, could be heard playing something a bit religious. In the past, Jake thought to himself, this would have made quite a plausible setting for a down-market spiritualist séance, though there of course your feelings would have been rather different – more certitude of tangible benefit and so on.

The room he and Brenda went into made much the same impression, but with more emphasis on things being dirty and damp. It also had Rosenberg in it. The little psychologist slipped to the floor from the sofa-like object on which he had been perching and shook hands with the curious warmth he always showed on meeting, not quite false and yet not right, off target, appropriate to some other relationship, perhaps that of a nephew.

'And how are we now?' he asked. 'Do make yourselves comfortable.'

In the circumstances this was self-evidently out of the question but Jake and Brenda made no demur about taking off their topcoats and throwing them across a chair that could have come from his rooms at Comyns, and then settling themselves side by side on a kind of bench that had the attraction of being not far from a tall electric fire. This gave off a hasty buzzing sound from time to time.

'Whose house is this?' asked Jake.

'It belongs to Mr Shyster,' Rosenberg seemed to say. He spoke with an air of self-satisfaction.

'Does he run the . . .' – Jake set his teeth – ' . . . Workshop?'

'He does not,' said Rosenberg, shocked that anybody at all should need to be set right on this point. 'The facilitator is called Ed.'

'The what?' asked Jake delightedly, having heard quite well.

'Facilitator. We like to avoid words like organizer and leader. They have the wrong associations.'

'Whereas facilitator has exactly the right ones. I see.'

Brenda looked hard at Jake. 'Does it matter what he's called?'

'Oh indeed it does, Mrs Richardson, indeed it does. Words embody attitudes of mind.'

'I was making the very same point the other day,' said Jake with a respectful nod of the head. 'And who is Ed? Apart from being the facilitator of the Workshop, that is.'

'Well, he had a brilliant and extremely creative career in the United States and came to this country just over a year ago. He says he thinks it's his duty to stay because the need for him is greater here. They're streets ahead of us over there in this field, as you might imagine.'

Jake had subvocalized an oath. Funny how everything horrible or foolish was worse if it was also American. Modern architect – modern American architect. Woman who never stops talking – American ditto. Zany comedian. Convert to Buddhism . . . 'Oh yes,' he said when Rosenberg paused.

'I asked you both to come a few minutes early to tell you a little about this work. First of all I take no part, I merely observe. Ed's object is to induce the participants to express their emotions, to confess what he or she thinks he or she is really like or what's wrong with him or her, or to say what he or she feels about another participant. Or the others may help him or her to a more intense experience. Things of that nature. The essential point is that the emotion should be expressed in full – no holds barred, as we say. Also it must be *emotion*: Ed'll be listening not to what you say but how you say it.'

'So it's all right if I talk nonsense,' said Jake.

'Oh indeed, Ed wants to know how you *feel*.'

'I don't think I can feel much about nonsense except that it is nonsense.'

'You were saying just now what we said was meant to be important,' said Brenda. 'Words embodying things.'

'That's the mental aspect. It's the emotions we're on to now.'

'Oh.'

'Now the purpose of Workshop activity is twofold. The first applies in equal measure to every participant. It enables him or her to achieve release and gain insight into himself or herself. The second purpose is individual and is different for

154

every participant. It helps him or her to overcome his or her special problem. In your case, Mr Richardson, it's the overcoming of sexual guilt and shame. You'll find that by –'

'You keep saying that,' said Jake in some irritation, 'and I keep telling you I don't –'

'I keep saying it because it's true and you won't accept it. Look at yourself at the McDougall.'

'I have, and what of it? Anyone would have felt the same.'

'Wrong. As you'll come to see. You think it's disgraceful that your libido has declined. Yes you do. As you'll come to see it's no more disgraceful than catching cold. But I mustn't lay too much stress there, that's just on the surface. Deeper down you feel that the slightest little deviation from any sexual norm is cause for guilt and shame, as your fantasy showed. There are parts of your sexual make-up you still refuse to let me see.'

Jake slowed himself down. 'Look, Dr Rosenberg, if I have got any parts like that I don't know what they are. As I've explained to you before, I don't particularly object to oral sex or anal sex or the rest of the boiling, I just don't enjoy that kind of thing as much as the . . . straightforward stuff. Didn't enjoy it, I should say. No desire to be a voyeur or be at the receiving end of one. Et cetera. And what of it if I had? And I had to eke out my fantasy with adjectives and so forth because what I was imagining was too simple to run to the number of words you asked me for.'

'Please just listen. Deepest down of all you think everything about sex is unpleasant as a result of your puritanical upbringing.'

'Good . . . God.'

'Excuse me but we must get on. Mrs Richardson, your problem is inferiority feelings. You agree with that, I think.'

'You bet I do. I feel completely hopelessly –'

'Save it for the Workshop. The only other thing I have to say – well, two things. You two are the only participants with directly sexual problems, and everyone is selected with great care – vetted. Some people will try to enter this kind of work for the wrong motives: to acquire a sexual partner or just to enjoy the dramatic aspect or plain curiosity. One of the ways in which Ed is so good is he can detect those fellows as if it's by taking one look at them. Ah.'

A muffled thumping indicated a new arrival and a series of loud creaks the progress up the passage of Mr Shyster, if indeed it was he. A double series of creaks coming the other way duly followed, there was a light tap at the door and a girl of about twenty came in. She was dressed rather unfashionably (Jake decided) in a terracotta-coloured trouser-suit and frilly green shirt and carried a long umbrella with a curved handle.

'This is Kelly,' said the doctor. 'All Christian names is the rule here. Kelly, this is Jake and this is Brenda.'

'How do you do Jake, how do you do Brenda,' said the girl in a pleasant expensive-upbringing voice, shaking hands firmly and looking each of them straight in the eye. Considering her ease of manner, healthy skin and teeth and at least perfectly adequate features (good unsoft mouth), hair (reddish) and figure (far from flat-chested), he found it hard to imagine what her special problem could be.

While Rosenberg was filling in about what Jake did and where Kelly lived (just where Orris Park merged into Hampstead) another person's approach was heard. It proved to be that of Geoffrey Mabbott. He showed not the least surprise at finding the Richardsons there, a very Geoffrey-like reaction but so total that Jake's first thought, soon to be corrected, was that he had been told of their recruitment. Jake's next thought, rounded out later that day, was that he wasn't as surprised to see Geoffrey as he ought by rights to have been, and not just because after all Geoffrey was a bit touched and lived locally. No, the real reason was that Rosenberg always reminded him of Geoffrey. Since bringing to light at their first session that Rosenberg didn't know where Freud functioned, what had happened in 1848 or who James Bond was, he had established with varying degrees of certainty that Rosenberg had never heard of the *Titanic*, haggis, T. S. Eliot, plutonium, Lent, Vancouver (city, let alone island or chap), Herodotus, Sauternes, the Trooping of the Colour, *The Times Literary Supplement*, the battle of Gettysburg, Van Gogh, Sibelius, *Ulysses* – (a) good going for an Irishman (b) and no doubt Ulysses too – chlorophyll, Florence Nightingale, the Taj Mahal, pelota, lemurs, Gary Cooper and Hadrian's Wall; theoretically, on the face of it, in the strict sense there was no reason why you shouldn't never have heard of one or other or even all of that lot and still be a good psychologist; after all, he hadn't never heard of pornography, parents, marriage, erections and sex; and yet somehow ... (By the way, how had he ever got to hear of sherry-and-Oxford, even sherry and Oxford?) Geoffrey wouldn't never have heard of most of the items on the list but he would tend not to have much idea of who or what they were, scoring not very near misses with the same consistency as Rosenberg showed in not recognizing the target at all. In Geoffrey's world Eliot would be a famous actor of Victorian times, Vancouver a lake in Rhodesia, chlorophyll a newish health food, Florence Nightingale a campaigner for female suffrage. These magpies of his were seldom associated with the wrong bullseye, Eliot not being taken for a female novelist nor chlorophyll for an antiquated anaesthetic; Jake would have felt easier in his mind about them and about Geoffrey if they had been.

This morning he had dressed in the dark as usual: chocolate-brown corduroy trousers, navy-blue cable-stitch pullover, black shoes and the jacket of his dark-grey suit. His manner was friendly but slightly restless, again a familiar combination. Jake lost no time in asking him whether Alcestis was expected to join them.

'Alcestis?'

'Yes. Is she joining us?'

Geoffrey frowned and shook his head. 'No,' he said with an upward inflection. 'Where did you get that idea from?'

'I didn't get –'

'I mean why should she be joining us?'

'Well, Brenda's here, and I thought –'

'I know, Jake, I know Brenda's here, I've just this moment spoken to her,' said Geoffrey, gently enough but with some triumph at having so readily diagnosed the acute senile dementia that must have caused Jake to be brought to this place.

To distract himself from restraining himself from kicking Geoffrey in the balls Jake said, 'What's whatsisname like, Ed, the fellow who runs these do's?'

First Geoffrey dilated his eyes. Then he drew in his breath in a long hiss, slowly pouting his lips as he did so. Next he clenched his fists, raised them slowly again to shoulder level, lowered his head until it was between them and pounded his cheekbones rhythmically, meanwhile slowly once more expelling his breath. After that he unclenched his hands, indeed made them quite flat, pushed them out horizontally in front of him to the length of his arms and cut the air with them a number of times. Finally he dropped them to his sides and gave Jake a nod that showed he had finished.

'Oh I *see*,' said Jake. 'My goodness, he does sound an interesting sort of chap.'

When the facilitator arrived a few minutes afterwards he was at once distinguishable as such from the two or three other men who turned up at about the same time. Jake didn't quite know what he had expected beyond somebody designed to be as offensive in his sight as possible: hairiness, uncleanliness, youthfulness, jeans, beads, hat, etc. The reality was the opposite of all that without being in consequence the least bit more encouraging. Ed turned out to be in his late thirties, heavily built, dark after a Spanish or Italian fashion, wearing an oddly cut oatmeal-coloured suit that was none the less a suit, moving in a way that put you in mind of a cross between an experienced actor and a man well used to responsibility. He soon showed he had a trick of stroking his face in detail while he peered at you. When he spoke it was in a deep slightly wheedling voice.

'All right everybody, let's get to work,' he said. 'We have a couple of new participants today, Brenda and Jake. Hi Brenda, hi Jake.'

Salutations of differing amplitude came from the rest of the company, now seated in a rough square with Ed on his feet in the middle. Counting him and Rosenberg there were twelve persons present, seven men and five women.

'Now let's just introduce you around. This is Lionel, who steals things out of stores and says he can't help it, and this is Winnie, who's so shy she can't stand to talk to anybody even although she comes here every week, and this is Ivor, who's afraid of the dark and being alone and a whole raft of other things, and I have word you know Geoffrey, who gets worried because he's figured out he's an asshole, and this is Ruth, who doesn't have anything to do except cry all the time, and this is Chris, who doesn't like the human race, and this is Kelly, who can't run her life, and this is Martha, who has to look after her mother and says her mother is mean to her.'

It wasn't that Ed recited this in a lifeless or even a neutral tone, it was simply that Jake couldn't tell whether he was amused or compassionate or bored or contemptuous or generously indignant. Those so briskly characterized showed no signs of surprise or resentment: Lionel, who stole things, even blinked and pursed his lips in a self-deprecatory fashion as if he thought Ed had in his case been somewhat over-gracious.

After a moment, Ed went smoothly on. 'What's with Jake is that he can't get it up any more, and what's with Brenda is she thinks it's her fault for having gotten middle-aged and fat, so she feels bad.' (Jake knew they were all looking at him but he didn't look back at any of them.) 'Now since we have our two new participants we'll make today a salad. For openers, scanning pairs. Jake, Brenda, that means each of you looks another person over and they do the same with you but no intimate physical contact. You start with the eyes – the others'll show you. All right – Ivor, Winnie . . .'

In due course Jake found himself standing near the window and facing Martha, the one with the mother. Her eyes were fixed on him in an unbroken stare. He stared back for quite a long time on the view that this must be what was required but in the end got fed up with it and shifted his gaze. Ed appeared at that very juncture and caught the tiny movement.

'No no no,' he said, and again he might have been feeling impatient or sympathetic or anything else. 'Hold it at eye to eye until I give you the word to break.'

It went on for a period that could have contained without substantial cuts the whole of an evening's viewing from Batman to Closedown, or strictly speaking that was how it seemed to Jake. Strange things happened to his vision: at one stage Martha's face went two-dimensional, became a rough disc floating against a background of dark clouds or water, at another it receded a whole mile but grew in size proportionately so that the space it occupied was unchanged. His mind could do nothing but announce its distress to itself: silent recitation of Catullus or poems from the Anthology was about as useful an idea as thinking about sex. When, hardly looked for any longer, the word came to break it suggested at short notice a breaking wave of relief, but as waves do this one quite soon receded. He felt shaken up, uncoupled from the outside world. If Ed had wanted to do that thoroughly but without resorting to shock tactics he had succeeded to the full.

He had also, perhaps without meaning to, stated a major theme of the Workshop's activities, namely that every single one of them without any exception whatsoever lasted for very much longer than you would ever have thought possible. The next stage was a first-rate case in point. It was called free scanning, which meant in practice that you and your yoke-fellow inspected each other's faces with a thoroughness that would have made it possible to count the pores on them if required. Martha's was the face of a woman of forty or so, neither pretty nor ugly. Subjecting it to this kind of scrutiny meant that conventional details of general shape of nose or mouth went unregarded; if Jake were to pass Martha in the street the next day he would have been less not more likely to recognize her as a result of this experience.

The face business was not of course the end of it: Martha took and examined each of Jake's hands in turn, and he hers. Then she walked very slowly round him like an exalted tailor. He looked out of the window on to a patch of knee-high grass with things like discarded clothes-horses and oil-stoves showing here and there and said quietly,

'What does your mother –'

'No talking,' said Ed, 'there'll be plenty of time for talking in a little while.'

There was, though the bit about the little while turned out to be relative. At last Ed clapped his hands above his head and called on Chris to make the rounds.

'Make the rounds?' It came out high-pitched and querulous.

'Yeah, you know. Start with Winnie and end with Jake and Brenda.'

Chris was the one who didn't like the human race, young, pale and (happily) on the small side. He went and stood in front of Winnie, swaying backwards and forwards slightly in apparent thought. Then he got off the mark, telling her she was a bloody bitch and Christ he'd be shy if he was her and much more of the same. It was a full six minutes by Jake's watch before Chris moved on. At that rate it would be close to an hour before the rounds were finally made, and at *that* rate, not allowing for intervals, it would be close to ten hours before everybody had had or done his (or her) turn, but long before then one participant at least would have suffered irreversible brain-damage from rage and boredom. Chris's tirades were repetitive in the extreme, but of course it was the tune that mattered, not the words. By the time Chris had moved on again Jake had spotted a periodic element in that tune, a repeated decline from the expression of apparent fury to a mere ill-natured jeering. But was it jeering? More significant, was it fury? Would Ed know?

Jake's interest perked up when Chris returned his attention to Geoffrey, on the basis that even the unobservant couldn't fail to observe a few things about him that would be just right for a truculent harangue, if only his witty clothing, but there was nothing worth attention apart from an all-too-short passage of Joycean word-play about assholes towards the end. Geoffrey appeared dumbfounded at most of it, but then he would have found your visiting-card a pretty tough nut to crack. Kelly was next and Jake's interest perked back up for a different reason – what reason? Oh, just interest. She stood perfectly still with her arms folded and stared Chris in the face throughout his speech to her. The folded arms brought her bosom into prominence. It was good all right. There was something about her, perhaps starting with the clothes, that separated her from others of her age, made her the opposite of Miss Calvert, helped him to see that she was attractive. He went on looking at her after Chris had shifted to Lionel, had his eye caught and looked away. When he looked again, sidelong this time, she was giving Ivor one of the cautious bits of appraisal he had earlier noticed her sending him and Brenda. Kelly wanted to know what Ivor felt about what was taking place between Chris and Lionel. Ah.

Chris finished with Lionel and started on Ruth, who was the oldest person there and was sobbing within seconds. Jake wanted to stop it and went on wanting more and more. So did Brenda, he could see. Kelly he thought did, but wasn't sure. Nobody else showed the smallest sign. Rosenberg didn't look up from the journal he was reading; Ed was peering and squeezing his chin. Suddenly he looked at his watch and said in his usual tone.

'All right, cut it, Chris. Go to Jake.'

Chris did as he was told at once. He said nothing for much longer than he had said nothing to any of his previous victims, his small features working their way through a limited range of expressions of loathing.

'Who do you think you are, you old bastard?' he inquired finally. 'Who gave you the bloody right to be so fucking superior? You think I'm dirt, don't you? Bloody dirt. Don't you? Come on, don't you?'

Jake thought it was rather clever of Chris, considering Chris, to have worked that out but kept the view to himself. 'I haven't any particular –'

'No talk-back, Jake,' said Ed.

Without turning round Chris made a shushing gesture that told of ingratitude or preoccupation. 'Eh hevvn't ennair pahtierkyawlah ballocks. You know what you are, don't you? You want to know what you are, what you really are? You're just one big lump of shit.' After that he descended to personal abuse. So far from waning in vigour as before his displeasure mounted. Then he fell abruptly silent. When he went on it was in a tone he hadn't used before, one unmistakably (to Jake) indicating real anger and so reducing all his earlier behaviour to some kind of charade. 'If you don't take that look off your face right away,' he said slowly and quietly, 'I'm going to ...'

It helped Jake that he had once been quite a good tennis-player and was still pretty nimble for his age, also that he had noticed Chris glance over towards Ed for an instant; anyway, when the punch came he was almost ready for it, just managed to deflect it past his ear. Ed was there in no time and gave Chris a tremendous slap across the face so that he cried out and nearly fell. That was about when Jake saw what a good thing it was that Chris was undersized. He felt a sudden sharp twinge of total lack of pity for him.

'Bad boy,' said the facilitator blandly. 'Around here we don't play it that way, okay?'

'You didn't see the look on his face.' Chris was close to tears. 'He was looking at me as if he thought I was a lump of shit – you should have seen him, honestly.'

'Well, you called him one.' (This feat of memory, for Chris had used quite a number of other expressions, impressed Jake. He realized he hadn't seen Ed take a single note.) 'Maybe he does think you're a lump of shit. Maybe you *are* a lump of shit. Now get yourself together and go to Brenda.'

'Not going to. Not fair.' (Twenty-five if he's a day, thought Jake.)

'You are going to. In my Workshop people do as they're told.'

That was believable. Chris's resistance crumbled within ten seconds. In ten more he had gone to Brenda and rather perfunctorily set about calling her old, fat, etc. She faced him with a look of open contempt; Jake's contempt had not been open, or so he believed.

The next ingredient of the salad was called Winnie in the cool seat. Each participant participated in making her feel better, more relaxed, more *wanted*. One by one they told her nice things and were allowed to stroke or hug her but not to enter the sexual area. Chris mildly surprised Jake by being no worse at this than anyone else, telling Winnie first that she was great and then that she was, you know, great. When it was Jake's turn he took her hands and said,

'The thing to remember is that a good half of the people you meet are shy too, it's just that they don't show it, or rather don't show it in front of you. There was a famous –'

'Hold it right there Jake,' said Ed. 'That's thought bullshit. You have to get away from reason and logic. No because or although or if. The only good conjunction is and.'

So Jake reproached himself for forgetting Rosenberg's warning and told Winnie a lot of things he didn't mean much because they didn't mean much and everybody else seemed satisfied. When she finally vacated the cool seat Ruth replaced her as the centre of attention, though Jake missed the official title of what she was doing or being. Not that that could have mattered: she told them in the simplest terms that she had nothing to live for and went on to explain just as simply the circumstances that had brought about this state of mind. She was seventy-one and her husband was dead and her son had been killed in an industrial accident and her daughter was in a home for the feeble-minded and she lived in one room and nobody came to see her and she couldn't afford to go out or to have television and she'd never taken to reading (Jake took this to mean she was illiterate or near enough). She wept frequently during this recital and so in varying degrees did all the other women and Lionel and Ivor. Jake found that this time he could turn his mind to Catullus and the Anthology. When Ruth had apparently got to the end Ed made her start again. This he did twice more. Then he put Ivor in the hot seat. Ivor gave an unannotated list of the things that frightened him, which besides the dark and being alone included underground railways and any other form of tunnel, lifts, buses and large buildings, and after that the others took it in turns to reprehend him as severely as they could for being cowardly, spineless, ridiculous and babyish. When Jake started on him he gave him as many furious Ernie-sized winks as he could before Ed, warned perhaps by something in Ivor's expression, moved round so that he could see Jake's. Ivor, who had looked pretty hangdog at the outset, was showing healthy signs of boredom before the end.

To limit the danger of cardiac arrest from indignation and incredulity Jake had made an agreement with himself not to look at his watch, but while Brenda was gamely trying to sound as if she despised Ivor he (Jake) looked out of the window and saw, not the Queen-Moon on her throne, but bright or brightish daylight. Soon after that Mr Shyster came in with a tray of food and Jake relaxed his rule: two minutes past one. Night must have come and gone unnoticed. A queue formed. It was soon established that Mr Shyster was supplying sardine or cheese sandwiches at 50p each Jesus Christ, cardboard cups of coffee at 25p each Jesus Christ, and a lot of whisky-vapour free. Jake and Brenda had one of each sort of sandwich each – she contriving to leave most of the bread – and agreed in due time that the sardine ones were better or less bad than the cheese ones because the nasty sardine still eluded modern science for the moment. But that agreement was not yet, for Ed accosted Jake, Ed with Rosenberg at his side, both chewing savagely as if they were a couple of those Third-Worlders you read about who earn $15 a year.

'Well, Jake, what do you think of our work so far?'

'I think it's interesting.'

'Interesting. I do like that word, don't you, Frank? It's a great word. Yes, Jake, your hostility was very evident. That happens.'

After a stage of wondering who Ed thought Rosenberg was Jake remembered that poxing stuff about Proinsias/Francis and was able to answer fairly normally.

'What happens?'

'Hostility. Happens a lot. Don't worry about it.'

'I'm not,' said Jake. It was all that training with Miss Calvert and some of his other pupils, all that not going for them with the sitting-room poker at each new display of serene apathy, which restrained him now, he would have alleged, from jumping feet first at Ed's face.

'Well anyway don't worry about it. Now I expect you've got a few questions you'd like to ask, Jake.'

'Yes, I have, but I'm not sure this is the right time and place.'

'It is. I say it is.'

'Very well. Except right at the end that fellow Chris didn't seem to me to be really . . . cross at all.'

'Hey, he got that, Frank, how about that? Very good, Jake, you're coming on. Chris is just frightened. He's small and he's not a raving beauty and he's afraid he doesn't count, so he gets his blow in first. The more I make him act aggressive the more he sees he doesn't feel it. I'm just showing him to himself. Oh and he wasn't really what you called cross at the end either. What it was, Jake, you got him a little annoyed and he tried harder, which was useful.'

All this, at any rate on immediate hearing, sounded so appallingly reasonable that when Jake spoke next it was with something less than the perfect self-possession he had been trying for. 'I suppose you were showing Ruth to herself too.'

'That's right. This is only the third time she's been along and it's going to be pretty painful for everybody for a while yet, but they're a nice gang and they'll take it. You see, Ruth is all eaten up with self-pity – okay, she has plenty to be unhappy about, though not everything she says is true, right Frank?'

'That's quite correct. People in the same house visit her now and then and Lionel has called on two occasions. The second time he found she'd been invited in to watch her landlady's TV.'

'Which isn't a hell of a lot, but . . . She needs to be shaken up and made to do things, Jake, go out and find friends, it's possible, there's plenty going on in a neighbourhood you don't have to pay for, nothing wrong with her physically, she rides free on the buses – and so on. I'm going to wait until everybody knows her story by heart and then put her in the hot seat and have the group tell her she bores the balls off them. And if you're worried about Ivor, Jake, he's ashamed of his fears, thinks he ought to face up to them like a man, pull himself together. Which is impossible. You don't know how his psychiatrist had to work on him to come here at all. He has to learn he has a troublesome but not very serious sickness which he acquired through no fault of his and which can be cured, and he can't learn that until he sees how fucking stupid it is to call him a coward or whatever. Which we just made some progress in showing him.'

Ed stopped speaking abruptly, thus exploiting his advantage over Jake, who was thoroughly taken down by his further discovery that the facilitator at least seemed to want to facilitate mental health rather than bloodshed and raving lunacy, much too thoroughly to set about questioning on the spot the practicality or wisdom of the measures taken and proposed. Trying for a loftily non-committal tone, he said, 'Thank you very much for the various explanations,' but it came out a bit lame.

'Any time, Jake.'

The afternoon session began with Lionel's round table. Ed
stage-managed or rather produced it more closely than any
of the morning's events, calling on Lionel himself to answer
questions like whether or how far he thought stealing was
wrong and one or other of the rest to comment positively
(bear-oil him) or negatively (crap on him). The emotional
temperature again was lower than before but without any
more sense being talked as a result. Several comparatively
interesting things did emerge in passing, however: that
Lionel was head of a small building firm, for instance, that he
was forty-three years old, that he lived with his mother, of
whom he was fond, that he stole things he liked the look of,
that sometimes he went weeks without stealing so much as a
paperclip and then spent a couple of days stealing away like
billy-ho – things like that. Jake also noticed a couple of
inconsistencies in Lionel's account of himself and more than
a couple of hesitations when somebody pressed him for
details of when and where and the like. Nothing came up to
challenge the surmise that Lionel had never contemplated
theft for a moment and was probably an inactive queer in
search of a like-minded companion, having picked on
kleptomania for his cover as simple and unobnoxious. In
that case what happened to Ed's renown as a sham-detector?

The round table was dismantled and Geoffrey's self-
draining announced. Jake's curiosity flared up at once, nor
did it ever burn low during what followed. Geoffrey began
with some information new to Jake, and perhaps to all the
others too, namely that he had been educated at home
because of his elderly father's adherence to the doctrines of

Charles Bradlaugh. Asked to explain the rationale of this he disappointed Jake slightly and surprised him a lot by not stating that Bradlaugh had been, say, a pioneer of vegetarianism, and then again by not classing as a freethinker an opponent of the corporate state. The home educator, by some associated twist of paternal whim, had been not a tutor but a governess (who must have taught him everything he 'knew' from T. S. Eliot's Victorian-thespian status onwards and downwards – wrong, as it was to turn out). There followed a passage in praise of women so intense, categorical and of course long that a confession of hyperactive homosexuality seemed almost boringly inevitable. Wrong straight away, or straight away by the standards of the occasion: women had one defect – they could be loved, they were there for men to love them, but they couldn't be heroes. Geoffrey gave one of his frowns at this point as some verbal or other nuance swam towards his ken and away again. Hero-worship, he now affirmed, was an integral part of any lad's growing-up but it should be worked out or through or off at the normal time and place: school. He hadn't been able to start his hero-worship till he got to Cambridge and that had been too late, in the sense that once acquired the habit had proved impossible to shake off – none of this had been clear to him at the time and for long after, and he had only recently identified its consequences.

Where on earth Geoffrey's narrative would lead was quite obscure – perhaps it would bend back to buggery after all – but it was making a bit of a kind of sense in itself, at any rate enough, it might have been supposed, for Ed to have denounced it as thought bullshit; no, he held his peace and massaged the side of his neck. What, Geoffrey went on to ask, had those heroes of his in common? Strong individuality. They were unlike the mass of mankind, and also one another, in many of their opinions, their interests, their likes and dislikes, even their tastes in food and drink. A would wish the United Kingdom to apply for admission one day to the United States, B spend his week-ends studying the behaviour of social insects, C endlessly re-read *Pilgrim's Progress*, D refuse all dealings with Roman Catholics on principle, E eat only fish and fruit and F mix alcoholic cordial of cloves with his Scotch. With a humility that might have disarmed some people Geoffrey admitted he hadn't the talents to belong to the A–F class but was so vain that he wanted to seem to belong to it. He must therefore light upon some views and practices that were unusual without being too outlandish and also hadn't been pre-empted by the A–Fs. No easy task, this, and one complicated by the fact that, as he soon found, he held no views and neither practised nor hankered after practising any practices that weren't conventional to the point of banality. To create the right sort from scratch had been tough, too (for him at any rate), so he had left things to chance and kept his eyes and ears open. Almost at once - this must have been while he was still at Cambridge, or soon after – Fate had smiled on him. He had accidentally barged into a nurse in a crowded street and knocked a bag of groceries out from under her arm and she had called him a clumsy oaf. At a stroke he was in possession of a whole network of A–F type material that had extended itself over the years from simple antagonism towards nurses and the mention or portrayal of them in print or on screen to points of view about the National Health Service, pay increases, equal opportunities, the right of those operating essential services to strike and even immigration. His biggest stroke of luck, and one of the happiest passages of his life, had come a year or two before with the success in London of a film representing unfavourably a nurse in a mental hospital; he had felt a sense of vindication. So he had become a sort of G, the chap with the terrific thing about nurses.

(The inverted pyramid of piss exposed, confirmed, systematized! For Brenda's benefit Jake worked like a black at dissembling his fascination and glee, hoped he had started to in time, went on listening just as closely. There must be more where that came from. Perhaps there was to be a definitive pronouncement on the Hollands gin/KLM/cream cakes question.)

No such luck, though Geoffrey did not let fall that his supposed admiration for the works of Dvořák, always likely to be proclaimed when music, the nineteenth century or Hungarians (*sic*) came up, rested on nothing more substantial than a pubescent crush on an American film actress of that surname. Well, that was the end, he implied, of Part I. In Part II he talked about his ignorance, a subject that could have kept them there all night and well into the next day, but he was commendably brief. About the time of his setting out to acquire simulated individuality it had dawned on him that the A–Fs, and plenty of others too, were always referring to things – places, works of art, important events – and men and women living and dead, especially though not by a big margin dead, that he'd never heard of. So he had started to read through the encyclopedia, not every word or every article but essential subjects like ... history – English history. When after some years he was about a third of the way through he had experienced another dawn: to put it more succinctly than he did, he still knew very, very little more about Africa and the battle of Bosworth and Charlemagne and *Dombey and Son* than he did about Xenophanes, Yaksas and Zoutpansberg (and had stopped reading forthwith). Until quite recently he had put this unalleviated uninformedness down to a bad memory. That brought him to Part III.

One evening he had been extolling Dvořák in the musical context when a woman had asked him, to all appearance quite innocently, if he didn't think that the something sharp minor melody in the middle of the something movement of the, er, the New World Symphony was as fine in its way as the famous tune played by the something in the first section and that only the ... the syncopations and the something elses in it, which made it hard for the uninitiated to sing, had stopped it being as famous. He had said quickly (and Jake could imagine with what stiffness) that in such matters he always followed the popular view and the subject had dropped. But afterwards he had started thinking and had realized that, although the existence of the New World Symphony and Dvořák's authorship of it were as firmly settled in his mind as the establishment of the principle of evolution by (steady) Darwin, he knew nothing about it, of how it might differ from its composer's old-world symphonies if any, of how the least part of it went, of how many decades had gone by since he had last heard it, assuming he ever had. How then had work and musician come to hold their curious importance to him? For the first time since God knew when the lovely Ann Dvorak had returned to his mind and it was in that moment (he must have read a book or two of a sort at some point) that he understood how he had acquired what he had thitherto thought of as his opinions. All these disappeared as such instantly and reverted to what they had always been: things he said so as to seem to be someone.

'But I wasn't anyone and I'm not anyone,' said Geoffrey. 'I don't just mean I'm not important, though I'm certainly not that. I'm completely cut off. Oh I don't mean in a personal sort of way – I've got a wife whom I adore and we get on very well and I have some very nice friends.' He looked affectionately at Brenda and Jake. 'But they're all like just sort of comforts, marvellous to have around but I don't want to know anything more about them than I do already. They don't interest me. Nothing ever has – I've never wanted to know anything at all. That's why I couldn't remember what I read in the encyclopedia: I had no reason to and I wasn't concerned with knowing for the sake of knowing. It was different with my governess and exams and so on. But now I've got nothing to think about and I realize it, nothing except myself and that's very dull. There's nothing *in* me. I'm contemplating my own navel – I remember reading that or being told it, I suppose everybody has to remember some things or we couldn't read at all or even speak or function in any way – and my navel's a pretty boring subject.'

That seemed to be all for now. From the familiar lively manner of his in which he had talked of his dealings with nurses and Dvořák, a manner quite reconcilable with a keen curiosity about himself and the workings of his own mind, Geoffrey had in the last minute or so fallen with some abruptness into a hollow, lugubrious mode of speaking that matched the content of what he said. This – the tune, not the words – recaptured the attention of his audience which, apart from Jake, Brenda and Kelly, and in a different way Ed and Rosenberg, had stopped listening at about the Bradlaugh stage. Even Chris might well have noticed the change. There was a pause, during which facilitator and psychologist conferred inaudibly; then Geoffrey was thanked for his efforts rather as if he had just failed an audition by a small but distinct margin. Poor old bugger, Jake thought to himself, at least you're a cut above Miss Calvert and that lot. To them, the failure of things like knowledge to win their interest constituted a grave if not fatal defect in the thing itself.

Martha's one-to-one followed. She was herself and you were her mother and there were slanging-matches which she always won. Jake did his best when it came round to him but he was a bit distracted by wondering, and also beginning to nourish a man's-hand-size-cloud-type suspicion of, what the good Ed might have in store for him. He also wondered, not so hard but still quite a bit, what would be required of the person whose turn must intervene between Martha's and his – Kelly.

Time, plenty of it, came to the rescue here: Kelly was to engage in self-expression. In Jake's vocabulary this was a vague term applied to activities like swearing and children's art but in the present context it evidently meant something more specific. The girl at once left her chair, sat down on one of the more affluent patches of carpet and clasped her knees.

'All right, Kelly.' The note of coaxing in Ed's voice was intensified. 'Your assignment is to give us yourself. You gave us a whole lot last time but now you're going to try to give us all of it, the piece, Kelly. Whenever you're ready.'

After half a minute of inert silence she uttered the first of a great number of loud howling noises. If this was self-expression it was hard to name the part of the self being expressed, its fear, its rage, its grief, its pain, its hatred or its disappointment or some other thing. Jake had never heard the cries of a maniac, far less those of a damned soul, but he thought there might be some common ground in both cases. The girl thrashed about on the floor, arching her backbone to a degree a trained gymnast might have envied and thrusting her trunk forwards and down between her parted thighs. The movements of her head were so rapid that it was hard to catch anything interpretable in her face, though there was a moment at which he saw clearly what he had seen only once before in his life, when the small child of a colleague had fallen in a Summertown garden and cut its knee: a tear spurting from a human eye. Next to him Brenda shivered or shuddered and reached out and took his hand.

At last the howls were reduced to moans and then to long gasping breaths; Kelly wiped her cheeks with her fingers and Ed helped her to her feet and told her that maybe that wasn't quite all of it but it was damn near and congratulations. Jake was bracing himself for the fray when Mr Shyster, fetched as it now seemed by means of a bell-push beside the disfigured fireplace, came in with more refreshments. This time there were cups of tea at the everything-must-go price of 20p and biscuits Jake didn't bother with. He saw that Geoffrey was unattended and crossed over to him.

'I thought that took some doing, what you did.'

'Took some . . . Oh. Oh, it wasn't all that difficult. Did you think it went down all right?'

'Who with?'

'Ed's in a funny mood, he didn't seem at all impressed, not even with the last bit, and that really was rather difficult. I was really trying then.'

'To express emotion, you mean.'

'But then he said hardly anything to Lionel either. It's probably just his mood. He's only human like the rest of us, after all.'

'Geoffrey, there's just one thing that –'

'Yes.'

'Er, well I was just going to say there was one thing that sort of puzzled me a bit in what you said – which was all absolutely fascinating, I don't mean that. It was about . . . you not going to school because of your father's ideas, which I quite . . .'

'No no, my father was *against* my going to school, any sort of school. It would have been contrary to his principles for me to be taught scripture and go to chapel. I thought I'd explained all that.'

'Oh I think I understood. But what I was going to ask you, I took you to mean you wished your father had let you go to school, because if you had, you'd have been able to get your hero-worshipping done while you were still there. Surely if you had, you'd have seen through the whole thing that much sooner and realized that much sooner, which is quite a long time, that you only got your opinions and all that from imitating the way your hero-worship chaps went on. Which wouldn't have been at all a good thing, would it, because you'd have seen you were whatever you said, nobody in particular, years, decades before you did in fact. In reality. As it happened.'

'Jake – everything you advance as an argument is quite true,' said Geoffrey weightily. 'But with respect you seem to be missing the point. It was *because* I didn't go to school that I *failed* to meet all those people. If I *had* gone to school I'd have met them *sooner*.'

'And realized you were imitating them sooner, that was my whole –'

'No no, if you go over it in your mind you'll see I'm right.'

What Jake did see was that he had fallen into his old error, still quite common with him even when dealing with pupils, of supposing that because somebody used things like verbs and conjunctions he (or she) could follow what others said. Changing tack he said, and meant it, 'Amazing how you managed to get that much insight into yourself and not be afraid to follow it up.'

'How do you mean?'

'Realizing how you'd come by all your views and that you've got no thoughts of your own. It took courage to face that.'

'Oh well, there we are.' Geoffrey had been frowning but now his features relaxed and he smiled cheerfully. 'I haven't the faintest idea what you're talking about. Just not my day.'

'How's Allie?' asked Jake to cover his renewed wonderment.

'Allie?'

'Yes. How is she?'

'She's all right. Why?'

'Nothing, pure interest.'

'She's never been better as long as I've known her. Why shouldn't she be?'

'No reason. If you'll excuse me I must just have a word with Brenda,' said Jake, who at that stage would have welcomed a word with Ernie, Mrs Sharp, anybody at all. But he didn't get his word because Ed declared it was time to be getting on, nor was the least disagreement voiced. After the tea-things had been collected and removed, he said,

'All right, Jake, strip.'

An expected or, as in this case, not really unexpected piece of nastiness is not thereby rendered less nasty; so at least it seemed to Jake at the time. Another point that struck him with almost equal force at about the same moment was that a piece of nastiness that has been preceded over a period by several other roughly comparable pieces of nastiness is not thereby rendered less nasty either. He said he wouldn't (do as he was told) and was disconcerted to hear how petulant and fatuous it seemed to sound.

'Wasn't I just telling you about yourself suffering from sexual guilt and shame?' This of course was Rosenberg, his little nose lifted in triumph.

'It isn't that, it's just embarrassment. For a ... with a female with sex in mind, that's a different matter.'

'Why so? You may have forgotten, but you once gave me an assurance that you had no objection to exposing your genitals in public.'

Imprecations suggested themselves in such profusion and variety that Jake was silent quite long enough for Ed to say in his calmest tone,

'Cut the bullshit. Jake, I said take off your clothes. So take off your fucking clothes.'

He caught Brenda's eye, which stated with the utmost

clarity of diction available to eyes that it would be measurably better for him if he complied with the facilitator's request. Everyone else was clearly expecting it too. So in the end he complied, marvelling a certain amount that he had had the unconscious predictive power or something to make that a clean-underclothes day. Well there he was, grey-and-white chest-hair, elliptic areolas round the nipples, some broken veins on the chest, a perceptible if less than gross pot-belly, pimple-scars on the thighs, yellow toenails and all, not forgetting those parts that had once so interested him and from time to time others. For a moment it didn't feel too bad, and then it felt too bad.

Acting on Ed's orders, the nine other participants came up to him successively and stroked or squeezed various parts of him though avoiding the genital area oh I say how frightfully decent; in practice his shoulders and upper arms got most attention. While they were doing that they were supposed to tell him things like he was all right. Kelly looked and sounded sorry for him, Chris, whom he had been looking forward to least, told him that he was all right and then that he was definitely all right, and Brenda seemed pleased with him, but he didn't take much notice of any of them because he was concentrating so hard on stopping himself from trembling all over. That was a help in a way. When they had all finished and he got dressed what struck him was how much less better he felt now he had got dressed than he had expected. He had some difficulty in giving his full attention to Brenda when, complying with Ed's request to conduct a self-draining (so you could have two of the same sort of thing in the salad), talked for twenty-five minutes about how unattractive and stupid and incompetent and ignorant and unattractive and useless and silly and unattractive she felt all the time. But he got the main drift.

When the Workshop broke up at half-past six Brenda asked Geoffrey if he would like to come with her and Jake for a cup of tea and a drink. He understood her fully and at once thanked her but said he had to be off to his own home to change and take Alcestis to a theatre. However he showed no disposition to be off in a hurry, hanging about in the room they had spent so long in and near the front door (at a spot from which another room was to be seen with only a wicker-covered carboy and a ping-pong table in it) and asking the other two if they didn't think that one or another part of the proceedings had been particularly good and saying he thought it had been. This minor delay made them the last to leave, just behind Rosenberg and Ed, who were exchanging fare-wells in the 'porch'. On their conclusion Rosenberg startled Jake by wheeling away the child's bicycle that had been parked there, mounting it at the kerb and riding off on it – startled him till he saw that of course a child's bicycle and a Rosenberg's bicycle would be indistinguishable for practical purposes. And any bicycle would be quite effective in today's traffic and was much cheaper than a car, especially one modified for a two-foot-high driver.

Geoffrey promised to be in touch soon and went, walking with his characteristic head-down gait – because he doesn't want to see anything, thought Jake. He said to Brenda,

'I'd give a few bob to know what he's changing into.'

'What? A suit, I imagine. Why?'

'He's got half a suit on already. For the theatre I should think he'd go for, er . . . a safari jacket with a frilled shirt and velvet bow-tie, jeans, tartan socks . . .'

'What are you talking about?'

'Well you must admit he does dress extraordinarily.'

'Honestly, just because he doesn't dress like anybody else . . .'

'You don't overstate the case. No, it's more than that. It's one of his character-trait substitutes like pretending to hate nurses and like Dvořák. No . . . it's not that either, if that was what he was after it would be much easier and less ridiculous if he just always wore white or bright red or had a collection of outlandish ties, say. Ah, you were right after all, not dress like *anybody* else. Perverseness! An instinct, a compulsion to get things wrong. That's why . . .' Jake's voice tailed off; he understood now about Geoffrey's magpies, Lake Vancouver and Florence Nightingale throwing herself under the King's horse at the Grand National, results of an endless series of drawn battles between memory and the will to err, but as he felt at the moment he couldn't face explaining all that from the start. He went on fast instead, 'That's why he's such a pest to talk to, always on the look-out for chances of getting at cross-purposes with you. In fact there was the most amazing –'

'Why are you so against him?'

'Darling I'm not *against* him, I'm just interested in him. You never know, we might even be able to help him.' (It was true enough that Jake didn't consider himself to be more against Geoffrey than any reasonable man ought to be and was indeed interested in him, but the mention of helping him was pretty pure hypocrisy.) 'You saw I was talking to him in that tea-break? Well, I congratulated him on sort of seeing through himself – that's what he said he'd done if you remember, there was nothing in him, he said. Anyway, he said he couldn't make out what I was driving at. That really staggered me, because I thought, when he said that all his views and everything were just to make him seem interesting, which struck me as absolutely dead right, perhaps it was sheer chance he got it right, he didn't really mean it, all he was doing was saying another thing that was supposed to make him seem interesting.'

'Bit of a coincidence, wouldn't that be, or have I got it

wrong? I expect I have. *I* just thought he was terrifically brave.'

'Perhaps he was. I told him I thought so, which can't do any harm, I suppose, though he didn't seem to take it in much.'

They were nearly home now, hurrying through the rain that had begun to fall. Two car-loads of Asians dawdled past. Brenda said hesitantly,

'What did you think of the other stuff, the other people?'

'Oh I really don't know, don't ask me yet. I'm what Ed would no doubt call too close to it.'

'All right. But you were good. Can't have been much fun.'

'Thank you darling.'

As soon as they were indoors Brenda slipped out to the kitchen and put the kettle on; Jake followed.

'You can't have tea at this time,' he told her, 'it's a quarter to seven.'

'Oh can't I, you just watch me. It's either that or gin and it had better not be gin. Not for a bit anyway.'

'What I could really do with is a cigarette.'

She gave him a glance of sympathy but said nothing. After a moment he picked up her discarded coat and head-scarf and put them with his own hat and coat in the hall cupboard, which had a floral china door-knob on it. An aeroplane went slowly by, or rather not slowly at all but staying in earshot for about three-quarters of an hour. With greater intensity than ever before he wished he still had his 'libido', because if he had he and Brenda would be on their way upstairs now to make love. Of course they would; nothing like the Workshop had ever come their way before but of course they would. The thing about you and your wife making love was that it made things all right, not often for ever but always for a time and always for longer than the actual love-making. In that it was unique: adultery could make life more interesting but it couldn't make things all right in a month of Sundays. And as for booze you must be joking – as well expect a fairly humane beating-up to do the job.

He went back into the kitchen where Brenda was spooning the Jackson's Earl Grey, one of their few indulgences, into the teapot, which was floral too.

'Look at me not making buttered toast,' she said.

'I do so, and I admire.'

'Twelve pounds I've lost in just three weeks. The Guzzlers say that's as fast as it's safe to go.'

'I'm sure they're right.'

The door-bell chimed. Jake always wished it wouldn't do that but would ring or be a buzzer instead; the trouble was it counted as being outside the house, which was his province, and he couldn't be bothered so it went on chiming. Anyway, when he opened the door he found Kelly was there, though she wasn't for long; she furled her umbrella and stepped across the threshold so promptly and confidently that he at once assumed that Brenda had invited her during one of the breaks at Mr Shyster's and for some odd reason neglected to mention it. Standing now by the cheval-glass the girl nodded and smiled inquiringly at him.

'We're in the kitchen,' he said; 'Brenda's just making a cup of tea.'

'Oh marvellous. Is it this way?'

Brenda had entered upon the very act of tea-making. The look she gave reversed Jake's understanding as fast as it had formed: the appearance of Kelly was a surprise to her, and not a particularly welcome one either. If the second half of this was noted it wasn't reacted to; Kelly walked over to the sink and stood her umbrella up in it to drain, talking eagerly the while.

'It's so kind of you both to let me just barge in on you like this, I hope you don't mind too much. You may be wondering how I found you, well I simply followed you from that frightful house. At a respectful distance, so I wasn't quite sure which gate you went in at but I got it on the second try. It's the most awful cheek on my part but I did so want to have a chat with you both.'

'What about?' asked Brenda in a colourless tone.

Kelly seemed to find this an unexpected question. 'That

ghastly session and the incredible things that happened and that criminal man Ed.' When neither Richardson responded immediately she hurried on, 'Of course if you're busy or anything I quite understand, I'll take myself off in a flash, you've only to say the word.'

Something like sixty-three and a half per cent of this last bit was directed at Jake, who didn't say the word. What he did say (and when taken up later on the point by Brenda said truthfully that when he said it disinclination to chuck someone, anyone out with no decent excuse in sight came first among whatever motives he might have had) was, 'No no, we're not doing anything special, stay and have a cup of tea with us.'

'Oh thank you, you are nice. You see, the reason I've come to you like this is there's really nobody else I can talk to. The others are all very sweet people, even poor little Chris, his bark's worse than his bite, but they're not what you'd call intellectual giants, well, Ivor's no fool and Martha's quite sensible except about her mother, but you can't sort of *talk* to them, so up till now I've had to work on my own.'

'Work at what?' asked Brenda as before.

'It may sound silly to you both but I want to expose Ed. Oh not so much Ed personally but the whole Workshop bit. So I, what do you call it, I infiltrated this one. Jolly easy it was too. I just went to my GP, who's a silly little man, and I spun him a yarn about not being able to keep a job or settle to anything and having rows with my parents, and he passed me on to that even sillier little man Rosenberg who passed me on to Ed, and there I was, simple as that. I've been going to these get-togethers for six weeks now. Oh I say what a beautiful room, it must have taken you absolute years to get it like this, Brenda, I do congratulate you.'

The room in question was naturally the sitting-room into which, Jake carrying the tea-tray, the three had now moved. General praises were followed by plenty of particular ones lavished on glass paperweight, trailing plant, some sort of candlestick, some sort of miniature and like lumber. It all went

182

down well enough with Brenda, though it fell some way short of winning her over. Jake put up with it as long as he could before moving back towards a matter that had started to interest him, not a lot, but more than any bleeding paper-weight or miniature was going to.

'This business of exposing the Workshop,' he said in a slender interval between such articles. 'You mean publicly? In court, for instance?'

Brenda, as she was apt to whenever he tried to take a conversation back to an earlier point, gave a look attributing to him either slowness on the uptake or pedantry; for her, things must run on, not back, unless of course Alcestis had a 'story' to finish. But Kelly turned eager again at once and he was touched with surprise and gratitude as the variegated awfulness and fatuity of the day sank for the moment out of sight.

'Well yes,' she said. 'Well, I don't know, I haven't found out enough yet, but how it began, a friend of mine at work went to another Workshop round Sloane Square, and it was absolutely appalling she told me, people beaten up and, you know, group sex and everything, so she stopped going. Then I heard from someone else about Ed, don't repeat this either of you because it may not be true, but this person said that after one of Ed's sessions a chap had gone straight home and killed himself with sleeping-pills. So I thought somebody had better look into it, so I joined as I said and, well, you've both just seen for yourselves.'

'Seen what?' asked Brenda.

'Well, him, Ed, encouraging Chris to be aggressive when what he needs is a damn good smack-bottom and being told not to be so boring, and poor Ruth, you're not going to tell me being made to do all that crying does any good, *made* to do it, four times over, and Lionel, after this afternoon the only thing he can be is more confused than when he started. And Ivor ought to stick to proper treatment and not . . . And making Jake strip,' – straight to Brenda in a relaxed informal interested conversational tone – 'just to humiliate him. He did the same thing to Chris two weeks ago after he'd ticked Ed off without being told to. I noticed you talking to him when we stopped for lunch, Jake – how did you hit off with him?'

'He said it was obvious I was hostile.'

'Exactly. Getting back at you. But he doesn't really need that, even, something to set him off. It's just power, hurting and embarrassing and generally abusing everybody and all in the name of therapy and no one to stand in your way.'

Jake offered more tea and was accepted. 'I think in fairness I ought to remind you of what Rosenberg said to me when I resisted. About ... shame and guilt. You could say there was a connection.'

'In this business everything's connected with everything else. I forgot why it was supposed to be good for Chris to strip but I could soon run up an explanation, couldn't you, either of you?'

'Another thing it might interest you to know is that during our chat in the lunch-break he told me his plan for Ruth. What she needs is a shake-up, you see, so when the time comes she'll be put in the hot seat and told what a bloody bore she is. A great help to be told that when you're old and lonely and frightened.'

'The swine. Anyway, thanks for telling me. One more bit of information.'

'He can be very plausible, though. He had me thinking it might be a good idea, and the same with Chris and Ivor.'

'Exactly.'

They looked at each other in silence for a moment, Jake on the corner of the velvet-covered sofa and Kelly sitting animatedly forward on what had used to be called a pouf or pouffe but obviously couldn't be these days; she reminded him for an instant of someone he had recently met, he had no idea who. Brenda had been standing by a carved plant-table near the window; now, announcing by her move that she would join the conversation for a strictly limited period and purpose, she perched on the arm of the chair in which she normally watched TV or read. Her voice was rather livelier than before when she said,

'Er . . .' – leaving an empty space where Kelly's name would have fitted – 'do you mind if I ask you a question?'

'No, Brenda, of course not.'

'You say you, what was it, you infiltrated the Workshop so as to show it up, so that means you faked being somebody who needed therapy, psychotherapy.'

'Yes, I went to quite a lot of trouble actually, but I needn't have bothered, it was as easy as pie, as I said.'

'So when Ed asked you to do whatever it was and you cried and writhed about and so on, you were faking that too.'

'Oh absolutely.'

'But you really were crying, real tears, I saw them. And you still look slightly weepy, as if you've been crying.'

'Do I? Oh yes, they were real tears all right, but I was faking them at the same time. What I mean is, it was a performance that included crying. I can cry at will, always have been able to. My dad says I get it from him, he's in the theatre, he says it's all a matter of being self-centred enough. I studied acting for a year until I realized I couldn't stand the people.'

'I see,' said Brenda. 'How can we help you?'

'Well really just knowing I've got the two of you on my side is a big help in itself. And you can both keep your ears open for anything you may hear, from Rosenberg and so on, and if I can't make it one Saturday I'll need someone to watch Ed for me. That sort of thing.'

'And when you've got enough information you'll decide whether you're going to sue him or not.'

'I might sue him or I might write about him in a newspaper.'

'What would you sue him for?'

'Well, I'm no legal expert, I'd have to find out about that but I'd have thought one could get him for fraud. After all he *is* a fraud isn't he?'

Brenda said nothing to that. Jake hesitated before he came in.

'An intellectual fraud certainly. All this stuff about getting away from logic and reason which he isn't even consistent about. And *of course* when a crowd of people tell you on instruction that you're nice you're not going to feel in the least less shy when you meet a crowd of other people you've never seen before. And whatever any of them may have got off their chests will all be back on their chests by now. *And* he makes a hundred and fifty quid a time out of us and God knows how many other lots he runs. But he hasn't got a contract with me, he hasn't even said he might be able to help me. So I don't really see quite how we . . .'

'Neither of you know the first thing about it so I think it'd be better if you shut up and gave him a chance.' Brenda spoke in a livelier style than ever. 'You say you've been six times and today was our first, it seems to me perfectly ridiculous to expect any results for several months, Dr Rosenberg said we shouldn't. And there are always rumours about these sort of things which I don't think should be passed on. And I don't care what rot anybody talks if they make me feel better and I dare say you won't believe me or think it matters but I felt really better after saying my piece even if it didn't last very long.'

She got up from her chair-arm and not very quietly began putting the tea-things together. The speed with which Kelly delivered thanks and good-byes, fetched her umbrella from the kitchen, made for the door and vanished, all without appearance of hurry, impressed Jake. In the passage he had to step lively to avoid being run down by Brenda with the tea-tray before her and no eye for him.

'What's the matter?' he called after her.

'Nothing.'

'Oh Christ.'

Again he followed her out to the kitchen, where she dropped the tray on to the draining-board from a height of several inches and turned round with the speed of a wide-awake sentry. Then she slowed down.

'I suppose it's not your fault.'

'Oh bloody good, what's not?'

'What do you think she wanted? Would you like another cup?'

'Yes I would, thank you. What do you mean? To get us on her side – I don't know how serious that was. Or just to have a chat.'

'To get the pair of us, both of us, the two of us, the couple of us on her side, you mean. She overdid it there. No, it was you she was after.'

'After?'

'Some girls like old men. I'm not being nasty, you're not an old man to me but you obviously are to her. She could see you thought the Workshop was a joke at best and didn't like Ed, oh don't be ridiculous, anybody could have in five minutes, so she cooked up this story about exposing him as a fraud and wanting our help. Sod that.'

'Fancy me when she'd seen me starkers? Thanks.' They were for his fresh tea.

'That probably gave her the idea. No really darling, I should say you're pretty good for your age-group. What?'

Jake was shaking his head. 'Just ... You see I was thinking the other day, before this business came along, girls, women would look me over a bit, I don't mean send me an invitation but at least look *at* me. Now they don't. Literally. Well they do when they have to, when I'm talking to them, pupils and so on, but only the minimum. Obviously the normal man sends out little signals all the time, not lecherous glares, just saying he's not against the idea. So I must be sending out signals saying I am against it, and they pick them up, without realizing it of course. So if you're right, why hasn't Kelly?'

'Because she's a howling neurotic with all her wires crossed. Do you honestly believe what she did back there was faked by as much as one per cent? Ed said she couldn't run her life.'

'Mm. But wouldn't she have held back a bit if she was planning to get us to believe she was faking?'

'She got carried away, or she reckoned we'd take her word for it. Or she just forgot.'

'Mm. She's so bright. Seeing that in Ed's world everything's connected with –'

'Neurotics very often are bright – Dr Rosenberg said. By the way, what happened to you being too close to it to discuss it, the Workshop? You were discussing it pretty openly with her just now.'

187

'I know, but that was her, she was the one who brought it up, for Christ's sake.'

'You still needn't have. Do you fancy her?'

'Darling, have I got to tell you again I don't fancy anybody?'

'Funny you brought up signals, anyway I just thought the ones she was sending you, because she was even though she was trying not to in front of me and thought she wasn't, I thought you might have picked them up and that would sort of take you back. I wouldn't mind. She'd be a dangerous girl to get involved with but that would be up to you. What I mean is you wouldn't have me to worry about. However this business ends up neither of us are going to have that kind of thing coming along much more in our lives. And if you did get interested in her it might be a way of you getting interested in me again.'

Jake put down his cup, went across the kitchen and embraced her, mouth against neck.

'So that's life as lived by me at this moment in time,' said Eve Greenstreet. 'No worse than that of many under late capitalism, I'm sure. Not very onerous tasks in the Secretary's office, bun-fights in Rawlinson Road attended by ladies who wear hats indoors, actually I can't remember when I last went to a bun-fight in Rawlinson Road or anywhere else but it's that *kind* of thing and in point of actual fact the percentage of ladies wearing hats indoors will probably be down to single figures by the end of the year, like inflation, or rather not like inflation, and, said she still miraculously keeping her balls in the air, being married to Syd.'

'Syd?' said Jake with a grin. 'I thought he was called –'

'Oh, he has a name for formal occasions and when I'm putting him in his place but in a non-variform-conditions situation he's Syd. Can it be that the fact has failed to penetrate you? After Sydney Greenstreet as the extremely wicked and extremely fat man in the star-studded cast of famed movie classic *The Maltese Falcon*. You remember. Upon my soul sir you are a character. Said to one-time screen idol Bogie-bogie. I'm sorry but I just can't resist calling him that. Shiddown, shweethat, and shtart shingin. That's enough. End of nostalgia bit. Syd, my Syd that is, what is Syd? Well to begin with of course he's Syd. Then he's a bank manager, no connection with the university except as customers, nothing queer about our Syd. And when you're looking at him you're looking at a bank manager. But hey there Jacob old boy, you have already received notification of this phenomena among others. We had you and your charming wife come for dinner at our delightful Headington home one time shortly after our marriage.'

'That's right, of course.' He had completely forgotten and didn't remember anything about it now.

'Well, as I say, when you look at Syd you see a bank manager. Unless that is you happen to have cultivated one of the strange powers of the mind that man has possessed since the dawn of his days but some hidebound and blinkered scientists continue to deny. If you *had*, cultivated and so on, you'd see not just a bank manager but a bank manager with a noticeable and most efficient distinguishing organ of sex, one with an unusually low turn-around time too. You better believe it, Jayqueeze buddy, when Syd fucks you you stay fucked.'

'Really.' Jake poured wine.

In one sense he was able to do this because he and Eve were dining in a restaurant, not as planned La Sorbonne, which had been booked up when telephoned, but a perhaps rather Spanish place recently opened in the strange quarter sprung into being after most of the oldest part of the city had been gleefully hauled down a few years before. Here, where once you could have sworn there was nothing but a couple of colleges, some lodgings and an occasional newsagent or tobacconist, stood hairdressers' and clothiers' and trumpery-bazaars of a glossy meanness formerly confined to the outskirts of the large cities. Here, within these walls, were dons and undergraduates and others in statu pupillari dressed for fishing expeditions or semi-skilled work on the roads, and most of them had females with them, but Jake took no notice of any: other matters filled his attention.

It was the evening of the Tuesday after the Workshop, Eve's mother having proved not to be starting to die for the moment. They (he and Eve) had met at the restaurant at seven-thirty, and at seven-forty he had ordered a second sherry, with a third destined to follow before the arrival of the sort of paella – yes, it must be Spanish – and the bottle of red wine. Or rather the first bottle of red wine: they were now half-way through the second. Three-quarters of the amount so far drunk was inside him. She had remembered his habit of moderation and asked him if he had changed his ways and he had said not in general but this evening was a special occasion.

Eve told him a little more about her husband's abilities, then dilated her eyes and clapped her hand to her forehead. 'Hold it right there,' she said in vibrant tones. 'Rewind.' She stabbed with her forefinger as at a button or switch and made high-pitched gibbering, quacking noises that were not so very much unlike those made by a tape revolving at high speed. After a time she made more finger-motions, saying, 'Clunk. Replay. Clunk,' then went on in the baritone register and in an accent Jake thought over-refined, 'Eve old girl, there's something I'd like to chat to you about. Would you do me the honour of letting me take you out to dinner? Well yes Jake that would be extremely nice of you thank you very much indeed,' the last series of words delivered in the kind of whining monotone to be loosely associated with imitations of footballers interviewed on television. The performance ended with switching-off noises and motions.

Jake gave a laugh. 'That's a new one, isn't it? Yes, I remember the scene you so vividly evoke, but there's nothing to it really. It was just an excuse to take you out to dinner after these God knows how many years.'

'Cock,' said Eve firmly. 'Uh-uh. No, as they say, way. It was a sadly shaken and deeply disturbed Jake Richardson who, that cold, rainy, windy morning in April, encountered his one-time close friend Evelyn Greenstreet at her place of work and sepulchral was the gloom wherewith he answered her polite inquiry as to the well-being or otherwise of his wife, right?'

'Well, we had had quite a nasty row, it's true, but once I'd –'

'Boom-boom-boom-boom-boom,' said Eve, this time like a tommy-gun and with appropriate arm-vibrations. You talk now or you talk later, but understand one thing, just one thing. You talk.'

And Jake did talk, though not till he had ordered cheese and a third bottle of wine. Eve demurred at the wine and asked if he was trying to get her drunk; he said he wasn't trying to do that, that these Spanish reds were very light and that they needn't drink it all.

'I'm worried about Brenda,' he eventually said. 'She goes on complaining I don't show her enough affection.'

'Are you showing her enough erect male member?'

'What?' He half turned away from her as if he had thought for a moment that somebody across the room had waved to him. 'Oh yes I think so. I don't think that's the problem.'

'You say you think.' Eve was now peering at him over phantom half-moon glasses of a forensic stamp. 'Am I to take that as indicating that there is doubt in your mind on this head?'

'No, that would be . . . No. Of course none of us are what we were.'

'Not each and every one of us at all events. No, I asked because affection and the erect male member tend to go hand in hand, if you'll pardon the expression.'

'That's just the trouble.'

'Eh? eh?'

'I mean . . . they probably do for most people. Yes, I quite agree they do for most people. The, er, the thing is they don't seem to for me. At least that's what Brenda says. According to her I'm the type of man who hasn't really got much time for women except as creatures to go to bed with. In fact I only want one thing, always have. According to Brenda.'

Jake's demeanour now was rather that of a motorist in an unfamiliar town who, after a couple of wrong turnings and the odd near-collision, suddenly finds himself on a route that will get him there after all. If Eve saw any of this she didn't make it known, instead examining him from a wide variety of angles, at one moment with her cheek and ear almost resting on the tablecloth, at the next bolt upright with her head thrown back so that she stared at him down her cheeks. While she did this she clicked her tongue at different pitches. He used the time, which must have been getting on for a minute, to appraise more fully than before the degree to which she had kept her looks. Pretty high, he decided: the streaks of grey in her hair only witnessed to the genuine blackness of the rest, her skin still had a pale glow to it, and nothing had gone wrong with what he could see of her neck, which wasn't its entirety because of the very jolly reddish blouse or shirt she was wearing. It had gold bits on the collar and cuffs. Compiling this inventory made his eyes feel tired. They also felt hot when he closed them, or perhaps it was that his eyelids were cold. But why should they be?

Eve finished her inspection. 'I wouldn't have thought, well as you know all too thoroughly I always wouldn't have thought given half a chance, that's just poor little Evie for you, but I wouldn't have *thought*, balls in the air again, that our Brenda had very much there or thereabouts. From what various purblind and reactionary elements would no doubt regard as my somewhat discreditably wide experience I would have said, and as you know equally well I would always have *said*, that my old compeer and associate the Reader in Early Mediterranean History, how about that, woman's got a mind like a razor, was, balls yet again, and I would wager still is, one of those whose interest in womankind extends well beyond the small central area designated by that notoriously short and unattractive little word. You managed to put up with me with great good cheer when bedtime was far far away and I was in full verbal flight – oh yes, little Evie knows she makes considerable conversational as well as other more shall I say corporeal demands on her swains. So I venture to suggest, paying due regard to the interests of our partners in the European Economic Community, the provisions of Phase III of the Incomes Policy, the recommendations of the Race Relations Board and the findings of the Budleigh Salterton Tiddleywinks and Action Sculpture Committee, that on the matter at issue our trusty and well-beloved Brenda is talking through her sombrero.'

'Let's have some brandy,' said Jake.

Jake woke up suddenly in total darkness. At first he thought he was in bed in his rooms in Comyns. Certainly and more pressingly he had a severe headache, his mouth was dry, he needed a pee and he knew something awful had happened. He was also lying in an uncomfortable position and un-wontedly was naked. As soon as he moved he found that the pillow under his head was thinnish where his Comyns one was fattish and the bed itself, the mattress, was slightly concave where his Comyns one was very slightly convex. He was on his right side with, as it soon proved, one edge of the bed within a few inches of his chest. What about the other edge and, more to the point, the intervening space? At the speed of a foot a minute he pushed his left hand out behind him. When the back of his middle finger touched what was probably a bare bottom he didn't do what instinct might have led him to do and recoil as from a nest of serpents, because he had already made up his mind that he could hardly be any-where else but in Eve's bed with Eve; he drew his hand back in good order and adjusted his position as far as he could without setting off the fear that he might wake her, which wasn't at all far, hardly any distance really.

Memories, half-memories, inferences, questions, emotions, prospects, interrupted now and then by self-abandonment to passive suffering, came at him in great profusion. To method-ize the inextricable, he determined that he had begun to feel drunk, as opposed to merely recognizing with benefit of hind-sight that he must have been drunk, some time before they left the restaurant. Then they must have left the restaurant. Then he had tried to insist that they should go to a pub not only to have another drink but also to buy a bottle for later, with what success in either regard he had no idea. There had also been something about getting a bottle from the Comyns buttery instead because the pub was shut or too far or unwilling to sell bottles, or might have turned out to be one or other of these, but quite likely the thought had never attained action or even utterance. Later there had been the interior of a taxi or other vehicle of that size and the general construction with him kissing Eve in it, and after that a room that also had him kissing her in it – a downstairs room, with a clock. Then he had found himself lying naked half on top of her on a bed, doubtless this bed, and doing the most extraordinary things to her with his hands and mouth. He knew he had done closely similar things to her and other women innumerable times in his life, in fact the two sets of things were virtually identical except for the recent one being so extraordinary, not seeming, being: what on earth could have possessed him? He had wondered that then and he wondered it now, on and off.

Finally, or rather 'finally', since it came circling round his mind every half-minute or so, the awful part. He knew nothing about it except how it felt, but that was quite enough. Oh, he did know it was awful in a non-new way, so he hadn't strangled Eve or pleaded with her to tie him up and whip him or pee on him. That was something, though again it didn't feel like much. Reason pointed to fiasco-plus-reproach, fiasco-plus-her-being-decent-about-it and fiasco as the most promising contenders; emotion pointed away, anywhere away from speculation about what it was. On each of its reappearances he tried vainly to assure himself he was better off in ignorance.

Actually there was one more thing he knew about the awful part: it asserted without fear of contradiction that he must do all he could to go on seeing to it that Eve stayed asleep as long as possible, till there was light enough for him to find his clothes, the door, the stairs, the kitchen at least. He wasn't going to go off without facing her but he must face her as his daytime self. A close consequence of these necessities was that any sortie for the discharge or intake of fluid, with its entailed voyage across a totally uncharted bedroom, was ruled out. O Iuppiter irrumator. O tetrakopros. Oh bugger. Wait a minute. In fact it was two or three before his inquisitive hand, moving as slowly as it could while still describable as being in motion, found a glass of something, presumably water, on something or other. Ah – but then he hesitated. To drink would alleviate one of his discomforts, but wouldn't it aggravate another? Not so's he'd notice: in his present condition the liquid would be doing fine if any of it reached his stomach, let alone his bladder. So he drank (it was water), and sure enough by the time he had settled the glass back again he could feel the first faint dryness returning to his tongue and throat. Just then his headache gave him something to think about for a change by taking a turn for the worse. From the start it had been one of the localized sort, well entrenched above the right eyebrow and the area slightly to the left of there; now it started pushing downwards into the top of his nose and the inner corner of his eye-socket. He rubbed and squeezed at the place, finding that the pain and the action together did a little to divert him from the short mental loop he was constantly tracing and retracing.

Where was Syd? Not around; that much was plain and little more seemed needed – Eve could be trusted to have seen to it that he wasn't going to cease to be not around at any sensitive stage. In fact that little more was all there was going to be: Jake never knew where Syd was that night and so likewise never knew whether his absence had been engineered or merely taken advantage of. He wondered about that for a bit till he saw it didn't make much odds. Where was here? He had forgotten anything Eve might have said to him or the taxi-driver that indicated which direction it was or how far it was from wherever they had picked up the taxi, though he could well remember having been in the taxi for at least fifteen seconds. When he listened he heard a distant vehicle, then another – no clue there. She had mentioned Headington, sure, but in a connection that implied past rather than present domicile. He wasn't approaching the problem in a spirit of pure disinterested inquiry. In the end there could presumably be expected to be a morning; when it came he would be all right if he was in Rawlinson Road, but if he was in a cottage half-way between Thame and Aylesbury he might find some difficulty in getting back to Comyns and picking up his lecture-notes in time to make it to Parks Road by eleven, this on the assumption that Comyns, lecture-notes and the like still existed.

Round about this point something he hadn't bargained for happened: a light went on at the other side of the bed. He went into a distinguished underplayed imitation of a man sound asleep, breathing deeply and regularly *nearly* all the time, not being lavish with grunt, sniff and swallow. So matters seemed to rest for a couple of minutes; not having sat up or made any other detectable move she could hardly be reading. When the minutes were up she got out of bed without the flurry he had half-expected and was to be heard walking away. A swift blink showed her naked back-view going out by a doorway in the far corner. He looked about: his clothes, or most of them, seemed to be on and around a chair next to a dressing-table at the window. And he now knew where the door was, but to gather up clothes and exit either instantly or later, in the dark, wasn't worth considering, so he looked about the room further. It was quite a big room with a certain amount of probably expensive furniture in it, and some pictures, paintings – he did notice them. Clever old Syd and lucky old Eve.

He heard a cistern flush and revivified the role of sound-asleep man. Quietly but audibly she came back into the room and over to the bed, this time to his side of it. Silence and stillness. What was she doing? He opened his mouth a little and shut it again. Nothing continued to happen. The moment at which he would have to scream and thrash about approached and arrived and prolonged itself. After he had given up hope she sighed, made a small wordless noise that might have indicated contempt or affection or sadness or pity or almost anything else but pleasure, went round the bed, got carefully back into it and switched off the light.

The return of darkness had the effect of informing him

authoritatively that he wasn't going to sleep again that night. The soporific effect of the alcohol he had drunk had long since been dissipated, his Mogadons were far away and the bottom sheet had become strewn with little irregular patches of hot semi-adhesive sand. More than this, his recent struggles to breathe regularly had fucked up some neural mechanism or other so that he now seemed to be breathing by conscious control alone: in, hold it, out, hold it, in. He kept trying to yawn but couldn't fill his lungs to the point where he could turn the corner, get over the hump and exhale naturally. So exhale anyhow, hang about and try again. He didn't know whether to be glad or sorry that he hadn't looked at his watch while he had had the chance.

In the end he came to a state of which it could be said with more truth than of any other in his experience that it was between sleeping and waking. He had thoughts; no, there were thoughts, each one of an unmeaningness, of a neglect of any imaginable kind of order that caused him leaden wonderment, numb doubt whether he would ever be able to go back to proper thinking. They came along at a regular moderate pace, each one a dozen or twenty words or word-semblances long and lasting a few seconds before being overlaid by the next. Most of them posed as statements of remarkable fact or hitherto unformulated views and beliefs, though a few were pseudo-questions that it was out of his power to begin to try to answer; the nearest comparison was the sort of stuff they gave you to read in dreams.

They receded sharply at an abrupt clashing sound and a voice saying Tea but didn't go away altogether for the first few seconds after he opened his eyes and at once started to come back when for excellent reasons he shut his eyes again. He struggled up to a sitting position, having to take his time about it because of the way his head rolled about like a small baby's unless he concentrated hard, and concentrating at all was no light matter. The curtains had been drawn back and it was full day, in fact, as he saw when he had hauled and crammed his glasses on to his face, seven-forty. There was indeed a cup of tea on the bedside table and he got it to where he could drink from it without spilling a drop outside the saucer. The state of his bladder had become something he could live with, given his present standard of living, so he sat and sipped and felt the hot sweet brew sinking into his tissues and doing him no good at all. When he had finished he got up, put on his trousers, soon found the bathroom and thank Christ. After that he drank, by way of tap and tooth-glass, something approaching his own weight in water. There was a metal cabinet above the basin, in the mirror of which he gained a first-rate view of his face. It looked as if it had been seethed in a salt solution for a time and then given a brisk buffing with sandpaper, but it felt as if it had also been lashed with twigs. He bathed it gently, which left it none the worse. More extensive ablutions would have meant deferring the time when he should be fully clothed and that would never do.

Back in the bedroom he got trousers off, pants on, trousers back on double-quick, then slowed right down, his head pounding. The ache in it was now firmly established in the top of his nose and had even moved on to the inner end of his left eyebrow, but it had relinquished a little of its former territory on the other side of his forehead. As he started to get up after easing on his shoes a wave of giddiness pushed him forward in a sudden crouching run that, if not checked, might well have sent him out of the window. The move brought him a view of what looked very much like part of North Oxford: one fear disposed of. He tied his tie and combed his hair, thereby making his arms ache a lot, put on his jacket and went.

He found Eve in a large well-equipped kitchen reading the *Daily Telegraph*, which she lowered when she saw him. Her glance and tone were pointedly neutral.

'You look bloody awful,' she said.

'Yes.'

'How do you feel?'

'If you don't mind I think I'd rather not try to answer that question.'

'Spirits don't seem to agree with you.'

'They differed from me sharply this time.'

'Would you like some breakfast?'

'No thanks, I must be on my way.'

'Cheerio then.'

'Look, I'm sorry about last night.'

'Which part of it?' When he didn't speak she went on, 'You don't remember much about it, do you? I might have known. Well, at your urgent insistence we went to bed, an act of sexual intercourse duly took place, and you immediately turned –'

'Oh really?'

'Yes really. If that's what was bothering you you can forget it – honour was satisfied. In fact considering how pissed you were you did quite well. It was what happened afterwards that you might consider feeling sorry about.'

He waited but in the end had to say, 'What was that?'

'Fuck-all. You said Good night love, turned over and went to sleep.'

'I was tired. And pissed.'

'That's when we show what we're like. You practically went on your knees to get me to play, when you'd promised not to try when you first asked me, right? and I told you twice at least I'd be breaking eight years of being faithful to Syd, yes we've been married quite a bit longer but it took me a while to give up my old ways, and then you do that. A nice man would have tried to make a girl feel it had been worth while, however tired and pissed he was. No that's not fair, a man who sees more in women than creatures to go to bed with, a man who doesn't only want one thing. So you see I've rather come round to Brenda's way of thinking. Suddenly. Before last night I couldn't have agreed with her less.'

Again he could think of nothing to say, though on a larger scale than before: he had the awful part squarely in front of him now.

'Don't worry about me.' Eve picked up the paper again. 'I'll get over it. You're the one with the problem. Turn right outside and you'll be in the Banbury road in three minutes.'

He found his raincoat in the hall and saw himself out.

When he got to the Banbury road he saw he was only about half a mile north of St Giles', say a mile all told from Comyns. It wasn't actually raining and a walk would do him good. It did, in that it brought about in him an additional form of physical exhaustion to help his mind off his other troubles. He stepped through the wicket with what alertness he could muster: he must not run into Ernie, be found by him entering college at a quarter to nine in the morning. At first sight there was nobody about. He tiptoed over to the lodge and had a peep: one of the under porters behind the glass partition. Moving quite naturally now he went in, nodded good morning, wished he hadn't nodded anything, went to his pigeon-hole and was turning over a couple of pieces of mail when he heard the approach of a familiar and dreadful creaking sound. Perhaps he could just . . . He was still a yard or two from the doorway when Ernie was there, filling it, well not filling it but making it hard for any creature much larger than a rabbit to get past.

'Morning, Ernie,' said Jake, taking a half-pace diagonally forward as if he somehow expected the porter to make way for him.

'Morning, Mr Richardson.' Of course he didn't budge. 'You're up early.' He looked more closely; it wasn't going to do Jake any good not to have been actually witnessed at the gate. 'Had a night on the tain have you sir?'

'Staying with, with friends.'

'Yes, you always were a bit of a night-ale, like, but never much of a . . . If I didn't know you better I'd have said you'd been draining your sorrows. I just hope you don't feel as lazy as you look.'

'Oh yes. No. Now if you –'

'Oh well, in for a penny, in for a bloody –' Ernie advanced suddenly and with a loud creak, his head twisting round over his shoulder. 'Sorry sir, I didn't know you was there.'

'Well, now you do, now you do. Morning, Jake.'

It was Roger Dollymore, looking offensively fit and spruce. The sight of him was an instant reminder of the College

Meeting to be held that afternoon and the hortations to be delivered there for and against the admission of women. No doubt Dollymore's was already prepared. Jake's wasn't. He stumbled off to his room to see if he could think of anything to say.

He thought of something quite soon and wrote it down on the spot, and that was a good idea, because not long afterwards he was just wondering whether he could possibly feel worse, given present circumstances, in other words not given epilepsy or impending execution, when he put his mind at rest about that by starting to feel not only worse, but worse and worse. The newcomer among his sensations was anxiety. By the time he reached the lectern in Parks Road it was advanced enough to reduce his entire audience, the little bastard from Teddy Hall along with the rest, to immobile silence. They were all keyed up for the moment when he should collapse and die or start screaming and tearing off his clothes. But he disappointed them. When he had finished he cancelled his tutorial with the Bradfordian, savoured an all-too-brief moment of self-congratulation at his own sagacity and fought his way back to Comyns through a medium that seemed appreciably denser than air. In his sitting-room he ran his eyes over the print of some of *The Hippogriff Attaché-Case*. He wanted to lie down but what he didn't want was another dose of those bloody thought-substitutes.

Having (purposely) missed breakfast he decided he had better try to eat some lunch and managed to get quite a decent way through a portion of steak-and-kidney pie with cabbage and mashed potatoes. It was slow work but he left the SCR in bags of time to get over to his rooms, throw up and stroll back so as to arrive in the Grade Room on the stroke of two. Inside him there continued to lie a dissolving Mogadon, taken with the object not of inducing sleep, which your true-to-form College Meeting could do on its own, but of soothing his nerves: Curnow had said when prescribing the stuff that it was a muscle-relaxant, which surely must mean that it relaxed the muscles, and offhand he couldn't think of any muscle of his that couldn't have done with some relaxation bar his sphincter, which for the last few hours or so had notably excepted itself from the tension that possessed him.

Lancewood was already settled in his usual place, half-way down the left-hand vertical, so to speak, of the hollow square of baize-covered tables, at the top horizontal of which sat or shortly would sit the Master, the Dean, the Senior Tutor and other holders of office. Jake went round and joined Lancewood, who at first sight of him said,

'Hallo, how terrible you look.'

'Ernie was saying much the same thing this morning.'

'Even Ernie is right sometimes. I think it's your eyes mostly. No, that's too easy – it is your eyes, but it's your mouth mostly. Its shape has changed. What have you been up to?'

'Oh Christ. Are you in to Hall?'

'Yes, and at a loose end afterwards. Skip dessert and come straight over to my rooms.'

'Christ. I mean thanks.'

Very soon afterwards Marion Powle came in and took his place at the centre of the top table. He announced that the minutes of the last meeting had been circulated and asked if he might sign them as correct. Jake could find no more objection than anybody else. Then Powle recited the names of lazy bastards who had said they weren't coming. After that part the Estates Bursar was called upon to introduce Agenda Item 3. (They mean Agendum 3, thought Jake.) The item or agendum in question concerned the sale of some college property in a part of the kingdom that had until just the other day borne the name of an English county but was now known by some historically authentic title that meant as good as nothing to anyone. The price quoted ran into six figures and was immediately agreed by those assembled. It was a very different story when the next item-agendum came up. This time the focus of attention was the proposed new chairs for the library, the joint proponents of the proposition being the Domestic Bursar and the Mods don who doubled as the Librarian of the college. A prototype was brought in by a menial and examined with some closeness, several leaving their own chairs to see it better. At first it seemed to gain some approval, and when Wynn-Williams sat on it and it didn't collapse its adoption looked almost certain. But then the cost was asked for and given as £125 and all over the room there were wincing noises, rather like but in sum louder than those made by Brenda on getting into a cold bed. For a chair! they all kept saying – for a chair? Not quite all. *Of course* it seems a lot, said Jake to himself, but haven't you noticed that *everything* seems a lot these days, you fucking old fools? In the end the Domestic Bursar, after he had made it plain that it would be no use going back to the maker and trying to beat him down, was instructed to do just that.

The next topic was described simply as Stanton St Leonard Churchyard. All Jake knew about Stanton St Leonard was that it was a village to the north-west of Oxford, that the living of its church was in the gift of Comyns and that by way of consequence a part of its churchyard was set aside for the remains of Fellows of the college, an amenity not much in use for however long it was since they had been permitted to marry. Probably the local authorities wanted the place concreted over and a community centre or skateboard park built on the site.

The Master looked round the meeting with a serious expression. 'Now I'm afraid I have a rather serious matter to draw to the attention of Fellows,' he said seriously. After explaining about Stanton St Leonard for the benefit of the recently elected, he went on, 'During the vacation a certain Hoyt H. Goodchild, a citizen of the United States, was visiting relatives in the village when he suddenly died. It seems that these were his only relatives; at any rate, there was silence on the other side of the Atlantic and the family in Stanton decided to bury Mr Goodchild in the churchyard there. By a most unfortunate and grievous coincidence the rector was away at the time and the sexton ill, and evidently neither had briefed his substitute in full, because on returning to their duties they found Mr Goodchild buried at the Comyns end.'

There was a general gasp of consternation, almost of horror, in which Jake couldn't quite prevent himself joining. Funny how we all overact at these get-togethers, he thought to himself: what ought to be of mild, passing interest attracted passionate concern or a facsimile of it, ordinary care for the interests of the college came out as crusading zeal. All part of being donnish.

Powle was continuing, 'Both men have expressed their profoundest apologies but that's hardly the issue. I must have some guidance here. Senior Tutor?'

'No difficulty that I can see,' said Dollymore. 'He'll have to come up, won't he?'

Wynn-Williams and some of the other senior Fellows showed their agreement.

'I don't really think we can quite do that,' said Powle.

'*We* won't have to do anything, Master, it's up to those two in Stanton to set right their mistake.'

'There would have to be an exhumation order, which might not be easy to obtain. And there are the feelings of Mr Goodchild's relatives to be considered, surely.'

'They'll be village people, I don't expect much obstacle there. And as for the exhumation, the authorities are bound to understand our historic right not to have a total stranger and an American at that, in our own sacred ground. Why, some of those graves go back to the time of the Civil War.'

'I think everybody here understands that, Senior Tutor, but I very much doubt if the authorities would, to the point of taking action that is. They'd be nervous of the publicity and I couldn't blame them.'

'It's out of the question, sir,' said the political scientist who ran a current-affairs programme on TV.

'Out of the question to do what is fully within our rights and in conflict with no law?'

'I'm afraid that in this case we'll have to bow to the opinions, the prejudices if you like, of ... outsiders,' said Powle.

'Good God,' said Dollymore. 'What a world it's become.'

'You're proposing that no action be taken at all, Master?' asked Wynn-Williams.

'Not necessarily. Are there any suggestions?'

There were none for half a minute. Then a natural scientist of some sort asked where Goodchild's grave was in relation to the others and was passed a marked plan of the churchyard. On examining it he said,

'As one might have expected it's at the end of a row and it also happens to be near the yew hedge. One might be able to plant a section of hedge, or transplant one, better, so that the intruding grave is as it were segregated from the others.'

This suggestion was debated at some length; in the end it was agreed upon. But Roger Dollymore hadn't finished yet. He said defiantly,

'It'll be all very well until the autumn.'

The writer in residence, who had often declared that he had done no writing at all as yet and had no plans for doing any while in residence, and who was wearing a red-and-black upper garment the material of which had been fashioned by human ingenuity, and who had uttered a loud yelp of deprecation on hearing Dollymore's first proposal for the treatment of the offending cadaver, said, 'What happens in the autumn then?'

Dollymore said as to an imbecile, 'The leaves fall.'

'And?'

'And cover the ground.'

'So?'

'So somebody has to clear them eh-way.'

'Like?'

'Like? Like?'

'I mean who, you know.'

'Oh who. Well not the sexton is what I'm suggesting.'

'Why not?'

'Because his responsibility is to us, not to Mr . . . Goodchild or his relations. He must have nothing to do with that grave and it'll be an ugly sight by Christmas.'

'I think we can probably come to some compromise

arrangement there,' said the Master with a confident smile. 'Now – Garden Committee to report on the south lawn.'

So it went. Nearer and nearer came 12: Admission of Women, and step by step Jake's anxiety mounted, some of it now detaching itself and identifiable as anxiety about his anxiety. What the bugger was wrong with him? He hadn't had a hangover for thirty years but he could have sworn that today's was a radical departure. Well, thirty years were thirty years, weren't they?

Finally, by way of closed scholarships, a report from the Wine Committee, a discussion of a vile sculptured thing some people wanted put in the front quad and stuff like the recommendation from the historian of drama (the one who put on plays full of naked junior members of the university torturing one another) that the library should start a sexism section, 12 arrived. It opened innocuously enough with a summary of what the other colleges had done in the matter of admitting women and what their policies for the future were, as far as these could be discovered or inferred, all ably presented by young Whitehead. And it went on, if not innocuously then at any rate not leading to physical violence, with Dollymore back in the limelight outlining what he saw as the case against admission. Quite radiant with hypocrisy he led off with the point made by Smith in Jake's hearing a couple of weeks earlier, that to let women into men's colleges reduced the status of the women's colleges. After that he mentioned the harm he thought would be done the academic performance of Comyns undergraduates by the distraction from their studies he thought they would suffer. Then he unwisely stressed the opposition of the college staff to the scheme, unwisely because it was hard to think about the college staff without thinking first and foremost of Ernie, and if there was anything that could have united that motley Governing Body it was that whatever Ernie was opposed to you were for. As his final argument he dilated on the incompatibility between a mixed college and the kind of intimate communion which members of Comyns had enjoyed for seven centuries; undergraduates came and went, but Fellows lived their lives here. 'All that,' he ended, the dramatic effect heightened rather than the reverse by his bleating tones, 'all . . . *this* . . . would be lost – for ever.'

There was a general murmur of appreciation of a case well put or at least strongly felt even if not necessarily found convincing. 'Thank you, Senior Tutor,' said the Master. 'Now I call on Mr Richardson to put the other view.'

'We are dealing here with an example of something we have all encountered more and more often over the last twenty or thirty years: a trend.' Jake spoke a little inexpressively because most of his attention was concentrated on getting the words out with their syllables in the right places. 'I would say two things about trends. One is that while many or most may be undesirable and on those grounds to be resisted, a trend is not undesirable per se. The other is that while no trend can be said to be irresistible until it is altogether dominant, there are trends to which resistance seems likely or very likely to be vain. In such cases it may be better, more advantageous, to yield at once rather than fight on. So we don't resist a policy of admission just because admission is the trend, nor do we resist it if we have no or virtually no chance of winning. In my view that chance disappeared five years ago or more if it had ever existed. I therefore appeal to the anti-admission party to yield at once, thereby giving itself the chance of doing what it would no doubt call salvaging something from the wreck rather than being finally compelled and so losing the option.

'Such is the pragmatic case, and discussion there will turn on the resistibility or irresistibility of the trend. But before we come to that let me briefly state the human case. I see it as divided into three. One, from what we were hearing earlier, both men and women undergraduates are overwhelmingly in favour of admission in general. As with trends, this is not sufficient grounds for resistance. Two, when they arrive here these young people still have some growing-up to do, and to be able to do it in close daily proximity to members of the opposite sex is a clear and considerable benefit.' (There was a faint stir of rallying, chaffing, etc. at this but Jake didn't notice it.) 'Three, admission to men's colleges is the only way so far devised of providing more places for women while leaving relatively intact the present collegiate and university structure.'

It was done. He found he was panting and leaned forwards over the table, head lowered, while he tried to recover his breath unnoticed. There was a handy interval before and while Dollymore asked if he might ask a question, was told he might and asked it.

'I'll take up Mr Richardson's *relatively* intact collegiate structure in a minute; for now I'd like him to tell me if he would whether he regards the provision of more places for women as a, as a clear and considerable benefit.'

'Indeed I do,' said Jake, grinding it out. 'Mr Whitehead's figures show clearly the disparity against women.'

'I take that point: women candidates are competing for a proportionately smaller number of places. What assurance have we that to increase that proportion will reveal a similar or comparable increase in the proportion of those found acceptable?'

'I'm afraid . . . I suppose . . .'

'More fundamentally, doesn't Mr Richardson's clear and considerable benefit rest on what I will persuasively call the faith that academically acceptable women are as numerous or about as numerous as their male counterparts?'

Jake's fists were tightly clenched under the table. 'In posse if not in esse.'

'A dangerous concession, surely, but let that go. May we hear some evidence for this academic parity or approximate parity?'

'The view I'm advancing can't be supported by figures or by self-sustaining facts, only by an adequate number of individual indications that woman is the intellectual equal of man, that her powers of observation, analysis, induction and so forth are on a level with his, and that her admittedly inferior performance numerically . . . er . . . results from a number of . . . social factors of which one is that they can't, I mean she can't get into a university as easily as a man.'

The writer in residence spoke. 'Look, are you trying to tell us –' He checked himself at something said to him by the philosopher who was co-editor of a London weekly paper, then went on, 'Sorry, got it wrong. Is – what? – is Mr Richardson trying to tell us he believes that? About women being equal to men? Does he believe it?' He looked round the room as if pleading for enlightenment. 'I mean, you know, like really *believe* it?'

'I think –' began the Master but Jake rode over him. He didn't know or care whether the writer in residence was trying to do more than demonstrate the impartiality of his contempt and/or simply draw attention to himself: he (Jake) saw in him a slight physical resemblance to the little bastard from Teddy Hall, who was little in worth, not size, but who by some association led him to think of Chris at the Workshop and even of Rosenberg. Rage and dizziness struck him together.

'Of course I don't believe it, you . . .' He stopped just in time to avoid technically calling the Master what he had been about to call the writer in residence. 'I was asked to put a case and I put it, that's all. No doubt they do think, the youngsters, it'd be more fun to be under the same roof, but who cares what they think? All very well for the women no doubt, it's the men who are going to be the losers – oh, it'll, it'll happen all right, no holding it up now. When the first glow has faded and it's quite normal to have girls in the same building and on the same staircase and across the landing, they'll start realizing that that's exactly what they've got, girls everywhere and not a commonroom, not a club, not a pub where they can get away from them. And the same thing's going to happen to us which is much more important, Roger's absolutely right, all this will go and there will be women everywhere, chattering, gossiping, telling you what they did today and what their daughter did yesterday and what their friend did last week and what somebody they heard about did last month and horrified if a chap brings up a *topic* or an *argument*. They don't mean what they say, they don't use language for discourse but for extending their personality, they take all disagreement as opposition, yes they do, even the brightest of them, and that's the end of the search for truth which is what the whole thing's supposed to be about. So let's pass a motion suggesting they bugger off back to Somerville, LMH, St Hugh's and St Hilda's where they began and stay there. It won't make any bloody difference but at least we'll have told 'em what we think of 'em.'

Only then, when he had in a sense finished, did Jake become aware of just how hard Lancewood had been squeezing his arm, of the pantomime of apology, helplessness, agreement and doubtless more that the writer in residence was putting on, and of what sort of silence had fallen. The Master thanked him with preternatural composure but Jake felt he couldn't very well stay after what he had said and how he had said it, matters on which he was already not quite clear. His headache drove and twisted at his brows. He asked to be excused, hurried out and stood in the main SCR with both hands on the back of a chair. Lancewood was only a couple of seconds behind him.

'I'll just see you over to your rooms.'

'No I'm all right, you go back.'

'Don't be silly, it'll only take a second.'

'No Damon, if you don't go back straight away they'll think there's something really wrong. Tell them, say it's side-effects of some new pills. Please, Damon.'

'If you're really sure. But we'll talk later.'

'Yes. Yes, we will. Thanks.'

As Jake approached his staircase he met Ernie coming out of it. The porter gave one of his fiercest winks.

'There you are after all, sir,' he said. 'I told your visitor you probably wouldn't be arraigned for a bit, with the College Meeting and all, but she said she'd wait if that was allayed, and I couldn't find it in my heart to say her nay. She really does you credit, Mr Richardson, at your time of life – take a bay!'

'What? Oh yes.'

He hurried into his sitting-room, unable to venture even a surmise.

'Hallo, Jake,' said a strange girl in a green trouser-suit.

The next moment he saw it wasn't a strange girl at all but Kelly, smiling, coming up and shaking hands. It bothered him, made him think himself senile, that even with the trouser-suit clue he hadn't recognized her at first, though he tried to cover this.

'Kelly, how nice to see you. What are you doing in Oxford?'

'Paying a call on you, Jake. Actually I've been staying with an aunt in Woodstock, so I thought I'd look you up on my way back to London.'

'Jolly good idea, I could do with a bit of lively company. I've just come out of a meeting of such boredom . . .'

'You don't look well, Jake. I know one isn't supposed to say such things, but you don't.'

'Had a rotten night. I feel as if I hadn't slept a wink.'

'Bad luck. Of course if you're used to sleeping with some-one else it is that much more difficult on your own.'

'Yes,' he said, keeping to himself the fact that his troubles had come about in the opposite way. 'How did you track me down?'

She smiled again. 'Oh I'm good at that sort of thing. Remember how I ran you to earth in Burgess Avenue?'

'Finding me here must have been a damn sight more difficult.'

'Not really, Jake. Not to me.'

'You're a clever girl.' He looked at his watch. 'We could go out and have some tea soon.'

'It's a little early, isn't it?'

'I suppose it is, but I've got to be back here at five o'clock to talk to some undergraduates.'

'Can't you put them off?'

'Not possible, I'm afraid.'

'You could ring them up,' she said coaxingly, nodding towards the telephone on his desk.

'They're not in the same place, they're all over Oxford. I couldn't hope to reach them in the time.'

'Oh, what a bore.'

'I'm sorry, but if you'd let me know you were coming . . .'

. . . I still wouldn't have done anything about it, he finished in his mind. At her remark about the demerits of sleeping alone a little alarm-bell of uneasiness had sounded there; it continued to purr away as he came to recognize that she was talking and behaving in an entirely different style from the one she had used at Burgess Avenue the previous Saturday. No cheerful confidence or confidingness now, no long eager speeches; instead, languor with a querulous edge to it. Above all, the Kelly of Saturday would never have tried to get him to cancel his seminar, would on the contrary have offered to leave at once in case he had preparations to make. So he had been half justified in not recognizing her straight away. He had meant what he had said about being glad to see her; he only hoped that the uneasiness would turn out to be misplaced, that things were going to take a turn for the better after the last twenty hours or so, that she was no more than tired or perhaps shy without Brenda's diluting presence. Ah! – Saturday-Kelly would certainly have –

'How's Brenda?'

'Oh . . . she's fine, thanks.'

'I bet she doesn't come here much, does she? No, I thought not, she wouldn't be able to stand it and quite frankly I'm surprised you can, Jake. I mean look at this, pretend you haven't seen it before and look at it properly.' Kelly indicated the padded chair she had just got up off. 'Isn't it absolutely revolting?'

'I know it's not very nice, but I don't spend much time here, so . . .'

'What happens when you entertain? – oh of course you're going to tell me you don't entertain. I can't understand how a cultivated man like you can bring himself to live in such, well I can't call it squalor because it isn't actually dirty or damp or anything but it's pretty damn slummy you have to admit. Not even a picture to take your eyes off it. And honestly those curtains, you'd have thought ... Oh I say that really is something. How gorgeous.'

Jake joined her at the window where she was apparently admiring the buildings on the far sides of the quad. 'Yes it is pretty good, isn't it?'

'What is it, early eighteenth century?'

Christ, he thought mildly. 'Yes, about then.'

'It must make up for a lot, having that out there in front of you all the time. What's the other way?'

She turned and made for the open bedroom door, past which daylight was to be seen. He followed her.

'There's not a great deal, but ...'

'Do you mind?'

'No, go ahead.'

The bedroom window showed a stretch of wall and part of the rear quad of Jesus College. Kelly looked appreciatively at them for a few moments and started back to the sitting-room, or so Jake thought till he made to follow and found she had shut the door and was facing him with her back to it.

At first he felt only mild surprise and puzzlement. 'What ...?'

'Jake, listen to me, this is important and we don't have very much time. We haven't known each other very long but I feel we appreciate each other and I don't know about you but I can say I trust you. It's an old-fashioned expression but I wish you well, and that's good because I can do something for you, I can help you with your problem. You might not think so but I've had a lot of experience, you could almost call it training. You put yourself in my hands and it'll all work out. You just leave everything to me and I mean everything. Okay? Right, let's go.'

All this was said in such a friendly, reasonable tone that Jake couldn't believe she meant what he knew she meant until she crossed the room, a matter of no more than a couple of strides, quick ones in this case, and closed with him, her arms round his neck and what Ed and Rosenberg would call her pubic area pushing into his. Jake had had to evade or discourage amorous females before, though admittedly none as forceful as this, and without Ed and Rosenberg and all that, and in particular without Eve, he would probably have done better than do what he did do, which was to pull Kelly's arms away and thrust her from him and call on her in a frightened voice to leave him alone, leave him alone.

She showed her teeth; as he had noticed before they were good enough teeth, white and regular, but this time he saw something about the way they were set in the gums that told him beyond all doubt who it was she had reminded him of on Saturday. He was horrified and got ready to defend himself, crouching with his balls tucked between his thighs, but she didn't come at him, didn't throw anything at him, perhaps because there wasn't a lot to throw, no ashtray, no water-jug or tumbler and again no pictures. All she did was shove the bedside lamp on to the floor, which did no more than knock the shade off its frame, and abuse him verbally. She used not only what is often called foul language in great copiousness and diversity but also foul ideas, and produced surprising variations on the themes of old age and its attendant weaknesses. After some minutes she stopped all at once in mid-incivility and seemed taken by a fit of violent shivering. By degrees she moved to the side of the bed and sat down on it with her hands on her knees. Then she started to weep.

Jake had come across lachrymose females before too, but never one like this, never one who gave such a sense of intolerable pressure within, as if what was being wept over was growing faster than it could be wept away. 'Sorry,' she said as the tears flew from her eyes, 'sorry, sorry, sorry, sorry, sorry . . .' She must have said it a hundred times, each time if possible with a different inflection. Jake sat down next to her, though not very close to her, gave her a clean handkerchief out of his drawer, and kept telling her it was all right, and in the end she stopped saying sorry and merely sobbed continuously.

'You aren't planning to expose Ed or anything like that, are you?' he asked as soon as he thought she might be listening.

She shook her head violently.

'You're just one of his patients, and Rosenberg's, aren't you?'

This time she nodded so hard it involved her whole body.

'Were you just after me when you came to the house?'

Another nod.

'There isn't any aunt in Woodstock, is there? . . . Is it true what Ed said, that you can't run your life? . . . Have you been like that for a long time? . . . What's just happened here this afternoon, has it happened to you before? . . . Often? . . . But you have had a lot of men? . . . Have you enjoyed it? . . . Where do you live? – I mean you do live with your parents? . . . They're kind to you, are they? . . . But your father isn't in the theatre and you haven't studied acting?'

Each time he got the answer he expected. He looked at his watch: he had half an hour to get this creature fit to move and to move her before his class started to assemble. But none of it could be hurried. Meanwhile there was another question he wanted to ask, for no good reason that he could see, another yes-or-no question in form but to which he hoped for a more than yes-or-no response. When the sobbing had become intermittent he said,

'You came up from London just to see me? Just for this to happen?'

'I suppose in a way,' she said in a dazed blocked-up voice. 'But it wasn't all I did. I came up quite early and had a look round the shops and found a good place for lunch in that street where there are no cars, and then I thought I couldn't come and see you right away, so I went for a nice walk by the river first.'

He would very willingly have done without this information. 'But you did . . . expect me to turn you down?'

'In a way.' She sobbed for a little before she went on, blinking at the floor. 'I didn't use to get turned down much but now I nearly always do, but I still go on. Dr Rosenberg says that's what's wrong with me, I don't learn from experience, but I'm quite intelligent and I'm young, he says, so I might get better one day. I'm sorry I said those things, they were horrible and I'm ashamed. I didn't mean any of them.'

'I know, I could tell that. I didn't listen, I couldn't tell you what they were now.'

'I must go, I've wasted enough of your time, and with you feeling rotten after your bad night.'

'That's nothing. I'll get you a taxi.'

'No don't bother, I can walk.'

'Not in this rain. It's about a mile to the station.'

'I've got my umbrella.'

'No, listen, you come along here.' He took her slouching and subdued into the small bathroom that occupied the space of what until not at all long ago had been part of the bedroom. 'You freshen up while I telephone for a taxi.'

It sounded plausible enough; the trouble was that a telephone, a British telephone of the 1970s, came into it. Following procedure he dialled 9 and got to the exchange, then started on the number of the taxi firm he always used. After the first digit a kind of steady cooing noise sounded, which meant that according to the telephone tens of thousands of people in the Oxford area had had their line communications cut by fire, accident or flood or in consequence of mass non-payment of bills. Further attempts brought the same absence of result. He tried to raise the lodge with the idea of getting the porter to dial direct – no reply. A last go at the taxi number succeeded, granted that being told there would be a delay of twenty minutes was success. Well, he had better treat it as such: if all parties went strictly by the clock, taxi and seminarists would coincide at the lodge, but he was unlikely to be able to improve on the present offer in the time, so he said yes thank you and rang off.

Kelly didn't reappear for quite a while, which was bad because he wanted to be sure of getting shot of her, but good because he didn't want to have to talk to her or deal with her in any way before getting shot of her. He was about to go and give her a knock when she stepped quite briskly out of the bathroom, collected her long-handled umbrella from where he hadn't noticed it and came and stood in front of him.

'I'll go whenever you want me to,' she said.

He looked her over to see if she was presentable and then just looked. In general her skin was even better than at first glance, but there was some roughness near the eyes that he didn't think had arrived in the last half-hour, and he noticed a broken blood-vessel or two in her cheek.

'How old are you, Kelly?'

'Twenty. Twenty-one in September.'

It seemed a bit soon. 'Now I want you to know that when I turned you down it was nothing to do with you, it would have been the same with anybody. Ed got it wrong, it's not that I can't, I can but I don't want to. With anybody. It wasn't you, I think you're very attractive.'

'Don't worry, I shan't bother you again, I never try twice with the same person. You're quite safe.'

'That's not what I mean. If I fancied anyone I'd fancy you, believe me. I'm just old and past it. Ten years ago I wouldn't have turned you down.'

'You really haven't got to worry.'

'But . . . Oh very well, let's be off.'

'You've no need to come, I'm perfectly okay now. I expect you'd like to have things ready for your students.'

'I just want to make sure you get the taxi all right,' and also make sure you don't go and lay about you with your umbrella in the chapel or, more important, in the gift shop.

She used it for its intended purpose as they moved across the quad, protecting him from the light drizzle as well as herself. In a way that might have been natural she took his arm.

'If only I had a bit of sense,' she said thoughtfully, 'I could have quite an enjoyable life. For instance today, when you said let's go out and have some tea I could have said yes let's, and we could have had a nice talk and perhaps we might have arranged for me to come up another day and you show me round Oxford or something, and we could have been friends, and now we can't.'

'It would have been difficult anyway,' said Jake, not knowing a hell of a lot about what he meant.

They reached the lodge and stood about outside in the dry for a minute or two. The Bradfordian, always inclined to be early, came through the wicket, saw Jake and hesitated. He didn't look at Kelly.

'Carry on, Mr Thwaites,' called Jake. 'I'll join you in just a moment.'

'You'll have to go.' She had moved some feet away and spoke without looking at him, presumably in an effort to spare him the embarrassment of being associated with her. 'I can manage, honestly I can.'

It was true he would have to go in the end, but the taxi might not come for another twenty minutes or ever, and for some reason he shrank from the thought of her walking to the station after all. At that point Ernie appeared in the lodge entrance. Jake made straight for him.

'Ernie, I want a word with you.'

The porter made a half-revolution as smartly as a guardsman and with Jake closely following retreated into the inner lodge, behind the glass partition. 'Sir?'

'The young lady is a little upset. I've ordered her a taxi. I have a class in two minutes. Would you see she gets off all right?'

'Receiving you laid and clear, Mr Richardson. Send her in here to me and I'll do the necessary, you may be sure – skate's honour, sir!'

Outside again, Jake told Kelly the porter would look after her and then hesitated.

'Thanks. Good-bye,' she said, shaking hands. Her eyes were smaller than when she had arrived but not very red. 'Sorry again.'

'That's all right . . . Good-bye.'

'See you Saturday,' she said as he turned away.

Saturday? Saturday! Dies irae, dies illa solvet saeclum in favilla. And ballocks. Real ballocks. Very serious ballocks indeed.

'Eve, Eve, what is Eve? Well of course when we've looked at the books and got our sums right and done our bigs and wiped our bottoms and at the end of the day, Eve is Eve is Eve is Eve is Eve, and I don't mean the mother of mankind or any such form of words inconsonant with the meaningful and relevant vocabulary of our secular society in these the closing decades of the second millennium, no sir, no siree, ya bedder believe it, right on, daddio, you cotton-picking bastard, get with it, stay tuned as leading Oxford campus hostess and elegant conversationalist Eve Greenstreet, wife of uncontroversial ithyphallic banker Syd Greenstreet, goes on about what she's sorry but she simply can't avoid describing as her endlessly fascinating self, and why don't you piss off?'

Lancewood screamed quietly, as if half to himself. 'No. No. It can't be. It's not in nature.'

'I assure you I've reproduced it with toiling fidelity, the most aridly pedantic literalism conceivable. Except of course in point of duration. You'll have some idea if you imagine what you've just heard lasting about three hundred times as long.'

'I daren't, I'd go mad.'

'I'd had as much as flesh and blood could stand after five minutes,' said Jake. 'My most obvious counter was feigning illness, but that's not as straightforward as it may well sound. Any really serious disorder is ruled out – heart-attack, stroke, apoplexy, all of them most alluring, and in the circumstances extremely plausible, but quite apart from how you deal with the doctor you find you can't face the upset, the ambulance and all that. At the other end of the scale, headaches and so on have been worked to death. So you need a dose of something incapacitating but not dangerous, in the 'flu mode let's say. The trouble with that is you can't just suddenly start quivering like a jelly and saying you've got to go home – well actually in this case I'm pretty sure I'd have got away with it, but I didn't know that then. I thought then I'd need acting ability, again wrongly, and a reasonable build-up, call it an hour at least from the first passing shiver to deciding to pack it in, plus time for getting the bill, finding a taxi and being loyally seen home. And time was the very thing I couldn't spend any at all of, so I went on the booze.

'Now as you know Damon, I don't enjoy getting drunk and I absolutely hate being drunk, not understanding what you're saying and feeling as if you're moving about on the sea-bed but still able to breathe. But I didn't think it would come to that when I started off, you see. I was working on the principle of lowering the old critical faculty, blunting the responses and such to the point where she'd merely be boring the arse off me. But I never got there, I can't have done, I mean I can't remember what happened late on or even latish on and I can only reconstruct bits of it, but I must have got utterly smashed and found I still couldn't stand her and threw a pass purely and simply to shut her up, which I'd as soon have thought of doing before she turned up, throw a pass I mean, as fly in the fucking air, as you shall hear. I don't know why I didn't just go home instead because it must have been quite late by then and I don't know where I did the throwing but I do remember it worked, that's to say it shut her up. And also to say it was accepted, or since short of rape it's always the woman who decides, it was encouraged, never mind she hung out a don't-try-anything sign when I invited her and a rotten-sod-for-taking-advantage one this morning. This morning, Christ. Anyway ... encouraged. She couldn't have got it all worked out as a conscious strategy could she? If you want cock talk balls kind of style? No of course she couldn't.

'It wasn't just balls though, as I hope I conveyed to you. One's used to that. This is Oxford, let's face it, as she'd say screwing up her nose to show she was being witty. No, it was her thinking she was the thinking man's rattle that made me want to watch her being eaten alive by crocodiles. You know, don't be so dazzled by how terrifically brilliant it all is with all those frightfully clever little cameo parts and absolutely marvellous imitations and accents, don't be carried away by all that so that you don't see that underneath it's *bloody good stuff*, wickedly observant and cruelly accurate and actually very concerned about the state of the language and of our society too. Like Mencken only sexy with it. Oh dear oh dear oh dear. And the insensitivity. I've been given to understand in the last few weeks that I'm not as good as I used to think I was at disguising my feelings, especially when they're feelings of contempt, hatred, weariness and malicious hilarity as they are most of the time these days. Well with Eve, for the first hour or so, until my face got tired, I smiled and nodded and twinkled and tried to laugh, and then, but this was well *after* I'd realized she was going to bat through to the end, then I stopped bothering. Cold. And she didn't notice a thing. Brenda would say of course she'd noticed and that made her nervous so that she couldn't think of any other way of going on. Well I've had my nervous moments but I doubt if I've ever been so frozen with terror that the recourse of shutting my trap has fled my mind. But then Brenda's been . . .'

Jake paused. After a moment Lancewood got up and put two more logs on the fire, then went out carrying the electric kettle. The room was pleasantly warm and Jake's chair, his every time he came here, more comfortable than any in his own rooms or at Burgess Avenue. Beside it stood a small table bearing a teapot with an embroidered cosy, a Minton cup and saucer and plate, a silver dish with shortbread on it and a glass that had held Malmsey, the only after-dinner wine he really enjoyed. The lights were too low for him to see any of the pictures in detail but he liked them to be there. Outside he could hear rain and wind and nothing else. Physically he was almost himself again, and though it would be different soon enough he felt completely safe, not just secure from harm but in some positive sense he couldn't define. A passage of Horace stole into his mind unbidden, so he booted the bugger out again a bit sharp, and quite right too.

All manner of clocks started striking ten-thirty. Lancewood came back and plugged the kettle in at his side of the fireplace. He was wearing what he called his uppercrust old queen's smoking-jacket in mulberry-coloured velvet.

'One or two questions occur to me,' he said. 'For instance, since you seem to have started hating the lady very much almost as soon as she arrived, why didn't you just tell her you found you had a headache and must leave at once?'

'Oh, Damon. Chivalry. And a long way behind that, memory of the fact that I see her every other day I'm here in the course of duty. To have walked out then and there would have been an insult, whereas my later behaviour in taking advantage of her did no more than damage her self-respect a lot. And I didn't know what my later behaviour was going to be until later, if then.'

'Very well, why did you invite her to dine with you? Had you forgotten all about her? Or I suppose she'd changed out of all recognition, had she?'

'That's more like it, as a question I mean, or questions rather. I invited her because I wanted to confide in her on a matter soon to emerge. As regards her revoltingness, I did try the Marx-Brothers theory briefly, that she had been great fun then and had stayed exactly the same but the lapse of time, it must be fifteen years or more, had made me see her as bloody awful. Change of taste in the world at large, not just in me. It's tempting but I'm afraid it won't do.'

There was a longer pause. Lancewood made tea; it was a China blend you never saw anywhere else but in this room. Even before he had expected, Jake's sense of safety began to slip away from him. He said without much solid intention that he must be going soon.

'Soon or late, you're not going till my curiosity is entirely laid to rest, and if that takes another three hours, so be it. Drink your tea.'

Jake obeyed, which is to say he took a sip; it was delicious. 'Quite amazing, the consistency with which I saw everything about her as what it wasn't, I'm talking about the past. I mistook her egotism for sparkle, her knowingness for judgement, her cheap jeering for healthy disrespect and her ... vulgarity for plain speaking. Oh, Christ, and, something I haven't mentioned up to now, her habit of saying I know I talk too much and then going on talking too much, I thought that was engaging insight and disarming frankness instead of bullshit. She gets things wrong all the time too. Now the reason I never even rose to the level of giving her the benefit of a couple of dozen doubts whenever she did or said anything ... let's take it in stages. I hardly knew her before I started having a successful affair with her, I mean we suited each other physically. But it wasn't that, because I went on seeing her after it was over, on at least one occasion for a whole evening, and I thought I'd forgotten all about it but later on I remembered one thing, or realized one negative thing, I hadn't started wanting her to be dead the moment she opened her mouth – that would have stuck in my mind. And I'm sure, this I can't remember but I'm sure from experience with other ex-girl-friends that I didn't sit there goggling at her tits and thinking about how it used to be and what fun if we tried it again. No, it was just that in those days I was a normal man with a normal interest in women and now I'm not. Yes Damon, I've lost all desire, though funnily enough not all performance, so last night might have been worse. Different, anyway. But since I can't remember anything about it, not a hell of a lot. I'm undergoing "therapy" for my condition, needless to say without the slightest effect.

'You see the really awful part about last night wasn't anything that happened during it. I'll have to go back a bit. Without ever really thinking about it I'd been working on the assumption that the only reason women were tolerated was because the world was run by men, normal men who by definition didn't see them as they really were because they were looking at them through, er, a kind of distorting –'

'Horn-rimmed spectacles.'

'Sod you. Yes. Once I even played with the fantasy that the point of women being in season all the time with only brief interruptions, and even those aren't treated as interruptions among primitive peoples I read somewhere, anyway if they were like dogs or rather bitches with intervals of several months during which they aroused no sexual feelings at all then most of 'em wouldn't make it, they'd get their bloody heads kicked off before they could come on heat. Well that was all very well, quite harmless, the sort of thing a lot of men say on the understanding that they don't really mean it, not really, especially men who are ones for the ladies.

'Now we come to last night, the awful part about it. The reason I could be so wrong about her wasn't so much that I'd been looking at her through horn-rimmed spectacles as that I hadn't been listening to her at all, not a word she ever said, she just didn't interest me. And I could have sworn she did, I could have sworn I'd identified her as what did I say, lively and clever and plain-spoken and so on. But I'd really - only - wanted - one - thing. She told me so this morning and that's when I saw it. I don't even like them much. Women. I despise them intellectually - as the Governing Body now knows. Christ, that reminds me, I must write to the Master.'

'What about?'

'What about? Me blowing my top at the College Meeting, that's what about.'

'Oh, that. You did cause a bit of a stir at the time but these things soon blow over as you know, or rather as you would know if you'd always attended as regularly as I have. Behaviour that would be taken as evidence of madness or brain damage or the utmost malignity outside is just something that helps to make life interesting when we do it. Comes from being in college. Rather like the Army. For instance Wynn-Williams and the Jehovah's Witnesses, were you there or did you ever hear about it? I'll tell you another time. Go on about not liking women.'

'Yes. Well, last night was a sort of illustration of it. I

think in a nasty way I quite enjoyed it, at least until I got pissed, watching that female make an exhibition of herself. The thing is, it's not them, it's me. I don't see them as they are any more than I did before. I haven't got those spectacles any more but that doesn't mean my sight's improved. Is it possible to be objective in a case like this? What I feel is imagine me thinking I liked them all those years when I didn't really care for them one bit. Rather sad. Makes you wonder, too. I mean can it be only me? Eve used to screw around a lot at the time I knew her, so there must have been plenty of other blokes who failed to notice she was intolerable company. And blokes who screw girls who screw around a lot are usually blokes who screw around a lot, like me or rather me as I was. More support for the idea that woman-izers don't like women. Whereas in fact, in fact they are nice, aren't they Damon? You ought to know, you've never fancied them for an instant and you like them.'

'As you say, but Jake love, you're depressing yourself, it's not as bad as you think, you're still suffering from the various tolls that have been taken of you.'

'I'd better go to bed.'

'Not in your present mood. I understand now why your final contribution this afternoon was so emphatic. A lot of what you said was true but only as far as it went. There's one thing you ought to try to remember. Men have their own ways, just as efficient ways, of being evasive and over-bearing and dull and thoroughly unsatisfactory. Perhaps I see some of them a little more clearly than you do. That ought to make me more tolerant when a girl tells me she thinks Hamlet was a woman. I don't say it does but it ought to. What about Brenda? She's the only one who matters.'

'She says I only want one thing too. Of course I don't know how far she . . .' Jake spread his hands.

'Oh dear. That is rather untoward, I do see.'

'I'm supposed to be working out what I feel about her. I don't dislike her, which is a start of a kind. I like having her about the place. I like chatting to her, but I don't find myself wanting to tell her things - I remember in the old days whenever I read or heard or thought of anything funny or striking or whatever it might be, my first thought was always, I must tell Brenda about that. Not any more. I suppose I ought to tell her just the same – my "therapist" works on the principle that the way of getting to want to do something you don't want to do is to keep doing it. Which seems to me to be a handy route from not . . . pause . . . wanting to do it o not-wanting, wanting not, to do it. But I am paying him to know best. Brenda wants affection, physical affection. She also needs it and ought to have it. My chap is always on at me to go through the motions of it on the principle I've described. I'm a bit scared of being shifted from not-pause-wanting to do that to not-wanting to do it. Do you know what I think I am, Damon? A male chauvinist pig. Until the other day I'd never have dreamt of saying that about anybody, least of all myself. Just goes to show, doesn't it? I think if you don't mind I will bugger off, before I depress myself into a decline. But thank you.'

It was of Kelly, not Eve or Brenda, that Jake was thinking as he trotted through the rain to his rooms. How did she fit in? He didn't think he felt any affection for her, which might have had something to do with what she had said about things like his dick – easy to forgive, not so easy to forget – but he couldn't be sure while his main feeling for her was pity. She certainly aroused his interest, genuine interest as opposed to the testosterone-fed substitute that had graced his sometime dealings with Eve, but again that interest might well attach to her as a phenomenon rather than as a person. Oh well.

On arrival he shut his outer door in case Mrs Sharp should be on her way into college to hear from his very lips whether he wanted his study curtains washed, and took the plastic phallus out of the drawer where it had lain for the past fifteen days, out of sight all the time and out of mind too except when he had been in London or on his way there. With a paper-knife, a razor-blade and his bare hands he eventually reduced it to fragments too small for it to be made recognizable again by anyone but a three-dimensional-jigsaw-

puzzle grandmaster, should such a person exist. As he worked
Jake muttered to himself,

'Ah now me poor owld bogger, sure it's athackun your
own masculinithy yiz are. Ochone, ochone, yiz do be per-
formun an acth of sexual self-thesthroction, do yiz know.
Guilth and shame have been rakun havoc wid yiz so dey have,
acushla machree. Jasus, Mary and Joseph, de resolth of
inorthinathly sthricth thoileth-thrainun thoo be sure, wid
maybe a spoth of sothomy ath your poblic school trown in.
And bethath and be-fockun-gorrah, loife's a soighth aisier
dis way if yiz ron tings roighth.'

As well as Kelly's visit to Oxford, that day had seen ball lightning in Glasgow. Later in the month the weather improved, with long spells of sunshine that reminded Jake of one of his summer terms as an undergraduate before the war, he couldn't remember which. At the beginning of June, while Brenda stayed with her Northumberland cousins, he spent a couple of nights with Lancewood and his friend John at their cottage near Dry Sandford, sitting out on the lawn with them till an advanced hour. It didn't last: the rain came back, accompanied by cold and thunder, in nice time to damage Eights Week and plague examinees scurrying to and from the Schools. The last day of term, the last of that academic year, was one of the worst.

Even so, the Oxford end of Jake's life over those weeks had been normal, even satisfactory to the limited degree possible: he hadn't trampled Miss Calvert to death, the little bastard from Teddy Hall had taken to cutting (no doubt it was called boycotting) his lectures and it looked as if Thwaites, the Bradfordian, was going to get his First in Part I, as against which the Cardiff man had been offered the job and had accepted. The London end, beyond question the larger one, had in the meantime not done too well. Jake kept up his visits to Rosenberg who displayed, whether or not he really felt, great interest in the Eve episode; it was possible that his mill had been getting a little hard up for grist. Naturally he tended to concentrate on his patient's fragmentary recollections of the act of sex he had performed, trying to elicit more of them from him.

'Let's go over the whole thing again at a snail's pace,' he would say.

'I honestly don't think I can do it more slowly than last time.'

'Ah, you can try. Now you commenced manual manipulation of her breasts.'

'Yes, I thought pedal manipulation was ruled out one way or another,' Jake ventured to reply on one such occasion. 'For instance etymologically.'

'I'm sorry, I'm afraid I don't quite follow.'

'Never mind. Yes, manual manipulation of her breasts was just what I did commence.'

'And what were your feelings as you did so?' Rosenberg would pursue.

'I've told you. That it was odd, that it was bizarre.'

'You mean you found it disgusting.'

'No, again as I've told you, all I found it and everything else I can remember was odd or bizarre.'

'You suffered feelings of shame.'

'No, and not of guilt either. Not even whatever you called it, personally orientated guilt about my wife. I wasn't thinking of her at the time.'

Another recurrent theme had to do with Jake's fantasies, in the sense not of his private daydreamings but of his commissions of these to paper for Rosenberg's inspection. Each fresh attempt brought the same response, the same as the very first, the one about the fantastically beautiful girl with the unbelievable figure. The holder of that M A (Dip. Psych) shook his small head, drew in his breath and sighed, cleared his throat repeatedly and in general behaved much as Jake would have done if confronted by an essay attributing the origin of Mediterranean civilizations to colonists from outer space. There was the same effect of not knowing where to start.

'I'm a doctor,' was a favourite opening of Rosenberg's. 'I'm *your* doctor, Mr Richardson. I'm not going to be shocked, you know, by anything you think or say or write.'

'No, I believe that.'

'If you do – I beg your pardon, seeing that you do, why don't you come clean? Or rather – it was well worth watching, the deliberation with which he steeled himself the first time he leaped the yawning semantic chasm in front of him – 'come *dirty*!?'

'Well, that's the dirtiest I could do. You must admit I've made progress, cutting out all the soft and warm stuff and being heavy on the Anglo-Saxon.'

'True, true, but it's all too normal, too straight. I've never worked with anybody who hadn't some slight deviation, often more than one – voyeurism, fetishism, a very wide field there, sado-masochism, even more so . . .'

'I'm sorry to disappoint you, I must be a very straight man.'

'In some ways indeed you are, to the point of extreme bourgeois puritan conventionality partly resulting from your having attended a single-sex school.'

'Oh come off it, man.' Jake never quite got over his incredulity at this accusation.

Twice at least Rosenberg tried to support his view by referring to the goings-on at the McDougall. 'Several of the photographs that were shown to you there you found offensive. In particular one featuring the female sex organ.'

'Yes, I remember. I said it was ugly and so it was, to me, and I bet a lot of other men would say the same and to find it an ugly sight in a photograph isn't the same as finding the whole idea disgusting which I know is what you're working towards.'

That usually stopped that one, though Jake's eccentric and psychologically sinister dislike of undressing in mixed company was sometimes taken into consideration. Like all Rosenberg's others, this line of inquiry was continuously and abundantly boring but at least, by the relaxed standards of the matter in hand, it had some observable relevance. The same could not be said of an occasion when Rosenberg produced a machine either called something like a GPI or designed to do something called something like GPI. It was somewhat smaller than the nocturnal mensurator (itself long since returned to him and never mentioned since) and was supposedly designed to measure nervous tension. The thing worked by in the first place measuring something else, sweat, perhaps, or changes in skin temperature; Jake, who didn't listen to Rosenberg whenever it seemed legitimate, wasn't listening. Pads connected by wires to the machine were fastened on his thumb and middle finger, a switch clicked and a different sort of click, as from a small loud-speaker, followed. It proved to be the first of a series of such clicks, one every five or six seconds. Rosenberg took him on an imaginary stroll round Orris Park and the clicks stayed the same, sat him in his study and the rate increased slightly, put him in the bedroom with an undraped Brenda and the machine behaved like a Geiger counter in a plutonium shop. They didn't try that again.

Actually that happened on the first Tuesday of the summer vacation. The dating was fixed in Jake's mind because something much more extraordinary happened then too; there was a moment of mild interest, nothing to do with the 'therapy' of course. He had mentioned the end of the Oxford term as he sat down on arrival.

'Ah yes,' said Rosenberg, 'to be sure. That means you'll be having several months at your disposal which you'll be able to devote exclusively to research because of your free-dom from teaching responsibilities.'

He spoke with marked reluctance, indeed with sullenness, as if he had been offered too good a price for reciting those couple of dozen words to be able to turn down the job but wasn't going to throw in anything in the way of pretending to care. Jake came back with something like Yes and the psychologist's manner changed completely, became just that, in fact, as he set the ball rolling with a fervid inquiry after his patient's early morning erections.

He must have got an answer but Jake knew nothing of it. His mind had sped back to their very first encounter when Rosenberg had used the same grudging tone in talking of his ancestry, then forward again a week and a bit to their convivial chat in the Lord Nelson. There had been an air of resentment, almost of hatred, about the way he had planked down that couple of miserable facts about his friend (friend?

friend?) the editor of *Mezzanine* and how long he might or might not go on editing it – yes, in that way worse for Rosenberg in the pub, because pubs were places where you were supposed to have real convivial chats, not like consulting-rooms or hospitals where you ran the show and need only waste a few seconds on tittle-tattle before getting on with *what really mattered*.

'No, no erotic dreams,' he said to Rosenberg. Another one was what he was saying to himself, another fucking displaced egotist. As the ordinary sort cared only for maintaining or advancing their own position, judging always in terms of what was useful, never of what was interesting, so this sort put a cause or subject in place of self, identified with it to a degree seldom envisaged by those fond of that term and made everything an example of something, some theory, generalization, set of facts already in their keeping. He had run across plenty of them in his time at Oxford, as he had half-remembered while he ordered his drink in the Lord Nelson: atheistical religionists who talked, not all that much better than Eve had done, about the hidden powers of the mind, philosophasters, global-equality persons – all or any of whom Rosenberg had reminded him of on the same occasion. That was today and yesterday; the day before yesterday had been far less daft, with Marxists of various sorts predominant or thought to be: as an undergraduate he had had pointed out to him a not very old man at Exeter to whom all evils flowed from what he still called Bolshevism.

Some of this occurred to Jake on his way home after the consultation. It was then too that he reconsidered Rosenberg's fitness for his job. He had tentatively decided, that time when the Workshop was assembling, that a psychologist could afford not to know a great deal outside his subject and still do well enough within it. What about a psychologist who didn't care in the least for the world outside it, even resented its existence? There were fields of study in which indifference or antipathy to all other matters could be no handicap, those fields in which the presence of an observer had a negligible effect on what was observed – astronomy, for instance. Jake felt that psychology must be a different case, so much so that he now doubted his earlier view. Any student of the mind would surely be a good deal hampered by lack of all acquaintance with some of its more note-worthy products – art, for instance. But he didn't bother to pursue the thought because whatever conclusion about Rosenberg he might arrive at he was stuck with him.

And that was because of Brenda. It would be unfair to say that she had faith in Rosenberg; to her, he was simply the expert whose instructions must be followed regardless. No, a little more, in that to query any of those instructions was seen as captious at best, as showing less than a burning desire for sexual betterment. Other things were similarly seen, most of all Jake's persistent refusal to accompany Brenda to the Workshop after the first try. Ed had it in for him, he said; there was no knowing what the man might get up to next, given the chance. He also said he was uncertain, unhappy, unconvinced, things like that about the procedures followed, pale versions of his real feeling that if Rosenberg was a bit suspect Ed was a ravening charlatan. (Didn't Rosenberg's readiness to send his patients to work with Ed make Rosenberg worse than a bit suspect? Not quite necessarily: he might find he gained fresh insight that way, might be standing by to intervene should the facilitator require one of the participants to be disembowelled by way of smartening him up. He – Rosenberg – got a mark for not having put any pressure on Jake to resume attendance.)

Another thing Jake didn't tell Brenda was as much as the bare fact of Kelly's call on him in Oxford. His silence was variously motivated. Admitting in effect that she had been right and he wrong about the girl would have gone against the grain, though he minded that sort of thing less than most men. It would have distressed him too to recount the incident in full, and although some people might have con-sented to be fobbed off with a fifty-word synopsis, Brenda was certainly not one of them. There was also the good rough rule that said that telling one female anything at all about your dealings with another was to be avoided whenever possible. And there was a fourth reason which eluded him at the time. Anyway, keeping quiet was another discouragement from changing his mind and starting to go to the Workshop again: one little extra apology for having invaded him, accidentally or accidentally-on-purpose within Brenda's hearing, and that would be shit. Well, he wasn't exactly palpitating with hunger for Kelly's company but he did want to know how she was getting on, for which his only source was Brenda – Rosenberg had gone all professional-ethical on him when approached. Since he couldn't hurry things up by admitting his interest he had to sit through Brenda's weekly bulletins with the best grace he could muster, and recent experience made him see to it that his best was pretty bloody good.

'Well, we started with scanning pairs and free scanning as before,' she said on the first Saturday evening, 'and then we did parents and children.'

'What's that?'

'First you're your father and then you're your mother and then you're yourself as a child.'

'How do you mean?'

'You act it. You pick somebody of your own sex and talk to them as if you were your father talking to you.'

'Oh yes?' said Jake, leaning forward eagerly. 'What about?'

'Whatever Ed decides. About your father, about sex - you try to remember what he did say. Telling you off. A good deal of that.'

'Really. It must call for quite a bit of acting ability.'

'You'd be surprised how good some of them are. Lionel was marvellous as his mother, he even managed to look like her. Well you know what I mean.'

'Yes of course.' He gave himself a mental pat on the back for having detected intimations of queerdom in Lionel.

'Martha was very interesting when she was her mother – you remember her mother's horrible to her, but Martha wasn't horrible at all, when she was being her mother I mean. You know, reasonable and kind and everything. Most odd.'

'Mm. It sounds absolutely –'

'Your friend Kelly was really the star turn.'

'Was she?'

'As herself as a child. Honestly it was quite frightening. The voice was particularly. If you'd shut your eyes you could have sworn it was a child speaking. She was different from the time before. Much madder. Of course she wasn't putting on a show for you today. She asked after you in the lunch-break.'

'That was nice.' Quite safe, he thought; Brenda wasn't one to save things up, very much the contrary.

'She hasn't been round here since last Saturday has she?'

'Good God no,' he said, sounding shocked. 'Whatever gave you that idea?' He wasn't acting; his shock had come from the immediate perception that only the luck of the draw had made Brenda ask what she had asked instead of whether Kelly had dropped in on him, say, and from the thought of how he might have reacted if the draw had gone against him. Anybody would think I was having an affair with the bloody girl, he said to himself irritably.

'Just the way she asked after you. I expect that was to get at me.'

'Why should she get at you?'

'Because she's after you, or was. Probably moved on to somebody else by now. You're still not falling for that investigative-journalist impersonation, are you?'

He frowned in thought. 'I don't know. Anyway, if you're right she sounds a rather pathetic character.'

'Oh yes she is, some of the time.'

'Sorry darling, I'm afraid I don't quite get you.'

'I mean she has a pathetic act to go with her bright act and all her other acts. She's never genuine. That's what's wrong with her.'

He didn't dispute this aloud and the talk moved on, eventually reaching Geoffrey and causing Jake momentary but keen regret at not having been there to see for himself. Perhaps Brenda had sensed his interest in Kelly, because in subsequent Saturday debriefings she would tend to mention her late and cursorily or not at all. To take it out of him deliberately in such a way didn't quite fit her character as he had come to know it over the years, but then she seemed as the weeks went by to be changing in other ways too, nothing spectacular or even easy to pin down, in fact the nearer he got to doing that the sillier it sounded. She was becoming more friendly and at the same time less intimate; amiable and talkative, never anywhere near chucking crockery about and yet not, or not so much, or not so often, or perhaps indeed not turning her eyes on his in the full deep glance he had known before. He found something comparable in her behaviour during the non-genital sensate focusing sessions on which, after the almost total failure of two successive genital dittos, Rosenberg had ordered them to fall back.

'Is that nice?' she would ask, stroking his chest. 'Or at least comparatively nice, I know this isn't your kind of thing much but there must be degrees, quite good and not so good. How is it?'

'Oh, quite good.'

'Or would you like it sort of harder, you know, pressing down more?'

'No, that's fine as it is.'

'You're meant to be really relaxed to benefit from it. I'm sure it's beneficial anyway, in general, I mean. Anything that reduces stress must be, don't you think?'

'Well, so people keep saying.'

'I think it's generally accepted . . . Right, my turn, but let's have a kiss first . . . Now you do my hip. Let me show you. All the way from here down to here and up again, slowly. Try it . . . That's it but not quite so lightly. I find it helps at first to shut your eyes and think of something peaceful, like a garden or a lake. You ought to try that.'

This matter-of-factness helped Jake. He still didn't look forward to the focusings but the gloom their prospect had aroused in him was somewhat alleviated. The hard work he put in each time not to seem to be gritting his teeth seemed to have its effect: there were no more complaints of lack of affection. On the two occasions when Brenda went with him to see Rosenberg in Harley Street and was asked what she thought of her marital situation, she answered in summary that it could be better but was coming along not too badly. Even her reproaches for not coming to the Workshop fell away. He began to feel occasional stirrings of hope, though his relief each time Rosenberg didn't order a return to genital sensate focusing was as heartfelt as ever. Funny how it had worked all right with Eve, he thought to himself more than once, or perhaps the difference was simply that then he had been free, responsible to nothing and nobody.

Over the week-end after the end of term the same small thing happened three times: the telephone rang, Brenda went to or across the kitchen to answer it and was hung up on as soon as she spoke. She mentioned burglars; Jake said they'd be wasting their time. He would have forgotten all about this if a not-quite-so-small-thing hadn't happened on the Monday evening while he was watching the nine o'clock news on BBC 1. The telephone rang; cursing mildly he made his way out and answered it.

'Is it possible to speak to Mrs Richardson please?' asked a very hoarse voice with at least two accents in it, one foreign, another perhaps regional, and a couple of speech impediments.

'I'm afraid she's out.' Earlier, Brenda had said she was going to a film about gypsies with Alcestis, the sort of thing she had done two or three times recently, if not a spiffing scheme in itself then a bloody sight better one than bringing Alcestis here.

'Can I get her later?'

'She won't be back till eleven at the earliest. I suggest you –'

Click. Jake would have forgotten all about this too if, ten minutes later, the door-bell hadn't chimed and it hadn't turned out to be Kelly who had caused it to do so.

'Jesus Christ,' he said.

'It's all right, no trouble I promise you, I'm perfectly okay, I can only stay a minute, can I just come into the passage?'

He looked at her. She seemed to have shrunk a good deal since he left her to Ernie, perhaps because of the head-scarf that flattened her hair against her skull and the tightly drawn raincoat, but her manner was much what it had been then. Anyway, what could he do? He stood aside and shut the door after her.

'What do you want? Was it you on the telephone just now?'

'Yes. Brenda hates me. She's probably quite right. Have you told her about me coming to see you in Oxford?'

'Certainly not.'

'Good, I didn't think you would have done. I haven't told anybody, not even my parents. What I wanted to ask you was about this week-end Workshop.'

'What? What week-end Workshop?'

'Didn't Brenda tell you?'

'No. You'd better ... You can't just stand there, take your things off and come and sit down.'

'It's okay, honestly.'

'Do as I tell you. Now what's this all about?'

'It's the week-end after next, starting on the Friday evening, the 8th, at least that's when we're supposed to get there so as to be able to start work in good time in the morning. The place is near Salisbury.'

'I see.' He saw more clearly that she had had her hair cut very short like a kind of rufous helmet. It took three or four years off her apparent age.

'Funny Brenda not telling you, Ed and Dr Rosenberg announced it last Saturday week. I ...'

'What?'

'I expect it slipped her mind. Why did you stop coming after just the one time?'

'It's simply struck me as frightful rubbish and a complete bore.'

240

'Oh I quite agree, but . . . What I wanted to ask you, do you think you could possibly come to it, the week-end Workshop I mean?'

So many expressions, most of them impure, tried to get out of Jake's mouth at once that for the moment he said nothing articulate.

'You see I'm absolutely dreading it, I can't tell you how much, but my parents want me to go and they're so sweet to me I really can't not go, and I thought if you were there, just there, somebody I trusted, I wouldn't feel so bad. I wouldn't, you know, do anything, I couldn't with Brenda about all the time, could I?'

'I'm sorry, Kelly, but you must realize it's quite impossible.'

She got up at once from the corner of the settee where she had been sitting for less than a minute. 'Never mind, it doesn't really matter, I'm sure I'll manage all right, it was just a thought, of course it was ridiculous to expect you to, I quite understand.'

'I am sorry,' he said, following her into the passage.

'No no, don't be, forget it, I shouldn't have asked, put you in an embarrassing position, just thinking of myself as usual.'

Being an erstwhile successful womanizer Jake had acted against his better judgement a number of times, but never more directly and more consciously than when he said, as he did now, 'All right, sod it, I'll see if I can fix it up.'

Fixing it up was not straightforward. To approach Brenda –
yes, why *hadn't* she mentioned it? – with stuff like thinking of
popping up to Dry Sandford again about the 8th or 9th
would be to put in an urgent request for trouble. Luckily the
next day was Rosenberg-day, though here again care was
needed: no Kelly-told-me or Rosenberg might in his
innocence or whatever it was drop that one in front of Brenda.
After a résumé of his latest self-abusive adventures Jake
casually let fall that he was thinking of another try at the
Workshop, not on the Saturday to come because he had to
be in Oxford then, but on the one after, the 9th. Expressing
no surprise at either his ignorance or his change of mind and
not the heartiest approval of the latter, perhaps because it
damaged his guilt-and-shame thesis, Rosenberg gave some
particulars of the proposed week-end and went straight on,
or rather straight back since they had been there several times
before, to Jake's early sexual feelings and experiences. Of
these he had managed to remember a very fair amount he
thought he had forgotten without thereby changing his
condition in the slightest.

When he brought the week-end up with Brenda she did
express surprise, saying she had told him about it on the
evening of the day she had herself been told, but now she
came to think of it it had been at the end of the evening, most
likely after he had taken his Mogadon and so was in a drowsy
inattentive state. Her approval was a shade warmer than
Rosenberg's but not unqualified: he had always said the
Workshop was rubbish so what had happened to change his
mind? Well, he had been thinking, and couldn't help being
impressed by the fact (it was a fact) that she constantly said

she was the better for the experience, and a week-end in the country would be nice. All right, but he wasn't to piss on the proceedings; he promised not to.

No sooner was the thing fixed up than the tonic effect of the actual fixing-up subsided and his qualms began to mount. It was true that Brenda's reports had included much activity that was daft, pointless, unpalatable and (wait for it) boring but nothing positively unsafe, lewd or illegal; just give that Ed bugger a free hand for forty-eight hours though, in a house as comparatively remote as the one designated seemed to be and for openers, as he would say, you'd be getting off lightly with gladiatorial games. And what might Kelly get up to? He turned his mind away from that, concentrating it on the thought that whatever dire possibilities occurred to him he couldn't fail her, not appear. Once, he was hard at it when he fancied he recognized the extra reason why he hadn't told Brenda about Kelly-in-Oxford: if he had he would never have been able to get away with wanting to join in on the week-end. Funny what you could see coming without knowing it.

As the day approached it began to look less baleful. He had found out by indirections that Geoffrey was to be of the party, so a touch at least of entertainment and satisfaction of malice was guaranteed. Then there was plain curiosity. And then there was the weather, hot and sunny all week long. When Friday arrived with more of the same and the time began to move along to six o'clock Jake felt little tingles of expectation, as he had once done before every out-of-the-way journey with the prospect of someone new and wonderful at the end of it.

Almost dead on the hour a fair-sized yellow car of foreign manufacture drew up as arranged outside 47 Burgess Avenue. It was driven by Ivor, whom Jake wouldn't have recognized after their one meeting a couple of months before. He turned out to be in his thirties, tallish, fairish, serious-looking and doing quite well in a building society. Beside him was Geoffrey. As could be seen when he emerged and came to the front door, he was most peculiarly got up in a sports jacket and flannel trousers, a shirt with an unobtrusive check, a plain woollen tie that matched his socks, and brown brogues; it was almost as if he had *tried* to choose clothes appropriate to a week-end in the country. Mind you, he must be bloody hot in them, there was that to be said. While giving a hand with the Richardsons' luggage, shutting the boot, getting in beside Jake at the back and waiting for Brenda, he explained with a thoroughness such as to defeat all misunderstanding that he had left Alcestis their car, his and her car, to do with as she pleased; this one, this car, the car they were sitting in, belonged to Ivor, was Ivor's car.

Jake remembered very well the senile-dementia treatment he had had meted out to him at the original Workshop and wondered whether Geoffrey intended his last few hundred words as more of the same with more yet to come. If so, he was going to be in trouble quite soon, but before Jake had fixed on just what kind he caught sight of Brenda hurrying up the tiny garden path and forgot all about Geoffrey for the moment.

After so many weeks of conscientious dieting she had lost something like two and a half stone and could no longer be called fat. With the weight she had taken off some apparent years too and would have passed for forty. She was wearing what must be a new dress in pale green silk, some not very serious brown-and-white shoes and an openly frivolous white hat. How fetching, how pleasant, how *nice* she looks, Jake thought to himself; must remember to tell her so at first opportunity.

There was some trouble with the hat when she got in beside Ivor but it passed off easily enough and they were soon on their way across town to get on to the M20. The traffic was thickish, though not so bad as it would have been if most of the people motoring out of London to the West of England countryside and resorts hadn't downed their shit-shovels about noon (Jake decided).

'What a glorious day,' said Brenda in a dreamy voice. 'And how lovely to be driving; just think of fighting one's way on to a train at Paddington in this heat. I mean to be driven. It is kind of you to take us, Ivor dear.'

'Not at all Brenda, I had three empty seats, and this is the only way I can travel. Has that come up, incidentally? My psychiatrist says it's quite common, chaps who can't face any kind of public transport or even a car or even being driven by someone they trust in their own car aren't bothered at all driving their own car. To do with being in control apparently. Isn't that interesting?'

It interested Jake, who remembered now about Ivor's phobias, in more than one way. As soon as they reached the M20 they moved into the fast lane and stayed there. Jake wasn't at all a nervous traveller but after a few miles he did start wondering what substantial fraction of the speed of sound they had reached. The object seemed to be to overtake everything else going in their direction: container trucks, articulated lorries, quite serious-looking private cars appeared in the far distance, swelled hectically in size and in effect hurtled past them like express-trains. Beside him Geoffrey stirred, shifted and made sudden darting movements with his head in pursuit of items that, seen clearly enough for long enough, might prove to arouse his puzzlement or dissatisfaction. At one point the momentary placing of a tall vehicle in an inner lane meant that he clearly missed a sign that Jake had happened to catch.

'Services in so many miles,' he said, pretending to be trying to be helpful. 'I couldn't see how many.'

'What?'

'Services some distance ahead.'

'What distance?'

'Services,' Jake began, then noticed that Geoffrey's frown, in being from the start, deepened slightly at this third utterance of the noun. 'Services are things like food, cups of tea, facilities for –'

'Wouldn't it be better to push on until we're nearer the other end?'

'I'm sure it would, I was just explaining about Services. As well as food and tea they have petrol and probably –'

'Are we low on petrol, Ivor?'

'No, I had a full tank when I picked you up, Geoffrey.'

'There you are, Jake.' Geoffrey gave a hesitant smile. 'Right as rain. Nothing to worry about at all.'

'I wasn't worrying for Christ's sake, I was telling you about Services because of that sign.'

'Sign?'

'Yes, Geoffrey: *sign*. The generic name for flat objects, often rectangular in shape, on which instructions or as in this case information –'

'Do please shut up, Jake,' said Brenda.

Jake held his peace. After about another three minutes' driving they came off the motorway and found to their surprise an authentic old-fashioned family and commercial hotel where it proved possible to dine. All the dishes were firmly in the English tradition: packet soup with added flour, roast chicken so overcooked that each chunk immediately absorbed every drop of saliva in your mouth, though the waterlogged Brussels sprouts helped out a bit there, soggy tinned gooseberry flan and coffee tasting of old coffee-pots. Jake wasn't hungry anyway: foreboding had driven out his earlier feelings of looking forward and there was some tension among the party, no doubt as a result of his surely pretty mild brush with Geoffrey in the car, so he didn't say much. The only one who did was Ivor, whose prowess behind the wheel had made them early and who had filled in the spare time with a few large gin and tonics.

'I don't think these psychiatrist chaps are much good,' he said a couple of times in his agreeable fully modulated voice. 'Or perhaps the phobia lot are particularly lousy. I'm on my third and none of them have made a blind bit of difference. In fact ... well never mind. Do you know what my latest one tried to tell me the other day? You don't mind me going on about this do you? I don't often get the chance.'

'You go on as long as you like, my dear.'

'Thanks, Brenda. Well – do you know what this bloke tried to tell me?'

'No,' said Geoffrey on brief consideration.

'Well you wouldn't would you Geoffrey? Now you've heard me go on about how I don't like the Tube, the Under-

246

ground. Right, he took me down there the other week, we went all the way from Warren Street up to Hampstead and I was fine, didn't turn a hair. Next go-off, next day I've got to make the return trip on my own. I went down in the lift and on to the platform and in half a minute I was absolutely terrified. I got myself over it in the end with that deep breathing, but it wasn't funny. So I said all this, and he was *surprised*, because I'd done so well when we went together. And him with a syringe in his pocket with half a gallon of tranquillizer in it, enough to calm down King Kong. And he's *surprised* it makes a difference. That wasn't it though, the really marvellous thing he told me. Now ... I'm an only child, it was a difficult birth, looks as if my mum and dad decided not to take any chances, I don't blame them. We've been through all that. Anyway, he asked me, when I said I'd been frightened he asked me if there was anything in particular I was frightened of, and I said yes there was, there was nothing on the indicator, no train signalled, and I thought, oh my God it'll never come, I'll be down here for ever. And he said, now this is it, he said, me being afraid of nothing arriving in my Underground was all to do with my mum being afraid of something arriving in her Underground. Isn't that marvellous? Especially nothing being the same as something. I tell you, that cheered me up, it really reassured me, I thought, I may be a bit peculiar but at least I'm not as bloody barmy as to come up with that.'

Jake, who had enjoyed the opening of this speech too, laughed a good deal, more than either Geoffrey or Brenda. Soon afterwards Ivor said they still had to find the house and he'd like to get there in the light, so the bill was called for. To Geoffrey's perplexity but without eliciting anything from him in the way of protest, thanks or contribution, Jake paid it; he considered that to save every spare penny for his retirement, every penny, every time would do its bit towards shortening that retirement. They went off. In less than ten minutes, before the sun was quite down, they had pulled in the large asphalted front yard of a fair-sized red-brick building that must have dated from about the year 1900.

Various creepers ran up its walls and there was an ochre-coloured lichen on part of its tiled roof. It was situated near the top of a slight depression that ran down from the main road to Salisbury. Ivor said interestedly that it looked a bit on the big side, to which Brenda demurred; Jake heard later that the place had once been a nursing-home and was now hired out for conferences and other enterprises of that kind, many of them no doubt perfectly serious and useful. They went inside.

In another ten minutes the four were reassembled in one of a pair of rooms run together by the disposal of folding doors. Both had the look of meagreness attached to being used rather than lived in: large table to discuss business round, dark-green leather armchairs to hold informal discussions in, reproductions of abstract paintings to do what with? Surely not look at; perhaps to be flattered by, flattered into fancying yourself a cultured person. Ed was on hand to greet them, giving Jake a smile not so much of geniality as of amusement; Rosenberg, little legs atwinkle, must still be pedalling gamely down the M20. The others already arrived were Lionel (stealing), Martha (mother), Winnie (shyness) and three men and a woman Jake had never seen before and whose names he didn't bother with for the moment because he would get to know them so very well the following day. After the introductions he stuck to Ivor, whom he had rather taken to and who seemed to need to talk to somebody.

'We're going to be sixteen altogether and that won't fill this house. It really is big.'

'Is that bad?'

'Not as such, but it means parts of it will be empty so that I can't sort of account for them.'

'I think I can see what you mean. But there's bound to be quite a large staff at a joint like this, and offices and so on.'

'That's true, I hadn't thought of that. Thank you, Jake.'

'Don't pills help? Tranquillizers?'

'Yes, but my bloke's made me give them up. Just gloss over the problem, he says. I take his point in a way, but I'm the one that needs them, not him.'

'Is there anything I can do?'

'It would be good if you could tell me you wouldn't mind if I came up to you and started talking rather fast and saying some pretty silly things.'

Jake had just told Ivor he wouldn't mind when a taxi drew up outside the window near which they were standing. It delivered Ruth (despair), Rosenberg, Kelly (you name it), an unnecessarily tall young woman with a head designed for somebody almost as short as Rosenberg, and not Chris (aggression or something), which was nice. When in due course Kelly came into what called itself the conference-room with the other new arrivals she had just the same easy amicable manner as on first meeting Jake. She greeted everyone in turn, leaving him till last and taking a step or two beyond him so that he had to turn about to face her. Over his shoulder she gave Ivor a superb experienced-hostess look that apologized for removing Jake and at the same time indicated her confidence that the need to do this would be understood.

'Jake, we may only have a second or two so please don't interrupt, all right?'

His mental alarm-bell started up. It was some comfort that the chatter of other voices and the opportune arrival of a trolley with coffee and sandwiches would prevent their being overheard for the moment; not a lot, though. 'All right, but make it quick.'

'I'm in room 33, second floor just next to the landing. There's something I want to show you. It won't take long, five minutes, ten at the very outside, but I think it really must be in private. Will you come to my room, number 33, and look at it for me? Leave it till everyone's bedded down, midnight or later, I won't mind, I've got something to read.'

'You must be . . . You must think I'm off my head.'

'Listen Jake, did I enjoy you turning me down? Would I enjoy it any more the second time? . . . Well there you are.'

'What do you want to show me?'

'A letter. Well, a kind of letter. I'd like you to read it for me.'

'Brenda's a light sleeper, I'd be almost certain to wake her up.'

'Has your room got a loo attached to it? Mine hasn't.'

'No.'

'Well there you are. Only five minutes. I'll expect you. Hallo Brenda, hallo Geoffrey, isn't this marvellous weather?'

Geoffrey understood without apparent trouble and said it was, but Brenda said in that colourless voice of hers, 'How are you getting on with your plans for exposing Ed? It's been a long time since we discussed them.'

'Oh, that.' Kelly laughed in a relaxed way. 'More or less on ice these days.'

'Really. You were quite keen on them before.'

'Yes, I do rather act on impulse, I'm afraid. I get crazes.'

'I see.'

'But it's not only that. I've pretty well completely changed my mind about Ed. I've come to the conclusion he's rather good. He's helped me.'

Jake would have chuckled if he had dared. The girl might be a bit touched but nobody could have improved on the deftness with which she had taken the initiative away from Brenda by forcing her into agreement. Add to that the way Geoffrey was looking from face to face, not merely unable to deduce anything whatso-bloody-ever from what he had heard but seeming to think that not to be in prior possession of every relevant fact about anything at any time was a novelty, and a shocking one – add this and you had the makings of quite a jolly party as long as you didn't add anything else. After constraining Brenda to extol Ed's qualities an extra couple of times Kelly took herself off, first to the snacks trolley and not long afterwards out of the room, presumably in the direction of bed.

Other people were drifting away too, just as presumably to allow for the early start promised for the morning. Jake's bedtime was at least an hour ahead, preferably more. He was about to go up and fetch his week-end reading (another slice of sizzling suspense by the author of *The Hippogriff Attaché-Case*) when he caught sight of what looked like, and proved indeed to be, a TV set in the further conference-room. To his considerable surprise it was in working order and could be switched on. He was soon settled down to a just-about-endurable film about Paris in 1944; it had in it Kirk Douglas, whom he didn't mind, and Charles Boyer, whom he minded a lot, and there was also some female. Two of the strangers and Martha and Ivor watched with him. Unusually for her, Brenda sat up too, but she was in the other room talking to Geoffrey. Ed and Rosenberg were also to be seen there. It was after midnight when the party dispersed. Before it finally did, Jake told Ivor he was to come and wake him at any time if he wanted company. Their rooms turned out to be on different floors – Jake's on the first, Ivor's on the second – but there wasn't a lot to be done about that.

Upstairs was a little more homely than downstairs but not much. The Richardsons' room had twin beds, plain curtains, a plain rug, papered walls that would have been nicer plain, a dressing-table of military (World War II junior officers' quarters) appearance and a few other things. Jake sat on his bed and told Brenda what Kelly had asked him to do, wishing he had also told her of the Oxford encounter at the time: too late now.

'Whether you go or not is entirely up to you,' said Brenda in a friendly tone, answering his question. 'You remember I told you to feel free; that still holds. But you know what she's like, or rather I don't think you do quite, not as well as I do, seeing her every week. Of course a straight pass is what it looks like but with somebody like that you can never be sure. This five or ten minutes business . . . If she's got it in for you for any reason, and people like that don't need a proper reason, then she might do anything. Rush about screaming you tried to rape her, anything. But it's up to you, completely.'

In the end, what with one thing and another, he didn't go.

'Jake, Jake, wake up!'

It was Ivor. The light was on. Jake got out of bed very fast saying things like steady and calm down, but Ivor said there was nothing wrong with him, it was Kelly. Brenda sat up in bed. The two men ran out and up the stairs, where it was dark, and into another room with the light on. Kelly was lying in bed on her side with her eyes shut and breathing deeply. Ivor handed Jake a page torn from a pocket diary with a few words written on it in ballpoint in a rather neat script. They were Sorry everybody, but it's better this way. Then Ivor handed Jake a small empty bottle made of brown glass. The label said Mogadon – Miss J. V. Gambeson.

'Do you know where Rosenberg's sleeping?' asked Jake.

'No.'

'Go into every room till you find him. I'll call an ambulance.'

He remembered seeing a telephone near the front door and hurried down to it. The emergency-services operator answered in three seconds. Within another twenty or so he had passed his message and was walking back upstairs when he noticed it wasn't completely dark outside. He looked at his watch: thirty-one minutes past four. And still hot, or hot already. In Kelly's room he found Brenda and Rosenberg. Kelly was lying on her back now. Brenda came over and squeezed his hand but didn't speak.

'Ambulance on the way,' he said. 'Any idea of her chances? Doctor?'

Rosenberg shook his head. In pyjamas and with his hair ruffled he looked about nine. 'I don't understand, there's something crazy about the timing. We'll have to wait for

Ivor. Oh, her chances, we don't know how many she took or how long ago she took them so medically nobody could say at this stage. If that bottle was full when she started it would have held around eighty of the things, quite enough to do for her.'

'I thought you couldn't die of an overdose of those,' said Brenda.

'I grant you it isn't easy but it can be done, that is if you've been taking other pills as well, which she no doubt was. The trouble is it's very widely believed that there is no fatal overdose. If she believed it . . .'

Jake made an effort. 'I noticed she was one of the first to go to bed. She could have been swallowing them by ten-thirty.'

'If so they'll be well into her by now. She can't have wanted that.'

'How do you mean?'

'Her object was not to die but to punish someone or call attention to herself or both. Unfortunately . . .'

He stopped speaking as Ed hurried in with Ivor. The note and the bottle were produced. Ed stood still for a moment and looked at the floor. Then at the sound of approaching voices he went active, moved to the threshold and said, 'Hold it there, fellows. Kelly's been taken sick and will have to be moved to the hospital but she's going to be okay. And that's all.'

'Anything we can do?' asked somebody who sounded to Jake like Lionel.

'Yes there is. There's an ambulance coming – you go down to the front door on the double to let the men in. You stay right where you are and don't let anyone past. I don't want a crowd in here. Thanks.' He shut the door and looked round the room, at Brenda in an unluxurious armchair, Jake standing near the head of the bed, Rosenberg sitting on its foot, Ivor by the boarded-up fireplace. 'All right Ivor, let's have it all and in the right order.'

'Jake kindly said I could wake him up any time I felt bad,' said Ivor at a brisk rate, as one who has worked out in advance the best and shortest way to impart a set of facts. 'I woke up suddenly and I was frightened because it was a strange place. I started to go to Jake but his room's on the floor below and I needed somebody at once. So I went into just the nearest room, I didn't know whose it was, and I turned on the light and it was here and she was like that and I saw the note and the bottle. So then I stopped feeling frightened about myself and fetched Jake and he sent me for Frank and I found him almost straight away.'

'So: she had no way whatever of knowing that you even might come bursting in at four a.m.'

'None.'

'What woke you?' asked Rosenberg.

'I don't know, I just woke, found I was awake.'

Ed rubbed his cheeks alternately with one hand after the other. 'It's off pattern, Frank.'

'I agree. What's worrying is that you can kill yourself with those things but hardly anyone –'

'Is that right, I didn't know that.'

'There you are, if you didn't know there's a good chance she didn't either.'

'So she goes for a cut-me-down, a joke, a phoney attempt without knowing what she's using can be deadly.'

'She could have found out about that,' said Jake, hoping even as he spoke to be taken as stating a rather obvious general possibility rather than showing special knowledge.

'Maybe. We'll know more later. You did well, Ivor. You too, Jake. Now you can all go along to bed. Frank and I'll take care of everything here.'

It struck Jake then that he wanted to stay and see Kelly safely taken off the premises, but he felt he couldn't argue the point so he glanced at her, saw that one of her cheeks was reddened, where Rosenberg might have slapped it to try to arouse her, but nothing else of significance and left with the other two. When asked, Ivor said he would be fine now because it was nearly light. As soon as he had gone Brenda said,

'You're not to blame for that in any way at all.'

'If she dies I'll be responsible. That stuff has had three or four more hours to work on her because of me.'

'You're not responsible. Either she is or God is or nobody is, not you. It's nothing to do with you except in the sense that she did it to get you involved with her and make you feel awful about her, and she picked you because she knows you quite like her or have a bit of time for her and nobody else does.'

'All right, but poor little bitch.'

'You can't afford to think that. Dangerous little lunatic is the only safe thing to think about her. Remember, it's *not your fault*. You couldn't possibly have foreseen what she was going to do, how could anyone?'

They heard the ambulance approaching. Neither spoke while it came up and halted outside the building and, after what seemed a remarkably short time, drove off again. Jake had heard no voices or footfalls in that time and wished he had, feeling that that would have been some sort of guarantee of Kelly's actual departure. By now he and Brenda were tucked up in their beds, or rather lay there in the hot twilight each covered by a single sheet.

'Do you think I did right not to tell them about her asking me to go and see her?'

'I should think so, darling. I suppose it might be a bit awkward if it ever came up, but I can't see why it should. And it doesn't make any difference, does it?'

'Not now.'

'I'm going to rest. I shan't sleep but I must rest or I'll feel terrible in the morning. I mean later on. Try not to worry. As I said, you're not to blame in the least.'

Jake agreed with Brenda about resting and sleeping but got it wrong: he dropped off almost at once and was woken by the heat four hours later. Much the same turned out to have happened to her. On the feeling-terrible front his achievement was well above par, nothing on the scale of the morning after Eve but with similar all-round coverage of the physical, mental, emotional, spiritual, moral. As for worrying he was well into that by the time his eyes were open, so far that he couldn't get round to considering whether he was to blame or not: perhaps he was an innocent instrument but there was no doubt whatever that he was an instrument.

If breakfast was to be had at all he must do no more than dress, comb hair and pee before plunging downstairs. With Brenda at his side, full of complaint about how ghastly she looked, he found something called a dining-room. The sun shone brightly on the non-prestige furniture, plastic table-cloths and haircord carpeting. There was a kind of sideboard with doll's-house packets of cereal, quarter-pints of milk, 'sachets' of sugar and other easier-for-them items that recalled the Comyns buttery. No cooked food was available. You got your coffee out of a machine, and having done that you couldn't get it back in.

The room was set with tables for four, only about half of which were to any degree laid, so Ivor had been right in his estimate of the non-fullness of the house. Here he was now, hurrying over to them.

'Ed and Frank would like to see you in the committee-room as soon as you're ready – same side of the hall as this at the back,' he said and was gone.

Brenda had agreed with Jake that it would be more comfortable to discuss Kelly's case as little as possible, so they picked the table already part-occupied by Ruth and Winnie, an ideal pair for the present purpose at any rate. On his left Jake had a window that gave him a view of a stretch of lawn in need of cutting, a tall thick hedge and then nothing until some low hills with a few trees and clumps of bushes and what looked from here like smooth densely growing grass, and sky of course, in no way remarkable but quite grand on such a bright day. And yet not so grand, he felt, as the same scene would have looked to him five or ten years ago. *Then* it would have been apparelled in ti-tum ti-tum, the glory and the freshness of a dream. Was that what Words-worth had been on about without knowing it? How old had he been when he wrote the Ode? Thirty-something? But then he aged early in other respects. Get on to Lancewood.

Within five minutes both Jake and Brenda had had enough 'breakfast', he not wanting much, she not allowed much. They soon ferreted out the committee-room, which might well have once been the office of the chief administrator of the nursing-home, though most likely not designed by him: it was low-ceilinged and, even on a morning like this, dark enough to need artificial light. A minor obstacle to the natural sort was afforded by the panel of stained glass that took up the top third of what there was of a window. Although several degrees below the ones at Comyns it was the only thing in the entire place, large or small, inside or out, that might stick in the mind for ten seconds after the eye had passed over it. Human figures were represented but making out who they were, if anybody in particular, wasn't easy, at least to Jake.

Rosenberg and Ed, who was wearing sunglasses of the deepest dye, sat together behind a table with a telephone on it and enough in the way of notebooks and pens to establish them in a business-conducting posture. Ivor was in attendance, also, unexpectedly, Geoffrey. As he took one of the identical straight-backed chairs with dark-green seats, Jake asked if there was any news of Kelly.

'Not yet,' said Rosenberg. 'There won't be for hours.'

'Have her parents been informed?'

This time Ed answered. 'She has no parents. Not in any real sense. Her father died of drink and her step-father, who lives with her mother in Belfast, won't have her in their home after she tried to burn it down the second time.'

'Everybody please understand that's confidential,' said Rosenberg.

'The only person to inform,' Ed went on, 'is her landlady in Hampstead, and that can certainly wait until we know more.'

Jake nodded his head. He looked at the stained-glass panel. It was divided vertically into three scenes: a kneeling girl above whom a heavily robed male figure was raising a sword, the same figure with lowered sword contemplating a quadruped about the size of a large dog, and the girl from the first scene accompanied by someone of uncertain sex carrying a curved wand and directing her towards a classical portico. He knew the subject but couldn't place it.

'We asked you to stop by,' Ed was saying, 'to let you know we decided on a cover-story for Kelly. Suicide, even a fake one, well, it depresses a lot of people, just the thought of it, and we want the folks to get on with their work without being bothered. Frank and I have staked a lot on this Workshop and we want it to be a success. So we pass it around that Kelly's suffering from an acute allergy that needs hospital attention but isn't dangerous.'

'With a very high fever as the main symptom,' put in Rosenberg.

'She woke up, knew she was sick, found Frank, he got her back to bed to wait for the ambulance. Long as we all tell the same tale if we're asked we'll be okay.' Ed gave a quiet reflective laugh. 'Isn't it great? Allergy. They'll swallow anything. And I go for that, it solves our Kelly problem nice and neat.'

The last phrase made Jake speak more sharply than he had intended. 'I take it you have been in touch with the hospital?'

'Like Frank said, Jake, they won't know anything for a long time.'

'You mean you haven't rung them up.'

'That's what I mean, Jake.'

'Well I suggest you ring them now. They'll know whether she's alive or dead, I imagine.'

'If she was dead we'd know soon enough.'

'Quite possibly. All the same I'd like to be told one way or the other.'

'Anybody else like to be told?' asked Ed, looking round the room.

Brenda didn't speak. Geoffrey had obviously seen through the cunning attempt to betray him into indiscretion, and likewise kept quiet. Ivor said he'd like to be told.

'All right.' Ed looked through a ring-spine notebook, drew the telephone towards him and began to dial. While he was doing so he said without looking round, 'Ivor, go tell the folks we'll be starting late, like fifteen minutes. We're having

. . . administrative problems. That'll hold 'em . . . Good morning, I'm inquiring after a Miss Gambeson, a Miss Janet Gambeson who was admitted as a casualty around five o'clock this morning . . . No, I'm afraid I don't.' He turned towards Jake. 'Her name isn't Kelly. I doubt that it's Janet either. Or Gambeson. Not that it matters worth a damn what she calls herself . . . Yes? . . . Thank you.' He rang off. 'She's still unconscious. Just like we said.'

Ivor had come back in time to hear this. 'Well, that's something.'

After a pause, Ed said pleasantly, 'That's all we need you for, Brenda, but we'd like Jake to stay.' When she looked inquiring, he added, 'There's a little bit of digging we'd like to do about Kelly.'

'I wouldn't mind staying for that too, unless you . . .'

'No no, fine, you stay if you want, you'll probably be able to help. Now Frank, do you want to carry the ball for a bit?'

'Thank you, Ed.' Rosenberg did want to. He didn't actually grasp the lapels of his unsightly cream-coloured linen jacket, but his tone made up for that. 'Now as some of you may know, when a person of this kind enters a suicidal situation there are two main aims or objectives. One is to arouse attention and concern, the so-called cry for help. The other objective is to carry out an act of revenge on some other person, usually for a sexual or family reason, to make that other person feel guilty, anxious and so on. An invariable accompanying feature is that the subject takes very careful precautions against dying. If that does happen, it's an accident. Something has gone wrong – the person in the next room doesn't smell the gas, the rope round the neck doesn't break.'

Jake had now identified the subject of the window. The curved wand was a bow, its bearer was Artemis, the portico was that of her temple at Tauris, the girl was Iphigenia, daughter of Agamemnon and Clytemnestra, and the beast was the deer supernaturally substituted for her by Artemis to forestall her sacrifice at Aulis. Shockingly rendered, but then. For a moment he felt pleased with himself.

'Now I strongly suspect,' continued Rosenberg, sounding very Irish for some reason, 'that that was what happened in this case, but I don't know what went wrong. If that second person, the one on whom an act of revenge was intended, if he exists, who is he? He might be somebody we don't know of, somebody who was supposed to telephone at midnight, say, but telephones are too unreliable and I just don't believe it. Since this happened here, I strongly suspect that the second person – if he exists – is also here. Here in this room. I've . . . eliminated Lionel.'

'I'm your man,' said Jake at once. 'She asked me to come and see her some time after midnight to be shown what she called a kind of letter. Which it was in a sense. I talked it over with my wife and decided it would be safer not to go.'

There was silence. Ivor looked incredulous, Geoffrey puzzled for once in his life. Brenda glanced at Jake and gave him an approving nod and smile. Ed did the same in his thank-Christ-quite-different manner and said,

'Good, Jake. Excellent. I hope you're not feeling bad about it? We all understand why you didn't go along. None of us would have – I hope. You were absolutely right not to.'

'How can you say that after what's happened? *Of course* I'm feeling bad about it.'

'Jake, you mustn't, you mustn't!' Ed spoke with great and impressive earnestness. 'Can't you see, you idiot, it's what she wants, it's her malice and her awful . . . You're falling for it, you're playing it her way by feeling bad. She's *sick* Jake, it's not like you've mistreated some normal human being as we all do all the time and pay the penalty. See it for what it is, a vicious child's game with you cast as loser. Have the flexibility to . . . oh, God.'

'She won't die, darling,' said Brenda. 'You can be quite certain of that. I'm sure there are accidents as Dr Rosenberg says, but Kelly isn't going to have one, she's too bright in the way she's bright. You said last night, I mean earlier this morning, you said she'd have found out about the dose. Indeed she would, she'd have found out what was a completely safe dose, and it doesn't matter to her if it's a laughably safe dose and everybody knows it was that *afterwards*. She'll have had her hour and made her point and be on to something else by then.'

'Right, Brenda. Very good.'

For a moment Jake tried to push out of his mind the memory of a weeping face, then stopped trying. He had wondered at the time what Kelly had been 'expressing' at Mr Shyster's; now he knew. Hatred. Of whom or what? Of self. But there could be no such thing: all that could be meant was the hatred felt by one part of the self for another. Perhaps in her that hating part was powerless, able to do no more than look on aghast at the acts the other displayed and to grieve at them. How dismal, if true.

'Er, may I ask a question?' This was Geoffrey. He was frowning. 'There's something I'm afraid I can't quite follow.' (Like the arrow to the Gents, you sodding moron, thought Jake.) 'If, er, if Kelly was revenging herself on Jake, what was she revenging herself for, I mean because of what? Had Jake offended her or something?'

'Yes I had. She tracked me down in my rooms in Oxford and offered herself to me, Christ, bloody well tried to rape me, and I . . . fended her off in a very ungraceful, ungracious way, and she called me every filthy name she could lay her tongue to and said everything she could think of that she thought might hurt me . . .' He turned to Brenda and said, 'I'm sorry I didn't tell you before, I wish I had. I was going to and then it sort of got too late.'

'I understand perfectly.'

There was an edge to her tone he didn't much care for but he forgot about that when Ed, who had been nodding slowly and sapiently in time with Rosenberg, butted in by saying,

'Then I guess we got the hysterics and tears and self-reproaches bit, right?'

'Right, I mean yes. And then, I suppose it was the pathetic bit.'

More nodding. Geoffrey held up his hand like a schoolboy.

'Er . . . It must have been a very unpleasant experience for you.'

'Good, I'm glad I managed to get that across.'

'Well then, why did you come here when you must have known you'd be bumping into her?'

'Because she asked me to,' said Jake, raising his voice. 'Because she came round and saw me and did her pathetic *bit*.'

'After what had happened in Oxford?'

'Precisely. That was the order of events.'

'All right, you two,' said Ed. 'We're all finished here. Very good Jake, you seem to have it straightened out now. And thank you for straightening us out, me and Frank. We have everything we need. Case closed. Come on everybody, let's go do some work.'

'Just a minute if you don't mind.' Jake's voice was back to its normal level. 'What exactly do you mean by case closed?'

'That there's nothing more to be said. With your help we have assembled one classic sortie of one type of hopeless neurotic.'

'I can think of one or two more things to be said. Doesn't either of you feel any sense of responsibility for what's happened?'

'We feel concerned, of course, since she's our patient, in very different senses in our two cases.'

'Do you now? But I was talking about responsibility. Anyway, how long has she been your patient in very different senses?'

'Just over a year,' said Rosenberg. He seemed curious to know where this discussion might lead.

'Since March.' Ed seemed to know roughly where and not to mind.

'And has she made one of these suicide attempts or phoney suicide attempts before?'

'Not that I know of,' said Rosenberg.

'Well you know of one now. Doesn't it strike you at all that that means she's got worse while you've been "treating" her? While she's been undergoing your "therapy"?'

Ed squeezed his chin and said rather wearily, 'It might have happened at any time. Any time at all.'

'And you've always been and always will be quite powerless to prevent it or render it to the slightest extent less likely. Which matters a bit, some people might think, because even a phoney suicide attempt is quite a serious matter, not just a fairly interesting example of something, which is all you seem to see in it. As your mate was saying, they do sometimes succeed. Kelly isn't alive yet.'

'No let him finish, Frank. After all, he's our patient too, remember.'

'Only for the next couple of minutes, and that only in case I may say something I'd prefer to be privileged, if that still counts at all. Let's try a spot of adding up. You've done less than nothing for Kelly. How about Ivor? Ivor, have you improved since you started going to Ed?'

'I think I'm about the same, thank you Jake.'

'Nothing for Ivor. What about Chris? Perhaps you cured him and sent him on his way rejoicing. Did you?'

'Jake, I don't deal in cures.' Ed sounded angry but in full command of himself. 'Did I offer you a cure? I aim to release checks on emotion and to improve insight, that's all.'

'Funny how it's got about that both of those must be good. Stop bottling up that emotion that makes you want to hit your wife with a sledge-hammer. Gain insight, you're bound to like what you see. To prefer it to what you couldn't see before. Let me tell you, *Ed*, there's no such thing as a totally phoney suicide attempt. They all want to be at least a little bit dead for a little while. If you were Kelly and found out more about yourself, how would you feel? More likely to knock yourself off or less? And talking of Kelly, there's a small piece of her that can see properly, of course there is or what is it that's gaining insight, but you'll never reach it, not with your methods. Methods, Christ. You just make it up as you go along, which I suppose you call being empirical if you know the word, and there'll always be plenty of applicants, lonely pansies like Lionel who want a nice chat and poor old dears like Ruth who want a good cry and fatheads like Geoffrey who want to show off. What you're up to is hideously boring to anyone without wants or needs of that sort. But then on the other hand it's intellectually beneath contempt – I should have made it clear that the whole of this bit applies equally to your undistinguished colleague. As against all that what you do is dangerous in the extreme. And yet when you come to weigh it up it's funny too, in other words it would be impossible for anyone with a grain of humour in them. All you have, but in abundance, is arrogance and effrontery. Oh, and a certain amount of greed.'

'Have you finished?' asked Ed.

'I think so. Should there be more?'

'You're the best judge of that, Jake. I've let you run on because anybody can see you have this most painful conflict between concern for a martyr-figure and anger at having been made the victim of a –'

'I'm not letting you run on, old boy, I can't have you explaining me, that would be, as you would certainly say, too much. I cease to be your patient as of this moment. And also, in a very different sense of course, Junior's patient too.'

'Mr Richardson,' said Rosenberg, 'may I talk to you in private for just a few minutes?'

'Certainly. Hang on.' Jake moved across to Brenda and tried to signal or will her to leave the room with him, using every means short of verbal directive, but she sat on in her chair next to the doorway and looked at him without curiosity. It occurred to him that in the last couple of minutes he had rather pissed on the proceedings, thereby breaking a promise, and pissed on Geoffrey, shown himself to be at least momentarily against him, too. 'Sorry,' he said to her, feeling hard up for words. 'Things sort of got on top of me. I'd better be off, get a train. Sorry.'

'I understand,' she said as before.

'Well . . . cheerio, love. See you when? Tomorrow night? Okay, fine.'

As he made to kiss her cheek she seemed to relent and kissed him on the mouth with some warmth. He waved in a general fashion at the rest of the room, looking at nobody, and went. After a word to Ed to start without him, Rosenberg followed.

'I suggest we move outside,' said Jake. 'You probably wouldn't want us to be overheard.'

There was a door near by. A gravel path with bald patches took them to a rough lawn that was much larger than the one to be seen from the dining-room. It gave extensive hospitality to buttercups, daisies, dandelions, chickweed, groundsel, charlock, viper's bugloss, plantain, moss and couch. Near its middle stood a large elm tree which might well have been on the point of toppling over from disease but for the moment kept the sun off satisfactorily.

'It's most important –' began Rosenberg.

'First me, then you,' said Jake. 'I don't want to hurt your feelings unnecessarily or say anything I might regret, so I'll just tell you you're a disgrace to the medical profession, which admittedly is saying something. As practised by you, sexual therapy doesn't exist. There are things that are merely treated as parts of a figment called that, the pathetic bits and pieces of machinery and pornography and genital and non-genital sensate focusing and early sexual experiences and fantasies and Christ knows what that you've tried to make me mistake for a technique, a coherent method. Yes, those fantasies. You were quite right about them, not that it matters in the very least, that stuff I wrote for you wasn't "serious" at all. I told you I have no homosexual feelings, no sadism or anything like that, I'm not a voyeur, anyway not in the usual sense, but I am given to thoughts of subjecting women to certain indignities, I'll say no more than that. Except that I've never put those thoughts into practice and never will now. I knew none of it would have shocked you, but that's not the point: it's private, you see. And I don't think the fact that I was born in 1917 has any bearing. Plenty of my contemporaries wouldn't have minded telling me all about such matters, let alone you. And there must be the same division among youngsters, though I'm sure you apply the same "method" to everybody. People's behaviour changes, "society" changes, but not feelings. And while we're on "society" let me remind you of something you said to me in that terrible pub, something about repressive attitudes making me feel sexually unrelaxed. Repressive? In 1977? I was doing fine when things really were repressive, if they ever were, it's only since they've become, oh, permissive that I've had trouble. In the old days a lot of people, men as well as women, didn't know quite what to expect of sex so they didn't worry when it didn't work too well. Now everybody knows exactly what's required of them and exactly how much they've fallen short down to the last millimetre and second and drop, which is frightfully relaxing for them. No wonder you boys have got enough trade.

'Hence guilt and shame at inadequacy – all quite superficial according to you. Do you still think so? As regards the other lot, I mean my alleged deep-down guilt and shame about sex itself, what makes you think that what's deep down is more important than what's up top? Anyway, I suppose it is possible they'd been there all the time but totally screened by my libido, which eventually receded and left them in full view. But if that's what they are they're only the foundation of something quite different, as I tried to explain when I was telling you about that woman I had in Oxford.' He paused again. 'What outlandish bits of anatomy, what an extra-ordinary thing to do, what curious reactions you keep saying to yourself. It's like being a child again, when an older boy's telling you the story and it all seems too unlikely for words. And when you do it, any of it, it's as if it's abnormal, almost monstrous. I know it isn't really. You can't imagine how you ever . . .'

Jake gave it up. A scream sounded from the house, no doubt uttered by a participant occupied in self-draining or ensconced in the hot seat.

'And you wouldn't have minded being overheard telling me any of this?' Rosenberg had received Jake's strictures with a composure that indicated an extreme of either humility or complacency.

'Good for you, Frank. No, because I won't be seeing any of them again.'

'Except your wife.'

'Yes, but that's rather different. Now you must excuse me.'

'What about my turn to speak?'

'I've cancelled it. Nothing you could say would interest me.'

'Mr Richardson, if we were to go on from where you've just brought us, I'm sure we could make a very –'

'No we couldn't, you'd never reach me, I say, that sounds like one of your words, any more than you could reach Kelly. Not really the same sort of person as I am. I'd think about that if I were you, doctor.'

'I'd be glad to recommend other practitioners with different approaches.'

'Thank you, but for one thing they'd all be too unconventional and unpuritanical for me. Good-bye.' There was a handshake. 'You know, now it comes to it and I realize I shan't be coming to see you any more I can't help feeling, how shall I put it, full of fun.'

Jake's last sight of Rosenberg had his little figure standing under the elm in sad thought for a moment, then violently slapping the back of his neck at the assault of some serviceable insect. It was the only fully human thing he had ever seen him do and it seemed to show up his total nullity as a person. The house was very dark after the glare of outdoors. No sound came from the conference-room. Jake telephoned for a taxi, went upstairs, shaved and packed his bag. He thought of writing a note for Brenda but soon decided against it: if he was to say anything he would have had to say a great deal, and he would be seeing her the next evening.

Shortly after five o'clock that afternoon a nurse told him that Miss Gambeson was now sleeping normally. He said thank you, declined to leave a message, went to the station and was back home for a full Saturday evening's viewing.

Brenda didn't get home till midnight on the Sunday. She explained that there had been a little party after the official closure of the Workshop, nothing very wild, just a few bottles of Italian wine. Thanks to Ivor's abilities and the lack of traffic they had made an amazingly quick journey. Yes, all things considered the week-end had been a great success. These and other matters were treated with the affable remoteness he had begun to observe in her recent behaviour. Soon they agreed that it was getting late and retired to their separate rooms as usual.

The next morning Jake awoke rather before his usual time, but feeling more rested than he had for weeks, so instead of turning to and fro in bed on the off-chance that a girl would cross his mind he got up, put on dressing-gown and slippers and went down to the kitchen. While he waited for the kettle to boil he opened the back door. It was going to be another hot day, though with that faint heaviness of or in the air that can betoken the imminent end of a fine spell, especially to someone who has just read in the paper that unsettled weather is forecast. He looked at the garden, advanced a step or two into it. Rain or shine the grass would have to be cut soon, the chrysanthemums staked and all the roses dead-headed, and ideally much else done besides, but in the last four or five years even this tennis-court sized plot had begun to be too much for him, not physically but mentally or morally – he couldn't be fucking bothered. These days what he did do he did largely to prevent it being said that he had let the place go to rack and ruin. Once, Brenda would have given him a hand with the light jobs just as he had done his bit indoors; now, their respective spheres were theirs almost exclusively.

Thinking of things being too much for him stirred the thought that he was going to be sixty the following week. This seemed to him an indefensibly ludicrous proposition; there must be some mistake. If, when he was in his twenties, anybody had advanced to him, except as a puerile joke, the notion that one day he would be sixty – not survive to be, just be – he would have told him not to be a bloody fool. Sixty was what all those old people were. It was something he ought to have taken steps to postpone indefinitely, if not evade altogether, while there was still time. Six-oh. LX. What a silly bugger. Well, at least no one could say he was wiser or more sensible or understood anything better along with it.

He made tea, poured some of it into Brenda's favourite Diamond Jubilee mug, remembered with a morsel of self-satisfaction not to add milk or sugar as formerly and carried the filled vessel to her, once their, bedroom. She sat up as he entered the room, thanked him and asked if he was doing anything special that morning.

'Not really. I thought I might stroll down to the bookshop in Philby Road. The fellow there has got some stuff for me.'

'What stuff?'

'Eh? Some *Greece and Rome* back numbers I've been after. Why?'

'Just wondered. There's something I'd like your advice about before you go, if that's all right.'

'Attend me in my sanctum.'

When he turned the corner at the top of the lowest flight of stairs he saw that Mrs Sharp, having let herself into the house with her own licensed latch-key, was standing in the passage with her back to him, a most sensible position to take up if what you wanted was to enshrine in your memory the look of the inside of the front door. As he went down the flight Jake trod more heavily than was his habit and cleared his throat a couple of times, but to no avail. The female turned, saw him and jumped, the third verb to be understood in a more literal sense than the context would suggest. She managed not to cry out, however. Her response would have been about right for one faced by a spectral Cavalier with his head firmly on his shoulders.

'Morning, Mrs Sharp. Sorry I startled you.' Perhaps a leper's bell fastened irremovably round the neck, he thought. Or were those hand-bells they had?

'Good morning, Mr Richardson. Don't worry, it's just my silly way.'

This said, she moved to her favourite station between the foot of the stairs and the kitchen, again hard to find fault with if you assumed that he had been intending to make for the street attired as he was.

'Excuse me.'

'Can you –'

'Just a –'

'There we are.'

'Thanks.'

There were further evolutions in the kitchen while he assembled his grapefruit and coffee and toast and she collected brooms, buckets and other matériel from this cupboard and that, but he got away in the end, even managing to dive into the bog under less than full scrutiny. He was feeling quite good when, shat, shaved, showered and wearing his green lightweight crease-resistant suit, he went into his study to find Brenda already there looking out of the window.

'Sorry the garden's in such a mess,' he said. 'I'll try and make a start on it tomorrow.'

'Good. Darling I don't actually want your advice, I just wanted to make sure of talking to you.'

He nodded, inwardly squaring up. There was a certain amount of ground to be covered and no mistake, not all of it coverable in any cosy spirit.

'I wish I hadn't got to say this. I'm leaving you.'

'Oh,' he said, and went and sat down behind his desk. He saw that she was trembling slightly.

'I'm going away with Geoffrey.'

'*What?*'

'I know exactly what you're thinking and please don't say

any of it or it'll make me hate you, and I don't want to do that.'

'All right.'

'You see ... he can perform, or he wants to, anyway he does.'

'Thanks very much.'

'Jake, I'm not a fool, not completely, I can understand how hard it must be not to take it that way, and of course it is the way, so ... But I'm only stating a fact, no I'm not only doing that but it is a fact. You've lost interest, your sex-drive, but I haven't, and I'm going to be forty-eight in October. I shouldn't think any sort of adventure will ever happen to me again. And it isn't only that. He's interested in me.'

'He's changed tack pretty fast then. At that Workshop I went to he said there were people he liked but they didn't interest him. His very words.'

'You mustn't take things so literally, he was having a gloom. Anyway he pays attention to me and he talks to me.'

'About himself. Sorry.'

'You used to talk to me about yourself and it was fine with me. I used to enjoy it, I didn't mind why you did it, I expect it was mostly because you wanted to impress me, like a clever schoolboy who's still a bit excited by finding out he's clever. In that sort of way you hadn't grown up and you still haven't, which was all right in those days, really rather nice, but it's not so hot when somebody's getting on. Anyway – it wasn't all like that, you talking to me. You thought it would interest me too, sometimes you probably even wanted to know what I thought. There's none of that these days. Do you remember, it must be three or four months ago, you brought a bottle of wine home and Allie was here and she asked for some and you did something in the kitchen, swapped the bottle or –'

'Got you to offer her some actually, and what I did was pour –'

'Don't tell me now, I don't want to know now. In the old days you'd have told me the whole story and we'd have enjoyed it together. But you couldn't be bothered, could you? And just this morning, an hour ago, you said you were going to the bookshop and I asked you on purpose what you were going to pick up there, and you answered as shortly as you could and wondered why I wanted to know. You'd have been sitting on the bed before I had a chance to ask and telling me all about it and what you needed it for, that's what you'd have done *then*. When you still fancied me. In the days when you used to take me out. Before you stopped wanting to talk to me.'

Jake was paying very close attention, but things from outside kept occurring to him, motives, explanations, even why when last seen Geoffrey had been garbed like an adult Caucasian.

'But what decided me was the Kelly business. Going back again, about eight weeks I suppose, that's right, I was talking about the Workshop and I mentioned her, and I've forgotten what was said but there was a moment when if you'd wanted to you could have ... I know, I asked you if she'd come round here again and you said no and I knew you weren't lying, you've always been a hopeless liar. I suppose it's because you've always thought the truth was very important, that's one of the things I respect about you. Anyway there was something, I thought afterwards there was something I didn't know, but then I thought there couldn't be, because you'd have told me.'

'Well, it would have been embarrassing, and I didn't want to –'

'I'm sure it would have been a lot of things, but the chief thing it would have been was boring. For you to tell me about it. A mad girl hunts you down in Oxford and tries to go to bed with you and has hysterics and God knows what else happens, and you'd rather watch television than tell me about it. Even though she might come round here in any sort of state at any moment, indeed *did* come round to con you into the week-end, I wonder how she made sure I wasn't going to be here, no don't bother. And even though you *knew* I wouldn't be angry or anything like that if you did tell me. Why should I live with someone who thinks I'm as bloody unrewarding as that?'

Jake didn't say anything.

'When I went on about you to Frank that time and when I gave you that lecture about being affectionate to me and how I'd be able to tell if you were one of those men who only take notice of women when it's to do with sex, that was all ... theory, Jake. A comparison. An awful warning. I'd met plenty of men like that, what woman hasn't, but I never thought you were going to turn out to be one. In the end. To have always been one, I couldn't believe that of you. I went through bits of thinking you were getting slack and a bit selfish in your old age and needed gingering up, being told if you weren't careful you'd find yourself turning into one of *them*. That's when I wasn't thinking it was all me. Well I've gone off physically but not all that much it seems, and I can't have got so many times more boring in just a couple of years, I worked that out over the weeks, and after I thought I'd warned you as clearly as I could and you went on just as before not talking to me except when you needed an audience and putting up with stroking me and me stroking you twice a week, well, the Kelly business just clinched it. Incredible.'

'Why did you keep on with those pissing sensate sessions?' asked Jake after a moment.

'Well, you know I love massage, I don't really care if it's badly done. And I'm like you, I tend to do what doctors tell me. And I sort of couldn't not go on without a showdown. And I kept thinking it might conceivably start to come right next time.'

'So did I.'

'Did you? Looking back I'd have thought you'd made up your mind none of it was going to be any good from the word go. You expect too much of people.' Brenda looked at him consideringly. 'You've changed, Jake. In other ways too I mean. Kelly again. I can't see you getting involved with a screwed-up little bitch like that in the old days.'

'I wasn't involved with her'

'Emotionally you were, and still are I imagine. No, you'd have seen through her from the start, because you'd have been observing her that much more closely. You'd have asked yourself what it would be like to get physically involved with her and have said no thanks, not with those complications round the corner. As it was, well, if it had been anyone else I'd have said they were a bit soft. It's odd, in one way you'd have expected a man in your position to see things as they are, especially women. Take away love or sex and the impression ought to be clearer, not distorted by emotions and wishful thinking and so on. But it's the other way round. You used to see as most men see, now you don't. Or it's more like . . . What's that stuff they put in ships to keep them from going all over the place?'

'What? Oh . . . ballast?'

'That's right. People's sex-drives are like ballast, they keep them steady. It sounds wrong, but they do. So as I say, you're worse equipped to deal with Kelly than you would have been before, not better.'

Brenda had long since ceased to tremble. With every sign of ease she sat down in the red-leather chair and went on talking in an interested tone, as if they had been sitting in a restaurant together. Her manner had lost what he now saw as the false amiability of the preceding weeks.

'So much so, in fact,' she said, 'that you virtually take her side against Ed. Now Ed has too good an opinion of himself I quite agree, but he does help people, or lets them help themselves which is just as good. I'm sure there are good reasons for saying he couldn't or he shouldn't or he doesn't really, but he does. For instance Martha now regularly tells her mother where to get off, goes out at night and all that. Anyway. I've got over it now, but I felt rather jealous of Kelly at one stage. Indignant too. You cared more about a destructive delinquent than you had about me for years. Not your fault and not the same sort of thing, I know. But let me give you a parting piece of advice – she's spilt milk, Jake. If she comes here again, chuck her out. Call the police if necessary. Do you think you can do that?'

'I don't know. I haven't thought. When are you off?'

'Probably about the end of the week. Geoffrey thinks he has a temporary place for us in Highgate. Are you going to stay on here?'

'I haven't thought about that either.'

'No of course you haven't. I should if I were you, stay on.'

'It would cost quite a bit to set up a new place.'

'That too. I mean I might come drifting back one day.'

'And put up with being found unrewarding?'

'Oh, I shouldn't be surprised. I like you and I don't care for being on my own as much as you do. And we might get on better with neither of us expecting you to find me rewarding. The thing is, Geoffrey hasn't said anything about divorces and Alcestis has always had a pretty strong grip.'

'On Geoffrey or in general?'

'Both really.'

'I thought her first husband left her.'

'Only physically. Allie gave him the boot.'

'I didn't know that. You must tell me the story before you go.'

'Actually there's not a hell of a lot to it.'

'Pity.' Jake got up from his seat at the desk. 'I'll miss you.'

'Without any malice in the world, darling, it'll be interesting to see how much.' Brenda too rose. 'Frank Rosenberg told me you said you weren't going to go to anybody else for treatment.'

'I probably said that in the lukewarmth of the moment.'

'I hope so. Another piece of advice. Don't let yourself not mind being as you are. Do a lot of thinking about the old days. Will you be in to lunch?'

'I expect so. I mean yes.'

'See you then.'

When she had gone he went on standing by his desk for a time. What hurt him most, and also shamed him, was her not having said she would miss him because she wasn't going to. Then he started remembering a holiday they had had in 1971 in Bodrun, where a gang of Danes had been excavating a fresh part of the ancient Carian city of Halicarnassus that had stood on the site and by so doing had involuntarily made it possible for him and Brenda to semi-diddle the taxman over their expenses, Brenda too because she had been designated his research assistant. The weather had been lovely, the Turks very agreeable and the scrambled eggs with tomatoes one of the best dishes he had ever eaten. They had stayed part of the time in a sort of private house infested with mosquitoes and Germans and, to anybody reared in the West and no doubt others besides, most remarkable for its lavatory. The night sound-track had been remarkable too: goats, chickens, donkeys, cattle and naturally dogs separated from them at times only by the thickness of the outside wall, together with, towards dawn and some yards further away, scooters. But they hadn't really minded any of that. To look back on it now was a bit like looking at a museum postcard of some archaic wall-painting or mosaic: you knew the official version of what the figures were up to and un-questioningly believed it, but found it hard to imagine with any clarity how they had felt about what they had been up to. So perhaps it wasn't really in order for him to be hurt a lot about Brenda not going to miss him.

Eventually Jake decided he might as well go and pick up the back numbers as he had planned. He needed them, the walk would do him good and it would probably be raining tomorrow.

The week passed in a flurry of tedium. There was the money to be settled: all four parties had some, Jake what there was from his academic posts and the odd bob from his books, Brenda a little from her family, Geoffrey a competence from the recklessly spendthrift chutney-merchants, Alcestis something from her terrifying tenure of a post as a social worker and perhaps something too from shares. What held things up was everyone being decent; a touch of rapacity here or stinginess there would have worked wonders. As it was they got no further than deciding that for the moment you hung on to what you had. In the same sort of way the furnishings of 47 Burgess Avenue were to be left as they were down to the last china cat till Brenda had somewhere else to put them, or rather a yet-to-be-agreed proportion of them. She could have the bloody lot as far as Jake was concerned but he couldn't say so.

Several times he considered getting the hell out and making for Oxford, not just for now but for the rest of his time there, letting the house despite Brenda's guarded forecast and doing up his rooms in Comyns and perhaps finding a cottage later. But he always came up against the thought that Oxford wasn't very nice really, not any more, and he had as many or as few friends in both places, and he might not enjoy the garden exactly but he wouldn't like to be without it, and there was the club, and above all he was used to being here, though admittedly not on his own.

There was some minor hitch in Geoffrey's arrangements when it came to it and Brenda didn't leave till the following Monday. The days in between had been normal to a degree that might have been comic: television, desultory work, the club, to the Thomsons' for drinks Sunday midday, the garden, television. Finally he was standing in the bedroom among her packed suitcases.

'That's the lot for now,' she said. 'I'll be back tomorrow for another load if that's all right. I'll ring you first.'

'Yes of course. Er, it's a bit late, but you remember that evening we went to the Bamboo Bothy?'

'How long ago?'

'Well, it must have been the same night you gave me the pep-talk about affection. I was waiting for you downstairs after we'd had a ... You came in and I said you looked beautiful.'

'Yes, I remember that all right. What about it?'

'You were touched and so was I. I thought if that could still happen, after all it's only a few weeks ago, then we still have something, and we could sort of build on it and make more of it. Oh I mean have your fling now but perhaps in a month or six weeks ...'

'We'll always still have something darling, after all those years but it wouldn't be enough, it wouldn't, you know, come round often enough. It would be very nice when it did, but at the moment I honestly can't see ...'

'No, I suppose not, you're right. I thought I ought to mention it, though.'

'Yes, I'm glad you did. It was sweet of you.'

'Good. Well I'll get this stuff down.'

'I can take these two.'

'No, leave the zip one to me. You take that one there.'

There was a horrible interlude in the sitting-room while the driver of the pre-ordered minicab sat in traffic, couldn't find the house, stopped for a hamburger, chatted-up a bird, anyway didn't appear. In the end of course he did appear and proved most surprisingly willing to deal with the luggage. While he did so Brenda walked round the room crying. Jake knew that she was crying because of the room and the house and her life there rather than because of her life with him. That part didn't take very long. When it was over he went out into the front garden with her. The air was cool and the sky covered with cloud but no rain was falling.

'I'm sorry,' he said. 'For it and about it.'

'You are a silly old Oxford don.'

'Off you go now. Good luck. Hey, hold it. I've just thought, we're mad. You have the house, you've put so much into it and made it so nice, you must have it. I'll find a couple of rooms somewhere and you can move back in. Give me a week or two to look round. Thank Christ I thought of it. Insane.'

'What about you and the garden?'

'Well I'll miss it but nothing like the way you'd miss the house. That's decided then. Ring me tomorrow. I'll be here all day.'

Back in the sitting-room he thought about Geoffrey properly for the first time since hearing that Christendom's premier fucking fool had taken his wife off him. Not that there was a great deal to be said about that circumstance, because it was so hard to imagine anything of what it must be like. Geoffrey and Brenda out to dinner at a restaurant, Geoffrey handed the menu, Geoffrey baffled not by the language or by where a Dover sole came from but by the concept of choosing what he wanted to eat from a proffered list of available dishes. Geoffrey and Brenda off on a trip to the land of the mango and the tamarind, Geoffrey with his papers at the airport – incidentally there must be someone at his office who knew which way up to hang a map of the world and had the authority to stop him darting off to the Yukon or Monte Carlo to do his shopping. Jake's mental two-shot of Geoffrey and Brenda regularly cut to a close-up of Geoffrey frowning as some aspect of reality came to his attention. That was just as well; long might it remain so.

One o'clock: nearly time for lunch. What had Brenda – but Brenda had gone. All the same she might well have left something for him in the larder, in fact now he came to think of it she had said as much. He went out to the kitchen and found a saucepan of brown soup (oxtail? chocolate?) on the electric stove. He turned the ring under it on full, thus ensuring it would be warm enough to eat by nightfall. The larder revealed most of a cold leg of lamb and a salad; he carved the meat and made a dressing, then uncorked the remains of the Médoc they had shared the previous evening. All this was very fine but things would assuredly take a turn for the worse in a few days. In pursuance of the principle that those who are always about when they're not wanted are never about on those admittedly very rare occasions when they are wanted, Mrs Sharp, who had been known to collect the odd pound of sausages on her way to work here, was going to be on holiday for the next three weeks; her usual replacement had fallen out at the last minute and Jake didn't know how to find a replacement for the replacement, at least he knew how to summon candidates for the situation but not how to separate the thieves and arsonists from those at the other end of the scale, the merely idle and inefficient. But perhaps he would find a lodging before any of this should start to matter; he had no idea how long it would take.

While he was assembling his lunch things, which included a jar of sweet pickle with the name of Geoffrey's firm on it, on the little round table Jake heard the door-bell chime. His immediate thought was of Kelly, Kelly couched till a moment ago in a hide in a neighbour's garden and now, with Brenda well and truly gone, moving in if not for the kill (and better not be too bloody sure about that) then certainly for the fuck-up. But it wasn't Kelly, it was Alcestis.

'Christ,' he said in simple surprise and dismay. He had thought vaguely that one (on its scale considerable) offset against Brenda's departure would be to see no more of the Mabbotts, by which term he would really have meant Alcestis, because Geoffrey was quite good value for the mean-minded, but of course that was, well, wrong.

She looked at him with her eyes slightly narrowed and her mouth bunched up in an awful Churchillian grimace about finest hours and fighting on the beaches. 'Hallo, Jake,' she said gruffly and with a tremendous amount of quiet courage packed into three syllables. 'Mind if I come in?'

He minded a lot but was still too taken aback not to go along with convention. 'No, no of course not, do come in.'

'Am I interrupting your lunch?'

'I was just going to start, but I haven't actually ... started.'

In she surged; he noticed she was carrying a supermarket plastic bag. *Christ*, he thought, that's her nightie in there, she's come to start the other half of the wife-swap, and fought down a squeal of panic. Not knowing quite what else to do he followed her out into the kitchen, where a lifetime of experience showed in the way she grasped the state of his soup. With that on the record she sat down at the table next to the place he had laid himself and here eventually he had to join her. Asked if he could get her anything she shook her head slowly, staring out into the garden with eyes that were now slightly wider than normal and looking like some picture of a hundred years before called *The Bereaved*.

'Well, Jake, there's not a great deal to say, is there?'

'Almost nothing.'

'Except perhaps this.' As Alcestis paused, the sound of a jet engine began to be audible. At the exact point where it prevented you hearing anything else she started to speak again. Jake watched fascinated as her expression and movements went from tender to grim and back again, from indignant to forgiving, wistful, desolated, philosophical, wry, brave, as amid the huge uproar she bit her lip, clenched her fist, bowed her head, lifted it, frowned, raised her vestigial eyebrows, sighed, half-smiled. He nodded and shrugged and so on repeatedly and farted once. As the jet started to wane she said, 'Which as far as I'm concerned is an end of the matter.'

'Well, I don't think anyone could put it better than that, Allie.'

'No. Thanks. Well. Now. Right. Go. Here.'

She stood up and successively took out of the supermarket bag and planked down on the table a pork pie, a packet of cereal, half a pound of butter, a tin of tomatoes and half a dozen other unelaborate foods. Finally and more ceremoniously she produced a tear-off pad with a hard back and a pencil attached by a cord.

'Don't know what you've got,' she said, 'don't know what you want. Get a copy of your front-door key made and drop it through my letter-box. Anything you need, just whack it down here and leave it on the table. I've got to fetch my own stuff, no point in two of us at it and I've got a car. Yes, I've been left that. However. Settle at the end of the week or whenever you like. You can be in your study when I deliver, no need for us ever to meet. We can't help each other emotionally but I can help you practically, so why not?'

'Well, Allie, that is most kind of you, I do appreciate it very much.'

'Rubbish, man, nothing to it. So long. No, I can see myself out.'

And in a moment the front door banged. Curious thing, human nature, Jake thought to himself as he started on his cold meat and salad. You get someone like that, by no means the most attractive of women, in fact pretty plain and full of irritating mannerisms, to all appearance entirely self-centred, and then she comes in at the end, so to speak, to show that underneath it all as so often there's more than a spark of decency – and of shrewdness too. Yes, that was certainly a legitimate view. On the other hand it might be tentatively argued that old Smudger was still just as much of a raving monster as she had ever been, or rather substantially more of one with her 'shrewdness' seeing him as a threat to her charter to talk balls all the time and her 'decency' trying to make him feel bad with a coals-of-fire job. He was delighted at this confirmation that she knew he hated her like hell and hoped devoutly that shopping for him would cause her great inconvenience. What about a couple of hundredweight of cement for a birdbath or something in the garden? It had begun to look as if finding somewhere to stay, somewhere really satisfactory and also cheap, would be no easy matter. He poured out the last of the wine and took it in front of the television set.

Later that year, in the November, Jake became troubled with excessive shitting. He would have to go seven or eight times a day and between those times his innards were never quiet, popping, chuckling and fizzing their head off and emitting moans of poignant grief that attracted the concern or the interest of his classes and pupils. A preliminary exploration of his bum by Dr Curnow proved inconclusive; he must pay another visit in the third week. So one afternoon he duly made his way through rainy gusts to the bus stop and, preceded on board by two pairs of coffee-coloured children, the first in the charge of a white woman, the second of a black man, was soon being carried towards Harley Street.

Not much had happened to him in the intervening months. He had cancelled his holiday in Sicily in favour of a trip to Crete with Lancewood and his chum. There he had accused the hotel staff corporately of having stolen his money, traveller's cheques and passport a sufficient time before their discovery under his mattress, where it could only be that he had stowed them out of some freak of caution put beyond recapture by retsina and Mogadon. Brenda was settled in the Burgess Avenue house with Geoffrey, Jake in a perfectly bearable couple of rooms in Kentish Town, nearer the centre of the 127 route. He often wondered how much he missed her but never for long at a time. Wynn-Williams fell down dead. Two days before he (Jake) moved he had had a very brief visit from Kelly, first in what Brenda had called her investigative-journalist persona and on being told to go away straight into the apologizing self-accusing waif he had had two previous doses of. Then bugger pity, he had said to himself, lest you let a fiend in at your door. But he was always going to feel he had let her down, or rather not always, what crap, just to the end of his days, not nearly as long. He finished his article about Syracuse and sent it in.

The bus passed between the tiled façade of Mornington Crescent station and the roughly triangular paved area with the statue of Cobden near its apex, pitted and grimy and lacking its right hand, Richard Cobden the corn-law reformer and worker for peace and disarmament, too famous for his Christian name and dates to be needed in the inscription. Almost at the foot of the plinth what looked like the above-ground part of a public lavatory, black railings draped with black chicken-wire, bore a notice saying London Electricity Board – Danger Keep Out and gave a limited view of a stairway with ferns growing out of it and its walls. Two bollards painted in rings of black and white were to be seen not far off, their function hard even to guess at. Weeds flourished in the crevices between the paving-stones, a number of which had evidently been ripped out; others, several of them smashed, stood in an irregular pile. Elsewhere there was a heap of waterlogged and collapsed cardboard boxes and some large black plastic sheets spread about by the wind. Each corner of the space was decorated with an arrangement of shallow concrete hexagons filled with earth in which grew speckled evergreen bushes and limp conifer saplings about the height of a man, those at the extreme ends crushed by traffic and the greenery run into the soil along with after-shave cartons, sweet-wrappers, dog-food labels and soft-drink tins. Turning south, the bus stopped at its stop across the road from Greater London House, through the windows of which fluorescent lighting glared or flickered all day. It stood on ground filched from an earlier generation of dwellers in the Crescent who had woken one morning to see and hear their garden being eradicated.

Fifteen minutes later Jake was walking down Harley Street, buffeted by damp squalls as he went. He noticed a man and a woman in Western dress before he got to Curnow's place and was admitted. Thanks perhaps to the default of a bashaw or begum the receptionist showed him in straight away.

'Sit down, would you please?' The doctor made it sound as if this procedure would quite likely be painful and was certainly unusual but would turn out to serve his patient's interests better than any alternative soon come by. 'And how have things been?'

'Oh, not too bad. A slight improvement on the whole.'

'You've kept to your diet?'

'Pretty well. I've laid off the fruit and the spices but I have backslid a couple of times with the wine.'

'You must cut it out altogether. You've passed no blood or mucus or anything of that character or nature?'

'No, nothing of that category or description.'

'Any pain? Good. Now if you'll just take down your trousers and pants and lie on the couch.'

Curnow pushed a light up Jake's bum and had a look round there while Jake made hooting noises to relieve his fairly marked discomfort. When Curnow came down again it felt as if he had brought far, far more than his light with him but this proved not to be the case. Soon Jake was back in his chair and very glad of it too.

'Well, there are some unformed stools up there but nothing abnormal. Keep on with the Lomotil and the diet and it should clear up. But remember: no wine,' said Curnow doggedly, adding with extreme reluctance, 'for the time being. If you must drink stick to spirits.' He paused, following up a memory perhaps set off by a glimpse of Jake's genitals a few minutes before. 'Ah – your libido. I sent you to Dr Rosenberg, didn't I? What was the result?'

'Nothing whatever. No, that's not quite true. My ... libido declined further during the "therapy" and has gone on doing so since.'

'I gather from that that you have ceased the therapy. Why?'

'Things like it being offensive and nonsensical.'

'I could recommend you elsewhere. There are others in the field.'

'If any of them could help me I shouldn't need to go to them.'

The doctor said impressively, 'Let me suggest an altogether different approach. When I measured the level of your testosterone in the spring, it was average.'

'You mean that hormone test you did?'

'Yes. It's been established more recently that what is significant is not the crude testosterone level but the level of that part of it that isn't bound to plasma protein. It would be perfectly simple to establish what yours is. If it's below average it can be supplemented artificially.'

'You mean it may be physical after all? And cured just by taking something?'

'Yes. As I said, we'll have to run tests.'

Jake did a quick run-through of women in his mind, not of the ones he had known or dealt with in the past few months or years so much as all of them: their concern with the surface of things, with objects and appearances, with their surroundings and how they looked and sounded in them, with seeming to be better and to be right while getting everything wrong, their automatic assumption of the role of injured party in any clash of wills, their certainty that a view is the more credible and useful for the fact that they hold it, their use of misunderstanding and misrepresentation as weapons of debate, their selective sensitivity to tones of voice, their unawareness of the difference in themselves between sincerity and insincerity, their interest in importance (together with noticeable inability to discriminate in that sphere), their fondness for general conversation and directionless discussion, their pre-emption of the major share of feeling, their exaggerated estimate of their own plausibility, their never listening and lots of other things like that, all according to him.

So it was quite easy. 'No thanks,' he said.

Kingsley Amis

LUCKY JIM

Kingsley Amis has written a marvelously funny novel describing, through one young adventurer in particular, an attempt of England's postwar generation to break from that country's traditional class structure. When it appeared in England, *Lucky Jim* provoked a heated controversy in which everyone took sides. 'I am told that today rather more than 60 per cent of the men who go to universities go on a government grant. This is a new class that has entered upon the scene. It is the white-collar proletariat. Mr. Kingsley Amis is so talented, his observation so keen, that you cannot fail to be convinced that the young men he so brilliantly describes truly represent the class with which his novel is concerned' – W. Somerset Maugham, London *Sunday Times*. 'No one has been so funny in this vein since Evelyn Waugh was at his best' – Arthur Mizener.